A SPARKLE OF SALT

A SPARKLE OF SALT

Evelyn Hood

A *Time Warner* Book

First published in Great Britain in 2003
by Time Warner Books

Copyright © Evelyn Hood 2003 .

A CIP catalogue record for this book
is available from the British Library.

ISBN 0 316 86084 0

Typeset by Palimpsest Book Production Limited,
Polmont, Stirlingshire
Printed and bound in Great Britain by
Clays Ltd, St Ives plc

Time Warner Books UK
Brettenham House
Lancaster Place
London WC2E 7EN

www.TimeWarnerBooks.co.uk
www.evelynhood.co.uk

Acknowledgements

My thanks to Isabel Harrison, David Mair, Bill Pirie and Jimmy Sinclair, and to the committee and members of the Buckie and District Fishing Heritage Museum for patiently answering my many questions about fishing and fisher-folk.

I also wish to thank Sheila Campbell, chief librarian at Elgin Library, and the staff of Buckie Library, and I am especially indebted to Lorna McAllister MA, who gave me access to her own research into the role of women in North-east Scotland's fishing communities from the 1850s to the 1930s.

I owe the people named above a great debt of gratitude, and I dedicate this book to them.

Contact Evelyn Hood, or find out more about her novels, at her website:

www.evelynhood.co.uk

Lowrie Family Tree

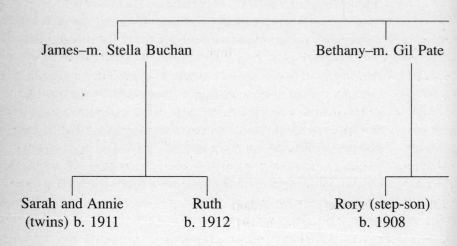

James–m. Stella Buchan   Bethany–m. Gil Pate

Sarah and Annie   Ruth   Rory (step-son)
(twins) b. 1911   b. 1912   b. 1908

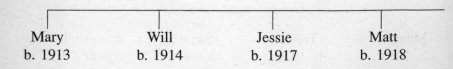

Mary   Will   Jessie   Matt
b. 1913   b. 1914   b. 1917   b. 1918

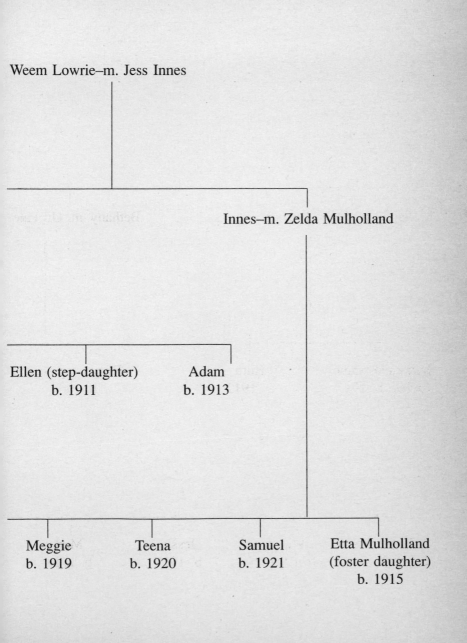

Weem Lowrie–m. Jess Innes

Innes–m. Zelda Mulholland

Ellen (step-daughter)
b. 1911

Adam
b. 1913

Meggie
b. 1919

Teena
b. 1920

Samuel
b. 1921

Etta Mulholland
(foster daughter)
b. 1915

Glossary

afore	before
an'	and
a pretty pass	a fine situation indeed [*sarcastic*]
arles	a binding financial agreement between curers and gutters
atween	between
aye	yes, always
ben the hoose	in the next room
bubblies	fish oil or paraffin lamps
ca' al	cold
cran	a basket used to measure the weight of herring
curer	the owner of a curing station where herring are gutted and packed
farlin	large wooden trough
fin	when
fit	what
gatherings	social events
greeting	welcoming, and also crying or complaining
know fine	know well
hoosie	house
ken	know
loon	boy or man
loupin'	jumping or throbbing

maskin'	letting a pot of tea stand, so that the liquid becomes stronger
Ne'erday	New Year's Day
quine	girl
shot	a fishing boat's catch
sneakit	sneaky, sly
staves	shaped wooden sections from which a barrel is constructed
thole	tolerate, bear
thrawn	difficult, stubborn

1

November 1918

The three Lowrie girls rushed along the street as though their lives depended on it, skirts tangling round their legs, faces red with exertion and arms swinging. Fetching up on the doorstep together, they became a clump of limbs and bodies thumping against the door, each determined to be the first in.

'I got here first!' Ruth shrieked as the twins, some eighteen months older and a full head taller than she was, tried to push her aside.

'No you didnae, it was me,' Annie panted, while Sarah claimed, 'I'm the oldest. I should tell her!' Then the latch gave way and they almost fell into the kitchen.

'Have you lassies got no sense at all?' Stella Lowrie scolded, pulling her daughters apart and setting them on their feet. 'Roarin' down the street like tinkies!'

'He's here, the boat's here,' Ruth gasped. 'He's back!'

'Who's here? What boat?'

'My faither,' Annie yelled.

'Don't be daft, of course he's not here!'

'He is, Mither,' Sarah insisted. 'We saw the *Fidelity* comin' in when we were playin' up the braes.'

'We ran down tae the harbour tae see it,' Ruth gabbled.

'And it's in a terrible mess,' Annie chimed in.

'Wait!' The one word came from their mother's lips like the crack of a whip and the three of them fell silent, the excitement fading as they saw that her brown eyes were huge

1

in a suddenly pale face. 'Wait,' she said again, and then took a deep breath. 'You're sayin' that the *Fidelity*'s comin' intae the harbour now?'

'She's already in,' Ruth told her. 'We went there.'

'You saw your father?'

'He came up the ladder tae the harbour wall and Mr McFarlane was waitin' for him.'

'Who else?' Stella Lowrie demanded to know.

'A whole lot of folk. I wanted tae talk tae my faither but Sarah made me come away.' Ruth glared at her sister, who glared back.

'I should think so too. What would he have thought if he'd seen the three of you lookin' like that? Off tae the wash house this minute and get cleaned up.'

The backyard was reached by a narrow passageway that ran down the side of the house. As the girls scrambled out of the street door Stella hurriedly checked the pots simmering on the stove. There was just enough meat for one more serving, and plenty of soup, but as for the potatoes . . . she started to peel more, tossing them into the pot as quickly as she could. James had written to say that the *Fidelity* – the steam drifter his father and Uncle Albert Lowrie had bought the year that she and James married – was to be decommissioned now that the war was drawing to a close, but he had not said that he would be home so soon.

She threw one final potato into the pot, now filled perilously close to the brim, and put the lid on before casting a quick look around the kitchen to make certain that all was ready for the man of the house. The newly blackleaded range shone, the blue and white patterned plates ranged along the dresser shelves were evenly spaced and the Stafford figurines that had belonged to her own mother were free of even a speck of dust.

She almost went to the mirror hanging on the wall, but stopped herself just in time. Once, knowing that James was on his way home would have been enough to send her rushing to study her reflection, pinching her cheeks to highlight them with colour, smoothing her brown hair, pulling the collar of her blouse straight. But not now. She had been a foolish young lassie in those days; now she was a wife, and a betrayed wife at that.

She could have done with one more winter of freedom, she thought as Ruth scampered back into the kitchen, her small face shining and her hair smoothed down by damp hands.

'Is he here yet?'

'D'ye see him?' her mother asked tartly, and when the child shook her head. 'Then he's not here, is he?'

'I'll go and look for him—' Ruth turned towards the door, almost colliding with her sisters on their way in.

'You'll stay here and mind your manners. Annie, set another place at the head of the table for your father. Sarah, see that there's a basin of water and a bar of soap ready in the wash house,' Stella ordered. 'He'll want a wash before he eats. And take a towel in with ye!' she added as her daughter made for the door again. 'D'ye expect the man tae dry his face on his shirt tail?'

Then she jumped as an ominous hissing rose from the stove, where the overfull pot of potatoes had started to boil over, and ran to tilt the lid and let some steam out.

Down at the harbour James Lowrie had lingered on board the *Fidelity* long after his cousin Jem and the rest of the crew had scaled the narrow iron ladder set into the harbour wall, to be met at the top by their families and friends and borne off to their homes.

They were all delighted to be home again, but James had mixed feelings. In one way, he never wanted to see Buckie again, and yet he knew that he was for ever tied to the place.

He looked about the silent drifter that had been his home for so long. The war and the part that the *Fidelity* had played in it as a minesweeper had kept him fully occupied day in

3

and day out over the past four and a half years. There had never been time to think of anything but the moment, and for James that had been a good thing. Heedless of whether or not he survived, he had taken chances; as a result, the *Fidelity* and her skipper had been mentioned in dispatches. But that meant nothing to him, for as far as he was concerned the real battle was here in Buckie, and always had been.

Time was passing, and he knew that although Stella had not been waiting on the harbour wall to welcome him along with the other wives, someone would have told her, by now, of the *Fidelity*'s arrival. It was time to go. He sighed, and hoisted up the shabby wooden box – his seaman's kist – that had travelled everywhere with him since his first trip at the age of fifteen, just as Jacob McFarlane, who had gone into partnership with him the year before the war started, came down the ladder, moving briskly despite his advancing years.

'Welcome home, lad.' He held out his hand. 'It's been a long time – and they've been hard years, eh?' Then, nodding at the strip of blue painted around the *Fidelity*'s funnel, the mark among fishermen of respect for a lost crewman, 'I see ye're honourin' Charlie.'

James set the kist down and shook Jacob's strong, hard-skinned hand. 'He deserved it. The boat's not been the same without him.' He had grown up alongside his cousins Charlie and Jem; they had gone to the fishing together as lads not long out of school, and Charlie had become the *Fidelity*'s mate when James took over the boat in 1913.

Charlie's love of life and everything in it had made him popular everywhere he went. While on minesweeping duties he had willingly volunteered to go out on another boat when one of its crew fell sick; the boat picked up a mine that exploded as it was being towed clear of the shipping channels, sending the vessel to the bottom immediately, with all hands.

'I'll have tae go and speak tae Uncle Albert about Charlie,' James said.

'He's no' the man he used tae be, I can tell ye that.' Jacob shook his head. 'For all that Albert has by-blows all around the Moray Firth, Charlie was his favourite. He's taken the lad's death hard. Ye think when ye're young that old folk can deal with death easy enough, bein' that bit closer tae it, but losin' folk ye've known all yer life seems tae get harder as ye get older. Look at me – I cannae tell ye how much I miss yer mither, James. I wish ye'd been here tae say goodbye tae her at the end.'

'It wasnae possible,' James said uncomfortably. He had been in Southampton when word of his mother's illness reached him and, had he wished it, he probably could have managed to snatch a few days' leave and travel home to Buckie. But he had decided otherwise.

'She went peaceful, with the rest of us here tae see her off on her final voyage. She's lyin' in the Rathven graveyard now, beside Weem.'

'The way she wanted it – safe in the ground by my faither.' Even after all these years James had to fight to keep the bitterness from his voice. Weem Lowrie, his father, had died at sea and James had wanted to return his body to the deep. Jess Lowrie's insistence on burying her man ashore, where she could tend his grave, had caused a bitter disagreement between mother and son that had never been completely resolved.

Jacob let the younger man's comment pass. 'The poor old *Fidelity*'s a sorry sight, is she no'?'

'She's been through a lot.' James rushed to the defence of his beloved drifter. 'We've scarce been on land these past few years. We did well tae keep her afloat at all, and we'd tae nurse her up along the coast tae here. That's why she was decommissioned early – she's worn out. But all she needs is cleanin' out and some repair work. New deckin', a good coat of paint, give the engine a good scour out and she'll be ready for the next fishin' season.'

'I was thinkin' o' puttin' Jem in as skipper of the *Homefarin*' next season,' Jacob said, naming the boat he had bought to replace the *Fidelity* during the war years, and then, as James looked at him sharply, 'He's ready for it, is he no'?'

'Aye, well ready, but that means that I'd have tae train someone else up as mate.'

Jacob spat over the side into the harbour. 'I bought a bonny drifter from a man in Rosehearty a month or two back. I renamed her the *Jess Lowrie* for yer mother, and got up a crew tae take her tae Lowestoft so's she could start earnin' for us right away. She's younger than the *Fidelity*, and I thought you could take her over next year.'

'I've already got my boat.'

'The *Fidelity*'s gettin' older, though. Time for ye tae move tae somethin' better.'

James felt his hackles rise. 'This drifter's got years in her yet.'

'I'm no' arguin' with ye there, lad, but that's the very reason why we should sell her now. We'd still get a good price for her, and then we can put the money towards buyin' a third boat, or mebbe even have one built at Thomson's yard. This is a good time for consortiums like us,' Jacob said earnestly. 'A lot of men arenae comin' back from the war, God rest them, and some that have got home again are too sore wounded tae go back tae sea. Boats are goin' at good prices. This could be our chance tae start buildin' up a smart fleet, and I've got it in mind tae set the *Jess Lowrie* at the head of it. But this isnae the time for such talk,' he went on before James had the chance to argue further, 'for ye'll be wantin' tae see Stella and the bairns, after bein' away for all these years.'

James seethed as he walked home from the harbour. The *Fidelity* was the Lowrie family boat, and although he himself had not put a penny towards the cost of buying her, he had sacrificed far more than money. In the days of sail, a fisherman and his sons or his brothers could raise the price of a sailed herring boat between them, mortgaging their homes to borrow the initial outlay and repaying the bank from their labours, but the high cost of steam drifters had put them beyond the means of many men.

When the *Fidelity* came on the market Weem Lowrie and his brother Albert, hungry for one of the new, fast steam drifters, had raised as much money as they could, but even with a loan from the bank it had not been enough. Then Weem thought of a fellow Buckie fisherman, Mowser Buchan, who was no longer fit enough to run his sailed boat. Mowser, a widower with an unmarried daughter, Stella, was in search of a lusty son-in-law who could keep him in his old age and ensure Stella's future, while Weem had a son of marriageable age. Through marriage to Stella Buchan, James had fallen heir to Mowser's herring boat, and the proceeds from its sale had made up the rest of the money needed to buy the *Fidelity*.

He had paid a high price for the drifter, James thought as he reached the little fisherman's cottage that had once belonged to Mowser, and he was not going to see her sold on, not after all he and the boat had been through.

To his surprise, the cottage was quiet and still, with none of the sounds that passers-by would normally hear, such as children's voices from behind the small windows, or the clatter of pots as the next meal was prepared. Perplexed, James lowered his bag and his kist to the ground and rattled the latch. The door was locked, and when he rapped on it there was no reply. He stepped back in order to look up at the chimney; it was without the usual welcome wisp of smoke curling from the lit fire in the range below.

'Fit are ye daein' at this end o' the toon, James Lowrie?' a voice shrilled, and he turned to see their elderly neighbour peering from her own door.

'I'm back home, and home tae a closed door. D'ye know where Stella's off tae?'

The woman stared, and then gave a cackle of laughter. 'Surely ye ken that Stella and the quinies have moved intae

7

yer mither's wee hoosie down in Buckpool? In the Main Street?'

'Oh aye, of course.' James felt his face redden. 'I forgot.'

'Bein' away frae this place has addled yer brain,' the woman said. 'Best get over there, lad. She'll be wearyin' for a sight o' ye.' Then, as he picked up his bag and kist and went past her, she laid a hand on his arm. 'I'm sorry, my loon, about yer mither. Jess was a fine woman.'

'Aye,' James agreed, and made his escape towards the old fishing village of Buckpool, now a part of Buckie.

As he walked along the shore road to the house where he had been born and raised, the house his wife now presided over in place of his mother, he felt his feet beginning to drag.

Stella's heart jumped into her dry mouth when the door latch rattled, but she stayed where she was, facing the stove and with her back to the kitchen. Only when her husband said awkwardly, 'Aye, Stella lass,' did she tap the wooden ladle on the edge of the big cast-iron pot, lay it aside carefully, and turn to face him, wiping her hands on her apron.

'So you're home.'

'We came intae harbour a wee while back.'

He was much the same as before, she saw in her first quick glance, still well built and broad-shouldered. Then as he pulled his cap off she saw that his hair had been cropped. The black curls that had once framed his square, tanned face had gone, and silver glittered about his temples.

'Ye'll be ready for some food.' Stella ran the back of one wrist over her face, which was flushed with the heat from the stove. 'It'll not be long. Sarah, Annie, Ruth!' she rounded on her daughters, who were clumped together in a corner, eyeing the newcomer. 'Where are your manners? Welcome your faither home.'

The twins murmured a shy greeting but Ruth went round the table to stand before him. 'I'd 've come tae the boat tae meet you but they wouldnae let me.' A backward jerk of her head towards her sisters sent a shock of light-brown curly hair swinging round a strong-featured face. This one had taken after him, James realised, while her sisters – glancing at the twins, he saw Stella in their round faces; Stella as she had been when they married, soft and pretty with serene eyes and a shy, hopeful smile. Now her cheeks were sunken and her brown eyes harder.

'Is this ye back from the war for good?' Ruth broke into his thoughts.

'Eh? Oh, aye, it is.'

'So it's over, then? Did ye beat the Kaiser?'

Stella turned to reprimand the child for her impertinence, but held her tongue when she saw that her husband's normally solemn face had been startled into a grin.

'Aye, nearly, though I had tae have some help.' James cleared his throat, searching for something to say to his three daughters, and finally ventured, 'Ye've all grown since I last saw ye.'

'That's what bairns do.'

'Ruth!' Stella snapped, while Sarah and Annie, clutching each other's hands, gasped at their sister's impertinence.

'I'm just sayin' the truth. I'm six,' Ruth informed her father. 'Not long since, but I'm tall for my age.'

'And cheeky for your age, too, ye wee lummock,' Stella said. 'There's soap and a towel ready for ye out in the wash house, James.'

'Aye. I'll just—' He nodded at the bag and the kist he had placed on the floor.

'Put them ben the house,' she said, adding as he went through to the room where his parents had once slept, 'There's space for your things in the wardrobe, and I kept the top two drawers of the cupboard empty for ye.'

'I went tae the old house first, and found it locked,' James said, when he was back in the kitchen. 'One of the neighbour-women told me ye were bidin' here now.'

'We've been here these six months past. I told ye about it

in a letter.' Stella didn't look at him, but he could hear the hurt in her voice.

'Aye, aye, of course ye did. I was so busy thinkin' of bein' back in Buckie that I let my feet take me tae the usual house.' It was a lame excuse, and he suspected that she knew it. He was not much of a reader or a writer, and her letters had been hurriedly scanned and then discarded, the memory of them leaving his mind as the paper fell from his fingers. His own letters consisted of brief reports that he and the rest of the crew were well and busy. Neither of them, throughout the past years, had written any words of affection, or even of comfort.

'I thought that since your mother had left the house to you as the oldest son, you'd want your family tae live here,' Stella said, then, 'The soup's ready. Ye'd best get washed.'

2

When James returned to the kitchen, his hair wet and his skin tingling from the cold water and the pummelling it had received from the rough towel, Ruth stabbed a small finger at the chair at one end of the table. 'That's where you sit. Mither says that's your chair and we never get tae climb on it, even though you havenae been bidin' here for a long time.'

They ate in silence, and when the meal was over James pushed his chair away and patted his stomach with both hands. 'That was good.'

'I'm glad ye enjoyed it,' Stella said formally, as though he was a guest. 'Lassies—'

'I'd best go and see my Uncle Albert,' James said as the three girls rose obediently to clear the table. 'He'll want tae know all about Charlie.'

'Don't stay away for long. Folk'll be comin' by tae see ye and hear about what's been happenin',' Stella said, and then, when he groaned, 'I know ye were never one tae enjoy a gatherin', James, but ye've been away for a long time and it's only natural for the neighbours tae want tae pay their respects.'

'Aye, I suppose so.' He pushed his chair back. 'I'll try not tae be too long.' There was no sense in antagonising the woman on his first day home, he thought as he went out into the street.

His father's brother, Albert Lowrie, was a confirmed bachelor who had fathered a large brood of children on a number of women up and down the coast of the Moray Firth, cheerfully acknowledging all of them. Charlie and Jem were both his sons, but Charlie, the older of the two by only a few months, had always been his favourite. When the *Fidelity* and her crew left Buckie just after the outbreak of war Albert had been a sturdy, active man; now he was a ghost of his former self, grey and silent, huddled in a big wing chair and looking as though he had somehow collapsed in on himself. Like a canvas bag that had been emptied and tossed into a corner, James thought, sitting opposite his uncle, trying desperately to think of words of comfort and knowing that none of them would help Albert.

'Jem's already been in tae see me.' The old man's voice was feeble, as though he spoke from a long way away.

'He's my mate now, in place of . . . he's a grand lad, Jem.'

'Aye, but Charlie was the one most like me. Can ye think of anythin' else tae tell me about Charlie?' Albert begged, hungry for memories to hold close in his heart.

James returned to Main Street, worn out by the old man's misery, to find the house full of neighbours with more filing in every few minutes, the womenfolk bearing plates and dishes and jugs to ensure a steady supply of food and drink for all the guests. The men were eager to hear about the *Fidelity*'s time down south on active war service, and James, never a great talker, was soon having to clear his throat again and again as his voice began to grow husky. It was a relief to him when the talk became more general.

Although there was an air of merriment about the gathering, there was sadness too. Hundreds of young men had, like James, gone from the Moray Firth to fight for their king and country, and many would never again return to their homeland. As the evening wore on their names were listed, names familiar to James – coopers and curers, fishermen and boatbuilders, carters and farm workers – all lost for ever.

As though the war was not bad enough, the Asiatic influenza that had begun to sweep across Europe as hostilities drew to an end had decimated those at home as well as those serving their country. Hundreds of the young servicemen who had miraculously survived the fighting succumbed instead to the insidious disease, while others returned home to find that parents, siblings, sweethearts or friends had sickened and died. Sometimes whole families were taken by the influenza, leaving empty, cold, dark and silent houses that had once been bustling warm homes. It was, the folk said, like the old Black Death they had learned about at the school.

When at last the well-wishers had all returned to their own homes and the girls were in bed in the upper room, James picked up a newspaper, flicking through its pages and glancing at Stella over the top of it as she put the kitchen to rights.

Her once comfortably rounded body was now slim, though still womanly, he noticed. The lamplight picked out grey strands amid the brown hair drawn loosely back into a knot at the nape of her neck, and at one point when she turned and lifted her head suddenly, as though listening for some noise from the attic bedroom above, he saw that her mouth, which had always been swift to tremble when she was upset, or quiver into a smile when she was happy, had firmed and there were new lines between her dark eyes. But then, the war had made a difference to them all.

Apparently satisfied that their daughters were asleep upstairs, and none of them needed her attention, she bent to pick something up from the floor, her breasts pushing against the front of her blouse. Recalling the feel of her soft body against his, James felt a sudden surge of desire and anticipation. He laid the paper down and cleared his throat.

'I'll just go out by and have a smoke before I go tae my bed.'

Outside, he leaned against the house wall, the smoke from his pipe twisting up from the bowl to lose itself in the darkness, and thought about Stella. He had not been a good husband to her, he knew that. From the very beginning he had resented being tied down to a loveless marriage. It had never occurred to him to wonder how Stella felt about their union, and if she was content. All he knew, as time went on and their three daughters arrived, each birth dashing his hopes of a son, was that Stella – gentle, biddable, anxious-to-please Stella – was not enough for him and never would be. He needed more, and he had found it where he should never have looked. And Stella had found out.

He gave a soft groan at the memory of those dark days. In a way the Great War had been a blessing because it took him away from Buckie, away from sinful temptation and from Stella's silent condemnation. But now, five years on from those hot-headed, hot-blooded days, James Lowrie watched the smoke from his pipe swirl and drift and disappear into the night, and wondered if he and his wife could make another beginning.

Part of his irritation with her had lain in her failure to produce the sons he wanted; laddies to be taken to the fishing and taught the ways of the sea and of the silver darlings that came each year in their huge shoals, and to take over when James finally became too old to haul in a net heavy with the dancing, shimmering herring.

Stella had lost two children in the six years since Ruth's birth, one early in her pregnancy and the other stillborn in the week war was declared. The second child had been the boy that they both longed for. Stella, her eyes sunk in an ashen face, had scarcely risen from her bed when James took the *Fidelity* to war.

But they were both still young, and fit, James thought now. There was time yet for them to produce a laddie, or mebbe two.

Boots clattered on cobbles and a neighbour went by on his way home. 'Aye, James,' he said cheerily. 'It's a ca'al night. Winter's comin'.'

14

'Aye,' James agreed, and knocked his pipe out against the house wall.

Stella was already in bed when he went back into the house, lying on her side, her eyes closed and her hair in a long plait that lay along the curve of her back.

James was not entirely comfortable about undressing in the room his parents had shared. The big chest of drawers and the bed had been there for as long as he could remember, though Stella had brought two chairs, a plain wooden upright and a low nursing chair, from her father's house. He eyed the nursing chair, recalling her sitting in it, years back, head bent over the baby cradled in her arms. He remembered the easy, natural way she drew her blouse aside, baring a breast white as the milk that made it even heavier than normal, and the beautiful, delicate tracery of blue veins against her alabaster skin.

She did not stir when he blew out the lamp and slipped into bed beside her. For a moment he lay still, listening to her even breathing, then he laid a tentative hand on her shoulder. The muscles tensed beneath his fingers, and her breathing stopped and then began again, slow and steady and controlled.

James took his hand away and turned over so that they lay back to back. It was a long time before either of them slept.

James Lowrie strode down to the harbour on the following morning, his studded boots striking sparks from the cobblestones. He was his father's son – never happy unless he was free of the land and the people on it, and besides, he had been away from the fishing for too long. After years of searching the seas for man-made, death-dealing mines he yearned to get back to his own trade.

The older men who hung about the harbour, clinging to memories of their own fishing days, tried to draw him into their talk, but he finally managed to escape them and get along to where the *Fidelity* awaited him.

For a few minutes he stood on the stone wall above her, trying to see her through Jacob's eyes. In the watery morning sunlight the drifter was a sorry sight, but she could be put to rights. The first thing to be done was an inventory of all the work that was needed.

James skimmed down the ladder, his booted feet landing on the deck with a satisfying thud, and then made for the rope locker immediately below the forrard deck. Normally it was used to house the coiled messenger warp that carried the fishing nets, but over the war years it had become a glory hole, where all sorts of bits and pieces had been tossed out of the way.

As he opened the double doors, not much larger than window shutters, he heard a skittering sound from the dark, smelly interior. James swore roundly, snatching at a bucket lying close to the door; he'd have no rats on *his* boat!

'Get out of it,' he roared, banging the bucket against the decking by the door. 'Filthy stinking vermin!' Then, as there was no reaction, not even the scampering and panic-stricken squeaking he had expected, he threw the bucket into the darkness of the locker.

'Ow!'

'What the—? Come out of there!' When there was no reply, James, almost bent double in his attempt to peer into the thick darkness, dropped to his knees and reached with a long arm. His fingers encountered cloth; reaching further, they closed round the material and the flesh and bone it covered.

'Ow-ow-OW!' came the protests as his captive was pulled willy-nilly through the clutter of boxes, buckets, ropes and rubbish. Then he was out in the open, dishevelled and dirty, blinking up at James.

'What are you doin' on my boat?'

'Just lookin',' the small boy said defensively.

'Aye, an' just takin' too, I've no doubt. Turn yer pockets out!'

'I will not! I never took anythin' from yer smelly old boat!'

The lad's impertinence took James aback. His grip slackened, and the child, taking advantage of it, wriggled like an eel and would have been off if James hadn't managed to tighten his hold just in time. Enraged, the little boy kicked out and one of his sturdy boots delivered a painful crack on the man's shin. Without stopping to think, James hit back, an open-handed slap that rang through the air as it landed on the side of the boy's head.

'Ow!' he yelled again. His knees sagged, and James had to catch him with both hands to keep him upright. For a moment the boy drooped towards him, then he rallied and glared up at his captor, blinking back sudden tears of pain and shock.

'You hit me!'

'And I'll hit ye again if I get any more of yer insolence, so mind that, my loon! You need tae be taught a lesson and if yer faither doesnae see tae it, then I will. Where d'ye come from?'

'Buckie, the same as you.' Although one ear was scarlet from the blow, the child had not lost his bravado.

'I mean, where d'ye live?'

The boy hesitated, biting his lip, and then, as James shook him, he blurted out, 'Cliff Terrace.'

'Cliff Terrace? And what are ye creepin' around my boat for, if it's not for mischief?'

'I just wanted tae see it.'

'Ye'll not see much in there.' James jerked his head towards the black hole that was the rope locker. 'What's yer name? Yer name, lad,' he repeated with another shake as the boy remained silent, his grey eyes flickering from side to side as though in search of a suitable answer. 'And I want the truth, mind. I can find out easy enough if ye try tae lie tae me.'

The child gave a heavy sigh, and then said reluctantly, 'Adam Pate.'

'Pate?' All at once, James felt the blood drain out of him, from his skull pan to the soles of his feet. He would not have been surprised to find it puddling on the deck around his boots. 'Gil Pate's boy?'

'Aye. An' when my faither hears that you hit me he'll come after ye,' the child stormed. 'He's a big man, an' he'll—'

'How old are ye?' James asked hoarsely.

'Four years past.'

Aye, that would be about right, James thought, releasing the boy, who rubbed at his sore arm.

'You're my Uncle James home from the wars, are ye no'?' he asked. 'I just wanted tae see the boat. It's a sorry lookin' thing.'

'Aye, well, so are you right now, and the *Fidelity*'s been through a lot more than you have. Come on.' James made for the ladder leading to the harbour. 'Up you go. I'm takin' you home.'

'I can go home by mysel'. I came down here by mysel'.'

'I'm takin' you home,' James said again, and scaled the ladder, leaving the lad to scuffle up after him.

They walked up the hill to Cliff Terrace in silence, James easing back on his usual stride to allow the boy to keep up, and Adam too busy running alongside to find the breath to talk. As they reached the terrace James stopped, swung the child round, but with a gentler grip than before, and squatted so that they were eye to eye.

'Ye'd best get tidied up afore yer mother sees ye,' he said. By good fortune, Stella had tucked a clean handkerchief into his pocket before he left the house; he himself had no time for such fripperies, but now he was glad of the snowy square of material. He held it out to Adam, as he had seen Stella doing with his own children, and after the little boy automatically spat on it James carefully wiped the worst of the rope-locker grime off his face before running his fingers through the dark hair, then tugging at the lad's jacket. Adam squirmed, little knowing that the attention he was receiving had nothing to do with making him more presentable – it was done solely in order to allow James to study him and to touch him.

The grey eyes, he now realised, were just like his father's and his sister's – and his own, if it came to that. The child had a tumble of dark hair; again, the same colouring as James and his own father Weem before him. His face was square-chinned and pleasing to the eye, and his sturdy little body held itself well.

'Are ye done now?' Adam finally asked, a pleading note in his voice, and when James nodded and straightened, stuffing the handkerchief into his pocket, the lad grinned his relief and turned to point at the row of smart two-storey houses built not long before on the hill above the harbour, facing out to sea. 'It's that house over there,' he said, and set off at a trot.

James stayed where he was, watching him.

'What d'ye mean, lassie – gone?' Bethany Pate asked from the stove, where she was ladling porridge from a large pot.

'He's no' in his bed, and nowhere tae be seen in the house,' the maidservant said. 'That sort of gone.'

'Mind your impudence. He'll be in the back yard.'

'I've looked,' Leezie snapped back at her employer.

'Rory, was Adam still in his bed when you came down?' Bethany appealed to her stepson, waiting patiently at the table for his breakfast.

'He was up before me. I thought he was down here with you, or out in the back yard.' Rory wanted no part of the responsibility for his young brother. It was enough to have to share a bedroom with Adam, who never seemed to be at rest, even when he was sleeping.

'Are his clothes gone or is he still in his nightshirt?'

'I didnae see his clothes but they might have been in the room.'

'Leezie, go and see – and look round the rest of the house while you're at it,' Bethany ordered.

'I thought I heard the front door closing when I was getting dressed,' Ellen offered, taking two plates of porridge from

19

the stove to the table, where she put one in front of her brother and sat down to eat the other.

'And you never thought to say?'

'Why would I?' seven-year-old Ellen asked. 'I thought it might be you goin' out early, or my faither home from Yarm'th.'

'He's not expected in as early as— The cooperage,' Bethany suddenly realised. 'That's where the wee imp of Satan's gone. Wait till I get my hands on him!' She stopped in the middle of ladling out her own porridge and hurried into the hall, while Rory and Ellen, used to their young half-brother setting off such alarms, rolled their eyes at each other and went on eating.

'Leezie!' Bethany shouted up the carpeted staircase. 'Is there any sign of him yet?'

The maid appeared at the top of the stairs. 'No there's not, but he's got himself dressed all right.'

'He'll have gone down to the cooperage.' Bethany began to unfasten her apron. 'See that Rory and Ellen get off to the school on time, lassie, and have your own breakfast. I'm away to the harbour to fetch Master Adam and give him the rough edge of my tongue!'

Snatching her jacket from the hallstand, she hurried out, pushing her arms into the jacket sleeves as she went. The first time Adam had found his way to the cooperage alone, when he was only three, he had not been noticed until one of the men caught him trying to peer over the edge of a vat of boiling water. There were so many dangers for a wee laddie in that place – the fires needed to bring the water to boiling point so that the steam could be used to soften the staves, the scalding water itself, the hammers – so many things to harm a small boy with an unquenchable curiosity and no fear at all.

She reached the gate and had gone through it to the road when she saw her son marching towards her.

'Adam? Adam Pate, ye wee imp!' She flew at him,

crouching down before him and taking his shoulders in her two hands so that she could study him and make sure that he was safe and unharmed. 'Where have you been?'

He shrugged himself free. 'I went tae see my uncle's boat.'

'Your uncle?' for a moment Bethany thought that he was talking of Gil's brother Nathan or her own brother, Innes, but neither man owned a boat.

Then, as Adam went on, 'He's come back with me,' and turned to point, she looked up to see her older brother standing several paces away, watching the two of them.

Worry and relief vanished, to be replaced by a strange sensation, as though time itself had stopped. Bethany got to her feet slowly, struggling to push her body upright through air that had become almost solid. She reached for Adam's shoulder, keeping him near to her, keeping him safe.

'James,' she said, and the word, dropping from her numbed lips, broke the spell.

'Ye look as if ye'd seen a ghost, Bethany.' He took a step or two towards her. 'Did ye not know I was back?'

'The bairns said they'd seen the *Fidelity* coming in yesterday,' she acknowledged, 'but . . .' She looked down at the child at her side and then back at James, who had pulled his cap off. Clutching it in one hand, he indicated Adam with the other.

'I – I found the wee lad down at the harbour.'

'I wanted to see what the boat looked like,' Adam prattled cheerfully. 'This is my Uncle James, home from the war.'

'I know who it is.' Bethany tore her attention away from her brother to her son. 'You're a bad laddie! I've a good mind to give you a whipping.'

'No,' James said swiftly, and then, as she glared at him he added lamely, 'He meant no harm. He was just curious tae see the *Fidelity*.'

'It's all right,' Adam assured him. 'She'd not really whip me. Anyway, my faither's comin' back today and he wouldnae let her.'

'Don't you be so sure of that, my loon,' Bethany spun him round to face the gate and then gave him a slight push. 'Go to the house at once and tell Leezie to get you cleaned up then give you your breakfast.'

'Come on in,' Adam invited James.

'He's too busy. Go on now before I change my mind about that whipping!'

3

'He only wanted tae see the boat,' James protested as the little boy went off.

'He knows that he's not supposed to go out of the house without permission.'

'Ach, he's a laddie, and laddies arenae good at keepin' tae the rules.'

'You're as soft as Gil is,' she said scathingly.

'It's been a long time, Bethany.' His eyes, grey like her own, and like Adam's, travelled over her face.

'Only four years.'

'But they've been long, long years.' He looked beyond her as he spoke, his eyes intent. Bethany turned to see Adam slapping the palms of both hands on the door panels. When Leezie answered the summons he pushed by her knees and disappeared into the house.

'That's a fine bairn ye've got there, Bethany,' James said, and she swung back to face him again.

'Gil's right proud of him.'

'Any man would be proud tae call that wee loon his son.' Her hands clenched by her sides. 'Why have you come here, James?'

'I told ye, I found the boy on the boat and brought him back tae ye.' He studied the row of handsome houses. 'Ye've done well for yersel'.'

'Gil's a good provider.'

'Aye – good at packin' and sellin' the fish that other men catch,' James said quietly. 'Did A— Did the boy say that he's comin' home today?'

'Later, from Yarm'th.'

'I'll see him then.'

'What d'you want to see Gil for?' she asked sharply.

'Ye neednae concern yerself. I'm not out tae cause trouble.'

'If you mean that, you'll keep away from this house, and from Adam. He's none of your business.'

'Are ye certain o' that, Bethany?' He studied her, his head tilted to one side, his eyes searching hers.

'Of course I'm certain. I'm his mother.'

'When I saw him down there on my boat just now—'

'That's enough, James!'

'You weren't always so cold towards me, Bethany,' he said, and colour rose up beneath the smooth skin of her face.

'We all make mistakes we regret,' she said, and turned back to the house, her erect back daring him to follow. As he hesitated, the door burst open and two older children erupted down the path and out of the gate.

'Uncle James?' The boy came rushing towards James, grinning, with his sister just behind him. 'It's me, Rory.'

'We saw the boat comin' in yesterday when we were all playin' on the braes,' the girl chimed in. Her name was Ellen, James remembered, then realised guiltily that he had identified his sister's stepdaughter more easily than his own daughters.

'I knew right away that it was the *Fidelity*,' Rory said proudly.

'Did ye?'

'Off you go, the pair of you, or you'll be late for the school,' Bethany snapped, and as they hurried off with a final grin at their uncle, she added, 'And if you'll excuse me, James, I've got a house to see to.'

As Bethany went into the house Adam shot out of the kitchen like a cork from a bottle. 'Is my Uncle James not with you? I wanted tae talk tae him!'

'He's too busy to be bothered with wee loons like you,' Bethany retorted. 'Especially loons that run out of the house and give their mothers a fright. You deserve a good skelp!'

'But I came back. I always come back.'

For now you come back, Bethany thought, her very bones melting with love for her only child; but the day would come when her most precious possession would go out into the world to make his own way, and not return to her. She picked him up and carried him to the kitchen, where the maid was washing the dishes.

'Keep him close by you, Leezie,' she said, and went into the front parlour to peer out from behind the snowy lace curtains hung over the bay window to ensure privacy for the inmates of the house. At the other side of the road the ground dropped down to the harbour below, allowing a good view of the Moray Firth, stretching to the far horizon.

From the side window she could just see James disappearing down the road. Almost at once he went beyond her sight, and she gave a small, soundless sigh, then turned to face the room.

Until he and his brother Nathan, a fish curer, had gone into partnership with Jacob McFarlane, Gil had been content enough to live in a small house in the Catbow, a district of Buckie. But the fortune Jacob had amassed during years spent travelling the world meant that the Pate businesses were able to expand, and it was then that Gil became ambitious. The need for food production during the war had been lucrative for both brothers, and had enabled Gil to buy and furnish the fine house Bethany now stood in.

The drawing room, with its carpets and its large, comfortable chairs and gleaming furniture, reflected its owner's success admirably. Tall vases the height of four-year-old Adam flanked the fireplace with its polished fire irons, and carefully selected ornaments were displayed on the sideboard and on the mantelshelf, where they stood on either side of a handsome clock in the shape of a pillared temple.

It was a far cry from the cottage Bethany and her two brothers had been raised in, and although she had been mistress of the place for the past four years she had never felt at home there, for she was still a fisherman's daughter to the tips of her fingers.

She smiled slightly as she heard a faint peal of childish laughter from the kitchen, then bit her lip. She was more severe with Adam than she had ever been with Rory and Ellen, her stepchildren, and that troubled Gil at times. But Bethany knew that it was nothing more than a defence against the passionate, overprotective love she had felt for the child from the moment of his birth. She would kill, if need be, to keep him safe from harm. Often she lay awake at night, fearful of some harm coming to him.

And now, with the *Fidelity* lying down in the harbour, she was doubly afraid for her son, and uncertain of her own ability to safeguard him.

She turned back to the window and stared out over the white-flecked sea, wishing that James had never come back to Buckie.

James went straight from the confrontation with his sister to the harbour, where he dropped down on to the *Fidelity*'s deck and then walked up into the bows, staring down at the smooth dark harbour water below. It had been a difficult home-coming, and now there was the lad, Adam, to reckon with. Recalling the child's bonny wee face and his eagerness to see the drifter, James wished that he could have the chance to spend some time with him. But he knew that Bethany would never allow it.

'Welcome home, James.'

He spun round and stared at the tall, lanky man standing on the harbour wall above. 'Innes?' he asked uncertainly.

'Aye, it's me right enough. Can I come aboard?'

'Surely.' James watched as his younger brother descended the ladder from the harbour wall slowly and carefully, making sure of each handhold and feeling carefully for every rung with his foot before trusting his weight to it. Finally Innes put a foot on the gunwale, hesitated, then just as James started forward to help, he managed the final drop away from the ladder and down on to the deck.

'Welcome home,' he said again, holding out a hand. He had aged more than the four or five years since they had last seen each other. Silver streaks glittered in his thick black hair, and his dark eyes – their mother's eyes – were sunk into their sockets. Innes had always been thinner than James, but now he looked as if a strong gale might blow him away. Even so, his grip was firm.

'Are ye well? Stella told me in a letter that—' James stopped, unsure of how to put it.

'That I was invalided out because the mustard gas went for my lungs.' His brother completed the sentence for him. 'I'm fine.' He thumped his own chest lightly. 'I'll always be damaged, but it doesnae trouble me overmuch.'

'Ye're back workin' at Webster's garage, then?'

'I'm at Thomson's boatyard now. I earn more there, and with the bairns comin' along sae fast we needed more money.'

'How many bairns d'ye have?'

Pride shone from Innes's face. 'There's Mary and Will and Jessie, and wee Matthew's the youngest. And there's another arrivin' at the turn of the year.'

'Jessie. She'll have been named for our mother?'

'Aye, she was born just months afore Mither died. She was right proud tae have her name passed on tae the wee one. Will was named for our father – and Zelda's father too, though she'll not admit to that, with him bein' such a thrawn old bugger,' said Innes, who had been beaten black and blue by Zelda's enraged father when he discovered that she was pregnant with no wedding ring on her finger. 'We've got a wee hoosie in Gordon Street. Zelda would be pleased tae see ye there, James, and so would Aunt Meg.'

'Aunt Meg's bidin' with you and Zelda?'

'The old soul's not fit tae bide on her own now, and she's

good company for Zelda,' said Innes. Then, studying the faded paintwork and the decking, gouged and splintered in places, 'You've had a longer war than I had – you and the *Fidelity*.'

'It wasnae an easy time,' James acknowledged.

'The whole town misses Charlie. He was a friend tae everyone – specially the lassies.'

'Aye.' For a fleeting moment the brothers exchanged faint smiles, then James said, 'I keep expectin' tae see him everywhere I go on this boat.'

A brief silence fell between them before Innes asked, 'How's the engine?'

'As good as ever it was.'

'I'll just have a wee look at it since I'm here.' Innes made for the galley, where an inner companionway led to the engine room.

Years before, James recalled as he followed his brother down into the bowels of the drifter, Innes had had such a fear of the sea, and of anything to do with the sea, that it had been a struggle to get him to look at the engines. James had thought Innes a coward, but the long, hard war years had taught him that bravery was not always obvious. By forcing himself on to the boat in those days Innes had shown courage. He had demonstrated it again when he held to his determination to marry Zelda despite being half-killed by her father, and yet again on the day he had faced up to James on the *Fidelity*'s spray-soaked, heaving deck.

That confrontation was not a memory that James enjoyed, for Innes had been the victor, and the memory of the utter contempt in his look that day still made James wince.

'They'll do,' Innes finally pronounced.

'Of course they will. The drifter herself'll be finished afore the engines give out.'

Innes's teeth flashed white in the gloom as he grinned. 'Ye're right there,' he said, and then wiped a hand across his brow. 'Let's get out of here and catch a breath of air. This boat still has the stink of fish about it.'

'It's been years since she was at the fishin',' James argued as his brother pushed past him. 'There's no smell of fish tae her now.'

'There is,' Innes told him, and began to climb. His progress became slower as he went up, and once back on deck he leaned his shoulder against the engine cowling, gasping, hands on his knees, head hanging and his eyes closed.

'Are you all right?' James asked, alarmed, and his brother nodded, flapping a hand as though trying to wave the questions away.

'Leave me . . . for a minute . . .' His voice was a low, painful wheeze.

It hurt to watch him struggle to draw air into his damaged lungs and not to be able to help. James took him at his word and went into the wheelhouse, where he loitered until, to his relief, he finally saw Innes straighten up and wipe his mouth with a handkerchief.

'I just need time tae catch my breath when I've been too active,' he said in a matter-of-fact voice when James joined him. 'Ye'll get used tae it, the same as I've had tae.'

'It takes a wee bit of gettin' used tae.'

Innes made as if to wipe the worst of the oil and grime from his hands with the handkerchief, thought the better of it, put the handkerchief carefully into one pocket and took a rag from another. 'The mustard gas made a right mess of my lungs,' he explained as he cleaned oil from his fingers. 'For a while I'd not have given a penny for my chances, but Zelda told me straight that she wasnae goin' tae be a widow sae young. She's a grand lass, is Zelda. She and Mither nursed me back tae health atween them.' Then, straightening to his full height, 'So when are ye goin' tae start puttin' this boat tae rights?'

'Jacob wants tae sell her. He's got a new boat,' James said, 'and he wants me tae skipper her.'

Innes nodded. 'That would be the *Jess Lowrie*. She's a fine wee drifter, a good few years younger than this one. But you're surely not goin' tae let the *Fidelity* go, are ye? I may not be a fisherman,' Innes went on as James shot a startled glance at him, 'but I know what this drifter meant to our faither and what it means tae you.'

'That doesnae seem tae mean anythin' tae Jacob, though.'

'Why should it? This is the Lowrie boat, James, and Jacob McFarlane isnae a Lowrie, he's a businessman. Granted, he's made sure he got his feet well and truly below the Lowrie table,' Innes said, 'and he started that by buyin' a big share in the *Fidelity*.'

'I don't see what ye're gettin' at.'

'Jacob didnae come back tae Buckie tae set up in business with you and Gil and Nathan. He came back tae marry our mither. The man told me about it himsel', just after she died. He was in a terrible state, poor soul, he had tae talk tae someone,' Innes recollected, pity in his voice. 'He grew up next door tae her and he never wanted anyone else but her. Only she chose our faither and Jacob went away then, for he couldnae bear tae see the two of them together. When he heard that she was a widow woman he came back and tried tae get her tae take him as husband, but she'd no thought of marryin' again. So, since he couldnae wed intae the Lowrie family, he used the money he'd made in his travels tae buy his way in.'

'Jacob McFarlane told you all that?'

'Not word for word, ye understand, but enough so's I could work it out for mysel'. I don't think he realised just how much he did tell me. So there he was, with the biggest share in Weem Lowrie's boat, Weem's son tae catch the fish, Weem's son-in-law tae pickle them and Nathan Pate tae kipper them. A nice wee arrangement.'

'An' what about you?'

Innes grinned. 'Mind that bonny motorcar he bought when he first came back tae Buckie? I'd a grand time drivin' him about in it and lookin' after it for him. Oh, it was a bonny motor, James! I was still bidin' with Mither then, so Jacob was anxious tae make friends with me. He even offered tae buy a garage for me when I wed Zelda, but I refused him, for I wanted tae make my own way in life.'

'So I was the fool that let him dae what he wanted with me, is that it?'

'No fool, for Jacob was your only chance tae get command of the *Fidelity*. But now that he's built up a bonny business here he's got no need of her, can ye not see that? This was Weem Lowrie's boat, and to my way of thinkin', Jacob's happy tae replace it with a boat he bought himself – and renamed the *Jess Lowrie*.'

James stared at his younger brother, marvelling at the man's shrewd mind and wondering why he had never noticed the way of things himself. Then he turned and looked along the length of the drifter.

'You and Bethany have shares in her,' he said thoughtfully. 'Our mither had, too, though I don't know who has her shares now.'

'She left them tae me,' Innes said.

'You could help me tae talk Jacob round.'

Innes shook his head. 'For one thing, nob'dy can change Jacob's mind once it's set on somethin'. If you want tae keep the boat ye'll have tae find a way tae buy Jacob out.'

'Buy him out? But steam drifters cost more than £5,000. That's more than I can afford – more than I can borrow, even.'

'You could find yersel' a partner. Not me, for I can't afford it,' Innes said as his brother looked at him with sudden hope. 'And I doubt if Bethany would be interested – not that she'll have the money either.'

'Ye both hold shares in her.'

'Aye, but we've always looked on this as our faither's boat, James, and now it's yours – and Jacob's. It was never mine or Bethany's – or even Mither's.'

'Are ye sayin' that ye'll no' help me?'

'I'm sayin' that I can't. Ye'll have tae find yer own solution – or go along with Jacob's plans.'

4

It was peaceful, Stella thought that night, with her on one side of the hearth with her mending and James on the other, reading the newspaper. It was the way she wanted it, for Stella was the sort of woman who needed love and security. She knew that his father had pushed James, a carefree bachelor who had always had a string of sweethearts, into their marriage, but even so, she had agreed to the union because she loved him and had loved him for years.

Being timid and unsure of herself, she had kept her feelings for the good-looking young fisherman to herself, knowing that he would never freely choose the likes of her as a wife. Weem Lowrie's need for her father's sailed boat and the money it represented to him had made a dream come true, and it had been her fervent hope that in time, James would come to love her. But she had never been enough for him. He had looked elsewhere, and—

Stella's mind flinched away from the memory of those terrible, hurting weeks, and she made herself blank it out by concentrating hard on the needle busily dipping in and out of a tear in Ruth's underskirt. As the turmoil within began to ease, she wondered if she should after all have turned to him in bed the night before, instead of denying him. Perhaps it was time to forgive the past, even if it could never be forgotten. The thought of the two of them going through the rest of their lives like strangers was unbearable.

'I was thinkin' about yer faither's wee hoosie,' James said just then. 'It'll fetch a good price.'

'I've no notion tae sell it,' Stella said, keeping her head bent over her work.

'What else would we dae with it? We cannae live in two houses at the one time.'

'I was thinkin' of hirin' it out.'

'Ye what?'

'Now that the war's over, the summer visitors'll be comin' back tae the Firth, and I thought I could hire the house out tae them. And there's all the folk that come here for the fishin' season too.' She glanced up at him, anxious to get him to understand. 'I can use the house tae earn my own way.'

'There's no need for that now I'm back home.'

'Even so.' She looked back down at her work.

'But we need the money we could get for it. There's work tae be done on the boat, and new nets tae buy, and—'

'That's for you and Jacob McFarlane tae worry about, surely?' Stella asked, and then as James stayed silent she looked up to see him chewing on his lower lip. 'Is there somethin' wrong between you and him?'

'He doesnae think the *Fidelity*'s worth repairin'. He wants tae sell her, and he wants me tae take one he's not long bought.'

'Is it a good boat?'

'I'm sure it is, but I'm happy enough with the *Fidelity*.'

'Then get Mr McFarlane tae change his mind.'

'He'll not do that!' James tossed the paper down and got to his feet, pacing the small room. 'We might be a partnership, but it's Jacob that holds the purse strings. If I want tae keep the *Fidelity* I'll have tae buy him out, and then find the money tae do the repairs mysel'.'

Suddenly, Stella saw where the conversation was leading. 'And ye can only do that by sellin' my faither's house.'

'Aye, that's about the strength of it.'

Part of her mind told her that this was her chance to heal

the rift between them. If she did as James asked, sacrificing her own hopes in the process, then he would be beholden to her. But the thought had no sooner shaped itself than the clear and logical part of her mind reminded her that grateful though he might be, James Lowrie was not a man to feel beholden to anyone. He would repair his precious boat, the boat he loved far more than he could ever love his wife, and he would take her back to sea, leaving Stella alone again. And nothing would change.

She took a few final stitches in silence before biting off the thread and smoothing out the petticoat, now darned so neatly that the tear in the material had completely vanished. She folded it, and then, at last, she looked up at him.

'That cottage belonged tae my faither, James, and his faither afore him,' she said, her tongue feeling so heavy in her mouth that the words had to be forced out. 'Now it's mine, and I want tae keep it.'

He stared at her, perplexed, and then threw his hands out in a swift, impatient gesture. 'If ye're so set on havin' it then we'll move back there and I'll sell this place. I'm no' bothered.'

She shook her head. 'No, James. This is your house and it's only right that your family should live here. Rentin' the other hoosie out will give us extra money. Mebbe Mr McFarlane's right. Mebbe it's time ye took on a new boat.'

'I don't want a new boat! I want the *Fidelity*.'

'Ye sound like a wee laddie that's lost his toy,' Stella said, and saw his face flame beneath its tan.

'I've just told ye – I need the money we could get from the sale of that house. You're my wife. You should be puttin' my wishes first!'

Stella's careful serenity suddenly evaporated. 'Your wishes, is it?' She stood up, the neatly folded little petticoat falling unnoticed from her lap to the floor. 'Your wishes? And what about mine?'

'Eh?' He gaped at her, taken aback. 'Ye've got a home and bairns and a man tae keep ye. What more can ye want?'

'Dogs have homes, James, and cats are kept. That's not enough for me! Why should you get what you need when I never have, and never will? You married me tae get what you and your faither and your Uncle Albert wanted – the *Fidelity*. And you got her. But what did I get in return – tell me that?'

'You wanted a husband,' he blustered.

'Not just a husband. I wanted a man tae care for me and for the bairns I bore him. But you're like your father, James Lowrie – nothin' matters but gettin' your own way. Now ye're tellin' me that ye "need" the cottage I was raised in, the place my faither left tae me, so's ye can keep that damned drifter? Oh no,' Stella stormed, remembering even in her rage to keep her voice low so that the children sleeping above could not hear her anger. 'Why d'ye think I want the money from the rent of the place? It's because I've made up my mind that if I can't get what I've needed from you all these long, empty years, I'll at least become my own woman and earn my own way in life!'

'Stella—' He began to get up, one hand held out in an attempt to placate her, but she stepped back swiftly, shaking her head. A tendril of brown hair broke loose from its restraints and swung down to brush her cheek.

'Stay away from me, James. If it's money ye want, why don't ye ask yer precious sister for it? I'm sure she'd be only too glad tae help ye.'

'Bethany? Why should she help me?'

'Because you and me both know well enough that the only two things you've ever cared for are the *Fidelity* – and her!'

The blood drained from his face. He came out of his chair with such a rush that for a moment she thought he was intent on striking her. With an effort, she stood her ground, waiting for the blow and in a way almost welcoming the prospect. At least a blow would demonstrate some passion.

But instead, James swallowed hard before saying thickly, 'Ye're haverin'!'

'Am I? You didnae waste much time runnin' up tae her fine, fancy house, did ye?'

'Who said I was there?'

'Nothin' happens in this place without someone knowin' about it. Nothin', James,' Stella said, her voice heavy with meaning. 'Ye were seen speakin' together, you and Bethany.'

'I found the wee laddie hidin' in the boat and took him back, that was all.'

'Oh aye, Bethany's wee laddie. A fine bonny boy, is he no', James? A real Lowrie, that one.' Stella, her heart aching for the tiny boy she herself had birthed and then buried within days; the son that might have made all the difference to her marriage, almost spat the words at him.

They stood glaring at each other, both breathing heavily, both with fists clenched. 'I'm goin' to my bed,' Stella said at last, and he made no attempt to stop her as she went into the back room.

It was only then that she remembered she had not gone through her usual procedure of setting the table for the morning meal and steeping oatmeal in water to soften overnight. They would just have to break their fasts with bread and margarine, she decided, dragging her clothes off and tossing them haphazardly over the small nursing chair, for she was not going back into that kitchen tonight. She pulled the pins from her hair, letting it fall about her face, and got into bed without bothering to brush it out or plait it.

She had expected to lie awake half the night but the sudden flash of rage had exhausted her, and when James finally came to bed more than an hour later, Stella was asleep, her hair scattered over her pillow.

James was sitting in the *Fidelity*'s cabin, a bottle of whisky and a tin mug on the table before him, when heavy boots thumped on the decking overhead. He looked up, and then decided to stay where he was. Jacob would find him soon enough.

But it was Gil Pate who came down the ladder. 'James!'

He shook his brother-in-law's hand vigorously, a huge grin splitting his round, red face. 'By God, man, but you're a sight for sore eyes.'

'So are you, Gil. Ye'll have a drink with me?'

'Ye're at the whisky early in the day, are ye no'?'

'It helps me tae think. And I've a deal of thinkin' tae do.'

Gil rubbed his hands in pleasurable anticipation. 'In that case I'll keep ye company, for it's no' wise for a man tae drink on his own,' he said, squeezing his bulk into the bench seat at the table. The fringe of greying hair about his bald head was now pure silver, James noticed as he poured the whisky, and his face was even redder than before, thanks to a mixture of weather and whisky.

'I'm glad tae see ye home safe from the war, James. And I was vexed tae hear about Charlie.'

'Aye. Ye're back early from Yarm'th,' James said, anxious to change the subject. He splashed some whisky into Gil's mug and then more into his own before he sat down.

'There's a timber boat comin' in and I wanted tae be here for the unloadin'. Nathan's down south seein' tae things while I'm away.' Gil took a big swallow of his drink.

'Can ye trust him?' James asked, with a lift of one eyebrow. Normally the fish-curer, and not the cooper, hired the gutting crews and ran the business, but Nathan Pate was notoriously lazy, and so Gil had taken on those duties.

Now his brother-in-law grinned and then set the mug down, wiping his mouth with the back of one hand. 'I cannae trust him any more than I could afore ye went away, but the men and the lassies know what's tae be done, an' I'll be back with them the day after tomorrow. He surely cannae make much of a mess of things in two, mebbe three days.'

'How's business been?'

'Very good,' Gil said complacently, stretching his thick legs as best he could in the small cabin. 'Beth'ny was sayin' ye called in at Cliff Terrace. I've got myself a fine new house there, have I no'?'

'It looks grand. I went up there with the wee lad after I found him here on the boat. Bethany wasnae very pleased with him.'

'She cannae keep up with him. I thought Rory was a handful, but Adam's worse. He's intae everythin'. I've tae watch him like a hawk when he comes tae the cooperage in case he falls intae a brazier or gets himself built intae a barrel. But there's no harm in the lad. Beth'ny and me are forever arguin' over him, for I think she's over-hard on the boy. Ye'd think that bein' his mother, she'd be more likely tae spoil him, but not her. I'll never understand women.'

'Ye're not the only one,' James said with all his heart, thinking of the previous night, and his normally placid wife's spitting fury.

'He'll be goin' tae the University when he's old enough – Adam, I'm talkin' of,' Gil went on. 'I've set my heart on it.'

'University? Ach, away! That's no ploy for a Buckie loon!'

'You think he should be a cooper, or a fisherman?'

'Why not? He was takin' a right interest in this boat.'

'No, no, James, this one's for the University. I fancy a son o' mine doin' well in the world, and he's sharp as a knife, that wee loon. You see if I'm no' right, James,' Gil boasted. 'Rory'll come intae the cooperage with me when he's older, and Adam'll be a scholar and make his old faither proud of him. I just wish my mither had lived tae see him.'

'From what I mind of the woman – no harm tae her, Gil – she'd have wanted him tae be a minister.'

'Aye, ye're right. Mebbe it's as well she's no' with us now. Did Beth'ny show ye all round the house?'

'I saw it from the street outside, just. I'd business with Innes so I couldnae take the time tae go inside when she invited me,' James lied.

'Ye'll have tae come for yer dinner some night, you and Stella and the quinies. It's a far cry from the wee cottage I used to bide in at the Catbow, eh?'

'Ye've done well for yersel', Gil.' Trust Gil Pate to look

out for his own comfort, James thought, and prosper while other men were fighting and dying.

'So has Jacob, and so will you, now ye're back home. And now that the world's found peace at last we'll all dae well,' the other man rattled on.

'Is the English fishin' good this year?'

'We cannae make the barrels fast enough, James. Ye should be there.'

'The boat isnae up tae it, with all she's been through. But she'll be ready in time for the next herrin' season.'

'Jacob was in at the house last night,' Gil said casually, his eyes on his brother-in-law's face. 'From what he says, he wants you tae take on this new boat he's bought, the *Jess Lowrie*. She's a trim vessel, James, and she's bringin' in good catches down south. She'd do even better with you as skipper.'

'I'll stay with the *Fidelity,*' James said, and then, as Gil looked round the dingy cabin, eyebrows raised, 'All she needs is some deckin' planks and a good coat of paint and a set of nets. I'll not see her sold when she's still got years left in her. If Jacob won't put out the money for the work she needs, I've a mind tae buy her from him and bring her back intae the Lowrie family.'

'Buy her? Ye must have made yer fortune in the war, then?'

'No,' James said, the germ of an idea beginning to form itself in his brain, 'but I was thinkin' that you and me could mebbe manage tae raise the money between us.'

Gil sucked air in through his teeth, eyes narrowing. 'I don't know about that, James, not with what I'd tae pay for that new house of mine.'

'You've done well durin' the war.'

'A bit, mebbe,' Gil admitted, 'but I've got the weans tae think of, and Beth'ny. And I'm no' a young man, James, no' near as young as you.'

'Come and have a look around,' said James, 'and then we might have another drink.'

*

39

Half an hour later they were back in the cabin and the level in the whisky bottle had gone down noticeably.

'I ken what ye mean, James,' Gil was saying, his words tending to run into each other. 'She's a bonny, sturdy wee drifter still, and she's brought back a wheen o' herrin' in her time—'

'And made you a wealthy man,' James put in quickly, refilling his brother-in-law's glass.

'No' entirely by hersel', but you an' the *Fidelity* aye made a good team,' Gil acknowledged.

'So d'ye not think that you owe her a wee bittie o' help in her time o' need?'

Gil chewed his lower lip. 'I could speak tae Beth'ny—'

'Best leave Bethany out of it,' James said swiftly. 'What dae women ken about business?'

'Oh, she's got a good head on her shoulders, has my Beth'ny. Every year she's on at me tae let her take over the hirin' of the guttin' crews the way she used tae, but I'm no' so fond of the idea. She's got enough tae do with the hoosie and the bairns – and I've got her a servant tae do most of the work about the place,' Gil added smugly, 'so she's got that lassie tae manage as well. Servants need trainin', James, and watchin'.'

'That's just what I mean.' James topped up his brother-in-law's glass. 'Men are best seein' tae the money and women are best seein' tae the hoose and the bairns – and the servant lassies.'

'But I think Beth'ny'd want tae help you, James. You're her brother, and when all's said and done she's still got a part share in this boat.'

'Aye, but women don't see things the way we do. They like tae tuck money away in the bank. Tae them, it's like puttin' a bairn tae its bed where it's safe. They don't realise that ye should send it out intae the world tae make more siller for ye.'

'Just like the bairns when they're grown, eh?' Gil rumbled

with laughter at his own joke. 'By God, James, would life no' be much easier if we could faither sovereigns instead of children, eh?'

'It would that.'

Gil held his glass up and owlishly studied the effect of the light shining through the small window and on to the amber whisky before saying carefully, 'There's nothin' gone wrong atween you and Beth'ny, is there?'

'What could go wrong with blood kin?'

'There's somethin' about the look she gets when I mention yer name. It's as if she doesnae like tae hear it.'

James turned a wince into a shrug. 'Me and Bethany always fought like cat and dog. We're too alike. But I've noticed that she's not as friendly with Stella as she once was. They've probably fallen out for some daft reason.'

'Aye, that's likely it.' Gil took another swallow of whisky. 'And ye're right about the money. If I do manage tae help ye out with a wee loan it's probably best tae say nothin' tae her about it. She can be right nippy when she doesnae agree with the things I dae.'

'I can promise you,' James said eagerly, 'that anythin' you put towards the *Fidelity* will come back tae ye safe and sound, and bring more with it forbye. She'll not be ready for the English fishin', but give me till next year's season's over and ye'll get yer reward. What d'ye say?'

'I suppose I could spare somethin',' Gil began. 'As for Nathan – we'll leave him out of it, eh? He's a decent enough brither, but' – he winked, and tapped one blunt finger against his temple – 'he's no' got much of a business head on his shoulders.'

'Best tae keep this atween ourselves,' James agreed. 'That way, you get all the profit when I pay back the loan.'

Gil's eyes brightened as he reached for the bottle and poured the last of the whisky into his glass. 'That's true, I will.'

'Here.' James opened a drawer and produced a notebook,

a pen and an old inkwell. 'Best tae get it all put down in writin' now, before we forget the terms we've agreed on, eh?'

'Aye,' Gil nodded, and then, frowning, 'Whit terms were those? All this talkin's taken them from my mind.'

'Don't you fret yoursel' about that,' James said. 'They're still clear as crystal in mine.'

5

There was nothing new in finding an unknown child in Zelda Lowrie's kitchen, for her door was permanently open in welcome to all who cared to walk in. But this child, Stella discovered, was staying.

'Etta's come tae bide with us and help me tae see tae wee Matt, haven't ye, my pet?' Zelda said cheerfully to the little girl who was rocking baby Matthew's cradle with one hand while keeping the thumb of the other wedged firmly into her mouth. The child gave a barely perceptible nod. Her dark hair, brown eyes and almost olive skin showed that she was a member of the large family Zelda came from.

'She's worth her weight in gold,' Zelda went on in the same bright, firm voice. 'But now ye've got the wee one tae sleep, my lambie, why don't ye go out the back and play with Mary and Will and Jessie? Poor wee soul,' she went on, the cheerfulness vanishing from her voice as soon as the little girl was out of earshot. 'She's an orphan, but she doesnae know it yet for she's only three years old. How can I tell her that her mother's gone?' Her eyes filled with tears. 'D'ye mind my sister Elsie, Stella?'

'Aye, I do.' Zelda had so many brothers and sisters that it was hard to keep track of them, but Elsie stood out in Stella's memory. Like her older sister before her, poor Elsie had become pregnant to a young cooper who, by the time she realised that she was carrying his child, was serving in the

43

army. Elsie's father had put her out of his house, and the young man's mother had taken her in. Sadly, the cooper had been killed before he could return home to marry his sweetheart, and Elsie herself had died in childbirth.

'That is Elsie's wee one?' Stella asked, and then, when Zelda nodded, 'I thought her grandmother was looking after her.'

'She fell poorly a year back and one of her daughters took her in. They didnae want Etta, so my mither got my faither tae agree tae take her. But he's that strict, and the bairn wasnae happy, Stella. So I said we'd take her and put an end once and for all tae her bein' passed from one pair of hands tae another.'

'Have you not got enough with your own four bairns?' Stella asked, and then, lowering her voice, 'Not tae mention—'

She nodded at the fireside chair where Meg Lowrie, aunt to Innes, James and Bethany, dozed. Widowed within months of marriage when her fisherman husband drowned at sea, Meg had earned her living with a variety of jobs: as a packer in a gutting crew, and either working in one of the local net factories or as a skivvy in domestic service between the herring seasons. In her prime she had been able to do as much work as any man, but years of hard physical toil had resulted in crippling rheumatism. Over the past few years Innes's mother Jess had cared for her, and when Jess died, Zelda and Innes had taken the old woman in.

'Ach, Auntie Meg's no bother at all, and neither's wee Etta.' Zelda's eyes filled with sudden tears. 'Elsie was only nineteen when she died, Stella, the same age as that poor lad of hers. And she didnae even live long enough tae hold her wee bairn in her arms. Anyway, what's two more mouths tae feed?'

'It'll soon be three more mouths.' Stella looked pointedly at her sister-in-law's swollen belly.

'But I couldnae leave her with my faither, Stella, not with her bein' a . . .' Zelda glanced at the old woman, who was snoring slightly, and lowered her voice, 'you know. Ye mind what he can be like – he would have it that Elsie's death was the Lord punishin' the poor lassie for her sins. When I went over there tae visit them last week he was talkin' about the wee soul's sins – as if it could be her fault that her mother and father got carried away with their feelin's for each other.' Zelda sniffed, and ran her arm across her face. 'She was that confused, Stella – ye could see that she didnae know what she'd done wrong. It fair broke my heart. How can anyone treat a wee orphaned lassie sae cruel?' Zelda seldom criticised anyone, but unmistakeable anger was creeping into her voice and her eyes.

Remembering the injuries Innes had suffered at his father-in-law's hands, Stella shivered at the thought of small, defenceless Etta living in his house and at his mercy.

'So I just took the few clothes she had, and I brought her home. I think my faither was pleased, and my mither too, because she felt as bad about the way Etta was bein' treated as I did – but she was never able tae stand up tae my faither.'

'How did Innes feel about you bringing the bairn back home?'

'He was fine about it. Why shouldn't he be?' Zelda poured tea from the pot that simmered on the range all day, ever ready for visitors.

'I can't think of Innes disagreeing with anything you wanted,' Stella said, and Zelda laughed.

'He's the finest husband any woman could have. Mother Lowrie used tae say that Innes was the best of the family; I suppose that that was because he was the youngest. You'd have thought that Bethany would have been the favourite, with her bein' the only lassie.'

At the very mention of her other sister-in-law's name, Stella felt her mouth puckering as though she had eaten something sour.

'Bethany was never easy tae like,' she said.

'Ye just have tae take Bethany as ye find her. I get on well

45

enough with her, but I've noticed that the two of ye go awful quiet in each other's company.'

Stella sipped at her tea, strong and hot. 'We've nothin' in common. Bethany's a fine lady now, with her house on Cliff Terrace.'

'Och, I'm sure ye'd rather have James and yer wee cottage than Gil Pate and his big house. I know I'd choose my Innes over the king that lives in London.' Zelda's pretty face took on a sudden glow. 'We made our marriage vows taegether an' neither of us would ever think of breakin' them.'

A surge of bitter envy flooded through Stella. She stared down at her cup, thinking of the quarrel between herself and James the previous night. Zelda would be shocked if she knew the things they had said to each other. But then, Zelda and Innes had married for love.

'Auntie Meg . . .' Gently, Zelda shook the old woman awake. 'Here's a cup of tea for ye – and Stella's come tae see us.'

'How are ye, Auntie Meg?' Stella went over to the chair, and took one of the old woman's hands in hers. The bony fingers were twisted and the skin covered with raised scars from years of packing herring in layers of coarse salt, but Meg's grip was still strong.

'I cannae complain, lass. They've been awful good tae me, Zelda and Innes.' Her voice, too, was still strong, with not a trace of the querulous note often adopted by the very old. 'They've got hearts of gold, the both of them, takin' an old body like me in when they've got a houseful of bairns tae tend tae.'

'Tuts, Auntie, there's always room for one more,' said Zelda, mistress of a house only a fraction the size of Bethany's.

'Your James was here not long since, Stella,' the old woman said.

'James – here?'

46

'It seems that Innes told him Auntie Meg was bidin' with us,' Zelda explained. 'He'd some dinner with us and then he went off on some ploy of his own.'

'He looks even more like Weem than he did before. It was as though my own brither was standin' there in front of me, rest his soul.' Meg's eyes suddenly glistened. 'I was sayin' tae him how much I miss Weem, and Jess. She was awful good tae me when the rheumatics began tae trouble me. I wish she'd no' been taken afore me.' She released Stella's hand in order to scrub the tears away before they overflowed down her seamed face. 'Its hard when the folk ye ken best go afore ye, lass!'

'Now then, Auntie, ye've got years left in ye yet,' Zelda admonished her.

'I hope no'!' Meg shot back at her. 'If the good Lord doesnae send for me tae go home soon I'll have somethin' tae say tae Him when I do get there!'

'I'm sure ye will, and I'd no' like tae be in His shoes if He doesnae please ye. Here.' Zelda folded the stiff old fingers carefully round the cup. 'Have ye got a grip of it?'

'Aye, aye, my quine, I'm no' in my dotage yet. You see tae yer bairn,' Meg ordered as wee Matthew suddenly jumped awake with a startled cry.

'I'll take him.' Stella lifted the little boy from his cot and sat down by the table. The baby stared up at her, yawned, and then settled back to sleep. It felt good to be holding a baby close again.

'He's worn himself out, the wee lambie.' Zelda brushed her son's rounded cheek with the back of a finger. 'He's on his feet now – imagine, and him only just ten months old! He's quicker than Mary and Will and Jessie ever were. Ye're goin' tae be a handful, aren't ye, my wee mannie?' she crooned to the baby. 'As tae the next . . .' She patted her rounded belly and then eased herself down into a chair with a sigh of relief. 'We'll just have tae wait and see.' Then, after a pause, 'I thought with James home at last you'd be smilin'

47

all over yer face, but ye're not. Is there somethin' wrong atween the two of ye?'

'It's just – there's times when I think that if I was his precious fishin' boat instead of just his wife James'd care more for me.'

'He's like his faither,' Meg Lowrie chimed in unexpectedly. 'The sea aye mattered more than anythin' else tae Weem. He was lucky that Jess understood that. I mind her sayin' tae me once that women cannae change men like that, and they can only destroy them if they try it. And destroy themselves at the same time. She was a wise woman, was Jess.'

'Aye,' Stella said. 'Aye, I think she was, Auntie Meg.'

Jacob McFarlane's comfortable house in West Cathcart Street was large enough to accommodate himself and his housekeeper, a widow of middle years. The soft carpeting and the thick curtains and the large chairs that all but swallowed a body up when she sat down on one impressed Stella, who had never been inside the place before.

She luxuriated for a moment in the armchair that Jacob had offered when she went into his study, then remembering that she had called on business, she struggled back to its edge and perched there, hands fisted on her knees.

'It's about James, Mr McFarlane, and the *Fidelity*. He wants tae buy out your share and own the boat himsel', since ye'll no' spend the money on repairin' her. And,' she hurried on as he opened his mouth to speak, 'I'd be grateful if ye'd agree.'

Jacob eyed her thoughtfully. 'Did he ask ye tae come here?'

'Ask me? He'd be in a right temper if he found out I was talkin' tae ye about his business. I'm here of my own accord.' Stella stopped speaking abruptly as the housekeeper brought in a tray.

'Thank you, Mrs Duthie.' Jacob waited until the woman had gone, closing the door noiselessly behind her, then said, 'Would you do me the favour of pouring the tea, my quine? It's no' often I've the pleasure of havin' a lady tae dae it for me.'

When the tea had been poured Stella asked, 'Will ye, Mr McFarlane? Will ye let him have the boat?'

'I'd not want tae lose James, for he's a good fisherman and a good partner.'

'You'd not lose him, not if ye handled him the right way. James knows every inch of the *Fidelity*,' Stella said earnestly. 'He's a good skipper, one of the best, but if he's made tae take over a drifter he doesnae care for, it'll spoil him. Ye cannae deny that the *Fidelity*'s more than paid her way over the years.' She cast a glance round the well-furnished room. 'You've done well out of her, Mr McFarlane.'

'I suppose I have.' He sipped his tea, watching her over the rim of the cup as though waiting for further argument. But Stella had already said what she had to say – more than she had meant to say; she was surprised at her own defence of James and the drifter that meant more to him than she and her daughters ever could.

Even though she had no notion for the tea, having drunk two cups with Zelda only an hour earlier, she sipped diligently, as though enjoying every mouthful.

Silence fell between them for a full four minutes before Jacob McFarlane laid his empty cup aside.

'Let me give the matter some thought. I'll not take long over it, I promise you.' He crossed to the fireplace and pulled at a bell rope; then, as they waited for the housekeeper to arrive, he added, 'I must say, my quine, that I envy your husband. I've never known the pleasure of a wife who cared enough tae go seekin' favours on my behalf.'

'Cared?' Stella felt her face colour at the very thought. 'Indeed, Mr McFarlane, it has nothin' tae do with carin',' she said sharply, hunting about for her gloves. 'It's just that the man can be like a bear with a sore head if anythin' comes between him and that precious drifter!'

It was late when James finally came home. As the clock ticked the seconds and then the minutes and then the hours away, Stella began to feel uneasy. Perhaps he wasn't coming back. Perhaps he had decided to stay on board the drifter rather than return to her and to their daughters.

She put the evening meal on the table, pushing her own food around her plate and snapping at Ruth when the little girl innocently asked where her daddy was.

The table was cleared, the dishes washed, the children sent to their beds, and still there was no sign of James. Stella put the kitchen to rights and then waited by the fire, her hands idle and her knitting neglected in her lap, ears straining for the sound of his return.

Several times, hearing studded boots clattering up the street outside, she picked up her knitting to give the illusion of being busy, but each time the feet went on past the door, the street fell quiet again, and the knitting was dropped back into her lap.

She was dozing by the time he finally returned, waking with a start when he knocked against a chair, scraping it over the floor.

'You're back.' She snatched up her knitting.

'I'd a lot tae see tae.' He shrugged out of his coat and hung it on the back of the door.

'I'll get your supper on the table while you get washed.'

By the time he returned from the wash house the meal was on the table and she was back in her chair, knitting busily.

'I hear ye were at Zelda's today.'

'Can a man not move in this place without everyone knowin'?' he asked, exasperated.

'Your Auntie Meg said. She was pleased tae see you.'

'Aye. She's no' as I mind her at all.'

'She's older. We all are. We've all changed,' Stella said.

'I saw Gil, too.'

'Is he back from England already?'

'So there's some things you don't know about?' James said, and she bit her lip, having the sense to keep quiet.

Jacob McFarlane arrived just as James finished his meal.

He pushed his plate aside and indicated the chair opposite. 'Sit down, man, I was just wonderin' if it was too late tae call on ye.'

'Never too late for business.' Jacob sat, and nodded his thanks as Stella put a mug of tea before him.

'Business, is it? Ye'd best hear what I've got tae say afore you tell me yer own business,' James said. 'I got Innes tae go over the boat with me this afternoon, plank by plank, and tell me what it might cost tae have her repaired. Then I went tae see the mannie at the bank and he's agreed tae take this house up as surety for a loan.'

'Ye've mortgaged the house?' The words were out of Stella's mouth before she could stop them. James gave her a cold smile.

'As ye said yersel', it's mine. Even if I cannae meet the loan – and I'll meet it – you and the lassies willnae be homeless if things go wrong, for ye've still got yer own cottage, have ye no'?' He turned back to Jacob McFarlane. 'So I'm offerin' tae buy your share of the *Fidelity*. Name yer price.'

'Well now, James, this is a right turn of events, for I'm here tae tell ye that I've thought things over, and I think we should keep the drifter. She's got years in her yet, as you said.'

James had been leaning so far back in his chair that, solid as it was, it had tipped back. Now he sat upright so suddenly that the front legs thudded to the floor. 'What made ye change yer mind?'

'I gave it a lot of thought,' Jacob told him smoothly, without so much as a flicker of a glance in Stella's direction, 'and decided that ye were right. We'll hold ontae her.'

Stella's pent-up breath had just started to go out in a long and silent sigh of relief when to her horror she heard her husband say, 'Ye'll not, for I want her for my own. I'm no' goin' tae give ye the chance tae do this again, Jacob. Name yer price.'

51

Jacob's thick, grey eyebrows immediately came together in a scowl. He was not used to being crossed like this. 'And if I refuse tae sell my share?'

'Then I'll keep on at you until ye change yer mind,' James said, his jaw set and his voice grim.

'James—'

'You keep out of it, Stella, this is men's business,' he ordered curtly without bothering to look at her.

'And if I ask for more money than ye can raise?' Jacob wanted to know.

'I'll find it, somehow.'

'Even if it means beggarin' yer own wife and bairns?'

James shrugged. 'I want the *Fidelity,* whatever the cost. I'll not have her and me held up tae ransom again.'

There was a silence, during which both men glared at each other, neither giving way, while Stella stood by helplessly. Then she jumped as Jacob slapped both hands palm down on the table with a sound like a gun being fired.

'By God, James, ye're a thrawn bugger,' he boomed. 'Aye, all right, ye've won.'

'Ye'll sell the boat tae me?'

'Aye, and for a fair price. We'll agree tae that in the mornin' for it's too late tae start hagglin' and bargainin'. Ye can pay half of it down now and I'll take the rest at the end of next season. I can't say fairer than that. There's two conditions, though,' Jacob said. 'The first is that I'll want ye tae go on sellin' yer catches tae Gil the same as afore.'

James grinned broadly. 'I can dae that all right. Better a contract than havin' tae hope for a good market every time. So what's yer second condition?'

'I still want Jem as skipper of the *Homefarin*', for tae my mind the mannie that's in charge of her at the moment would make a better mate nor a skipper.'

'But Jem's been my mate ever since Charlie was killed. We work well together, him and me.'

'I need him and I'll have him, or the agreement's off.'

52

Jacob's tone was inflexible, and Stella eyed her husband nervously, wondering if all the new plans were going to be for nothing.

James bit hard on the stem of his pipe, then said, 'Aye, I suppose it's time he'd his own boat. It's no' right tae stand in his way.'

'Good. That's that settled.' Jacob spat on the palm of his large, calloused hand then held it out to James, who shook it. 'And now I'm for home, and my bed. Come and see me tomorrow mornin', James, and we'll get the business finished. And I want you and Jem in Yarm'th as soon as ye can. You can take over the *Homefarin'* for what's left of the season, and it'll give Jem the chance tae get intae the way of her. Ye neednae fret about the *Fidelity*, for me and Innes can see that the work gets done.'

'It's a shame,' Zelda said as she watched Stella pack James's seaman's kist for his trip to Yarmouth, 'that your man's scarce arrived home and here ye are, losin' him again.'

'Aye.' Stella wondered if it was possible to lose someone she had never owned in the first place. But on the other hand, she had learned not to expect much else from her marriage to James Lowrie.

'Mind you, I'll mebbe be able tae get the chance tae talk tae Innes once James has gone,' her sister-in-law prattled on, pouncing on wee Matt as he toddled past and lifting him on to her knee. 'Your James has never been away from our house since Innes agreed tae see tae the repairs while he's down at Yar— Will ye get this bairn's hands off me afore he makes me bald?' Zelda winced as Matt reached out to tug hard at her black curls.

'Here, pet.' Stella cut a piece of hard crust from the loaf on the table, dipped it in her tea, and then into the sugar bowl before holding it out to the baby. Matt promptly let go of his mother in order to grab it. 'He's determined tae leave the boat in good hands afore he goes away.'

'It's in good hands, all right. It's funny how Innes cannae abide the boats when they're on the sea, yet he's as happy as a lintie workin' with them in the yard,' Zelda said. 'Not like me – I think a boat up on the stocks looks like a whale. It gives me the shivers. As far as I'm concerned, they belong in the water.'

Normally James Lowrie followed the fishing to the various ports by sea, but this time, since the *Homefaring* was already in Yarmouth, he and Jem had to go by rail. A carter passing through Buckie on his way to Aberdeen arranged to take him to the railway station, and he refused to let Stella walk to the meeting place with him.

'I cannae be doin' with goodbyes,' he said irritably, snatching up his kist and making for the door. 'I'll no' be away for long in any case, since there's only about four weeks left tae the English season.'

'You'll let me know how you're . . . how the new boat handles?' she said, and he nodded without looking directly at her. His relief at making his escape was so strong that it almost cut through the air.

'Aye,' he said, and was gone.

Alone in the kitchen, Stella bit her lip until it hurt, then went out to the wash house at the back, where water was heating in the big copper. Taking a pailful, she returned to the kitchen and began to scrub the floor.

They had finally lain together on the night before. There was nothing warm or loving about it – James had suddenly turned in the bed and reached for her, and this time she had not denied him. Minutes later they had been back to back again, with not a word said, but at least it was contact after all those years. As she scrubbed at the already spotless floor the following morning she wished with all her heart that there might be a result. A laddie this time, she begged the Fates from behind lips set in a thin tight line.

While his wife scrubbed and prayed, James waited for the

54

cart, his kist at his feet and joy in his heart. The war was all but over and at last he was free to escape to the sea where he belonged.

A week later Stella got her answer. There was to be no son to follow James to the fishing. Not yet, and possibly not ever.

6

If only, Bethany thought as she surveyed the bundle of scrap paper that Gil used to record his business transactions, he would give in to her pleas and demands and allow her to take charge of his paperwork. Instead, he insisted on seeing to it himself even though he knew that she was much better at figuring than he could ever be. Every time, he ended up having to turn to her for help when things got out of hand, and every time she had to spend hours putting the books to rights.

It was almost the end of November, and she had two weeks at the most before he returned from Yarmouth in which to transfer his scribbled records to the big ledger kept in the roll-top desk that dominated one corner of the parlour. Gil had tried to take the ledger down to the cooperage on several occasions but Bethany, knowing that it was not safe out of her keeping, had always managed to retrieve it. Now she thumped it on the desk, tutting as its arrival caused a waft of air that, in turn, floated several papers to the floor. She retrieved them and then settled to work. For once the house was silent, for the two older children were still at school and Leezie had taken Adam over to Zelda's for the afternoon.

An hour later she put the pen down and stretched her arms above her head and then rubbed her cold, stiff hands together, frowning over the neat lists of pounds, shillings and pence before her. The ledger was almost up to date but there was a discrepancy somewhere; a considerable amount of money unaccounted for.

Bethany picked the pen up again and chewed on it, her eyes flitting down page after page without finding the solution. She searched the floor around the desk, then began to pull the desk drawers right out. After emptying each drawer of its contents she reached into the cavities left in the desk to make sure that no papers had managed to get wedged out of sight.

Finding nothing, she went upstairs to the big front bedroom and took Gil's jackets and trousers from the wardrobe, laying them on the bed so that she could go through the pockets. At last, tucked into the small inner pocket of a waistcoat, she found what she was looking for – a piece of paper folded again and again until it was no more than a tiny square, little larger than her own thumbnail.

She unfolded it and ran her eyes swiftly over the contents. Then her jaw dropped and she sat down suddenly on the bed, heedless of crushing her husband's best suit. The handwriting wasn't Gil's, but the writer had signed his name in a clear, confident hand – James Lowrie.

Anger began to burn through Bethany as she took in the meaning of the paper, an IOU for money paid by Gil to James. A large sum of money, handed over without her knowledge or consent.

When Leezie brought Adam home a few moments later she found her mistress coming down the stairs, dressed to go out.

'Look after the house, Leezie, I've got business to see to.'

'I want to come with you,' Adam immediately clamoured.

'You'll stay where you are and do as Leezie tells you, for once.'

'When will you be back?' the maid asked.

'When I'm good and ready,' Bethany told her, and slammed the door on her way out.

*

57

'Never bother with tea for me, I'm not staying long,' she said half an hour later as Jacob McFarlane began to issue instructions to his housekeeper. 'I'm here on a matter of business.'

As soon as the door closed behind the woman she smoothed out the piece of paper she had found in Gil's waistcoat pocket and held it out to him. 'What d'you know about that?'

He studied the paper, then handed it back. 'Whatever it is, it's between James and Gil. It's not my concern, and surely,' he peered over the tops of the spectacles he now had to wear for close work, 'not yours, either.'

'I'm Gil's wife! He's got no right to be handing over that much money without speaking to me first!'

'Your brother's a man who'll honour his debts. And after all,' Jacob suggested carefully, 'it's Gil's money tae spend or lend as he thinks fit, and he'd never see you and the bairns goin' short.'

Bethany's temper boiled over. 'Gil's money, is it? He can only afford to save enough to hand out to other folk because I run his house for him, and I make sure there's never a penny wasted!'

'Sit down, lass, and we'll—'

'Time and time again,' Bethany fumed, pacing the room with a man's long steps, 'I've tried to get him to let me take over the books properly, and to let me hire the gutting crews the way I used to, but he just keeps insisting on doing it all himself. And now he's giving out money to anyone who asks for it, without a thought for me and his bairns!'

Jacob had been standing, as a gentleman should in the presence of a lady, but now his knees, plagued by rheumatism in cold weather, were beginning to protest. 'Sit down, Bethany,' he said again, 'and we'll talk about this.'

'Why would James be borrowing money from Gil?' she asked, ignoring the invitation.

Jacob gave up trying to be a gentleman and sat down behind his desk with a barely concealed sigh of relief. 'You know that James is buyin' my share of the *Fidelity*?'

Bethany stopped pacing. 'Buying her from you? Why?'

'Because I wanted tae sell her and put him intae the *Jess Lowrie* instead.'

At last he had her undivided attention. She came to the other side of the desk, planting her two hands on the polished wood. '*Fidelity*'s the Lowrie boat. Why would you want to sell her?'

With her wide grey eyes, dark brown hair slashed here and there with gold, and her comely figure, Bethany Pate was a strikingly attractive woman, Jacob thought. Even so, it was a pity that she had not been born a man, for her grasp of business matters and her strong temperament were to be envied.

Aloud, in answer to her question, he said, 'The boat's gettin' old.'

'Havers! She's got years in her yet!'

'That's what James thinks. That's why he wants tae buy her back from me.'

'But where would James get that kind of money?'

Jacob picked up the paper she had left on the desk. 'Some of it from Gil, as ye've just found out for yersel'. And he's mortgaged his house. He's already paid half my money and I'm tae get the rest at the end of next season.'

'Oh.' Bethany picked up the slip of paper, folded it and put it carefully into her pocket. Once again her eyes took on the cold, angry grey of a stormy sky. 'But even so, Gil had no right to lend this sort of money without consulting me first. I'll have something to say to the man when he gets back.'

'Poor soul, he doesnae know what he's comin' home tae.' A grin began to spread over Jacob's face.

'He does not,' Bethany agreed ominously. 'I'll bid you good day then, Jacob. No need to see me out or ring for the woman,' she added as he began to struggle up from his chair. 'I know how to turn a door handle.'

She opened the door and then paused, shut it again and

returned to the desk, a sudden light in her eyes. 'I hear that you're thinking of taking over that wee net factory in Buckpool, is that right?'

'I've already done it. My offer was accepted yesterday.'

'So you'll be looking for someone to run it for you.'

'I am.'

'I could do it,' Bethany said.

'You? Have ye ever worked in a net factory?'

'No, but I can mend nets – what fisher-lassie can't mend a torn net? I could learn about net-making fast enough, but what you need is an overseer, someone who can deal with folk. I can do that, and as for the bookwork, I've been doing Gil's books for years. You'll surely need someone you can trust to run it for you,' she added as he looked at her doubtfully.

'What would Gil say?'

A cold smile curled the corners of Bethany's mouth and she slipped a hand into her pocket and brought out her brother's IOU. 'I doubt if Gil can make a fuss about it,' she said. 'Not once he finds out that I know about this. Leave Gil to me. All you need to do is think about what's best for your new net factory.'

'I'm goin' tae have a look round the place tomorrow,' said Jacob. 'Why don't ye come along with me?'

'Are ye certain o' this?' he asked on the following day as he and Bethany emerged from the small factory.

'I am.' Bethany could scarcely keep her excitement under control.

'It'll be hard work for ye, lass.'

'Nothing like as hard as working at the farlins, and I could still do that if I had to. I want to earn my own keep again. I'll soon get to know the way of the business,' Bethany said earnestly, 'and then I'll see to it that the place makes enough to pay back the money you're putting out on it. I promise you, Jacob.'

'If ye're certain,' he began, then shrugged. 'Damn it, if ye're that eager, I'll away and see the lawyer this very minute. Will ye come with me?'

'Best you go alone, since it'll be your factory. Come to the house tomorrow and let me know when I start work. I'm off home to tell Leezie that she'll be in charge of the house from now on.'

The *Homefaring* was a fine wee boat, but she wasn't the *Fidelity* and never could be, as far as James was concerned. She handled well enough, though, and it was grand to be back at the fishing, but he had no sooner got the feel of the drifter and settled back into the routine of the Yarmouth fishing than the herring shoals moved on and it was time for the Scottish boats to turn towards home.

'At least it gave ye the chance tae try yer hand at it again,' Nathan Pate said, as the *Homefaring* butted her way through the choppy coastal seas.

'I didnae need tae try my hand at it. Fishin's like breathin' tae me; once I get back tae it, it's as if I've never been away,' James snapped. When Gil and Nathan had first arranged to return to Buckie with him it had suited him well enough, for the *Homefaring* was two crewmen short for her return trip. She had been one man short at the start of the fishing, and had taken on a Yarmouth deckhand who was staying in his hometown, while another of the crew had fallen for a local girl and opted to remain in England.

But Gil, who had been suffering from a bad cold when he first came aboard, had not been able to do his share of the work. As the drifter moved northwards his cold had become worse, and now he was tossing in his bunk, flushed with fever and with a chest that wheezed like a badly played squeezebox, as Jem had put it.

As for Nathan – James shot an irritated glance at the man now leaning against the galley wall and lighting his pipe – folk spoke the truth when they said that Nathan Pate was as lazy as the day was long. He had managed to get his pipe lit, and now he puffed out great clouds of smoke that were caught by the wind and blown back into James's face.

'Someone should go down below tae see how Gil is.'

'Ach, he'll be fine.' Nathan made no attempt to pull his shoulder away from the galley wall.

'I'll do it, then.' That pipe, James thought as he ducked into the galley, would finish Gil off completely and stink out the entire cabin into the bargain. All the men on board smoked, and James enjoyed the smell of pipe smoke, but for some reason Nathan's tobacco smelled vile.

His brother-in-law was asleep, his large body crammed into one of the shelf-like bunks and his lungs crunching and grinding as they sucked in air. When James put a hand to the man's forehead he found that it radiated as much heat as a coal fire. At his touch, Gil opened his eyes.

'Eh? Is it time tae get up a'ready?' He began to heave himself up from the bunk.

'No, no, man. I just came down tae see if ye wanted anythin'.'

Gil's furred tongue ran round his thick dry lips. 'I could dae with a wee sip o' water.'

The ship's boy had left a pan of water and a tin mug on the table. James filled the mug and helped Gil to sit up, then put the mug to his lips, refilling it when it was emptied. Halfway through the second mugful Gil sighed and pushed the mug away. 'That's enough.'

He was asleep by the time James had lowered him back on to the pillow. Realising that it was wet with sweat, he heaved Gil up again and managed to turn the pillow, cursing himself for agreeing to take the brothers home on the drifter. He was a fisherman, not a nurse!

Ellen erupted into the net factory and ran straight up the passageway between the looms and the net frames to where her stepmother sat at a small desk, writing out bills.

'My father's home.'

It was no surprise to Bethany, for the local boats had started arriving home from the English fishing several days ago.

'Leezie can surely see to him until I'm finished here,' she said calmly. 'Tell him that I'll not be long.' Let him wait on her, for a change. James's IOU, which she had been carrying about with her for safekeeping, seemed to glow in her pocket with eager anticipation. She was looking forward to having that little matter out with Gil. Not long to wait now.

'Leezie says to come now. He's not well,' Ellen said anxiously. 'He's got a terrible cough and his chest makes a funny noise when he tries to breathe. Leezie says you should come home and take a look at him.'

Gil was in his bed, with Nathan sitting on one side of the bed and James on the other, when Bethany and Ellen arrived back at the house. All three men held a glass of whisky, and the bottle was on the bedside table.

'I'm all right,' Gil wheezed peevishly as his wife went into the room. 'It's just a wee bittie chill, that's all.'

'He's had a bad cough for nigh on two weeks now,' James said, and Nathan nodded vigorously.

'That's the truth of it, Beth'ny. I tried tae get him tae come home early, but he'd have none of it.'

'D'ye think I was goin' tae leave when there was still herrin' comin' in and barrels tae be—' Gil started, before the words were overtaken by a fit of coughing that hauled him up and forward from the pillows to bend double, fighting for breath. James only just managed to save the glass of whisky from spilling over on to the quilt, while Nathan thumped at his brother's back.

'Easy there, man.'

'For goodness' sake, he's not a sack of chaff needing to be whacked into shape!' Bethany pushed Nathan aside and settled Gil back on the pillows.

'Where were ye?' he wanted to know when he finally got his breath back. 'It's no' seemly for a man's wife no' tae be

63

waitin' at home tae greet him when he gets back after bein' weeks away.'

She put the back of her hand against his forehead and realised that this was no time for a confrontation. 'I was at the shops, just.'

'But Leezie said—' Nathan began, and she moved slightly so that her back was turned towards him, and she was blocking Gil's view of him.

'You're running a right fever, Gil Pate. This is what comes of working around those braziers then going out into the cold wind with no jacket on. How often have I told you about that?'

'For God's sake, woman, I've done it all my life and come tae no harm.' His voice sounded as though his throat was made of sandpaper.

'Mebbe not, but you're not getting any younger, are you?'

'Aye, that's true, and it was bitter down there,' Nathan put in. 'A right snell wind, and sleet as well. Terrible tae work in.'

James shot him a steely glance. 'You should try haulin' the nets at sea in that weather,' he advised. 'Then ye'd know what cold really feels like.'

'And you should try standin' at the farlins for hours on end in the winter winds and the snow, James,' Bethany snapped. 'Out of here, the two of you. This man needs rest, not talk.'

'Come back tomorrow,' Gil wheezed, and then, as his visitors got to their feet, 'Where's my whisky?'

Nathan blinked at the two empty glasses on the small table. 'I think I drank yours by mistake, Gil.'

'Mistake? Ye can just pour me another one.'

'Later,' Bethany said. 'You can have a hot toddy later, but first you're going to get a poultice on your chest, and a plate of broth. Outside,' she added to the other two, shooing them before her from the room.

As they left the house James said, low-voiced, 'Ye'll let me know if ye need any help?'

'I doubt if we will,' she said firmly, and when she had closed the door behind them she marched into the kitchen. 'Leezie, bring clean lint and linseed oil and some meal for a poultice while I warm up some broth and put the kettle to boil. The steam might help to clear the man's lungs.'

Gil was so hot and so restless that night that Bethany was forced to make up a bed for herself on two chairs pushed together in a corner of the large bedroom. Not that she got much rest, for she was up and down all night, sponging him with cold water, making a fresh poultice and fetching cool drinks. The house rang with his harsh, barking cough, and on the few occasions when she did slip into a light doze the sound of his laboured breathing was constantly in the background of her fragmented dreams.

She woke from one of her brief naps to hear Leezie, always the first to rise in the morning, moving about below. Opening the heavy curtains Bethany saw that dawn had finally arrived, turning the warm glow from the bedside lamp into a wan imitation of its former self.

Gil slept, sprawled in a tumble of sheets and blankets. His breathing was still laboured, and when she laid a hand on his forehead it was so hot that she could scarcely bear to leave her fingers there for more than a few seconds. When he opened his eyes and looked up at her it was with a blank stare, as though he could not think who she was.

Then his eyes cleared and he complained, 'I'm as dry as a bone. Fetch the whisky, Beth'ny.'

'Never mind whisky, it's water you'll have.' She took the jug that stood by the bed and hurried to the bathroom to rinse and then refill it. He drank half the contents of the jug, and once his thirst had been quenched he was more like his old self. When Bethany suggested sending for the doctor, he flatly refused to allow it.

'It's just a chill, woman! Keep on with those damned poultices and the hot toddies and I'll be fine.'

He managed to eat some porridge and drink a cup of tea, laced, at his insistence, with a little whisky. Then he slept throughout the day, rousing only to take some broth and a milk pudding Bethany made especially for him.

Once again, she spent the night on two chairs, rising frequently to attend to Gil as he tossed restlessly.

As she bathed his face in the morning, he opened his eyes and looked at her as though she was a stranger.

'Fetch yer mistress, quine,' he said, so hoarsely that it was scarcely much more than a groan, 'Tell Molly that I'm no' feelin' too well—'

His eyes slid up until only the whites showed, and the lids dropped, but only halfway. His strong, stubby fingers plucked at the edge of the linseed poultice on his chest, trying to pull it off. Bethany hurried from the room and downstairs to where the maidservant, her face still puffed with sleep, was raking out the kitchen range.

'Leezie, I don't care what Gil says, I'm bringing the doctor in to see him. Run and fetch the man now.'

'But I've got the dishes tae put out and the porridge tae make and—'

'Just do as you're told!'

'Is he worse, then?'

'A lot worse,' Bethany said. 'He doesn't know me, Leezie. When he woke up a minute since he thought I was his first wife's maidservant. Tell the doctor to be quick.'

7

Gil Pate's funeral was a handsome affair, with four black horses pulling the hearse up the hill to Rathven Cemetery, followed by a long procession of mourners on foot. Although women were not expected to go to the graveside Bethany insisted on leading the procession, with ten-year-old Rory walking by her side. Zelda had taken Ellen and Adam to stay in her already overcrowded cottage until the funeral was over.

On the way to the open grave the procession passed the Lowrie plot, where Bethany's parents, Weem and Jess, lay side by side. Jess had kept her husband's grave neat, but since her mother's death Bethany had only paid one or two visits. She cast a swift glance at their headstone as she went by and saw that someone had been tending the graves. Zelda, surely, or Innes – it was the sort of thing that they would do, and she could not imagine James or Stella taking on the task.

She would be expected to do the same for Gil, she realised, and decided there and then that she would pay for his grave to be kept decent. Unlike her mother, she had no intention of weeding and cleaning and tidying her husband's last resting place. She would be too busy earning her way and feeding and clothing the children.

Rory stood motionless by her side, shivering slightly in the chill December wind as the coffin was lowered into the fresh grave that had been dug in the cold earth. When Bethany threw a handful of soil in after it he followed suit, his fingers searching for hers even as the earth rattled on the polished lid of the coffin, and as they moved away from the grave-side after the short service he glanced back several times.

Jacob, unable because of his rheumatism to walk up the hill to Rathven, had come in his motorcar. It was waiting for him at the cemetery gates, with his driver behind the wheel. Jacob had never learned to drive; he used the motorcar infre-quently, and when he did need it he hired a local man to drive it for him. He offered to take Bethany and Rory with him, but Rory opted to walk home.

'He'll be all right with me.' Nathan put a large hand on his nephew's shoulder. 'We're the men of the fam'ly now, eh, Rory? You and me are goin' tae have tae look after the womenfolk, are we no'?' His eyes were on Bethany as he spoke, and the gleam deep in their depths sent a shiver down her spine.

'This is a bad day,' Jacob said soberly as they drove down the hill. 'I never thought tae see Gil go so soon. He cannae have been much over forty years of age.'

'He was in his forty-first year, just.' Bethany spoke absently, unable to forget the look in Nathan's eyes, or the way his meaty hand had clutched Rory's shoulder, as though claiming the boy. She had never cared for her husband's brother; to her mind, Nathan was a sly, slippery creature, and more than once he had reminded her of the eels that were sometimes brought up in the fishing nets and writhed in the fisher-wives' creels, reaching out to catch and hold unwary folk.

'A fair bit older than yersel', then,' Jacob was saying.

'A good ten years.'

'Ye're young tae be widowed.'

'Not on this coast. There's many a lassie been widowed almost as soon as she wed. My own Aunt Meg, for one.'

'Aye, that's true.' He covered her gloved hand with his own for a brief moment. 'If I can ever help ye, ye know where I am.'

'You can help me,' Bethany said swiftly. In the dark nights between Gil's death and the funeral she had been laying plans. Now, she decided, was as good a time as any to speak in private to Jacob. 'Keep me on at the net factory,' she said, 'and pay me to keep the books for the curing and the coopering. You know that Nathan's no good at sums.'

'But surely ye'll have enough tae see tae—'

'I need to earn my way, Jacob!'

'But your man'll have made certain that you and the bairns are well provided for, surely.'

'Even so, I want to be my own woman, not Gil's dependant.' Bethany thought again of Nathan.

'If that's the way ye want it,' Jacob said, as the car drew to a halt before the house.

'It is.' Bethany had the door open and was out before the driver could assist her.

Four or five women were bustling about between the kitchen and the front parlour, where a long table held plates and glasses and trays of food. Zelda, usually the first to volunteer her services when help was needed, had stayed at home on this occasion to look after Ellen and Adam Pate as well as her own brood, but some of the neighbours had brought food for the funeral guests and stayed to help Leezie.

Stella was there, too, a black apron covering her black dress. When Bethany said, 'It's good of you to come, Stella,' her sister-in-law replied stiffly, 'It's my Christian duty tae offer help where it's needed.'

'Here, I'll take that in for you.' Bethany seized the tray of cold meats that Stella had been carrying from the kitchen. It was hard to believe, she thought as she went into the parlour, where a big table had been set up, that only five years ago, when the Pates lived in a cottage near the sea, Stella had almost driven her mad by calling in almost every day to chatter like a mindless sparrow about recipes and bairns and suchlike. Now the woman could scarcely bear to speak to her, and Bethany had no need to wonder why. A lot had happened in the past five years.

She put the tray down and stepped back to survey the table. Leezie had done her work well; the best cutlery and china and glassware had been set out, and there was enough food to satisfy even the largest appetite.

The guests began to straggle in, and soon she was too busy to think about anything other than the funeral tea. Nathan, she noticed, made a determined attempt to play the host and make sure that all the menfolk were kept supplied with drink, but Jacob had already appropriated that task for himself. Nathan finally resorted to sulking in a corner and trying to catch Bethany's eye. She ignored him studiously, though she was aware of his gaze following her as she moved around the room, making sure she spoke to each and every one of the people who had come to pay their respects to her late husband.

As always with funerals, the proceedings began in sombre silence, but as the meal progressed and the whisky bottles were passed around, tongues began to loosen, and what started as a low buzz of conversation steadily rose until they were all speaking at their normal level. Since many of them were outdoor workers – coopers, curers and fishermen – their normal level was loud enough to make the walls vibrate.

When they had eaten their fill, Jacob produced some bottles of port that he had brought with him, and Bethany judged it the right time to retreat to the kitchen, where the womenfolk were gathered about the table, drinking tea.

First, though, she made her way to where the coopers stood in a group, tongue-tied with shyness at finding themselves in their former employer's fine house.

'Thank you for coming, all of you,' she said warmly, shaking each and every one of them by the hand, 'and I hope that you'll stay on for a wee while and enjoy a glass of Mr McFarlane's port.' Then, turning to Wattie Noble, Gil's right-hand man, 'Wattie, could I have a wee word with you outside?'

In the hallway, with the parlour door firmly closed, she said, 'You make sure your men stay and have some port, Wattie, for I'm told that it's very good, though for now I'm more interested in having a cup of tea with the other women in the kitchen. I wanted to ask if you'd be willing to look out for the cooperage until Rory's of an age to serve his apprenticeship.'

'Me – take charge?' The big man stared down at her. 'I don't know about that, missus.'

'You can do it, can't you? You know as much about coopering as the master did – and he knew everything about it.'

'Aye, but . . . are you takin' it over, then?'

'I won't know that until the will's read tomorrow. It could be me and it could be Nathan Pate. All I'm saying,' Bethany said vigorously, 'is that I want to make sure that you're on my side.'

Understanding dawned on Wattie's face. 'It's like that, is it?'

'Aye, it is. And I'll be expecting you to consult me on everything, even if the place has been left to Nathan.'

The man looked uncertain. 'I'd not want tae get caught up in any quarrels, missus. I just want tae get on with my job.'

'There'll be a bit more money in your pocket from now on, besides your usual pay packet,' Bethany promised recklessly. 'I'll see to that.' And so she would, even if it took all the money she was being paid for her work in the net factory. She desperately needed to maintain control of the cooperage, for Rory's sake.

'In that case,' he said, 'I'll dae whatever ye ask, missus!'

'Good.' She gave him a push towards the parlour door. 'Now in you go and enjoy your drink. You've earned it.'

In the kitchen she hauled her hat off and flopped on to a vacant chair. 'Thank goodness that's over!'

'You mean you're glad tae see that poor man laid in his grave – at his age?' Stella asked, eyebrows raised.

'You know I didn't mean that, Stella. I meant having to

71

listen to the men talking and talking and never saying anything of interest or worth. Pour a cup for me, Leezie, I'm parched.' Bethany loosened the top button of her high-necked jacket and reached for a buttered girdle scone. 'Where's Rory?'

'He went upstairs a while back,' someone volunteered. 'He's missin' his faither, poor wee loon.'

'I'll look in on him later.'

A gust of laughter could be heard from the next room and a few of the women, Stella included, tutted and shook their heads. 'It's not seemly,' objected one of the neighbours.

'It's human nature, Mrs Marshall. What's done's done and Gil can't be brought back.' Bethany downed half a cup of tea thirstily and then bit into the scone. Suddenly she was weary to her very bones, and desperate to have the house to herself.

Eventually the guests in the parlour began to drift away and it was time for her to button up her jacket, put on her hat again and take up her position at the parlour door to shake hands and thank each of them for attending the funeral.

'D'ye want me tae take young Rory back tae the hoosie with me?' Innes asked.

'No, leave him here. I need to have a talk with him later. Besides, your house must be bursting at the seams.'

He grinned at her. 'It always is. I think the walls must be made of some stuff that stretches, for Zelda can aye manage tae find room for another body.' Then, serious again, he took both her hands in his. 'If ye need anythin', Bethany, ye know ye can come tae me and Zelda any time.'

'I do. Thank you, Innes.' She watched him go with a sense of wonder. She had never set much store by her younger brother, dismissing him as a weakling and a mother's boy, but Innes had grown to be a man with confidence in himself. He was a happy man too – it showed in his eyes and in his bearing. Innes was contented with his lot, which was more, she thought bitterly, than she and James had ever been.

'Bethany?' As if her thoughts had summoned him, James

stood before her, holding his hand out. She allowed her fingers to rest in his for only seconds before pulling them free. 'Stella's in the kit—' she began, and then stopped as James's wife appeared by his side. 'Thank you for your kindness, Stella.'

'It was only right, since we're kin by marriage,' the woman said sharply, and almost hustled James from the house.

Nathan was the last to go. 'I'm goin' tae miss Gil.' He took her proffered hand and held on to it. 'He was a fine, fine brither, Beth'ny, and a fine husb—'

'We'll all miss him.' She almost wrenched her fingers free of his grasp and moved swiftly along the hall to open the door. Today, at least, she was still mistress of the house, and could still decide who should be in it. 'I'll see you tomorrow at the reading of the will. Good day to you, Nathan.'

She closed the door behind him and stood staring at the stained-glass panel for a moment, biting her lower lip. She had searched high and low for a copy of the will, anxious to find out what it contained, but there was nothing, not even a scribbled note. It must have been left in the lawyer's keeping. She wondered, given Nathan's sly looks, if he already knew its contents.

Leezie and the neighbours had already begun to transfer the used dishes and glasses from the parlour to the kitchen, for all the world like a stream of ants, Bethany thought. She rubbed her hand down her skirt to rid it of Nathan's touch and then went upstairs to the bathroom, where she tore the hat from her head for the second time, heedless now of tousling her hair, and washed and rinsed her hands several times before drying them.

Turning back to hang the towel on its hook, she caught sight of herself in the mirror, clad in black from head to foot, her face flushed with the warmth of the house.

'The widow Pate,' she said aloud, and then again, tasting the words in her mouth. 'The widow Pate.'

Her hands, when she put them against the heat of her cheeks, felt pleasantly cool. She closed her eyes, inhaling the smell of the coal tar soap she had used, and then went on to the landing and knocked on the door of the bedroom that Rory shared with Adam.

'Can I come in?'

His voice, when he said, 'Aye,' was surprised. Normally, only the adults were allowed privacy in that house; Gil had considered it his right, as head of the house, to barge into any room he pleased, other than Leezie's tiny bedroom close by the kitchen.

Rory was sitting on his bed, working away at a sketch-pad. Two or three open books were strewn about the bed and he looked up guiltily as his stepmother came into the room. 'I was getting tired of bein' down the stairs. Nob'dy was talkin' to me—'

'You were quite right to come up here. Are you doing your homework?'

'Just drawing.' He had been clutching the sketchpad to his chest, but relinquished it when she held her hand out.

She sat down on the bed and stared at the drawing. 'What is it?'

'A steam engine. It's not very good,' the boy said apologetically. 'That's why you didnae recognise it.'

'I didn't recognise it because I know nothing of engines. I didn't know you did, either.'

'It's easy enough when ye just think about it.' Rory knelt up beside her, pointing with his forefinger. 'It all makes sense. See, that's the cylinder, and that long bit's the rod, and there's the crank that moves the rod, and here's the main condenser—'

'I still can't make head nor tail of it. How d'you know all this?'

'Uncle Innes showed me. Those are the engines that make the fishing boats work. He took me down tae the *Fidelity*'s engine room and explained it all tae me,' Rory said proudly.

'Did he indeed? Now,' she picked up one of the open books, a book on birds that his father had given him at the boy's own request, 'this makes more sense to me.'

'They're bonny, aren't they?'

'They are that. Bonnier than engines, and they sound better too.' Bethany riffled through the pages, stopping at one. 'What's that?'

'A yellow bunting. And that,' the boy pointed to a picture on the opposite page, 'that's a greenfinch.' Then, as she turned the page, 'That's a merlin and that's a mountain linnet. Some folk call it a twite.'

'Was it Uncle Innes who told you about birds, too?'

'No, Peter taught me all about them – Peter Bain.'

'He must know a lot about the countryside.'

Before marrying Innes, Zelda had worked as a maid at the Bain farm in Rathven. Peter, the farmer's son, was two years older than Rory.

'And the shore, too,' Rory said. 'And I'm learnin' from him. I like learnin' things.'

'Rory, you were grand today.' Bethany closed the book and laid it on her lap. 'Your father would have been proud of you. You behaved like the man of the family,' she hurried on as tears began to sparkle in the boy's blue eyes, 'and that's what you are now, the man of the family.'

'Me?'

'Of course. I'm going to have to work hard to make enough money to keep us, and that means that I'll be away from the house during the day.'

'Are you goin' to look after the cooperage?'

'No, I can't do that because I'm not a cooper. One of the men will look after it until you're old enough to run it. That's what your father wanted for you. I'll be at the net factory, and when I have to be out of the house Leezie will be here to see to the three of you. But it would help me if you'd keep an eye on the wee ones and let me know if there's anything wrong with them, or with you.'

A tentative smile tugged at one corner of the boy's mouth. 'I could do that, all right.'

'I'm sure you could.' Bethany got to her feet. 'Mr

Morrison's coming in tomorrow morning to talk to me and your uncles and Mr McFarlane about some things, then you and me can go and fetch the wee ones home. The sooner we get back to our usual ways the better. For now, I'd best go downstairs and help Leezie. You stay here with your books and your drawings.'

The three of them – Rory, Leezie and Bethany – dined that night on the remains of the funeral tea before going to bed early, worn out from the day's business.

Alone in the big front bedroom she had shared with Gil, Bethany stripped off her widow's weeds and stretched before pouring water from the china jug into the basin. The bathroom, Gil's pride and joy, boasted a proper bath, but tonight she preferred to use the basin in the privacy of the room that had become hers. At least, she thought as she tossed the uncomfortable clothing aside, she was still slender enough to avoid having to wear corsets.

After putting on her nightdress, she gathered up the discarded clothing from the floor and hung it carefully in her half of the big wardrobe. She would have to put it on again tomorrow for the lawyer's visit, but after that she would return to skirts and blouses in suitably muted shades.

Unpinning her hair, she shook it out about her shoulders and started to brush it with long, slow strokes until it lay about her shoulders, soft and shining, the ends curling slightly. The electric light caught the fair streaks she had inherited from her mother, turning them to gold among the rich brown. Normally she put it into a single plait for the night, but now, too tired to be bothered, she fetched a ribbon and tied it at the nape of her neck, then turned the lamp out and drew the curtains back before climbing into the double bed.

The sash window was open at the top to allow fresh air into the room. Bethany stretched her limbs luxuriously across the bed and contemplated the task before her – to raise three children single-handed and at the same time earn her keep, and theirs, by working for Jacob McFarlane and, if possible, running the cooperage.

The prospect of taking on all those responsibilities did not frighten her at all. Ever since her marriage, and especially since Adam's birth, Gil had done all he could to turn her into a housekeeper, dependent on him for every penny. But now she was free to become her own woman again, answerable to no man.

Bethany Pate, widow, smiled to herself in the dark before drifting into a deep, dreamless sleep.

8

Gilbert Pate's will was brief and to the point – control of the cooperage was entrusted to his brother Nathan until such time as Rory had served his apprenticeship and was capable of taking charge. The house went to Bethany and any moneys Gil possessed at the time of his death, together with his share of future profits from the business that the Pate brothers and James had entered into with Jacob, would be held in trust for the three children by Nathan, who was also responsible for allotting a monthly housekeeping sum to Bethany. On reaching their twenty-first birthdays each of Gil's children would take control of a third of the money in trust. Nathan and Jacob McFarlane were named as trustees.

Bethany sat straight-backed during the reading, staring fixedly at the lawyer's shoulder. Her face was expressionless, though her hands were clenched within their black kid gloves, and behind her calm exterior she seethed at the thought of being beholden to Nathan for every penny, just as she had been beholden to Gil.

All these years of looking after his children, her brain clamoured so loudly that she felt the words ringing in her ears, caring for his home, submitting to his needs whether she felt like it or not – and what thanks had she got for it? The man had left her as good as destitute, dependent on the goodwill of his brother for every morsel of food she put into her mouth and every stitch of clothing that covered her body.

All she had was the house, and she could not sell that, for it was the children's home.

She could tell by the way Nathan's eyes kept flickering towards her that the terms of the will suited him very well. If she had only known the way the wind blew she would have done whatever was necessary to make Gil change it. But it was too late now, and she would either have to become an independent woman or spend the rest of her life under Nathan's thumb.

The very thought of it made her feel as though she was stifling. The room seemed very stuffy and she longed to get away, but as soon as the business was over Nathan was by her side.

'I want ye tae know, Beth'ny, that I'll look after you and the bairns as if ye were my own,' he said into her ear, standing so close that his tobacco-rich breath was hot on her cheek.

'We'll manage fine, Nathan.' She made as if to move away from him, and then turned when she was at a safe distance. 'You'll know that I'm running Jacob's net factory for him now?'

'I'd heard, but I don't approve. Ye deserve better than that. Gil left ye in my care and it's my duty tae take over his duties as a husband and faither until the bairns are grown.' He put a faint but definite emphasis on the word 'husband', and as his eyes slid over Bethany's body his tongue flicked out to moisten his lips. 'After all,' he went on, 'every woman needs someone tae support her, and who better than yer man's brother?'

'There's nothing wrong with a day's honest labour for a day's wages. I've no worries about supporting the children,' Bethany retorted, and then to her relief she heard James ask Jacob when the end-of-season reckoning was to be held.

'I'm sorry tae be bringin' business up at a time like this, Bethany,' James added uncomfortably as she joined them, 'but there's wages tae be paid out and bills tae be settled. Folk need tae know where they stand.'

'Bethany knows that well enough,' Jacob said briskly, 'as she's always been the one tae write out the final reckoning for Gil. That's why I wondered, Bethany, if ye'd continue with the task of calculatin' the money due tae each boat – for a reasonable payment, of course.'

'Beth'ny?' Nathan spluttered, while her knees went weak with relief. 'But I'm the curer! It's my job tae do the books!'

'Mebbe so, but it was always Gil who took charge of them, was it no'?' Jacob said easily.

'Aye, mebbe it was, but now he's gone it should be me.'

'It's just that Gil always relied on Bethany here tae do the final reckoning, with her bein' better at the writin' than he was. That why I thought it only right tae ask her tae go on with it.'

'I've no argument against that,' James cut in. 'Our Bethany always had a good head for figurin'.'

'The books should be my responsibility!'

'Nathan's right,' Bethany said, and as all three men stared at her, taken aback, 'What does a woman know of men's business? You should take over the books Nathan. In fact, I'd be glad to stop working on them. Here—'

She opened the roll-top writing desk and heaved a large, thick ledger over to the table, dropping it from a few inches away so that it arrived with a hefty thud. 'You'll easily learn from glancing over pages for the past years how to write it in. First, you need to get all the bills and receipts from James and the other skippers, then you take a different page for each boat, and you write down everything they got on tick down one page. Every single thing, mind. Then you write the number of crans taken during the season on the other page, and work out the payment for each cran. That's not many boats, so it should only take you a day at most. But it has to be done soon, for as James says, the skippers have to pay out the crews' wages as soon as they can. There are the gutting crews too – the way you work out their wages is this—'

'I've no' got the time tae do all that!' Nathan protested, and Bethany gave him a sweet smile.

'Neither had Gil. That's why he left it to me.'

'Aye, well, mebbe you should go on with it, just until I find the time tae take over.'

'If that's what you want,' Bethany said demurely. 'But what about these? You'll want to take them over yourself for certain.' She turned back to the desk and deposited another two ledgers on the table before his horrified gaze. 'These are to do with the cooperage – materials bought in and barrels made and the work each man did on each day. You have to work out their wages from the hours and the number of barrels, but it's quite easy once you get the idea of it. And you must balance the materials bought in against the barrels sent out. There are the stock records to keep as well; it's important to make sure that you don't run out of timber because then the men'll have nothing to do. Gil was never over fond of paying his workers to be idle. And these,' a sheaf of papers landed on the table, 'are the bills still to be paid and the accounts waiting to be sent out. You have to balance them all in this ledger, and they'll have to be done soon, but even so—'

'Jings,' James said, grinning. 'I'm glad I'm just a fisherman, Nathan, and no' a businessman like yersel'.'

'You can keep on with the lot of them for the time bein', just until I get the time tae start doin' it mysel'.' Nathan flapped his hands at the books and paperwork on the table as though trying to make the untidy pile disappear, then added in an attempt to retain control over the situation, 'But I'll do the hirin' of the guttin' crews mysel'.'

'Now that's settled, if ye're willin', Bethany, I'll tell the skippers tae gather at my house a week from today for the reckonin',' Jacob suggested, and she nodded.

'I can have the books ready, if you'll make sure, James, that the skippers answerable to Gil and Nathan tell me what's owed and how many cran of herring they took. And now I'll go and tell Leezie to bring in some tea. I know I'm ready for it. Jacob, there's something stronger in the cupboard there, if anyone would care for a glass.'

Bethany watched from behind the parlour curtains as the three men walked along the road, Nathan and James flanking Jacob and walking slowly to accommodate him. Age was beginning to tell on Jacob, Bethany thought as she watched. He could do with an assistant – someone trustworthy and able.

She turned back into the room, a smile curving her lips as she glanced at the roll-top desk where the ledgers lay waiting for her attention. There was a lot of work to be done in the next week, but she could manage it easily enough.

She rubbed her hands together, and then went out into the hall. 'Rory?' she called from the bottom of the stairs. 'You can come down now. It's time for us to go and fetch Ellen and Adam!'

Passing the harbour on her way home from the factory on the following day, she saw that the *Fidelity* had been brought from the boatyard and was now moored in the innermost basin. She looked bonny in her new paintwork, with her name picked out in elaborately curling gold letters.

Bethany hesitated and then went to have a closer look at the drifter. Nobody else seemed to be around, but as she stood there, her mind seething with memories, James said from behind her, 'She's lookin' more like herself, eh?'

She spun round. 'I was just wondering how she was coming along.'

'Why not, since ye're a Lowrie, and this is the Lowrie boat?' The tide was in and the basin full, which meant that the drifter's deck was almost level with the harbour wall. James brushed past her and put a foot on the gunwale, then turned. 'Come aboard and have a proper look.'

'Leezie'll be expecting me home—'

'Bethany,' he interrupted with a touch of irritation, 'I'm

82

back in Buckie now whether you like it or not, and we cannae spend the rest of our lives tryin' tae avoid each other. Folk would notice, for one thing, and I'm sure you don't want tae arouse the gossips. So come and have a look at her.'

He leapt lightly to the deck and she paused for only a second more before following him. As she put a foot on the gunwale, hesitating in order to adjust to the slight bounce of the boat, he held a hand out to assist her. Instead of taking it she jumped to the deck almost as easily as he had, then steadied herself and looked up to see him grinning at her.

'Ye've not lost yer skill with boats, then.'

'I never will.' She began to walk along the deck, past the galley. To her relief James stayed where he was, leaving her to enjoy the sensation of being back on the boat that she loved every bit as much as he did.

The drifter shifted slightly beneath her feet, and, drawing off her glove to put a hand on the smooth, solid wood of the mast, Bethany felt the years drop away from her. The *Fidelity* was part of her life, and being on board again for the first time in many years reminded her fleetingly, disturbingly, of what happiness had been like.

The smell of strong tobacco drifted towards her on the stiff breeze. James had lit his pipe and now he was standing, half turned away from her, studying the other boats in the harbour. Bethany climbed up to the wheelhouse and went in, resting her hands on the wheel's wooden spokes and looking unseeingly through the window before her as she thought of all the men the drifter had carried out to the fishing grounds and safely back to shore, low in the water on the return journey, her holds full of the silver darlings.

Her father, Weem Lowrie, the man who had edged rather than pushed her into becoming Gil's wife in order to further his own ambitions, had spent his last years in this wheelhouse; her Uncle Albert had taken over from him and now the boat belonged to James, her brother. She tightened her hold on the wooden spokes, thinking of his hands resting there, strong and confident in the ability of his boat. The *Fidelity* was the only part of James's life that was at all certain, she thought, and wished that it could have been otherwise for the older brother she had idolised, fought with and cared for deeply – too deeply.

Looking up, she saw that he was watching her from the deck below. For a moment their eyes met before Bethany turned away. When she rejoined him, he said, 'Are ye not goin' below? The whole boat's been painted and varnished.'

'Leezie's expecting me back,' she said again, then stared, startled, as James suddenly laughed out loud. It was a sound she had not heard from him in a long time.

'Ye fairly sorted Nathan out yesterday.'

'The man's a fool.' She leaned against the wall of the galley. 'Gil propped him up for years and he'd no right to leave Nathan in control of the cooperage. It should have come to me!'

'Aye, I agree with ye.' James took the pipe from his mouth and moved to spit over the boat's side before turning back to her, wiping the back of one hand across his mouth. The moment's amusement vanished as he went on coldly, 'I didnae care for the way he looked at you when the will was bein' read. He thinks tae take over from Gil in more ways than runnin' the cooperage and hirin' the fisher-lassies.'

'Nathan's all eyes and no wits and I don't give that for him.' She snapped her fingers. 'As to the cooperage, I've had a word with Wattie Noble, and he's agreed to tell me everything that goes on. I doubt if Nathan will be any better at managing it than he would have been at keeping the books. I think I'll be able to control things in my own way.'

'But can ye control Nathan himsel'?'

'Of course I can.'

'Ye're probably right, but if he starts tae cause ye grief just tell me and I'll soon put a stop tae it,' he said and then, nodding towards the wheelhouse, 'Ye looked just right up there. It's a pity that quinies cannae fish the deep.'

'I've always thought that myself.' Bethany said, and then, remembering, 'I found this in one of Gil's pockets.' She held the folded scrap of paper out to him and watched his face as he read it. 'I found it while he was away in Yarm'th,' she said when he looked back up at her. 'I was going to face him with it when he came home, but I never had the chance.'

'The loan was arranged fair and square—'

'I'm not saying that it wasn't, but I wish that one of you had had the decency to tell me about it.'

'We thought it best tae keep it between ourselves.'

'Because women know nothing of business, I suppose.' Bethany's voice was sharp, and colour rose under James's tan.

'Jacob wanted tae sell her.' He gestured to the drifter they stood on. 'The only way I could keep her was tae buy his share and find the money tae get her put tae rights. I mortgaged the house but it wasnae enough, so I turned tae Gil for help.' He held the paper out to her. 'We agreed that I'd pay him back at the end of the next fishin' season. Now I'll be payin' you.'

Bethany took the paper and stood for a moment, considering it. She had meant to use it to give her bargaining power over Gil, and now that he was gone, it could give her some power over James, not to mention some welcome income in a year's time. But even as those thoughts came to her she was tearing the note across once, twice – and then she opened her fingers to let the little scraps of paper flutter free. James watched in astonishment as the breeze wafted them over the gunwales and then released them, allowing them to fall into the dark water between the *Fidelity* and the neighbouring boat.

'What did ye dae that for?' he demanded to know as the last tiny white scrap disappeared.

'Your debt was to Gil, and now he's gone. And, as you said, this is the family boat. We couldn't let her be sold.'

'But . . . you've three bairns tae raise!'

'I've still got my own share in the *Fidelity*. And I'll manage fine on my lone,' said Bethany. 'No need to fret about me.'

*

85

A week later, Bethany sat behind the big desk in Jacob McFarlane's study, the ledgers open before her and a pen in her hand, as the skippers and mates of the drifters contracted to sell their fish to the consortium headed by Jacob filed in to collect their money.

If they were surprised to see her there, they were also happy to accept the money due to each boat. It had been a good season for herring, and there was enough money to last them and their crews through the winter.

'We'll be seein' a difference after this,' one of them prophesied gloomily, 'because the Germans are no' buyin' the way they used tae afore the war. And nob'dy kens yet about the Russians, after what's been happenin' in their country.'

'That's for me and Nathan tae fret over,' Jacob told him, and Nathan, standing by the desk, shifted uneasily. At the outbreak of the Great War considerable numbers of foreign buyers had been in Britain to bid for the herring catches as they always did. They had left abruptly, taking as much fish as they could; in almost every case their debts had not been honoured and, as a result, fish-curers up and down the coast had been made bankrupt and forced out of business. Nathan had been one of the lucky survivors.

'I dae a bit o' frettin' mysel', havin' a fam'ly tae feed,' the man protested. 'What's tae happen next year?'

'We'll engage you and your boat same as we've done before, and guarantee tae buy your first hundred cran of fish for an agreed price as usual, and mebbe more. With fewer curers around and the fishermen back from the war, we'll have another good season,' Jacob prophesied jauntily. 'Away through tae the other room with ye, now. There's a dram waitin' there, just desperate tae be swallowed.'

The man's eyes brightened, and as soon as he had pocketed his money he made for the door, followed by the other skippers.

'I'm no' so sure that it would be a good idea tae take on too many boats next year.' Nathan girned as he collected the money due to the women who gutted and packed the fish. 'If we promise the men a fixed price for the first hundred cran they take we'll be layin' out a lot of money.'

'You don't get money in if you don't put it out first,' Bethany said crisply, irritated by the man's fear. 'And if Jacob thinks it'll be a good season next year then it will be. He knows the fishing better than you and me.'

'Away and have a drink afore it's all gone, Nathan,' Jacob suggested, and when the man had gone off, still muttering uneasily, he remarked, ' I doubt if Nathan's comfortable with the notion of havin' tae put siller intae other men's pockets instead of his own.'

'He never was. He takes after his mother.' Bethany shivered at the memory of her late mother-in-law, a formidable woman who had never, until the day she died, released her grip on her two sons. It was only Bethany's strength and determination that had kept Phemie Pate from gaining control over Rory and Ellen and Adam as well. Nathan, a bachelor, had lived with his mother in her small cottage in Findochty, a nearby fishing village, and had continued to live there in the two years since the woman's death.

'There's nothin' wrong with a man takin' after his mither – I take after mine,' Jacob said complacently. 'But she was one of the finest women you could ever hope tae meet. Euphemia Pate, on the other hand . . .'

He chuckled, then said briskly, 'Only your James tae come. He'll be down at the harbour, no doubt, makin' certain that the *Fidelity*'s goin' tae be set up for the new season. Then I suppose I'll have tae find a crew for the *Jess Lowrie*, because James is determined tae get back tae his own drifter.'

'D'you really think it's going to be a good year next year?'

'Ye can depend on it. There'll be a few more good years at least, though I'm not sure as tae what'll happen after that. For the meantime, I'll be takin' on as many boats as I can.' He tapped the side of his nose with a gnarled finger. 'It'll be worth the outlay. The secret, Bethany, is—'

'Never pay out all your silver,' Bethany said as she counted James's share of the catch. 'Always keep back a wee bittie against the cold weather.' Then, glancing up at his surprised face, 'I've run a house for years, Jacob; I know how to handle money.'

He grinned. 'You take after the woman that bore ye, lassie. I wish Nathan had your way with money. Sometimes I feel that I'd be better without him.'

'Mebbe you would at that,' she said, and would have said more if Jacob had not started to hoist himself to his feet, clutching at the edge of the solid desk for support.

'I'm away in tae have a dram with the others. Can I bring one through for ye?'

'A cup of tea will do me fine.'

Bethany busied herself with the books, going over columns of figures that had already been added more than once. Jacob's comparison between her and her mother displeased her, for she liked to think that she was her own woman, owing nothing of her nature to either of her parents.

James came in, hauling his cap off and glancing around the room. 'Is Jacob not here?'

The skippers traditionally put on their Sunday best for the ceremony of dividing out the season's money, but he must have come straight from the harbour, for he was still wearing his work clothes.

'He's in the other room with the rest of them. I've your money here, and the list.' She held out the sheet of paper and he took it, his eyes skimming down the page as Bethany briskly accounted for every penny earned and every penny spent.

'D'you agree with it?'

'It seems right enough.'

'It is, you can be sure of that,' Bethany was saying when Jacob came in, glass in hand and followed by his housekeeper with a tea tray.

'There ye are, James,' he said affably as Bethany cleared

a space on the desk for the tray. 'Thank ye, Mrs Duthie.' He lifted his glass to his nose and inhaled the whisky's aroma, then drank some down, watching brother and sister over the rim of the glass as Bethany counted the notes and coins due to James into his outstretched hand.

There was something amiss between these two; he sensed it in the air each time he was with them. He wondered idly if he would ever know what it was, and then shrugged it out of the way. James and Bethany were thrawn, the pair of them, but they were strong and they were ambitious – and that suited him well.

The more he thought of it, the more he liked the idea of Bethany allying herself with him. She possessed more intelligence than her husband and his brother Nathan put together.

'Come on through to the other room and have a drink, James,' he said, and paused to drain his glass before following the younger man out.

'To Bethany Lowrie Pate,' he said to himself as he drank the whisky down. 'To the future.'

9

'Isa Thain's at the door,' Leezie said. 'She's askin' if she can have a word with ye.'

'What is it she's wanting?'

'Tae talk tae ye. I just said.'

'Leezie!' Bethany, in a hurry as she always was these days, glared at the maid. 'I've to get to the net factory as soon as I'm . . . Oh, you'd better send the woman in. Tell her I'll talk to her while I'm finishing my breakfast. See that the children get off to school in good time – and make sure that Adam has a warm jacket, for it's bitter outside.'

Isa's thin face was pinched with cold when she came into the kitchen, and Bethany immediately went to the big dresser to fetch another cup and saucer. 'Sit down, Isa, there's plenty tea in the pot.'

'I'm no' here for tea,' the woman said stiffly, standing just inside the kitchen door. 'I'm here tae ask for work.'

Bethany, pouring out the tea, gave a small, silent sigh. Isa Thain had always been a difficult creature. 'You can ask for work just as easy sitting down and drinking tea, surely? You might as well, for I'm in a hurry to get to the net factory and I want another cup before I go,' she said sharply, and after a moment's hesitation the other woman did as she was told.

'That's better, now I'll not have to twist my neck looking up at you all the time.' Bethany sat down and took a sip from

90

her own cup before asking, 'Are you thinking to get work in the net factory for one of the quines?'

Isa, a widow, had three daughters, all in their teens, and she supported her mother as well. 'It's for mysel',' she said, warming her hands on the cup, 'an' the net factory's no use tae me, for I never worked there and I don't know the way of it. I'm lookin' for some skivvyin' work.'

'Skivvyin'? Here?' Bethany was unable to keep the surprise from her voice. Skivvying, kippering (smoking the herring) working in the net factory, baiting the lines for the white fishing, gutting and packing herring were all jobs open to women in the fishing community. Isa had worked for Gil as a packer for years and Bethany knew that the woman was highly skilled at the job. In a good year she could earn enough money during the herring season to keep her going for a month or two at least. But now, it was just two weeks into the New Year.

'What about your two eldest?' Bethany asked. 'Surely they're old enough to earn their way now?'

She could tell by the sudden colour in the other woman's face that the question had angered her. Isa Thain's worst fault was an inability to get on with other folk. Her sharp tongue often made her unpopular and in the days when she herself had been hiring the gutting crews for Gil, Bethany had had to act as mediator between Isa and the other women on many occasions.

When Isa finally managed to speak it was in a low voice, and she stared down at the table instead of meeting Bethany's gaze. 'Bella's already skivvyin' at one of the big houses out by Garmouth, but she's no' bringin' in enough tae keep us goin'. And Nanse hasnae been well enough tae work since she'd the bairn.'

'Your Nanse has a bairn? I didn't know that.'

'Aye, well, you've been too busy bein' a fine la—' Isa began with a flash of her usual self, then she stopped short and said, 'You've had things tae think of yersel', wi' Gil dyin'.'

'Aye, I suppose. What about Nanse, though?'

The story came out bit by bit. Isa's eldest daughter had fallen pregnant by one of the labourers who flocked to the coastline to make some money during the herring season. Who the man was nobody knew, for he was long gone before poor Nanse discovered that she was carrying his child. The girl had been at the Yarmouth fishing with her mother when the child was born prematurely.

'I should never have let her keep on at the packin', but she was scarce showin', so I thought it was all right tae let her follow the fishin',' Isa said. 'I kept an eye on her an' tried tae make sure she didnae have too much heavy work tae dae, but one day when I was at the mission havin' some right bad cuts dressed Nathan Pate made her an' some of the other young ones stack a whole lot of full barrels, an' that was enough tae bring her on.'

Bethany winced. The coopers usually handled full barrels, but when they were busy the women were expected to help. It was heavy work, too heavy for women, and many a fisher-lassie suffered later in life from medical problems brought on by the strain of heaving the packed barrels around.

'She'd the bairn that night and she lost an awful lot of blood. There was nothin' for it but tae bring her and the wee one back home, for he was a right peelly wally wee creature and he'd have died for sure if we'd kept him in the lodgin's with nob'dy tae look out for him while we were workin' at the farlins. Anyway, Nanse was awful ill. For a while,' Isa said, running her fingertip round and round the rim of her cup, 'I thought I'd lose the two of them. But the bairn's still with us, though whether he'll manage through the winter I don't know.'

'And Nanse?'

The birthing had been arduous and Nanse had never quite managed to struggle back to health. 'So, ye see, I've got tae bring in some money, with them tae look out for, and me and Nanse no' gettin' much money from the guttin'. That's why—'

'What d'you mean about the gutting money?' Bethany interrupted.

'With me havin' tae take her and the bairn home, it meant the two of us bein' away from the farlins,' Isa explained with a flash of irritation at Bethany's stupidity. 'It was a good fishin' too; there was that much herrin' that the quines were workin' from first light tae well after dark. But Nanse wasnae fit tae come back home on her own, let alone care for a wee bairn on the journey, so I'd tae bring the two of them back tae Buckie. The other lassies gave me somethin' from their own wages, but they couldnae spare much and it's all gone now.'

'Nathan only paid you for the time you worked?' Different curers had different rules, but Bethany had always seen to it that if a member of the gutting crew fell sick and was unable to work she got some sort of financial compensation, especially in a good season.

'Aye, snivellin' wee bastard that he is,' Isa snapped. 'I know he's kin tae ye, Bethany, but I've never liked the man.'

'Neither have I, and he was kin to my man, not to me.' Bethany thought hard, chewing at her lower lip, then said, 'If I took you on, Isa, you'd have to do as Leezie tells you, for she's the one that runs this place, with me being at the factory all day.'

'We'll get on fine,' Isa said, though Bethany doubted it.

'She'll put you to the dirty work – scrubbing the floors and suchlike.'

A faint smile touched the woman's thin lips. 'I'm used enough tae that.'

'Then you can start tomorrow. I have to go now,' Bethany said, and then, as they both got up, 'Will you and Nanse be going back to the fishing next season?'

'Of course we will, but it'll be for some other curer, for I'll never take arles from Nathan Pate again – nor will the other lassies if I have my way of it,' the woman said viciously. 'Not that he's likely tae ask me, for I told him a thing or two when I found out that he wasnae even goin' tae give my Nanse a decent pay for the hard work she put in afore she took ill.'

Isa's final words were still ringing in Bethany's mind when she reached the factory. The women, well used to the routine, were already at work when she arrived, and she eyed them thoughtfully. Most of them had started in this factory, and other local net factories, straight from school at the age of fourteen. Some stayed, but many left when they were fifteen or sixteen to follow the fishing, returning to the factory between the herring seasons. Now that Bethany came to think of it, some of the best gutters and packers in the business would be working for her during the next few months. And Isa would be in her own kitchen every day.

Her anger at the mean way in which Nathan had treated Isa and her daughter began to fade. She tapped the tip of a finger against pursed lips and then smiled broadly as she realised that long before the man even thought of going round the fisher-lassies offering them arles – a binding financial advance – to work for him during the coming season, she, Bethany Pate, could have made her own arrangements with each and every one of them. She knew those women far better than Nathan or Gil ever had, for she had worked alongside most of them.

It would give her great pleasure, she thought as she opened the order book waiting on her desk, to regain control of the Pate gutting crews while at the same time triumphing over Nathan.

'Isa Thain?' Leezie skirled. 'Isa Thain, in my own kitchen? I'll not have it, Mrs Pate!'

'Aye but you will. I'm the mistress of this house, and I've already told her she can start work tomorrow.' Bethany, caught up in the delight of knowing that she had found a way to take the gutting crews away from Nathan, had quite forgotten that she still had to face Leezie.

'She's a troublemaker! You know that as well as I do!'

'Isa's all right if you handle her properly.'

'The only way I'll handle that one's with the end of a broom. If she sets foot in my kitchen I'll sweep her out of it again!'

'Leezie, you need someone to help you now that I'm spending all my time at the net factory.'

'I'm managin'.'

'It's not right to expect you to see to the bairns and everything else into the bargain. I've told Isa that she'll be the skivvy and she'll have to do as you tell her. Just think, with her here you'll not just be the maidservant any more, you'll be the housekeeper. And,' Bethany added swiftly as the girl paused to think over what she had just said, 'there would be a wee bit more money for a housekeeper.'

'Aye, well,' Leezie said reluctantly, 'I suppose I could try her out. But if she causes trouble, Mrs Pate, she'll be out of that door – or I will!'

The herring shoals were congregating in northern waters as they did every June, and for weeks Buckie harbour had been buzzing with activity as the fleet was made ready for the start of the fishing season. There were nets to repair, boats to clean out, engines and sails to be inspected, stores to be laid in, drifters coaled in readiness for the new season and fresh chaff mattresses to be made for the crews and for the fisher-lassies who would follow them north.

Women were welcomed onto the boats only twice a year – in June, before the fishing season began in northern waters, and in October before the drifters went south to the English fishing. They streamed along the harbour wall, armed with mops and cloths and buckets, and stormed aboard drifter after drifter, a great invasion of skirted and head-scarfed pirates. Woe betide any man who had forgotten, before allowing his wife or mother or sisters or daughters on board, to remove the various pictures he and his crew had torn from magazines and pinned on the cabin walls to while away the lonely hours at sea.

In the Pate cooperage Wattie Noble and his men worked long hours in the heat from the braziers, rising at first light and arriving home late each night exhausted and soaked with sweat. Carts and lorries travelled back and forth between the cooperage and the harbour throughout the day, and the pile of new barrels waiting to be loaded on to the drifters grew daily. Herring barrels were never used twice, which meant that the coopers would be hard at work from now until the end of the season, six months away.

Men and women mended nets, either down by the harbour or at their doors or in their lofts, and as fast as the factories could produce new nets they were hurried off to have corks and ropes added, then to the barking yard, where they were seasoned and protected from the effects of sea water by immersion in a solution of boiling water and tannin. Once barked, they were hung out on every available piece of fencing to dry. This was only the first treatment – during the fishing season they would be barked every Saturday, as soon as the week's fishing was over.

Bethany's scheme, carefully hatched over the spring months, went smoothly. A word dropped into this ear and that as she moved about the net factory, the occasional visit to a fisher-lassie's house to deliver a parcel of Adam's old baby clothes here, a home-made cake there, and a solicitous interest in sick relatives soon brought the women she had once hired for Gil round to her way of thinking. When Nathan Pate finally stirred himself and began to make the rounds of the gutting crews to offer his usual arles in return for a commitment to work for him for the entire season, he found woman after woman, many of them with triumphant smirks about their mouths, turning him down.

'I've promised mysel' tae Bethany Pate,' was the refrain he heard again and again. And when he protested that they owed him some allegiance, having worked for him and his brother for years, they explained sweetly that Bethany Pate

96

had offered more money – and besides, the more experienced women pointed out, they had dealt with Bethany long before Nathan took over the hiring.

When he stormed along to Bethany's house she received him with haughty courtesy, taking him into the parlour and offering him tea as if he was some stranger instead of her own brother-in-law and protector.

'I don't want tea, I want tae know what ye think ye're doin', hirin' my guttin' quines!'

'They're there for whoever speaks to them first,' Bethany pointed out coolly. 'And they're not very happy with you just now, Nathan, not since you treated Isa Thain and her daughter so badly in Yarm'th.'

'It was me that was let down – the pair of them came back here and left me tae find two new packers!'

'They had to come home with Nanse's bairn. He'd have died down there in the cold, with his mother too busy working to care for him. And from what Isa says, it was Nanse being made to lift filled barrels about that brought the wee one on sooner than he should have been.'

'I'm a curer, no' a nursemaid,' Nathan said sulkily.

'If you'd just asked me, I could have told you that you can't get these women to work for you if you treat them badly. They're not dumb animals – they've got brains in their heads, and tongues too.'

'Mebbe ye've got them this year, but ye'll no' do that to me again.'

'That depends on the women. They'll choose who they want to work for, Nathan, and if it's me I'm happy enough to hire them.'

Jacob, when Nathan appealed to him, was just as unhelpful. 'It was always your place as curer tae hire the crews,' he said. 'But you left it to Gil and he was content tae let Bethany see tae it. So am I, for she built up a good crew. If they won't work for you, Nathan, then they're best with someone they will work for.'

And so Bethany gained another foothold in her fight for independence and won another small battle over Nathan.

Zelda and Stella went, together with almost everyone else in Buckie, to see the boats go out. Zelda with a clutch of children about her skirt as always and the newest baby, Meggie, in her arms. Stella had a tight grip on Ruth's hand to stop the little girl from falling into the water in her excitement.

'Not too far away from me, mind,' she told the twins. 'I'll not have you fallin' in and gettin' yersel's drowned.'

'They'd be more likely to fall onto a deck,' Zelda said. 'You cannae see the water for the boats. Look, the *Fidelity*'s just about ready tae go. Wave tae her.'

James Lowrie felt the old familiar tingle of excitement as he curled his fingers about the spokes of the wheel. The tingle ran from the soles of his studded boots, clamped firmly to the deck timbers, up through every muscle and every vein to the top of his head. Freedom, that was what it was, he thought exultantly.

He leaned to one side, poking his head out of the side window in order to watch his new mate, Siddy, haul in the forrard rope. As the *Fidelity* began to peel away from the wall he glanced up and saw Ruth, still tethered to her mother but straining so far forward that she seemed to be in danger of dislocating her shoulder, waving vigorously with her free hand.

James, in a benevolent mood now that he was heading out to sea, took off his cap and flourished it in reply. Her bright little face was immediately split by a huge, proud grin. He had grown fond of the youngest of his three daughters over the past few months; she had a lot of courage and a good brain in her skull. If only she could have been a boy.

He glanced at Stella, still as a statue, her face so expressionless that she might have been a figurehead from some old boat. He nodded to her and she nodded back. In the eight months since his return from the war they had settled into a form of domesticity that suited them both well enough. He had his boat and Stella was busy with plans to let out her father's cottage to summer visitors. They were as content as they could ever be.

He waved to the twins, who gave shy, decorous little gestures in return, then the *Fidelity* was nosing into her position in the great procession of boats, a mixture of steam and sail and motor boats, easing out of the harbour to the sea beyond. The drifter moved smoothly and decorously beneath his feet, but even so, he could have sworn that he felt a slight tremor run through her as though, like him, she pulsed with excitement at the thought of escaping from the shackles of the land.

They were almost at the harbour entrance when he glanced up at the wall and saw Rory, Ellen and Adam, all waving energetically. He waved back, looking for and finding Bethany just behind them. Although she was still dressed, as protocol demanded of a woman in the first year of widowhood, in dark clothes, she was hatless, and the sunlight caught the gold tints as loose strands of hair whipped about her face in the breeze.

For a moment her eyes met his, but neither of them acknowledged the other. Then the drifter was through the harbour entrance and into the Moray Firth, plunging forward to meet the first of the big waves with skittish, almost flirtatious excitement.

Buckie fell swiftly astern, and fell as swiftly from James Lowrie's mind as he set his face and his mind and his boat towards the long anticipated meeting with the herring shoals.

'Some folk,' Zelda Lowrie said breathlessly, 'are right dirty tinks.'

'As long as their money's clean I'm no' complainin',' Stella told her from where she was blackleading the fireplace. 'When ye've done with the windows I'll bring in the curtains an' we can hang them again. They'll be dry by now.'

'Nearly finished. I wonder if they're as dirty at home as they are when they're here on their holidays?' Zelda wondered.

'Mebbe not. Mebbe they arenae bothered when it's no' their ain hoosie. It's been a grand summer for me, Zelda,' Stella said happily. 'I kenned it was the right thing tae keep this place on an' let it out tae summer visitors.'

Her old home had been let almost constantly since the boats had gone off to the northern fishing grounds in June, just over two months earlier. Now the women were putting the place to rights before the next batch of visitors moved in. 'And then there'll be folk comin' here for the fishin' soon,' Stella went on, 'so that'll keep me goin' till the herrin' move south. And over the winter I can get this place set tae rights for next summer's visitors. With the money I've made I can afford tae buy in some extra bits and pieces.' Then, glancing at the younger woman, she asked sharply, 'Are you all right, Zelda?'

'Aye, I'm fine.' The younger woman had suddenly stopped work and was holding on to the back of a chair.

'Ye're lookin' awful hot.'

'It's a warm day. D'ye think ye could fetch me a drink of water?' Zelda ran one rounded forearm over her forehead and lowered herself into the chair. By the time Stella had brought the water she was looking more like herself.

'Mebbe you should go home and leave me tae finish off the work.'

'I might as well stay, for all we've got left tae do. And Auntie Meg likes tae see tae the bairns; it makes her feel that she's needed, bless her. Anyway, your quines are there tae help her.'

'Better helpin' there than here.' Stella seated herself on another chair for a moment's rest. 'Every time I bring them here tae work they end up playin' or makin' more of a mess than there is already.' She peered at the younger woman. 'Are ye feelin' better?'

'I'm fine.' Zelda hesitated, then confided, 'Stella, there's another bairn on the way.'

'Another? But wee Meggie's no' five months old yet.'

'She'll be on her feet by the time this one comes, for it's no' due till next year.'

'Does Innes . . . ?'

Zelda gave her sister-in-law a radiant smile. She looked as if someone had promised her the best present she could ever want, Stella thought, amazed.

'I'm goin' tae tell him tonight. He'll be pleased, for he loves bairns as much as I dae myself.'

'It's another mouth tae feed, Zelda. And you've already got Etta tae raise intae the bargain.'

'We'll manage fine. Every bairn brings its own love and its own blessings,' Zelda said, then got to her feet. 'I've cooled down now. Let's get back tae work.'

'I'll finish the windows. You fetch the curtains in and I'll hang them.'

As she watched her sister-in-law go off to the small back-yard, already adopting the leaning-back waddle of the pregnant woman, Stella was suddenly consumed by a sense of envy so strong that it hurt. Years ago, on the threshold of marriage to James, she had hoped for the sort of life Zelda now shared with Innes. In those days she had believed, in her naivety, that the children they made together would bind them together even though their marriage had begun with no love whatsoever on his part. She had been wrong.

She set her mouth into a hard thin line and started polishing the windows. At least she had something of her own now – the cottage, and the money it brought in. She'd show James, and Bethany too, that she was their equal.

'They're all dry,' Zelda sang out from the doorway, then buried her nose in the curtains. 'They smell of fresh air and sunshine. It's a grand day!'

101

10

It had been a good fishing. As Buckie came into view, James Lowrie settled his feet firmly on to the deck and knew a brief moment of contentment. The past few weeks had cleansed him of the bitter war memories; it was almost as if the *Fidelity* knew that she was back in familiar waters, for she had handled sweetly, even when the seas were mountainous and the wind blowing at gale force. He felt, as he and the others hauled in nets filled with leaping silver fish, that at last his world had come right again.

The engine throbbed with a strong steady beat as the drifter sped towards the harbour. There would be six to eight weeks of fishing from home, and then when the autumn began to turn to winter the boats would go south for the English fishing.

He stuck his pipe in his mouth and clambered up to the wheelhouse. 'I'll take her in, Siddy,' he said, and the mate relinquished the wheel.

It was a relief to Bethany when the official year of mourning for Gil ended and she was free to cast off her black clothing. Not that she intended to promenade along Buckie's streets dressed in all the colours of the rainbow, but it was pleasant to put on whatever she chose.

Today on her way to the factory she was wearing a warm grey jacket over her blue knitted blouse and grey skirt. The clothes felt free and light and comfortable after months of wearing only black and as she went along the street there was a new spring to her step.

Over the past year her life had settled into a pleasing pattern. All was going well at the net factory – Jacob was pleased with the way she ran it – and every day she made a point of calling in at the cooperage to have a word with Wattie Noble. Nathan's attempts to interfere in the running of his late brother's business had irritated the men, and this, like his treatment of the gutting crews, had played into Bethany's hands. She had made a wise decision when she had asked Wattie to supervise the cooperage, for the other coopers liked and trusted the man, and were happy to take orders from him. Now Nathan stayed away from the place, which suited everyone.

She had fared better in her handling of the cooperage than in her handling of her home. When Isa Thain first came in to help Leezie the two women had quarrelled and sparred like a pair of cats, but gradually, to Bethany's relief, a form of familiarity had crept into their rows, and now they got along well enough in their own fashion. When Isa went off to work at the Yarmouth farlins her place was taken over by her daughter Nanse, who had to bring her sickly, wailing baby with her since there was nobody to look after the child.

The baby's constant crying would have driven Bethany mad had she been at home during the day, but mercifully, Leezie had taken an interest in the little boy, and on more than one occasion Bethany had returned home to find Nanse working away while Leezie sat by the kitchen fire crooning to the puny wee thing cradled in her arms.

The first time her mistress came across her holding the baby instead of working, Leezie had glared at her, defying her to find fault, but Bethany had had the sense to hold her tongue. The arrangement between them had been that while she was at the factory Leezie was in sole charge of the house, and as long as the work was done, the meals made on time and her own three charges cared for, Bethany was content.

During the English fishing Buckie was almost emptied of fishing folk but now the streets were busy again, for the boats were back in harbour and the trains had brought the fisher-lassies home, bearing gifts for those who had been left behind. There were toys for the children, pipes and tobacco for the old men, scarves and gloves for the womenfolk, and handsome hand-painted plates and figurines to be displayed on shelves and in corner cupboards for visitors to admire.

Christmas and New Year – the main Scottish celebrations – were approaching and for two months, until the line fishing for haddock and halibut, codling, skate and whiting started in February, the fishing community was freed from the usual routine.

But first there was the reckoning to be done. The fishing could have been better but the boats contracted to Jacob McFarlane had been among the most successful, and Bethany had almost finished the task of working out the payment for each of the boats contracted to Jacob McFarlane.

Her mind was filled with these figures, together with a mental assessment of the day's work ahead of her, as she gave a brisk 'Good morning!' to two neighbours already on their way back from the shops.

'Did ye see the colour she was wearin'?' one asked the other as Bethany continued on her way. 'Awfu' bright for a widow woman, was it no'?'

'It must be a year past since the poor man died,' the other calculated, adding, 'But even so, it was awfu' bright, ken.'

'There's surely nae need for her tae go out tae work at all, no' when she's still able tae go on livin' in a bonnie big hoosie like thon. He must have left her well off.'

'Aye, but she never was like other women, Bethany Pate,' the second woman opined. 'I mind when we were all wee quinies taegither – she was happier swimmin' in the harbour with the loons instead of playin' with the other lasses. Always walked her own road, that one.'

'Even so,' her friend said doubtfully, 'that colour's awfu' bright for a widow.'

James, with no knowledge of the sort of gifts lassies and women might like, had asked one of the Buckie fisher-lassies to choose something for his wife and daughters. Back home and watching the three girls' pleasure as they unwrapped their new dolls, he felt an unexpected and previously unknown moment of pleasure, especially when Ruth, always the most affectionate and the least timid of the three, hurled herself at him and gave him a hug and a smacking kiss on the cheek.

When they had gone off to show their new acquisitions to their friends, he dug his hand into a pocket and then held a small package out to Stella.

'For me?' There was genuine surprise in her voice and in her face. She was not used to such gestures.

'Just a wee thing,' he said gruffly. She opened the wrapping almost warily and then gasped at sight of the little china shepherdess in her delicate pink and green gown, her small pretty face peeping out from beneath a wide-brimmed bonnet.

'Och James, it's bonny!'

'It'll do, then?'

'It'll do,' Stella agreed, her voice shaking with shock and pleasure. For a long moment she cupped the little figurine in one hand, stroking it gently, almost reverently, with the tip of a finger, before reaching up to put it on a high shelf of the kitchen dresser.

'So that the lassies won't be tempted tae play with it, for they'd be sure tae break it,' she explained, as she stepped back and looked up at it. Watching her, James was surprised to see that in her sudden happiness she looked very like the young lassie he had married all those years before. It was as though the years had fallen from her. He marvelled at how easily pleased women were.

Then Stella opened a small drawer in the dresser, where she kept the household money and important papers such as their marriage certificate and the girls' birth certificates. She took out a small brown paper parcel and put it on the table before him. 'This is for you. I was goin' tae give it tae you at Ne'erday, but you might as well have it now.'

'For me?' He opened it and then stared down at the small wad of banknotes. 'What's this?'

'The money I made from lettin' the cottage.'

His jaw dropped. 'Ye got as much as that?'

More than that, if the truth be known. Stella, stunned by her own daring and sophistication, had gone on the bus to Elgin to open her very own bank account in a town where nobody knew her or her business. She had put some of her earnings into the account, and given the rest, the larger share, to James.

'Now the war's by, folks are wantin' tae take the sea air again,' she said proudly. 'And a cooper from England took the place for all the time the boats were fishin' in the Firth, so's he could bring his wife and his fam'ly with him. They'll probably come back next year.'

'But it's your money, Stella, you earned it. I can support us all now that the *Fidelity*'s back at the fishin'.' He folded the paper over the money and held the package out to her, but she shook her head and put her hands behind her back.

'No, I want ye tae put it towards that mortgage you took out,' she said, then couldn't help adding, 'I was right tae keep my faither's hoosie, was I no'? This way, we'll have a wee bit extra comin' in every summer. And,' she went on, triumph creeping into her voice and adding sparkle to her eyes, 'now ye can see for yersel' that I'm just as able tae earn my own way as Bethany Pate!'

Every year since her marriage Jess Lowrie had celebrated the New Year by preparing a Ne'erday dinner for her family. In the earlier years her parents and her in-laws had been the main guests; as the years marched by the older members of the family passed away, so then it was the turn of her own full-grown children and their families to fill the seats round the table.

There had been no thought of a New Year celebration for the Lowrie family the year before because of Gil Pate's death, but as 1919 gave way to 1920 Jacob McFarlane insisted on reviving the tradition. When Stella pointed out with some reluctance that she and James, now living in Jess and Weem's former home, should be the ones to follow the family tradition, Jacob shook his greying head.

'Na, na lassie, you've got enough tae do all the rest of the year. Mrs Duthie's more than willin' tae set up a grand meal for us and I've got plenty room for the wee ones as well as the adults. I'd like fine tae invite ye all tae my table, even if it's just the once.'

Large though Jacob's house was, Bethany thought as she sipped at a small glass of sherry, it was still overrun with children. As well as her own three, and Stella's daughters, there were Innes and Zelda's fast-growing family: six-year-old Mary; Will, her junior by one year; Jessie, almost three years of age; Matt, almost two; and nine-month-old Meggie, not to mention Zelda's niece Etta, now five years of age and as much a part of their family as the other children.

It was abundantly clear that Innes and Zelda loved being surrounded by children – nephews and nieces as well as their own. Innes thought nothing of sprawling about the floor with them while his wife, so heavily pregnant that she only just managed to hold wee Meggie on what was left of her lap, beamed on the writhing, giggling mass of arms and legs, heads and bodies at her feet.

Jacob's housekeeper, assisted by a woman brought in for the occasion, had worked hard to produce a fine table. The meal began with two large tureens of broth, rich and steaming hot, followed by the traditional steak pies as well as chicken and every kind of vegetable imaginable, and, finally, fruit-stuffed dumplings, custard and jelly. There was wine for the adults and fruit juice for the children, who, once the meal was over, were given the run of the house and told to seek out the gifts that Jacob had hidden away for them.

They scattered, shrieking with excitement, and the house-keeper followed with Meggie in her arms while Jacob sat back in his seat, looking down the length of the table at his guests.

Meg Lowrie was in a place of honour at the opposite end of the table, as befitted a woman of her mature age. She was wearing her best black dress with a handsome jade brooch, Jacob's Ne'erday gift to her, sparkling on her generous bosom. The excitement of the occasion had brought colour to her cheeks and straightened her shoulders, and she looked a good ten years younger than normal. Innes flanked her on one side and Zelda on the other.

Marriage and bairns suited these two, Jacob thought, but, strangely enough, widowhood seemed to suit Bethany just as well. For all that she was past the first bloom of youth there was a glow about her that warmed her grey eyes and empha-sised her natural beauty. A stranger might be forgiven for assum-ing that a new love had come into her life, but Jacob knew that her air of well-being and happiness was brought about by nothing other than the chance, at last, to be the independent woman she had always wanted to be, answerable to none.

Stella, too, had changed for the better; her tight mouth had loosened a little and there was less sadness in her eyes. She had also found a way to stand on her own two feet and it had brought a new confidence that showed itself in the way she took part in the various conversations floating around the table, instead of remaining silent as usual. She was even pleasant towards Bethany, and once or twice Jacob caught her giving James a warm look.

James was the silent one of the group, but that had always been the man's way. He was almost as lost on the land as the herring he caught in his nets.

'Are ye goin tae the line fishin', James?' Jacob asked, and the younger man shrugged.

'I might.'

'Then ye'll find someone else tae bait your lines, for I'm not for it,' Stella said, without rancour. 'I used tae hate havin' tae bait lines for my faither. It's awful sore on the hands, shellin' the mussels then puttin' them on the line.'

Each line held about fourteen hundred hooks, with each hook requiring two or three mussels, which had to be shelled before they could be attached.

'When I see the women workin' on the lines I'm just thankful that Innes doesnae go tae sea,' Zelda put in, while Meg's voice boomed along the length of the table: 'Mind workin' the lines with yer mither and me all those years ago, Bethany? You were there and all, Stella. We mended the nets, too, in Jess's loft. Mind those jellyfish they call scalders, that got caught in the nets?'

'I do that!' Stella made a face. 'When they died they dried tae a powder that stung yer hands somethin' cruel. And if ye got any of it on yer fingers and then touched yer eyes they were near stung out of yer face.'

As the others talked around him James stared down at the tablecloth, lost in his own thoughts. The sight of Innes's two healthy, lusty sons hurt him in a way he had not expected. 'The way those two are goin',' he had heard Stella say with disapproval of his brother and Zelda, 'they'll soon be able tae fill the schoolhouse on their own.'

Just then young Adam rushed into the room, his small face rosy with excitement and his eyes shining like stars, to show his mother the wind-up dancing bear he had found. James watched hungrily as Bethany lifted the solid little body on to her lap and ruffled Adam's dark hair; then, aware that Stella's sharp eyes were upon him, he wrenched his gaze from his sister and her son and reached for the wine decanter.

'After you, James,' Jacob said, and leaned forward to take the decanter once James had done with it. He filled his glass and then sat back and sipped at the rich red wine, well content with the way his life had gone. If Weem Lowrie had not charmed Jess away from him, Jacob might well have been father to those young folk. If Jess had not insisted on remaining true to her marriage vows, even beyond death, he would at least have been their stepfather.

But despite their mother's stubbornness, Jacob thought complacently, his wealth had enabled him to become closely involved with the family that had been Weem Lowrie's.

Just as close as if they had been his own blood kin.

11

June 1931

'Ye'll wish ye'd stayed home and kept on workin' in the net factory,' Adam Pate said with relish.

'No I won't.'

'Aye but ye will, once that steamer gets out intae the open sea an' starts its pitchin' an' rollin',' said Adam, who had been to the northern fishing grounds the previous year.

'I like the sea, and I've been in boats before this and never been up nor down.'

'Mebbe so, but this is different. This time ye'll wish ye'd paid heed tae me an' stayed home.'

'Will you stop your teasin'?' Etta Mulholland, kneeling by the fine new wooden chest she had recently acquired for her first trip to the Shetlands as a fisher-lassie, glared at Adam, and when he grinned at her, crossed his grey eyes, clutched at his stomach and made choking noises, she appealed, 'Aunt Zelda, can you no' make him stop his nonsense?'

'Leave the lassie alone, Adam,' Zelda ordered her nephew fondly. 'She's made up her mind tae go and she's lookin' forward tae it. Don't spoil it for her.'

'I'm only warnin' her,' Adam protested. 'Mary, you've been up north tae the fishin', you tell this lassie what the journey's like.'

'It's fine,' said Mary, who had her mother's kindly temperament; then, as Adam gave a derisive laugh, 'Sarah never has any bother with the journey.'

'Sarah's a good sailor, I'll give ye that, but last year you and the rest of the lassies were as green as grass when you got off the boat at Lerwick, with the tossin' and tumblin' you'd had.'

'I'm sure you were just as green when you were makin' the trip in the *Fidelity*.'

'Not me.' Adam shook his dark head. 'The sea never bothers me, even when the boat starts tae roll an' toss an' dip and lift an'—'

Mary caught at a handful of her cousin's hair in one hand while the other brandished the razor-sharp gutting knife she had been about to pack into her own kist. 'Another word from you, Adam Pate,' she said sweetly while Meg Lowrie cackled like a hen from her fireside chair, 'and I'll be usin' your hair tae stuff my mattress instead of chaff. I doubt if all the lassies would be so quick tae run after ye if ye didnae have those bonny black curls.' Her grip tightened, and Adam yelped.

'Let him be, Mary,' her mother ordered. 'And as for you, Adam,' she reached up to administer an affectionate swipe at his shoulder, 'ye'd best get away back home before yer mither sends Leezie out lookin' for you. Anger Bethany, and she'll pack you back tae Aberdeen tae do some extra studyin' instead of gettin' tae the fishin'.'

'She won't.' Adam, released, rubbed at his stinging scalp. 'I've told her it's bad enough havin' tae go tae the university without extra studyin' in the summer too.' Then, making for the door, 'See ye in Lerwick, lassies. You too, Auntie Meg. You and me'll have a wee turn on the dance floor when we get there, eh?'

'Right ye are, son,' said Meg, delighted, and then when he had gone, 'He's a fine laddie, that one.'

'The quines all know that, Auntie Meg,' Mary said dryly. 'And they make sure that he knows it too. He's gettin' bigheaded.'

'I'd be after him mysel' if I was a wee bit younger.' Meg slapped a wrinkled hand on her bony thigh.

'You behave yersel', Auntie Meg, before ye make yersel' ill with yer nonsense,' Zelda scolded, laughing. 'Anyway, Mary, there's no harm in a lad of his age enjoyin' the lassies' attentions.' Zelda, like many of the women in the town, had a soft spot for Adam, who possessed an abundance of charm and high spirits as well as good looks.

'I don't see Aunt Bethany settlin' for a Buckie lassie as wife to Adam,' Mary said. 'Rory can wed whoever he wants, but I'm sure she's hoping that when Adam marries it'll be to some well-born Aberdeen lassie he's met at the university.'

'Adam Pate'll go his own way. He's like a young horse that's awfu' hard tae tame.'

'You're right there, Aunt Meg.' Zelda began to fold the skirt she had been ironing, and then put it down as nine-year-old Samuel rushed in, clamouring for food.

'Ye've not long had yer breakfast!'

'Aye, but I'm hungry again,' Samuel said plaintively, eyeing the tray of scones, fresh-baked and still warm, on the table.

'Here, son.' Zelda lifted a scone, split it, and began to spread it with home-made jam. Samuel was her youngest, and doubly precious because his twin sister had been still-born and Samuel himself, a mewling, pitiful scrap of humanity the size of his father's hand, had not been expected to live.

Nor had Zelda, for several days; the only thing that kept her going was her determination to raise the child destined to be her last. Samuel had spent his first few weeks in the oven with the door propped open, baking, as Zelda put it, at an even temperature, and had survived, to become a healthy, active boy.

Now as he snatched the scone from her outstretched hand, gave her a broad grin, and then rushed out again, yelling to his friends as he went, she said indulgently, 'He's a wee tyke, that one.'

'Only because you spoil him,' Mary said.

'Ach, a wee bit of spoilin' never did anyone any harm,' her mother protested, and then, as she returned to folding the skirt, 'As for Adam, if Bethany tries tae make that laddie travel a road he doesnae want tae go she'll have a rare fight on her hands, for they're both thrawn. Bethany aye wants her own way and Adam's more her son than Gil's.'

'He puts me in mind o' my brither Weem,' Meg said from her usual place by the fire. 'Once our Weem set eyes on Jess nob'dy could have stopped him from takin' her tae wife. James is just like his faither, and so's Adam. The loon's a right Lowrie, no' a Pate at all.'

'Is it awful bad on the steamer?' Etta asked nervously. She had started learning the gutting trade the year before, during the late-summer fishing season on the Moray Firth. This would be her first time away from home.

'Sometimes – but ye'll like it once ye get there,' Mary assured her. Seventeen, and a year older than Etta, she had already been north to the Shetlands and south to Lowestoft. 'Ye'll meet folk from all over and the company's grand. Now then,' she cast her eye over the box Etta was packing, 'are ye managin' tae fit everythin' intae your kist?'

'Are you sure I need all this?' Etta sat back on her heels, looking at the great pile of items on the floor and then at the box. It had seemed quite large when she first got it, but now it seemed small beside all the items waiting to go into it.

'Every bit of it. Ye'll need good warm clothes for workin' in because the weather can be cruel up there, even in the summer. And ye'll want oilskins for when it rains, and scarves tae cover yer head.'

'And somethin' decent for the kirk on Sundays and when folk come tae wee gatherin's at your hut,' Zelda chimed in, 'and good sheets for yer bed.'

The items were all in a heap by the kist, together with towels and soap and a hairbrush, knitting wool to keep Etta's hands busy when she was waiting for the boats to come in, cups and saucers, cutlery and a tablecloth, her sturdy working boots, her knitting needles, the leather knitting belt with a section padded out with horsehair where the needles were kept when not in use, and her sharp gutting knife.

'Are ye certain about the wallpaper?' she asked doubtfully.

'The huts we've tae live in are awful dreary. A bit of wallpaper makes them bonny,' Mary told her, 'and we have tae take curtains tae hang over the windows, else everyone that's passin' can look in on us. And don't forget the cloths for yer fingers.'

'I have them here, all ready for you.' Zelda triumphantly produced a large bundle of soft, strong strips of flour sacking that had been washed and then boiled to make them flexible. They were needed to protect Etta's fingers from razor-sharp fish bones and from the worst of the coarse salt that was liberally scattered over the fish that the gutting crews worked on.

After a lot of effort and assistance Etta managed to get everything packed into her kist, which was then closed and locked. Each kist had been set on a large piece of canvas, which was now folded tightly over it and stitched into place with large needles and strong thread. The canvas provided extra protection for the kists during the journey to wherever the girls were to work.

'This is excitin',' Zelda said as she helped the two girls to heave the completed kists over to the doorway to await collection by the curer's lorry. 'It's an adventure!'

Etta smiled at her. To Aunt Zelda everything was an adventure and a joy to be explored and savoured. 'Were you never a fisher-lassie yourself?'

'Me? No, no, I'm from farmin' stock. I spent all my workin' days at Bain's farm in Rathven. And your Uncle Innes was never fond of the sea, for all that his folk were fishermen. Mind you, I'd've liked fine tae have been able tae go travellin' about, meetin' all those different folk. I'm pleased tae see you lassies gettin' the chance.' Zelda clapped her hands and beamed at her niece and her daughter. 'Ye'll have a grand time!'

*

Jacob McFarlane and Bethany were busy estimating the cost of coaling and equipping and victualling the drifters they had engaged for the season. This year, as Bethany pointed out with considerable satisfaction, even more skippers than before were under contract to them.

'Mebbe more than we can manage.' Jacob sucked at his pipe. 'We've undertaken tae buy fish from every one o' these boats, mind, and that's goin' tae cost us a pretty penny.'

'We'll be all right. We're not putting out more money than we have, and if the fishing's good this year, we'll do very nicely.'

Bethany Pate came to life when she was busy, Jacob thought, watching her as she bent over her work again, pen in hand. She had been running the net factory for eleven years now, and he knew, though she had not complained, that it had been a struggle at first. Many of the workers had resented her as an outsider, but she had won most of them over, gradually weeding out those who were determined to wear her down and replacing them with newcomers more willing to accept her regime. Jacob had given her a free hand with the place while he watched from the sidelines and said nothing. Now she had won the trust and respect of all the men and women employed at the factory.

As the years passed she had gradually taken over more and more of Jacob's paperwork; this was another great achievement, for Jacob McFarlane was a hard-headed businessman and there were very few people he would trust with details of his financial life.

She herself must have amassed a tidy fortune over the years, he thought now as he watched her; enough, mebbe, to keep her in relative comfort, and yet she kept on working.

'Are ye fond o' money, Bethany?' he asked now. She looked up, startled.

'What a thing to ask a lady!'

'Ye're right, I dinnae ken why I said it.'

'Since it's you, I'll give you an answer,' Bethany said, then pursed her lips, considering. 'No, I'd not say that I'm fond of the stuff,' she said at last. 'Though it's always nice to have enough. It's knowing that I'm doing something with my life instead of just frittering it away.'

'Ye've brought up three bairns on yer lone; is that no' doin' somethin' with yer life, woman?'

'Aye, and it's been hard work, but it's not enough,' Bethany said, 'I like to know that I've earned every penny I spend, and I'm not beholden to anyone else for it.' Then she added, with a sidelong glance at him, 'The one thing I've not done yet is to deal with the fish merchants. When are you going to let me try my hand at that?'

'It's no' a job for a woman,' Jacob said as he always did, and she scowled at him.

'Women are fine in their place, but there are some things that only the menfolk can do, is that it?'

'Ye've got the right way of it there, my quine.'

'But surely you need someone to take Nathan's place?'

'I don't need tae fill his place, for he was never much help tae me.'

'You're right there,' Bethany said complacently. Regaining control of the gutting crews had only been the first step in her campaign against Nathan. Over the years he had become increasingly lazy and when, after years of careful hoarding and investment, she was finally able to offer him a good price for his curing business, her brother-in-law had accepted and gone off to Fraserburgh, where he had married a spinster of comfortable means and settled into a life of ease.

'Let me go to Yarm'th with you this year,' Bethany coaxed now. 'Leezie can look after the house on her lone.'

'I'll think about it,' Jacob said evasively. He was in his sixties now, and rheumatism was slowing him down, especially in the colder weather, but he wasn't ready to hand over the reins of power just yet.

Bethany was still trying to work out a way of persuading him to take her to Yarmouth as she walked home, loitering at the harbour to soak up the busy atmosphere. Boats, most of them steam drifters, crammed the outer harbour and the four inner basins, and from where she stood Bethany looked over a great patchwork of colours, with black and white and yellow and green subordinate to the vibrant shades of blues and reds most popular with fishermen. The name of each boat was carefully painted in flowing script edged with gold leaf – *Handsome, Mary Cowie, Trophy, Homefaring, Furze, Olympus, Fidelity* . . .

Even as Bethany identified the drifter a familiar figure emerged from the galley and went across the deck, his cap set to the back of his dark head. As James stepped up on to the gunwale and then to the next boat as easily as if he was strolling along a street, she turned and hurried away.

'Tae think,' Etta moaned, 'that I've aye liked the sea! What have I ever done tae it that it should treat me like—'

The steamer began to climb the steep slope of another large wave and she clutched her stomach with both hands and closed her eyes tight, knowing what was about to come.

Up and up the *St Ninian* struggled until it reached the top of the wave, where it hesitated for a moment, as though undecided as to whether it should go down the other side or fall backwards into the trough it had just left. Then it opted for a forward plunge, with a corkscrew twist added in for good measure.

'. . . like this?' Etta finished the sentence as the ship dived, and then almost bit her tongue as the vessel hit the next trough with a bang, causing her jaw to snap shut.

'You've done nothin',' Sarah Lowrie said cheerfully. 'The sea just likes tae show us that it cannae be taken for granted. Think what it must be like for the fishermen – they have tae spend most of their lives tossin' like this, up and down an'—'

'If you don't shut your mouth it's you that'll be gettin' tossed – over the side of this boat,' Ruth snapped from where she sat on the deck, leaning against the funnel. Her face, like Etta's, had a greenish tinge. 'How is it that for all that you and me's sisters, Sarah, I'm the only one that gets sick when we go tae Lerwick?'

'Mebbe it's 'cos God likes me better,' Sarah suggested. 'It's the same with Annie – she gets sick and she's my twin.'

'I wish my mither had kept me at home tae help with the summer visitors instead of Annie,' Ruth mourned. 'Why didn't she pick me?'

'Because Annie's the better worker. You'd be too busy eyein' up the lads tae dae anythin' else,' Sarah pointed out.

Ruth glared and began to say something, then as the boat shuddered and plunged once more she shut her mouth hurriedly and pressed her fingers against it, eyes closed. The prettiest and the liveliest of the three sisters, she had no shortage of suitors, and the previous year she had become very friendly with the son of the people who had rented out her mother's cottage. As the young man was already engaged to be married his parents had cut their holiday short and whisked him home and out of danger. To Stella Lowrie's fury they had also cut short the full rent agreed by letter before their arrival.

'Look at these poor dumb beasts,' Sarah went on as the boat lurched and then settled again. 'They don't even know why they should be here, and they're no' complainin'.' Then she laughed as one of the cows penned in one corner of the deck, staggering to the ship's roll, bellowed its misery. 'That one must've heard me.'

It was true, Etta thought, glancing round the deck. The poor sheep and cows being taken from the mainland to the Shetlands must surely be suffering even more than the fisher-lassies who, like herself, were huddled on deck. But feeling sorry for the animals didn't make her feel any less sorry for herself.

'I wish I hadnae come!'

'You've been fair desperate tae get tae the Lerwick fishin',' Sarah pointed out.

'I thought it would be fun.'

'It will be, once we get there and your stomach catches up with you. I'll just go and see if Mary's all right.' And Sarah sauntered off to where Etta's cousin was nursing her own misery in the confined space of a cabin.

Ruth put a comforting arm about Etta's shoulders. 'Ye'll be fine, pet, an' I should know, for I'm sick with every crossin'. But ye'll enjoy yerself once we're ashore. The Shetland season's good.'

'When will we get there?'

'Tomorrow.'

'Tomorrow!' The prospect of another night on the steamer made Etta's stomach lurch. That was all that it could do, since it had long since emptied itself over the side.

'You'll be all right,' Sarah assured her. 'Most of us hate the gettin' there, but it's worth it. Think of the money you'll earn.'

'All I can think is that I'll have tae do all this again, only goin' the other way next time.'

'Goin' back's not near as bad as goin' out, because then we know we're on the way home.'

Home. The very word made Etta want to cry. She would have given a king's ransom, had she had such a thing, to be back home in the warm, crowded kitchen, listening to Samuel going over his multiplication tables or helping Teena, aged ten, with her sewing.

Although the sea was rough it was a pleasant early-June day. Etta looked up at the sun and guessed, from its position in the blue sky, that just about now her Uncle Innes would be getting home from his work at the boatyard, ducking as he came in through the door, which wasn't quite high enough for him. Her pale lips twisted into a faint smile at the thought. She always liked it when Uncle Innes was home because then the family was complete.

'Here.' Sarah was back, brandishing a green glass bottle. 'Try this.'

'What is it?'

'Whisky. One of the quinies from Aberdeen gave it tae me. She said that it—'

Ruth had taken the bottle from her sister and sniffed at the contents. Now she turned even more green and, thrusting the bottle into Etta's hand, scrambled up to make a bolt for the side of the steamer, reeling from side to side as the deck rolled beneath her feet.

'She said it would help tae settle your bellies,' Sarah called after her. 'It's helpin' the other quinies.'

Etta sniffed cautiously at the neck of the bottle and screwed her face up. 'I don't know, Sarah . . .'

'Go on, it cannae make you feel much worse than you feel now, can it?'

'I suppose not.' Throwing caution to the winds, Etta tipped the bottle up and took a good swallow, the whisky burning her throat as it went down. For a terrible moment she thought that it was going to hurl itself back up, bringing her entire stomach with it. The back of her tongue seemed to buck and writhe and she had to swallow hard to keep from losing control. Then as the whisky settled she became aware of a warm, soothing glow spreading through her sore, empty stomach.

Sarah was watching her anxiously. 'Has it helped?'

The glow spread, creating a sense of well-being. Etta drew a deep, shaky breath and would not have been surprised if, when she breathed out again, flames had spurted from her lips. She swallowed again, and smiled tentatively at Sarah.

'Aye,' she said. 'Aye, I believe it has.'

12

The fishing boats, with the curers and coopers on board, had gone off to Lerwick before the gutting crews, and by the time the women arrived the drifters were already out in search of the herring shoals. Tired, stiff and still queasy from the sea crossing, Etta and the others began to clamber aboard the lorries waiting to take them to the wooden huts that were to be their homes for the next two or three months.

Etta found a space beside Mary, who still looked far from well. 'Are you all right?' she asked anxiously, and her cousin managed to summon up the ghost of a smile.

'I'll be fine once we get tae the huts. I'm always like this,' she said, and then, as the lorry started up, 'Just leave me be for a wee while, for I'm not good company.'

The trip to the curing station was uncomfortable, with the women thrown about as the lorry jolted along. It did nothing to ease Etta's fragile stomach, and it came as a relief to her when at last they reached the huts. As they spilled out of the lorries the more experienced women hurried to find the best huts. Etta, wishing she were back home in Buckie, trailed after Sarah. She didn't care where they settled as long as there was a bed she could lie on.

'We'll have this one,' Sarah decided.

Each hut held two three-woman crews. Etta and an older woman, Jenny Logan, known as Andra's Jenny to differentiate her from other women called Jenny, were both gutters, and Sarah was their packer. The other crew consisted of Mary, Agnes – another older woman – and Ruth as their packer.

At first sight the huts were bleak; little more than sturdy wooden shelters with a cast-iron stove. There were two solid, wooden bed frames, each just large enough to hold three women, and a table and some shelving made up the rest of the furniture. Etta's heart quailed as she surveyed the grim place, but the others took it all in their stride.

'Etta and me and Ruth in that bed,' Sarah decreed, 'and the other three can have that one.' Then, glancing out of the window, 'and here's our kists already, so we can start cheerin'' the place up a bit.'

'There's no chairs,' Etta said feebly, and was told, 'We sit on our kists once they're emptied. Besides, ye're not goin' tae dae much sittin' about, lassie.'

As the women went back outside to claim their luggage the coopers arrived to carry the sturdy wooden chests into the huts. 'Cheer up, Etta, it's not as bad as it looks,' Rory Pate said reassuringly at sight of her wan, worried face.

'Is it not?'

'Wishin' that ye'd stayed at home with Aunt Zelda?'

'I am that,' she admitted.

'Give it a day or two. You'll see,' Rory said. 'The lassies fairly know how tae turn a hut intae a wee palace. Which kist is yours?'

She eyed the growing pile. 'Er – that one.' A lump came into her throat as she identified the stitching – Zelda's handiwork – on the canvas cover. At that moment Aunt Zelda's warm, loving presence seemed very far away.

'And which hut?'

Etta pointed to the hut that Sarah had chosen.

'Right. Johnny, give me a hand here,' he yelled, and one of the other coopers came over. Even though the kist was full the two men handled it easily, and Etta followed them as they carried it into the hut.

Someone else was bringing in the mattresses and pillows

that had been brought to Lerwick on the boats. Etta eyed them hopefully as they were tossed onto the bed frames. After the shaking she had endured on the boat, it would be bliss to lie still and quiet for an hour or so.

But the others, even Mary, were already cutting the stitches and pulling off the canvas coverings so that they could open their kists and start hauling everything out. 'I'll take this bucket and start scrubbin' the floor,' Andra's Jenny was saying briskly, 'and you and Agnes can brush the walls down, Sarah. Ruth and Mary can get the stove goin' and the kettle on.'

'Could we not have a wee bit of a rest first?' Etta begged. 'A wee sit down and a cup of tea, even?'

'Lassie,' Andra's Jenny said as the others, all seasoned travellers, went about their various tasks, 'ye're surely no' goin' tae drink tea in this dirty place? Na, na, we'll have tae get everythin' decent first. Fetch that other bucket from the corner and give it a good clean out before ye fill it with water. There's a brush below the sink there. We can get the place scrubbed out twice as fast if we start at each end and work tae the middle.'

The prospect of all that work still lying ahead before she could rest sent Etta's heart plummeting to her sturdy boots, but there was no point in arguing, so she fetched the bucket and set to work, forcing her weary muscles and aching joints into action.

Little more than an hour later the hut had been scrubbed out and the walls brushed down and covered with wallpaper, tacked into place. The assorted curtains the women brought with them hung across the windows on lengths of string and the many nails already on the wooden walls were pressed into use as makeshift wardrobes. One or two of the nails held pictures and there was even a pretty paper fan pinned to one wall, adding a cheerful splash of colour.

Cups and plates and cutlery had been laid out on the table, the stove had been cleaned and lit and steam puffed from the big kettle. Someone was slicing a loaf coaxed from the cook-house, which catered mainly for the coopers and the fisher-men, and someone else was slathering the thick slices with jam. Although her back was aching and her knees sore from kneeling on the rough wooden floor Etta began to feel a bit more cheerful as she emptied her bucket out and rinsed it at the big stone sink standing below one window.

'Where do I put this?' she asked Andra's Jenny, who nodded at the long curtain someone had hung across the corner.

'Behind there,' she said, and then, smirking, 'That's the orra bucket you've got. It's our privy. The one Mary has holds the clean water.'

'Ye never had the lassie scrubbin' the floor from the orra bucket,' Sarah protested as Etta's stomach, which was improving but still fragile, gave a nasty lurch. 'That was a mean trick tae play on her, Jenny!'

'Ach, it did no harm. And she rinsed the bucket out first. Now it's got a clean start,' Andra's Jenny said airily.

Etta felt better once they were all round the table, using the wooden kists as seats, eating thick slabs of bread and jam and drinking strong, scalding tea.

'It's no' much of a meal, but it'll do for now,' Agnes said with satisfaction as she swilled down the last of her tea. 'And the place looks like a wee palace.' She gave the others a smug smile. 'If ye ask me, we've got the bonniest, clean-est hut of all now. We'll be fine here for the next few months.'

There was more work to do before they could go to their beds. During the fishing season, Etta was beginning to realise, there was always more work to be done as far as the fisher-lassies were concerned. While three of the women spread sheets and blankets over the beds she, Ruth and Mary set to work to peel a great pile of potatoes, which would be left in cold water and used over the next few days.

When all was done, Sarah stretched and yawned. 'I'm for

my bed. The boats'll start comin' in early in the mornin', and most of us have sleep tae catch up on.'

The mattresses, filled with chaff, and known to the lassies as 'caff mattresses' were not very comfortable when new, but even so, the other women in the hut were quick to fall asleep, judging by the low chorus of snores and groans and mumblings that floated through the hut. Etta envied them as she listened to their slumbers; tired though she was, she couldn't sleep for fancying that she was still at sea. The bed beneath her seemed to be lifting and falling and corkscrewing, and she had to dig her fingers into the mattress beneath her and concentrate on listening to the breathing, snoring and occasional mumbling as the other five sank into sleep.

Eventually the imagined movement of the bed began to slow, then settle, and her thoughts began to slow as well. She closed her eyes and floated into darkness.

'It doesnae seem fair on the lad, settin' him tae keep watch when he's got the cookin' tae do as well,' Siddy muttered to James as the crew prepared to turn in. Two miles of nets had been shot over the starboard side of the vessel, as tradition demanded, and lamps had been hoisted to show that the *Fidelity* was fishing. Now, as she drifted with the tide, the crew had a chance to snatch a few hours' rest.

'Ach, it'll do him no harm. He's the one that wanted tae learn what it's like tae be a real fisherman. Anyway, it's the way my faither taught me.' James only just managed to stop himself from putting the emphasis on 'my'.

'Aye, but that was different, for Weem was bringin' you intae the fishin',' said Siddy, an older man who had started his career as cabin boy for Weem Lowrie. 'Adam's only helpin' out till it's time for him tae go tae the university in Aberdeen.'

'All the more reason tae show him what real work's about,' James grunted, hauling off his left sea boot and letting it drop with a thud on the deck. 'If ye're so concerned for the loon ye're welcome tae stand his watch for him. It makes no difference tae me. Just mind that we've only got three hours afore we have tae get up an' haul the nets.'

His right boot thudded onto the deck.

'I'm no' that worried for him.' Siddy began to tug his own boots off. 'I like my bed.'

'Aye, I've noticed,' James said dryly, taking his jacket off and climbing into his own bunk. Fishermen always kept most of their clothes on, in case of emergencies during the night. There was no time to get dressed if the boat was going down. 'Now shut yer mouth and get tae sleep,' he advised his mate, dragging the blanket over his own shoulders.

To judge from the snores that echoed around the tiny cabin, Siddy and the others were asleep in no time, but James was restless. He soon tossed the blanket aside and turned on his back, hands behind his head, staring up at the bulging mattress only inches above his face and thinking of Adam, alone on the deck.

If, as Siddy said, he was hard on the boy, it was because Adam was a natural-born fisherman and James wanted to teach him as much as he could before Bethany whisked the lad off to resume his studies in Aberdeen. There was another reason, one that he could only admit to himself in the dark of the night, with nobody else around to read his mind. He had to be harder on Adam than on any of the other deckhands because it was the only way to prevent himself from being too lenient with the boy. Adam was the son Stella had never been able to give him, the lad who could, if Bethany would only allow it, keep the family traditions of fishing alive, just as James himself had been raised to follow in his own father's footsteps.

Instead, he was going to be sent away from Buckie and his heritage, and made to devote his time and his boundless energy to book learning. It was a terrible waste, James thought, tossing in his narrow bunk.

He remembered the day, in this very cabin, when Gil Pate

127

had first come up with the daft idea that Rory would go into the cooperage and Adam would become a scholar. James had thought that when Adam began to hang around the *Fidelity*, begging to be taken out on her whenever possible, Bethany would realise where her son's true interests lay, especially when it was what she herself had longed to do when she was a lassie.

He smiled slightly, remembering how angry she had been with Innes when after two disastrous trips on the drifter, he had refused to go to sea again. 'Why couldn't Innes have been the quine, and me the loon?' she had wailed. 'Then we'd both have been content!'

After Gil's death, Bethany could have dismissed the daft idea of university for her son, but for some reason known only to herself she had kept it on, even paying for a tutor to work with the lad during the school holidays. The smile broadened into a grin as James remembered all the times Adam had rebelled and gone to sea with him while his mother and the tutor hunted high and low for him. Many a scolding the boy had endured over these escapades, but that had never deterred him from doing it again.

Aye, James thought, turning over and settling himself down to sleep, Adam was a real Lowrie. His grandfather would have been proud of him. Mebbe Weem could have talked sense into Bethany, for she would not listen to James. The two of them had been close as children and close again for a while just before the war – too close, then. But now Bethany kept him at arm's length.

He slept at last, and woke while the others were still asleep and snoring. Gathering up his boots, jacket and cap he scaled the vertical ladder to the galley, where the huge teakettle, as always, was simmering on the stove. After putting on his boots and jacket and jamming his cap down over his head, he took the time to pour out two mugs of black tea, adding three heaped spoonfuls of sugar and a large dollop of condensed milk to each.

Sometimes the herring shoals were elusive and the drifters had to steam for miles in search of them; when that happened they could be away from the land for days at a time, and so their food rations had to be carefully hoarded. But tonight the boats were sitting over a large shoal, and once the nets were hauled they would head at full speed for the fishing station at Lerwick. James could afford to be generous with what was left of their stores.

He found Adam leaning against the wee boat kept in the stern, balancing himself comfortably against the drifter's continuous lift and drop.

'A fine mornin',' he said cheerfully as his uncle appeared. He took a long swallow of the sweet, piping-hot tea, and then lowered the mug. 'That's welcome!'

James grunted in reply and the two men drank their tea in silence, balancing their bodies easily to accommodate the boat's movements.

'I like the way she rides the waves,' Adam said after a long pause, 'as if she's just breathin' nice and natural. And ye get the sense that even when the sea's at its worst she can ride it out.'

'She can that, but ye've still tae taste a real storm at sea, lad.'

'Are ye ever frightened, Uncle James?'

James looked at the boy, his cap pushed to the back of his dark, curly head, his lithe body leaning back against the wee boat as comfortably as if he was at home in an armchair. 'Aye, often enough. When the seas are high and breakin' green over the bows and the wind's howlin' and the boat's bein' tossed about as if it was no more than a piece of grass I can be as scared as the next man. If I wasnae frightened I'd no' work hard enough at gettin' my boat and my crew back tae shore.'

'Are you ever scared for yourself?'

The question caught James by surprise. He took a while to think about it, and Adam was content to wait. 'I'm not scared for mysel' as much as for my crew and the boat,' James said at last. 'I suppose I'm like my faither – he lived on the sea and he lived by the sea and he always said that the sea owned him, and if it ever decided tae take him, it had the right and he'd not deny it.'

'But he's buried in Rathven Cemetery, is he no'? So after all his years at sea, he died on the land?'

'He died on this very boat, but it was a heart attack that took him. I'd have put him over the side there and then, and given him tae the sea like he'd always wanted, but my Uncle Albert was the mate then, and he'd have none of it.' James emptied his mug and put it aside, then began to fill his pipe with tobacco. Adam waited, sensing that he would be more likely to hear the end of the story if he kept silent. 'We took my faither back tae Buckie, wrapped in a sail,' James said when the pipe had been lit, 'and my mither had him buried at Rathven so's she could lie by him when her own time came.' Even now, long years after, bitterness thickened his voice as he added, 'I still say it went against the man's own wishes.'

Another long silence fell between them, while the boat rocked like a cradle beneath the touch of a loving mother. Finally Adam said, 'I think I'd have felt the same as you. Would ye just look at that?'

The first promise of a summer dawn was just beginning to draw a bright line across the horizon; here and there, appearing and disappearing as the waves lifted and then dropped them, they could see the lights of other boats spread over the vast fishing grounds. The brisk wind fretted at the tops of the waves, fraying them into white lace.

'There's nowhere else a man could want tae be, in life or after it,' the boy's voice was hushed.

'I'm more interested in here and now,' James grunted, suddenly embarrassed by the turn the conversation had taken. 'And what's happenin' down below us.'

'Ach, the nets'll be full. You said yourself that you could

smell the fish even before we saw the patches on the water. And you're usually right.'

'I wish I could be as certain as you. We need ten cran o' fish at least tae make this trip worth our while. Fishin' boats don't run on fresh air.'

'The old sailed boats did.'

'Aye.' Much as he loved his boat, James felt a moment's nostalgia for the great red sails that, with the wind to belly them out, had made grand engines.

'It'll be twelve cran,' Adam predicted cheerfully.

'Ten or twelve'll make no difference if we don't start haulin' soon.' James collected the mugs. 'Time we got started, or the other boats'll get tae Lerwick afore us.'

Five minutes later the rest of the crew had stumbled on deck, hauling their sou'westers on and knuckling sleep from their eyes. Murdoch, the boy, was despatched forward to the rope room, little more than a dark, cramped cupboard, to coil the lead rope as the steam capstan hauled it aboard, while the stoker and another crewman prepared to untie the buoys from the nets and toss them to one side. Siddy stood by to free the nets from the rope while three other men went into the hold to shake the fish loose from the meshes.

'Mind yersel', Adam,' James ordered as the lad leaned far out to watch for the first net.

'I'm fine.'

'I'll tell ye when ye're fine and when ye're no'!' James barked, then craned forward himself in time to see just what he had hoped for – a silvery glimmer a few feet below the plunging waves. The first net was full and with luck, this would turn out to be a good catch – a good shimmer.

The sun's first rays broke over the sea minutes later, just in time to turn the struggling fish to silver as the net broke the surface. The men waiting at the gunwales hung over the edge, arms at full stretch, hands straining to grasp the net and help to drag it over the side. As they hauled it towards the hold's gaping maw some of the fish dropped free, spilling onto the deck and flapping over its timbers, so that the men had to watch where they placed their feet for fear of slipping on the creatures and falling backwards into the hold, or forwards into the sea.

Hour followed hour and still the nets came in, each one carrying a handsome load of fish. The capstan rattled and roared and more steam was called for to help it to cope. In the rope room young Murdoch crawled frantically round and round the filthy, slippery floor, wrestling the great, thick soaking wet lead rope into coils. The men in the hold were thigh-deep in fish and those on deck were beginning to feel their muscles ache with tiredness. But it was a good catch, James thought exultantly, and to judge from the activity he could make out on the other boats in sight, they too were doing well.

The last few nets were on their way to the surface. Once they were aboard the *Fidelity* could make for the shore and the crew could snatch a hasty breakfast before turning to the job of clearing nets and buoys away, swabbing fish scales from the deck and putting the drifter to rights.

Then the next net broke the surface, and James's elation vanished at the sight of a sleek, dark back slithering among silver scales and torn, bloodied flesh. A wicked dorsal fin flashed as its owner managed to slide over the side of the net and disappeared into the depths.

James let out a howl of rage and despair as the net came up towards him, dead and maimed fish spilling back into the sea from the huge, jagged holes made by the marauding dogfish that had torn their way into the net in the dark of the night to eat their fill of the trapped herring.

13

It seemed to Etta that she had no longer closed her eyes than they flew open again to see early morning light streaming in through the drawn curtains. Someone was banging on the door and shouting, 'The boats is comin' in, lassies. Tie up yer fingers and get tae the farlins!'

The women scrambled out of bed, Agnes letting out a yelp as her bare feet landed on the rough floorboards. 'A splinter!' She sat back on the bed with a thump, hauling her foot up to examine it.

'Ye should have had the sense tae put down the canvas from yer kist at your side of the bed,' Andra's Jenny lectured her, hurrying to set the big tin teapot on the stove and rake through the ashes. 'It's still alight,' she reported, pushing kindling and coal into the stove.

'I was that tired that I forgot.' Agnes found the splinter and tugged at it. 'It's out,' she reported and began dressing.

There was just time for each of them to have a slice of bread and jam and a drink of stewed, reheated tea from the pot before they bound their fingers with the strips of cloth they had brought from home, securing them in place with strong thread. The cloths would stay in place until the day's work was done, even when they were eating.

Mary, mindful that her foster sister was still new to the work, insisted on checking Etta's bandages and making sure that there were no gaps to allow the tip of a gutting knife or a herring bone, sharp as a needle, to slide into unprotected flesh.

'They'll do,' she said at last. 'But mind now, if you get a cut you need tae tend tae it right away. Once the salt and the pickle get intae an open cut they'll eat the flesh off ye, right tae the bone.'

'Bread's the answer,' Agnes advised as they tied kerchiefs about their hair and strapped their leather knitting whiskers about their waists so that they had something to do should there be a lull at the farlins. 'A bit of bread well chewed an' then pushed right intae the cut keeps it safe and heals it too. It leaves its mark on ye for the rest of yer life, mind, but that's a sight better than havin' tae go tae the mission nurse and lose time away from yer work.'

A lorry tooted its horn outside and they hurriedly pulled on their work boots before scrambling out to climb aboard for the bumpy drive to the farlins.

It was a soft, cool morning with the air holding the promise of warmth to come. Some of the boats were already in, unloading their fish into wheeled carts known as bogies, while others could be seen hurrying shoreward across the serene waters. Sore though she still was from the journey, Etta felt her spirits rise as she and the other women jumped down from the lorries and went to the big wooden troughs, where the gutters immediately began the task of arranging the small tubs that would take the fish guts and the various sizes of herring, while the packers settled the first empty barrel into place and the coopers brought up the barrels of the salt that would be scattered over the fish on the farlins and between each layer packed in the barrels.

'Settled in?' Rory asked Etta as he and one of his men hoisted a salt barrel to its place. She smiled at him.

'Aye, I'm fine now.'

'Good.' He patted her shoulder and went on his way.

'That Rory's a nice lad,' Andra's Jenny said, watching him hurry back to the open shed where the coopers worked. 'We're lucky with him, for he's not like his faither and his Uncle Nathan.'

'Gil wasnae bad, just short-tempered and in a hurry all the time,' Agnes said, and Andra's Jenny nodded.

'Aye, I suppose you're right. Most of us kenned how tae deal with Gil. But his brother Nathan,' her lip curled contemptuously, 'that one thought he was better than us quines just because he stood on his hind legs tae piss. Most of us were pleased when Bethany began tae hire us again, the way she did when she and Gil were first married.'

'D'you like her, then?' Etta had always been in awe of her Aunt Bethany Pate, who had none of Zelda's warmth.

'I'd no' go so far as tae say I like the woman, but at least she was a guttin' quine hersel' afore she wed Gil, so she knows our ways. She's fair, I'll say that for her, and she's sly.' Andra's Jenny made it sound like a compliment. 'Mind that year she took the hirin' away from Nathan, Agnes?'

'I do that. Beth'ny came round early and engaged us for the guttin' sneakit like, before Nathan even began tae think about it. He aye left everythin' tae the last minute that one. By the time he came tae hire the crews we were all contracted tae Beth'ny. He near burst with rage, but there was nothin' he could do about it since we'd all taken arles from her.'

'He still found some crews of his own, though,' another woman further along the farlins put in, and she and Andra's Jenny roared with laughter.

'He did that, and my-oh,' Jenny said with relish, 'it was a right business! Beth'ny had made sure tae get all the best guttin' quines an' he was left wi' some that werenae so good. He was daft enough tae think that shoutin' an' bullyin' would make them work harder, but it went the other way. In the end, one of the lassies threw a fish at him, and then they all started at it. The man had tae run for his life, with everyone laughin' at him and fish fallin' like rain about his head. And then after a good while Beth'ny took over the curin' and the kipperin', just like she'd always wanted, if ye ask me. And

Nathan went off tae Fraserburgh with his tail atween his legs an' married some poor quine that's no doubt regrettin' the day she ever set eyes on him. Rory's nothin' like his faither nor his uncle – he's fair with the women, and the coopers forbye, as long as we all do the work we're paid tae do. Here we go,' Andra's Jenny finished as the first of the bogies arrived and the coopers took up their big wooden shovels and began to pile the fish into the trough.

Sunlight turned the salt being tossed lavishly over the fish into a sparkling shower of tiny diamonds and struck bright swords of light from the sharp gutting knives. The fish scales looked like silver mail and all at once it was easy, Etta thought, to see why the herring were known as the silver darlings.

She picked up her first herring and drew the knife's blade along the length of it.

The new season had begun.

The gutting crews always attracted bystanders fascinated by the speed the women worked at, and their dexterity with the gutting knives, but when a young man started setting up a strange contraption on three long, thin metal legs on the lassies' second day in Lerwick, Etta watched uneasily.

'What's that?' she asked the others.

'It's one of those fancy cameras. I've seen folk usin' them at Yarm'th,' Sarah said airily.

'He's going to take our photographs?' Etta suddenly felt very self-conscious. 'Why would he want tae do that?'

'Who cares why? It's nice tae be noticed,' Ruth said blithely. She smiled at the fair-haired young photographer and he grinned back at her before disappearing beneath a black cloth covering attached to the camera.

'Pay no heed tae him, pet,' Agnes advised. 'Folk can have all sorts of strange notions, 'specially those that don't have anythin' better tae do. Just go on with your work and pretend he's no' here.'

Etta tried to concentrate on what she was doing, but her gaze kept returning to the camera. To her, it was like a cold eye, recording her every move. Finally, in a desperate attempt to take her mind off the visitor, she asked the others, 'Are Yarm'th and Lowestoft as busy as this?'

'Busier, and with plenty folk gapin' round the farlins, so ye'll have tae get used tae bein' watched. Ye'll like the shops, though, and the music halls and the picture houses. My man doesnae like me goin' tae the farlins down south,' said Agnes, who was married to a fisherman. 'He thinks there's too much chance of me gettin' up tae mischief in a big place like that.'

'Why would he think that?'

Agnes grinned, the knife in her hand working at such speed that it was a blur. 'Because that's where him and me first met,' she said, 'so he well knows what I can be like when the mood takes me.'

In the time it took her to utter the sentence three fish had been split open and disembowelled, the guts tossed into a bin and the herring into one of the three tubs behind the gutters. Each tub held a different size of herring – full fish were large and with roe, matt was the name given to smaller fish with roe, and empty herring were known as spent fish. As the price of the fish depended on the different grades it was essential that the gutters selected the right tub every time.

Etta was becoming more skilled, and no longer needed the gauges used in the learners' farlins to help the girls to calculate the size of the fish, but she doubted that she would ever be able to work as fast as Agnes and the other experienced gutters. Even while they talked or sang a rousing hymn or a popular music-hall song their hands moved at speed, slitting, gutting and then flipping the finished fish into the correct tub without even having to glance round. Seagulls cheeky enough to touch down close to the gutters in the hope of finding fish that had landed on the ground instead of in the proper tub were seldom fortunate.

'Another catch comin' in, lassies,' Rory Pate said as he arrived at the farlins. 'An' this one's torn bellies.'

A groan ran up and down the rows of women. 'Torn bellies' was the name given to fish damaged by dogfish or conger eels that had got in among the nets in search of food. Those fish were difficult to work with, and brought in little money.

'Can we no' eat afore we start on them?' someone asked. 'It's intae the afternoon already an' my stomach's that empty I could take a bite out of a raw fish and enjoy it.'

Rory cast an eye over the farlins, now more than half empty. 'Aye, go on, the boat's no' started unloadin' yet. But ye'll have tae be quick.'

Several women, those detailed to do the cooking on that day for their huts, took to their heels and ran while the others went on with their work, heartened by the knowledge that they were soon going to eat. The coopers and fishermen had a cookhouse and a cook but the gutters and packers, being women, were expected to see to their own meals.

'I mind bein' here just afore the war,' one of the older women said as they worked. 'It was a bad year for the dogfish and we'd a lot o' torn bellies. But even so, the German buyers couldnae buy them up fast enough. We couldnae understand why, for they were usually particular about gettin' the best of the herrin'. Then they all loaded the barrels ontae their boats an' off they went, quick as winkin'. Next thing we knew we were at war wi' them. They'd already known it was comin' and they'd only been buyin' up all our fish, damaged or none, tae feed their own people durin' the war years. I hope it gave them the bellyache,' she added grimly.

As soon as the farlins were empty the women scattered to their huts to bolt down plates of herring and potatoes and slices of bread and jam, and drink as many cups of tea as they could manage before the lorries arrived to fetch them back to work.

Ruth loitered behind, arriving when the rest of the women were almost finished eating.

'Lost yer appetite?' Mary asked when the girl finally hurried in.

'I was talkin' tae that mannie with the camera. He's wantin' tae do a book,' Ruth said, glowing with excitement and self-importance, 'with pictures of women at work.'

'It's easier than doin' the work itself,' Sarah jeered, and her cousin glared at her.

'He says he could make a lot of money from it. His name's Jack Morrison,' Ruth announced importantly through a mouthful of bread and herring. 'He comes from Glasgow.'

'Ach, folk are always takin' pictures of the guttin' quine.' Andra's Jenny refilled her mug with strong black tea, and poured out a mug for Ruth. 'Ye'll have tae eat faster than that, my quine, for we'll be called back any minute now.'

The photographer was still there that afternoon, but as time passed Etta managed to get over her self-consciousness and soon she took as little notice of him as the others.

'How did ye like bein' at sea, Etta?' Adam Pate asked when he arrived at the farlins.

'It was fine,' she said jauntily, then as he raised his eyebrows at her she admitted, 'You were right, I didnae like it very much. I'm no' lookin' forward tae the journey back.'

'Ach, that'll no' bother ye so much because ye'll be goin' home,' Sarah assured her, while Agnes wanted to know, 'Should you not be at home, Adam Pate, and gettin' ready tae go back tae the university?'

The youth's handsome face twisted in a scowl. 'I'm not back there till September, and anyway, I'm tired of readin' books. All the time I was there last year I was hungerin' for Buckie.'

'And its bonny lassies,' Agnes gave him a near-toothless grin.

'Ye're right there, Agnes.'

'D'ye not want tae be a fine gentleman, then?' Ruth asked.

'Not if it means havin' to have my nose stuck in books all the time. It's all my mother's idea.' Adam nodded at the farlins. 'That's part of our catch. The dogfish got into the last of the nets. Ye should have heard my Uncle James cursin' when he saw the state the fish were in. And then when he saw the holes in the nets the air turned blue. We lost a lot of fish tae those damned creatures.'

'There'll no' be much money in your pockets, then,' Ruth said.

'That's where ye're wrong, for we're on wages. It's Uncle James an' Siddy and the engine driver that'll be out of pocket, no' me and the rest of the deckhands.' The skipper, mate and engineer were the only three crew members to be paid a share of the catch. 'There's one net that'll have tae go back tae Buckie for repair,' Adam went on, 'but we should be tae repair the others here. Uncle James sent me tae say that we could do with some help.'

'And when d'ye think we'll find the time tae mend yer nets for ye, my fine laddie?' Agnes indicated the farlins, still full of fish.

'Saturday, when the guttin's done?' Ruth suggested.

'We've got the hut tae put tae rights then, and clothes tae wash and food tae buy in, not tae mention gettin' a rest after the week's work,' someone else said peevishly.

'I'll help,' Ruth offered. 'And you will too, won't you, Etta?'

'I don't mind.'

One or two other women had volunteered their help before Rory brought a new barrel along, rolling it skilfully over the ground on its rim. 'Is this you keepin' my crews away frae their work?' he asked his half-brother.

'Ach, leave him be, he's no' gettin' in our way and we're enjoyin' the crack,' Andra's Jenny told the cooper amiably. 'We're women, we can work our tongues and our hands at the same time. It's men that have tae stop whatever they're doin' every time they open their mouths.'

'Well, since you're here anyway, Adam, you can just help Tod an' me tae take those full barrels away.'

'Have I no' done enough?' Adam complained. 'I was on watch all last night. I scarce got the chance to close my eyes.'

'You're young yet, ye can dae without sleep. Come on, give us a hand,' Rory ordered, and Adam shrugged and turned to wink at the women before taking hold of one of the barrels.

'It's lads like him that make me wish I was a bittie younger,' Agnes said, gutting so fast that the herring seemed to leap like salmon from her hand to their allotted tubs. 'He's grown intae a right fine man.'

'Ye'd need tae be more nor a bittie younger tae catch that one,' one of the other women scoffed, and Agnes wiggled her ample hips as she flipped another gutted fish into its tub.

'Ach, I'm sure a wee bittie would dae it, for the lad's more than ready for a taste o' fun with a comely lassie like mysel',' she said, and then, with a broad wink, 'an' if I was just young enough for him, I'd soon show ye why my man's no' happy about trustin' me in places like Yarm'th.'

Mending the *Fidelity*'s nets turned into a social event. Several of the younger women had volunteered, and since the weather was mild on Saturday afternoon they sat outside one of the huts, the nets spread around them, plying the bone needles filled with cotton yarn. The last net to be brought on board the *Fidelity* had been sent back to Buckie and would probably have to be remade, but the others, gashed in places, could be repaired.

Etta, too shy to join in the joshing that went on constantly between Adam and the younger lassies, flicked occasional glances at him as she worked. He was clever, and one of the best-looking men in Buckie with his dark, curly hair and his striking grey eyes and his smooth, brown skin. But to her mind he was too vain for her liking.

'Are ye comin' tae our hut the Sunday after next?' she heard Ruth asking the others. 'We're havin' a wee party for Etta here. It's her sixteenth birthday.'

'Ye don't need tae have a party just for me,' Etta protested, blushing as they all turned to look at her. 'It's just a birth-day!'

'It's a good excuse for a party, though. Will there be cakes?' Adam asked hopefully.

'Of course there'll be cakes, and jelly too. An' mebbe some dancin' if we can find the musicians tae play for it,' Ruth promised.

'I'd as soon not bother,' Etta said as the two of them walked back to the hut later. Ruth squeezed her arm.

'Listen, when folk work as hard as we do it's good tae have an excuse for a bit of a celebration. Anyway, this is your first time away from home, an' you deserve a wee treat.' Then, lowering her voice, 'Jack Morrison, that young man takin' our picture the other day, he's asked me if I'd like tae go dancin' in Lerwick with him on Monday night.'

'You'll be too tired for dancin'.' The fisher-lassies spent Mondays topping up the barrels of herring. It was heavy work, and on Monday nights they were usually too tired to do anything other than make their evening meal and then fall into bed to rest their aching muscles.

'I'm never too tired for dancin'.'

'But you don't know the man. You've not said you'll go with him, have you?'

'Of course I have.'

'What'll your mother say?'

'My mother isnae here,' Ruth said blithely. 'What she doesnae know won't hurt her, and Sarah knows better than tae try tae tell me what tae do. Goin' dancin's a sight better than staying in the hut with the rest of you. Etta, I've never met anyone like him before.' Her voice suddenly softened. 'He's really nice, and he's a right gentleman. How can I pass up the chance tae go out with the likes of him?'

14

Once she got into the way of the life at Lerwick Etta began to love every minute of it, even the long hours spent at the farlins. When the boats brought in good catches she and the other women worked from first light until nightfall and beyond, their hands stinging from the salt, backs aching and feeling as though they might snap in two at any minute; when the weather was bad they still worked on, their feet sinking into the mud and rain streaming down their faces and necks to trickle beneath their clothing and chill their bodies.

These trials were offset by so many pleasures – the screeching of the ever-present gulls and the smell, when the wind was blowing from the right direction, of the salt-laden sea and smoke from the drifters' chimneys. Her ears were filled with a mixture of accents – the soft, precise speech of the Highlanders, the Irish accents, sometimes gentle like the Highland way of talking and sometimes broad, depending on whether the speaker came from the north or the south; the broad vowels from the West of Scotland, and the differing English accents.

Although the heyday of the German, Russian and Dutch buyers was over there were still some visitors from those countries, putting their own stamp on the multicultural mix of folk drawn to the Shetlands by one common interest – the herring. As well as fishermen and coopers and curers and buyers there were salesmen and hawkers, lugging carpet bags filled with all sorts of treasure; ribbons and buttons and even hats and items of clothing as well as cheap jewellery. Etta had never seen so many things all together in the one place, and if Mary hadn't kept a close eye on her she would have spent every penny she had in the first week.

'It's easy tae part with the whole of yer wages,' her foster sister warned, 'for ye think at the time that ye've got a bargain. But ye'll soon find that there's always somethin' better in the next bag, so bide yer time and spend yer money wisely. God knows ye've had tae work hard enough tae get it!'

There were soft, fresh early mornings when the birds themselves had scarcely wakened and the world was still and at peace and it was a delight to be up and about. There were mornings when the fleet was in late and the womenfolk had time to walk to some pleasant spot where they could sit on rocks and grassy mounds, knitting as they watched for the first boats to appear.

There was the laughter and friendship and sing-songs and window-shopping in Lerwick when they could find the time, followed by the luxury of a cup of tea in one of the town's tearooms. There was Sunday worship in the Baptist Church in Lerwick, followed by gatherings in the lassies' huts or in the big hut where the coopers lived.

Sometimes a few of the lassies were invited onto one or other of the drifters for a sup of tea and a shop-bought cake, and occasionally they were entertained by local people who were then invited back to the huts or even the boats.

The other women in Etta's hut made a special effort on the Sunday she turned sixteen. They each presented her with a small gift – a little china brooch, a scarf, a ribbon, a wee doll dressed as a fisher-lassie – and set the table with plates of cakes and biscuits and plates of jelly with jugs of custard, all bought by Mary and Agnes, who had gone shopping in Lerwick after work on the Saturday. There were even home-made paper chains festooned from the dusty ceiling, and they all insisted on Etta getting first turn in the hip bath after work on Saturday when normally, as the youngest in the hut, she was the last to use it. It was a luxury to wallow in clean, warm water for once.

After she had washed her hair Andra's Jenny wound long strands of it around clean finger cloths, fastening each strand close to the scalp in a tight knot that brought tears to her eyes and made it almost impossible for her to lie comfortably in her bed that night. In the morning she brushed it out and tied it back with a piece of ribbon, and when they came back from church on Sunday, Andra's Jenny insisted on brushing it again before arranging it.

'It's fine just tied back,' Etta protested, but Jenny would have none of it.

'Na, na, lassie, ye've got bonny hair, and it needs somethin' different for yer birthday.' She sighed, running a glossy strand of black hair through her work-rough hands. 'I'd give a king's ransom tae have hair like yours. Make the most of it afore it starts tae turn grey, like mine,' she advised as she began to weave three strands into a thick plait.

When she had finished she fetched the hut's one and only mirror and held it before Etta. 'What d'ye think?' she asked as the others gathered again to study the new hairstyle. She had drawn Etta's long hair into two plaits and then wound them so that they cupped the girl's ears.

'It's bonny,' Mary said, and the others agreed.

Etta stared into the mirror, scarcely able to recognise the girl looking back at her. 'I look like one of those princesses in a fairy book, the sort that's doin' her sewin' while she's waitin' for her prince to come along.'

'That's all right then, because you're the princess for today,' Jenny said. 'And make the most of it, my lassie, because tomorrow ye'll just be another fishin' quine like the rest of us.'

It was a grand party. So many people crammed into the hut that there was scarcely room to move, let alone dance to music provided by an accordionist and a fiddler.

'I'm ready for my bed,' Agnes announced when the last of the guests finally departed. She gave a mighty yawn that showed the pink cavern of her mouth and the gaps where teeth had been pulled. 'There's the toppin' up tae do in the mornin'. We'll need all our strength for that.'

'We've got this place tae set tae rights afore then,' Andra's Jenny reminded her, and they all groaned. The bedding, which had been removed so that the beds could be used as seats, had to be replaced, and the table cleared and dishes washed before they could think of getting some rest.

'The sooner started, the sooner finished,' Mary said briskly. Then as Etta began to gather up the plates, 'Not you, it's still your birthday.'

'But that's not fair on the rest of you!'

'I know, but that's the way of it. Never fear, lassie, we'll make ye work twice as hard tomorrow tae make up for today,' Agnes promised. 'For now, just you sit down and play at bein' a fine lady while we put this place tae rights.' She grimaced and opened the hut door, wafting it to and fro on its hinges. 'The place is reekin' o' pipe smoke.'

A breath of cool, clean air from the door made Etta's mind up. 'Since I've not tae help I'd as soon go out for a walk than sit in here.' She reached for her jacket.

'Don't stay out too long,' Sarah called after her.

'Ach, the lassie's sixteen now, she can stay out as long as she wants,' Etta heard Andra's Jenny say as she went out into the night.

After the hut's stuffiness the night air was like a drink of clear, cold water. Etta drew it deep into her lungs as she made her way between the huts, each with lamplight glowing softly from behind drawn windows. Now and again she caught the sound of voices, a sudden eruption of laughter, a woman singing a snatch of song.

The moon was new, a crescent-shaped silver brooch pinned to the sky's black velvet cloak. Other than the lit windows and the stars scattered across the heavens there was little light, and she had to step carefully. As her eyes became accustomed to the darkness she began to make out the uneven shadows that told of grassy tussocks or bits of stone raised above the path she trod. The sea shushed softly against the shore, and as she moved towards it she began to make out glimmering lights where the moon's rays caught the wavetops.

Sixteen! She gloated over the thought, scarcely able to believe that she had finally made the step from childhood to womanhood. In another three birthdays she would be the same age as her own mother had been when she died.

She wished that she had known the girl who had birthed her and then died. She could remember very little of her father's grandmother other than a very old woman who moved slowly and painfully, but was kind in her own fashion. Her strongest memory of her early childhood belonged to the time she was with her mother's parents. Even at a very young age she was keenly aware of the tension that had settled over the farm cottage whenever her grandfather came home from his work, and the way her grandmother seemed to shrink into herself like a small creature trying to hide behind a stone whenever her husband was in the vicinity.

God ruled over her grandparents' home, a harsh and unforgiving God who used William Mulholland as His mouthpiece. Even though she had been little more than a toddler at the time, Etta knew that God was unforgiving because, for some reason she could never fathom, she was one of the people He could never forgive. She was expected to pray for absolution every night before she went to bed and every morning when she got up, and at the table her grandfather always begged the Lord to pardon Etta her sins before anyone was allowed to eat. Grandfather had also believed in cleansing the soul by punishing the body – she remembered the beatings clearly enough.

All the misery and bewilderment had vanished when Etta went to live with Aunt Zelda. In the Lowrie household God

147

was a kindly personage who loved little children – and goodness knew that there were enough children to love in that house. As well as those who lived in the small cottage, there were always friends and cousins coming about the place. Aunt Zelda, like her God, loved children.

When she was twelve and old enough to demand an explanation from her aunt, Etta finally discovered that her unforgivable sin had come about because her mother Elsie, Zelda's favourite sister, had borne her out of wedlock.

'But that wasnae your fault, pet, nor hers,' Zelda hastened to explain. 'She was goin' tae marry your daddy, only it was wartime and he was away fightin' when she found out that you were on the way. And he was killed afore he could get back tae Buckie tae marry her, poor lad. He didnae even live tae see his bonny wee lass, or his twentieth birthday.'

Zelda, in the middle of baking when Etta marched into the kitchen and demanded to know more of her past, had scrubbed moisture from her eyes at this point with the cloth she held. When she took her hand away her round, normally happy face was smudged with white powder. Etta, on the verge of tears herself at the sad story about her poor young parents, had laughed instead, and Zelda, looking in the mirror, had joined in.

Etta smiled at the memory, but she was still wondering about her mother and her father as she started to walk back to the hut. She had nothing of theirs to keep their memories in her mind, not even a faded photograph.

'Good evenin' to ye, missie.' The voice, coming from the darkness around her, made her gasp, and the man immediately added, 'Did I startle ye? Sorry, missie, I'd no mind to do that. I was just after wishin' you all the benefits of this grand evenin'.'

She could see him now, a vague figure standing to one side of the path.

'G-good evening,' she said uncertainly.

'Are ye on yer own, then?'

'I just stepped out for some fresh air.'

'Allow me to walk ye back to yer lodgin', ma'am.' His arm swept up to pull a cap from his head as he sketched a clumsy bow.

'I've not far to go.'

'The Scotch huts, is it? I can tell by the way ye speak. They're along here.' He replaced his cap and began to lead the way, saying over his shoulder as she hesitated, 'I know this place like the back of my own hand, even in the night. This way.'

Realising that she had lost her own sense of direction, Etta followed him, her initial unease lulled by his steady flow of talk about the peacefulness of the night and the beauty of the area. His soft accent told her that he was one of the Irish labourers scattered about the yards, working wherever they were needed.

A hut loomed out of the darkness. The man walked confidently round a corner and Etta followed, blinking as they came on a small fire. Although it was little more than a glow with a few flickering flames it dazzled eyes that had become accustomed to darkness.

'Where are we?'

'This is where I sleep,' her guide said. 'The fire keeps me warm when the night gets cold. The fire, and this.' His silhouette was partly outlined against the red glow as he stooped and then straightened again, tilting his head back and lifting the bottle in his hand to his mouth. She heard him gulp the liquid down once and then twice before he lowered his arm again. 'It's good stuff, missie. Here, have a taste of it for yerself. It'll warm your bones, so it will.'

'I don't want it.' Etta took a step back as the bottle was thrust beneath her nose. The stuff within had a sharp, gut-churning smell. 'I have to go,' she said nervously. 'I'll find my own way back.'

'Indeed and you will not. What sort of gentleman would I be if I let a pretty lass like yerself wander off on her lone in the middle of the night? One wee drink for friendship's sake,' he coaxed, moving in on her, 'and then I'll take ye right to yer door and wish ye a good night's sleep.'

'I have to go n—' The words were choked off as a long thin arm suddenly snaked about her shoulders. His hand cupped her upper arm, tightening its grip so that she was drawn towards the man's body.

'In a minute, I said.' She was so close to him now that his mouth brushed her ear. 'It's only friendly to accept a drink when it's offered. Just one wee drink.'

As the glass bottle was pushed at her face Etta closed her mouth. The neck jammed into her lips, forcing them painfully against her teeth, and she thrashed her head from side to side, dislodging the bottle from his fingers.

'Will ye look at that!' he said breathlessly, his now empty hand closing about her waist. 'It'll have spilled out onto the ground. Ah well, there wasn't much left anyway. But surely ye owe me a wee kiss in its place, eh?'

His breath reeked of raw whisky and his mouth was still wet with the stuff as it found hers and latched on to it. Wild with fear, Etta kicked out with a booted foot and felt it connect with his leg. His body jerked and he took his mouth from hers to say, 'Ah now, what did ye have tae do that for?'

Etta wriggled frantically and managed to free one hand. She reached up to the shadowed face glimmering above hers and dug her nails in, feeling skin tear beneath them as she pulled down as hard as she could.

Her captor let out an animal-like cry and reeled away from her, his hands to his face. Seizing her chance she turned and fled, one shoulder hitting the corner of the hut and sending a jolt of pain down her arm as she went.

Etta still had no idea of where she was or where her hut stood, but at that moment all she wanted was to put as much distance between her and the Irishman as she could. She was bolting along, stumbling over tussocks of grass and sending loose stones rattling into the darkness, her breath sobbing in her throat, when someone caught at her arm, jerking her to a standstill and sending another wave of pain shooting right down to her fingertips.

Blind to everything but the need to protect herself she whirled, ducking at the same time so that the top of her head connected hard with the person who had accosted her. She heard an 'Oof!' from above her head and then, as she bounced back from the collision, a stone moved beneath her foot and she went down, landing on her backside with enough force to jolt her to the top of her skull and make her see stars.

In falling she had pulled herself free, but before she had time to scramble up and take to her heels again a door opened, sending out a beam of light.

'Who's there?' a woman called.

Etta opened her mouth to scream for help and then shut it as the man standing over her, both hands clasped to his midriff, straightened with an effort and said, 'It's all right, Anna, it's just me.'

'Is that Rory Pate?'

'Aye, it is.'

'Who's that with ye?'

'It's me,' Etta called, and heard the wobble in her own voice. 'Etta Mulholland.'

'What are ye doin' on the ground? Rory Pate, are you up tae mischief with that lassie?'

'I tripped on a stone, just,' Etta shouted. 'Rory's walkin' me back tae my hut.'

The woman standing at the hut door turned and said something to the other residents and Etta heard a burst of female laughter. 'A fine night for it,' the woman called, then the door closed and she and Rory were alone in the darkness.

'What did ye have tae grab hold of me like that for?' Etta asked angrily. 'You frightened the life out of me!'

'I wanted tae know what was amiss with ye.' His voice still had a breathless wheeze to it.

'Are you all right?'

'I've been better,' Rory said. 'Ye've got a right hard skull.'

'And you probably spoiled that nice hairdo Andra's Jenny gave me for my birthday.'

He gave a brief laugh, then said, 'What happened, lassie? Ye came out of the dark as if the devil himsel' was after ye.'

A shiver shook Etta from head to toe. 'It was a man. He tried tae—'

'Tae what?' All at once Rory's voice was grim.

'Ye know fine what! I gave him a good kick and he let me go. I was tryin' tae get away when I met up with you. I thought it was him catchin' hold of me again.'

'Whereabouts was this?' Rory turned towards the darkness as though set on finding the attacker. In a panic, she caught at his ankle.

'Leave him, Rory, he's probably run off the other way. I just want tae get home.' Her voice wobbled on the final word, and he peered down at her.

'Are ye hurt? D'ye want me tae get help, or carry ye?'

'I'm fine. Just help me up, will ye? I'm sittin' on the hem of my skirt and it'll no' let me get tae my feet,' she said, and then, when he had reached down to put his hands on her waist, and lifted her as easily as if she had been a doll, 'Now, can ye help me tae find my hut?'

'Here, hold on to my arm.' He drew her hand through the crook of his elbow then said as they started to walk, 'What were ye doin' out on yer lone at this time of night?'

'I just wanted some fresh air.'

'The rest of them should never have let ye go out like that. There's all sorts of folk come tae the fishin', from all over. Did ye know the man?'

'No.' She didn't say that he was Irish because she didn't want Rory to go looking for him. 'He'd been drinkin'.'

'Some of them do, that's why it's no' a good idea for quines tae go out on their lone. If ye ever want tae take a walk at night again, tell me and I'll go with ye.'

'What were you doin' out?' she asked.

'The same as you, no doubt – in search of some fresh air and a bit of peace and quiet.'

'I was thinkin' about my mother,' Etta confessed. 'She died when I was born. I don't even know what she looked like, or my faither. He died afore I was born.'

'My own mother died when I was just wee,' Rory said, 'but I knew my faither, at least. An' there's pictures of my mother in the house.'

'It must be nice to have pictures,' Etta said wistfully.

'Aunt Zelda and Uncle Innes are as good as parents to ye,' Rory pointed out. 'And the important thing is who you are, not who your parents are.'

A sudden wailing sound in the distance made Etta's flesh creep and she clutched Rory's arm tightly. 'What's that?'

'Just an owl, out huntin' for his dinner. An' there goes a bat.'

'Where?'

'It just flew by yer head. Look, there's another.'

She peered into the darkness. 'I can't see anythin'.'

'Can ye not? The night air's full of them. There – and there.'

But try as she might, Etta could not see a single bat in the night sky. She was still looking for them when Rory said, 'Here we are. This is your hut.'

'Are ye sure?' She looked doubtfully at the black bulk before them.

'Of course I'm sure.'

'One hut looks like another in the dark. I'd not want tae go wanderin' intae someone else's.'

'It's yours,' he said, amusement in his voice. 'I'm the one that can see the bats, ken? I know where all the huts are, even in the dark. Go on in now and get some sleep. There's hard work tae be done in the mornin'.'

'Aye.' She started to go, then turned back. 'Thank ye for yer kindness, Rory.'

153

'Och, it was nothin'.'

'Ye'll not say anythin' tae the rest of them? I feel a right fool.'

'It's not you that's tae blame, it's the creature that caught you. If ye see him in the daylight,' Rory's voice was suddenly hard, 'just you point him out tae me. And you neednae fret about me sayin' anythin' tae the rest of them. I know when tae hold my tongue. Just don't go out on yer own again.'

'I won't,' Etta promised fervently.

15

It was the right hut; Etta knew that as soon as she slipped inside the door and heard Agnes's distinctive snore, a guttural intake of breath followed by a long sigh that ended with three emphatic 'Humphs!' Surely nobody else in the whole of the island snored like that?

She stood just inside the door for a moment, bringing the hut's interior to mind and picturing just where her bed stood. Then she moved silently and cautiously across the floor, her hands stretched before her and each foot testing the ground before she put her weight on it.

She managed to reach the large bed without falling over anything, and undressed swiftly in the dark before slipping in beside Sarah and Ruth. It was just as well, she thought as she curled against the warm, solid curve of Sarah's back, that she slept on the outside, and had not had to crawl over any of her cousins to get to her rightful place.

Because the Scottish boats never went to sea on the Sabbath there was no fish for the farlins on Monday. Instead, the day was spent in topping up the barrels. The coopers bored holes in the side of each barrel, and tipped it to pour out the brine resulting from the coarse salt and the herring. The lid was then taken off and the women added another layer or perhaps two of fish and some fresh pickle. After the bunghole was sealed the barrels were covered and rolled off to the side, where they were stacked three tiers high to await the lorries.

It was heavy work, and although there were always labourers willing to earn a few shillings by helping out, the women were expected to take their full share of the backbreaking toil.

Much to Ruth's delight her young photographer friend, Jack Morrison, returned with his camera. She willingly posed for him, now clutching the rim of a barrel as though about to manhandle it on her own, now rolling an empty barrel or placing an extra layer of fish or pouring pickle in through a bunghole.

'That lassie's got a great conceit of hersel',' one of the older women sniffed.

'Ach, leave her be, there's no harm in that at her age,' someone else said, adding longingly, 'It just seems like yesterday that I was as young and bonny as she is. Who'd want tae take my picture now?'

Ruth did look particularly pretty that day, Etta thought, watching the girl talking and laughing with the photographer. Her lightly tanned skin and her hazel eyes glowed with health, and her teeth, when she laughed – which was often – were white and strong. She had wound a blue scarf about her head and strands of her light brown hair, escaping from beneath it, tossed in the breeze. Her plain skirt and blouse, with the sleeves rolled up to above her elbows and unbuttoned at the throat, showed off a body as comely as her face. It was clear that the young man was quite smitten by her.

Etta envied the two of them their pleasure in the day and in each other's company. Her arm ached and she had to steel herself against the pain each time she helped to lift a barrel. She was suffering from lack of sleep and although the cool, fresh wind helped to revive her it could never blow away memories of the groping, grasping hands she had run from the night before. As she struggled with the laden barrels the sheer terror of it kept returning to haunt her.

'Are you all right?' Rory asked at one point as he helped

156

her and Mary to lift a barrel that had to go up to the second tier.

'I'm fine. Why wouldn't I be?' Her voice was sharp, signalling a warning to him.

'I just wondered, after the party last night.'

'If ye ask me she ate too much,' Mary said robustly. 'She had tae go out and walk it off last night, and even so, she scarce ate a thing this mornin'.'

'Mebbe she slipped out tae meet with her lad,' someone called from further down the row.

'I did not!' Etta concentrated on lifting the barrel, keeping her head averted from the others in an effort to hide the sudden warmth flooding her face. Then as the barrel settled into its proper place and they turned back towards the farlins she felt the blood drain from her head to her toes.

Agnes and one of the coopers were lifting the next barrel into place, assisted by a labourer whose skinny body, not much more than flesh and bone, was buckling under the weight he was trying to lift. As he put his shoulder beneath the barrel and struggled to heave it upwards, trying at the same time to prevent the thin, patched shoes he wore from skidding in the mud, his head was twisted to one side and Etta saw that four raw strips of lacerated skin stretched down one cheek from below his eye to the line of his jaw.

Just as the barrel rocked into its place and the boy stepped back Mary said something to Rory. The two of them burst out laughing and the noise brought the lad's head round. As he glanced across at the three of them Etta flinched back, her hands fluttering up to draw the edge of her headscarf over her face in an attempt to hide from him. But his gaze swept over and past her without recognition.

She opened her mouth to call Rory, who was walking away from her, and then closed it again, realising that the ragged, bony youth would be no match for the broad-shouldered, well-nourished cooper, especially if Rory was as angry as he had been last night.

Safe now in the knowledge that he had no idea who she was, Etta watched the boy as the morning wore on and saw that he was having a desperate struggle to keep up with the other men. On one occasion, after helping to lift a barrel into place, he staggered slightly and had to lean against the stacked barrels for a moment. His chest heaved and she could see that his face was slick with sweat. When one of the coopers roared at him to stir himself and lend a hand, it was an effort for him to straighten up and return to work.

To think that she had run from this poor creature, she thought, astonished. She could surely have bested him in any struggle. Then as she recalled the tight grip of his hand on her waist and the way he had dragged her closer and forced his kisses on her, the panic came sweeping back. She had to turn away from the others and pretend to be adjusting the cloths about her fingers until the irrational fear subsided.

Again and again that morning she found her eyes drawn back to the young Irishman. His clothes, shabby and worn almost paper-thin, were little protection against the wind, and his hair was an untidy matted thatch. She remembered the small fire and his soft Irish voice saying, 'This is where I sleep.' He must be living out of doors, sleeping on the hard ground with no roof over his head and little to keep him going other than the raw whisky she had smelled on his breath. She had heard that some of the Irish labourers were in a desperate state, suffering from poverty unknown to the likes of her, but she had never encountered it until now.

The fisher-lassies often gave leftover food to the itinerant workers for, as Mary said, no matter how poor you were there were always folk worse off. She should know, for her soft-hearted mother frequently had whole families, down on their luck and with nowhere else to go, living in the little lean-to in her back yard.

At the midday meal Etta saved her bread, which was no hardship since she was still without any appetite, and stuck the two thick slices together with a scrape of butter and a generous spread of jam. She wrapped it in a bit of newspaper and put it into her pocket.

When she got back to the farlins the boy was sitting alone in the shelter of some barrels, hunched over and with his arms locked about his bony knees. Etta went over to him and held out the little parcel. 'Here you are.'

He lifted his head slowly, as though it took an effort, and looked at her, not understanding.

'This is for you.'

'For me?' he asked, astonished, and then as she pushed the parcel towards him, he took it and unfolded the paper with dirty, long-nailed hands. 'Bless ye, missie,' he said in his lilting Irish voice before cramming a huge bite of bread and jam into his mouth. As Etta backed away from him he added thickly round the food, 'May the angels watch over ye for yer kindness.'

She turned and walked away, not looking back until she had gained the safety of the farlins and the other gutters. He had finished eating by then, and he was licking his filthy fingers one by one, making sure that not a crumb or a drop of sweetness was lost.

That evening, while the other women rubbed embrocation on aching muscles and bathed sore feet, Ruth filled a bowl with water and washed from top to toe, including her hair, 'tae get the smell of the fish off me'. Then she put on the pretty blouse and skirt she had brought from home for special occasions and tied green and red ribbons in her hair before going off to meet her gentleman friend, looking, as Andra's Jenny remarked enviously, as fresh as a daisy, and as though she had never in her life had to do a hard day's work.

They were all asleep long before she returned to the hut, but the next day at the farlins they heard all about the grand time she'd had, and how she had danced all evening. Even though she had not had much rest, her eyes were clear and her skin glowed as she deftly arranged the fish in the required pattern, tossing generous handfuls of salt over each layer before starting on the next.

'I hope you're settin' these fish right,' Rory told her when he arrived to inspect the work. 'You're no' here just tae get yer picture taken.'

Ruth stuck her tongue out at him. 'I know what I'm doin'. Have a look,' she invited, standing back. 'Have ye ever seen a bonnier barrel o' herrin'?'

He grinned at her, ignoring the barrel. 'I know you're one of the best packers we have, so on ye go,' he said, and then to Etta, low-voiced, 'It looks like bein' a grand evenin'. D'ye fancy a wee walk round by the shore afore it gets dark?'

'That'd be nice – if we get away from here early enough.'

All that day she watched out for the Irish lad, at the same time dreading the sight of him. But he must have been put to work in some other area, for she never saw him again. Even so, it was a long time before he ceased to haunt her dreams.

'It's not fair!' Ellen Pate stormed.

'Nothing's fair in this life.' Bethany told her stepdaughter coldly. 'We all have to work for our living and it's time you started. I need you to help me with the net factory.'

'But I don't have to work! I have money; my father left it to me.'

'You don't get that money until your twenty-first birthday next year. In the meantime you're living under my roof and it's time you paid for your keep.'

'Paid?' Ellen said the word as though it belonged to a foreign language and was beyond her comprehension.

'I put money into my mother's house every week when I lived there. Your cousins do the same for their mothers. Why shouldn't you?'

'That's different.' Ellen stamped a neatly shod foot on the parlour carpet. 'They're all working folk and I'm a cooper's daughter. Coopers' daughters don't have to go out to work.'

'No doubt if your faither was still with us he would be happy to feed and clothe and house you out of his own pocket, Ellen, but he can hardly support you in idleness from the grave, can he?'

'Rory owns the cooperage now. It's his place to look after me!'

'Then you can speak to Rory when he comes back from Lerwick. If he wants to keep his sister in comfort that's his concern. I'm just saying that I can't do it any more.'

'You mean you won't. You've plenty money!'

'I do,' Bethany agreed, 'but none of it comes from your father. He left this house to me in his will, Ellen, but I couldn't sell it because it was your home, and Rory's and Adam's. And he arranged for your Uncle Nathan to pay me a sum of money every month to feed and clothe the three of you. But I'm not like you – I don't like to live off other folks' charity. So I've paid my own way by running the net factory and the smokehouse and the gutting crews, and keeping Jacob McFarlane's books. I work for my keep,' Bethany said coldly, 'the same as I always have.'

'My father kept you well enough when he was alive.'

'You think I didn't work for my food even then?' Bethany raised an eyebrow. 'All married women have to earn their keep, Ellen. Mebbe they don't have to go out to work but there are other ways, some of them mebbe not to our liking, though we can do nothing about it. No doubt you'll learn about that for yourself, one day.'

Ellen stared at her stepmother, chewing her full, artificially reddened lower lip. 'Uncle Nathan won't be pleased when he hears that you're making me work for my living. I can get him to give me my inheritance now.'

'You can try,' Bethany told her dryly. 'I know that you can twist Nathan round your little finger, and I know fine where the money for most of your bonny clothes comes from, but I doubt if he'll be willing to hand over your father's inheritance before it's due. And when it is, I'd not be surprised to hear that he's already deducted all the money you've wheedled from him in the past few years.'

Her stepdaughter's face suddenly paled. 'He wouldn't do that!'

'You'll not know the truth of it until your next birthday. And until then, you'll either work or you'll go hungry.'

'How dare you say such a thing to me!'

'If you don't want to go to the net factory I can always turn Leezie off and let you run the house.'

'Me? A skivvy?' The girl's voice was contemptuous.

'What's wrong with that? Most of the fisher quines work as skivvies between fishin' seasons. At least they'll turn their hands to anything to earn their keep. We can call you the housekeeper if it makes you feel any better about it.'

Ellen fiddled sulkily with her stylishly cropped brown hair, then asked, 'What would I do in the net factory?'

'Nothing that takes skill, that's certain. You don't know how to wind the skeins of cotton for the looms, or how to weave, and it takes a good year to learn how to be a beatster. It's a skilled job, mending nets. I should know, for I had to do it when I was your age.'

'It was different for you, you were only a fisherman's daughter!'

Bethany's clear eyes suddenly took on the deep, threatening grey of an approaching storm. Although the parlour was warm, Ellen felt chilled as those eyes surveyed her.

'It's the herring fishers that made your father rich enough to buy this fine house and turn you into a lady, Ellen Pate.' Bethany's voice was as icy as her stare. 'Never forget that. As to what you can do in the factory,' she went on as Ellen began to wilt, 'you can see to it that the materials the workers need are ordered in time, and that the men and women are content, and getting on with what they're paid to do. Contented workers work better. And you can make up their wages. You should surely be able to manage the writing and figuring.'

There was a moment's silence before Ellen heaved a martyred sigh. 'I suppose I'll have to do what you want – until Rory comes home from the fishing, at least.'

'Good.' Bethany sat down at her desk, a sign that the meeting was at an end. 'You can come to the factory with me tomorrow and I'll show you what has to be done,' she said, picking up a pen and dipping it into the inkwell. Then she laid it down again, sighing, when the girl had flounced out, closing the parlour door behind her with unnecessary vigour. Ellen had been a placid, biddable child, but for some reason that Bethany could not fathom she had grown into a self-centred young woman.

It was true that men who owned cooperages as successful as the Pate's were usually wealthy enough to support their families. Coopers' sons and daughters normally led easy lives and dressed in the height of fashion, and if Gil had lived, Ellen could no doubt have played the young lady to her heart's content. But it irked Bethany each time she came home from the factory after a day's work to find her stepdaughter lounging in the parlour, leafing through magazines.

It seemed to her that children were more trouble as they got older instead of less. When it came to doing her bidding, the only one of the three who had not given her any worry was Rory, who had calmly served his apprenticeship in the cooperage and then taken charge of it, as his father had planned. Even when he received his inheritance, a tidy sum of money, he had put it away in the bank where, as far as Bethany knew, it still lay.

Adam was every bit as difficult as his half-sister. Every time he went missing she had known where to find him – down at the harbour and as like as not on board the *Fidelity* if the drifter was there. Once he turned fifteen he was desperate to go out on the boat, pestering and badgering until Bethany was forced to agree. She had hoped that he would take after Innes and be a poor sailor, and that one voyage would be enough for him, but instead he had come home

163

glowing with excitement, and determined to go out to the fishing whenever he got the chance.

'Let the loon have his way,' Jacob had advised her. 'The more ye go against him the more determined he'll be. James'll see tae it that he comes tae no harm.'

She had listened to him – and where had that got her? This summer Adam was off to the Shetlands with his uncle, and goodness only knew what sort of nonsense James would put into his head. When she was expecting her only child Bethany had longed for a son who would follow the fishing, thus fulfilling her own thwarted ambition, but when James returned from the war and she saw the hungry way he looked at the child she realised that, like her, he wanted Adam to follow in the family tradition. But that would mean that he and James would be in each other's company, and that she could not allow.

So she had adopted Gil's ambition for the boy, and now Adam, who had done well at the school, was attending Aberdeen University.

At least, Bethany thought as she went through to the kitchen, he would be well beyond James's reach there. He would meet new folk, follow new interests, and there would be no more talk of the fishing.

'What was all that about?' Leezie asked as her mistress walked in, and then, as Bethany raised her eyebrows, 'Ye neednae worry, I've not stooped as low as tae listen at doors. I didnae have tae, for I could hear the two of ye shoutin' at each other from here.'

'We weren't shouting, we were having a discussion.' Bethany took an apron from the hook on the door and tied it around her waist, noting with annoyance how far she had to reach to tie it at the back. She was into her forty-third year, and it seemed that every birthday brought with it a further slight thickening of her once slim waist. 'Ellen's going to be the new overseer in the net factory.'

'Ellen?' Surprise sent the maid's voice soaring. 'No wonder she was shoutin' at ye.'

'She wasn't shouting.' Bethany began to scrape carrots.

'That's as may be, but I'm certain sure she didnae come up with the idea on her own. That one's the laziest lassie in the town.'

'You mind your tongue. You're just a servant here.'

'I'm the hoosekeeper and I'm stayin' the hoosekeeper! Aye well, mebbe I did put my ear tae the door for a minute,' Leezie said as her mistress gave her a hard look. 'But I took it away again when I heard ye say that ye'd turn me off and give her my job.'

'You know as well as I do that she'd never have agreed to it.'

'Even so, it wasnae very nice tae hear ye offerin' tae put me out without a second thought.' Leezie underlined the words with a hefty sniff.

'I told you, it would never have happened so stop making such a fuss about it!' Bethany's knife bit into a carrot with such force that it pared off a large chunk of the red flesh. She swept it into the rubbish bucket before Leezie noticed. Leezie hated waste.

16

'It's about time that lassie was made tae do some work,'
Stella Lowrie said when Annie came back from the shops
with the news that Ellen was overseeing the net factory for
her stepmother. 'It's not right, her walkin' about the town as
if she owned it when she does nothin' for anyone. Did ye
get that soap?'

'Aye.' Annie put the bar of yellow soap and the few coppers
of change onto the table then returned to the task of blackleading the grate. The two of them were getting the holiday
cottage ready for the next lot of summer visitors.

'After all,' her mother ranted on as she rubbed beeswax
into the big dresser, 'she's no better than you and your
sisters. You were born in this very cottage, and she was
birthed in one just like it. What right has she tae put on airs
and graces?'

'Uncle Gil did well for himsel',' Annie ventured. 'Ellen
grew up in that fine, big house he bought, and he'd enough
money tae keep her in comfort. She didnae have tae work
for her livin' the way we did.'

'And what's come out of that? The lassie's got a right
conceit of hersel'. The devil finds mischief for idle hands,'
Stella snapped, and Annie took some comfort in thinking that
if that was true, the devil would never be able to get close
to her. 'She's spoiled, and so's that young brother of hers.
University, indeed! What about that ash pan?'

Annie hauled the metal tray out from underneath the grate and held it out for inspection. 'It's been emptied.'

'Aye, but has it been cleaned?'

'Ye don't clean ash pans, mither!'

'Ye do in my house,' Stella said. 'Take it out the back and give it a good brushing, then ye can wipe it over with a bit of metal polish when ye've brought it in again.'

Annie opened her mouth to argue, then closed it again and did as she was told, wishing with all her heart that she was standing at the farlins with her sisters Sarah and Ruth and the other fisher-lassies. A fine drizzle of rain was falling, but even if it was the same in the Shetlands, with mud under-foot at the farlins, she would have welcomed it.

'Rory's the only one that's turned out right in that family.' Stella picked up the conversation again when her daughter brought the ash pan back into the kitchen. 'He's not afraid of a hard day's work, that lad.'

'Aunt Bethany works hard too,' Annie pointed out, and Stella sniffed.

'I wouldnae call overseein' the net factory and the smoke-house hard work. Not as hard as carin' for a house, but she's fly enough tae have someone in tae dae that for her.'

'She does Mr McFarlane's financial books too, Rory says. And it was Uncle Gil that brought Leezie in tae do the house-work, surely.' Then, when her mother simply said 'Hmph!' Annie ventured, 'What did my Aunt Bethany do that was so wrong?'

'What did you say?' The words rattled out so quickly that Annie jumped. She turned away from the grate to see that Stella, too, had stopped her work and was staring at her, her eyes hard and her normally pale face looking almost yellow.

'I was just wonderin',' the younger woman faltered. 'She must have done somethin' tae make ye dislike her the way ye do.'

'Bethany Pate,' her mother said slowly and clearly, 'doesnae need tae *do* anythin' tae annoy folk. It's just her way of behavin' as if nob'dy's as good as she is – that's enough tae rile anyone.'

'Aunt Zelda gets on well with her.'

'Your Aunt Zelda would get on with anyone,' Stella snapped. 'How's that ash pan lookin'?' Then, when Annie held it out for inspection, 'It'll do. You can put it back.'

'It seems a shame tae fill it with ashes now,' Annie said as she obeyed.

'That's what it's for,' Stella was beginning when hurried footsteps rattled on the road outside, and the door was thrown open.

'Mind my clean oilcloth with your wet feet!' Stella skirled, but the order was ignored as Samuel Lowrie burst into the kitchen, heedlessly tracking prints from his muddy boots all over the scrubbed oilcloth.

'Mither says tae come at once,' he gabbled, his dark eyes wide with fear. 'It's Auntie Meg. She's sleepin' and when mither tried tae wake her she fell off her chair and we cannae get her up from the floor!'

Adam brought Stella's letter to James as he sat in the *Fidelity*'s cabin, enjoying a quiet smoke after a long night's fishing. 'One for you, and two for me,' the boy said, dropping the envelope with its familiar handwriting on the table and throwing himself onto the bench at the other side of the table. 'There's letters for some of the others, but Siddy took them.'

'And who's writin' tae you, then?'

Adam grinned. 'Ach, some lassies enjoy writin' letters,' he said, tearing open the first envelope. James watched him scan the single sheet of paper, remembering the days when he had been Adam's age and local lassies had written little notes to him while he was away at the fishing. Now, it seemed as if those carefree days had belonged to someone else entirely, he thought as he unfolded Stella's letter and began to read the contents.

He scanned the few lines once, and then went back and

read them again, unable to take in the news they contained. As he sat motionless, paralysed with the shock of it, Adam glanced up at him and then returned to his own letter; then, suddenly realising that something was wrong, he looked sharply back at his uncle.

'What is it?'

James tried to speak, but had to clear his throat and try again before he found his voice. 'It's your Auntie Meg. She's died.'

'Auntie Meg? But she wasnae ill when we left.'

'It was sudden, Stella says. She just went in her sleep. She'd reached a good age,' James said, his eyes still on his wife's letter. 'Longer than most. But even so, it's come as a bit of a shock.'

'Will we be goin' back tae Buckie for the funeral, then?'

James ran the back of his hand over his mouth and cleared his throat again. 'No, no. Stella says it's all in hand, and we'd not get back in time, anyway.'

'It'll seem strange, without Auntie Meg,' Adam said, and then, with the resilience of the very young, 'But she was a good age, as you said.'

'Aye.'

'D'ye want me to go and tell the others? Jem and Mary and the rest of them?'

'Aye, ye could. I've got things tae do here before I come ashore,' James said, and the youth departed, skimming up the ladder and whistling as he tramped across the deck overhead.

James put the letter down flat on the table, and sat stroking it with one finger, staring unseeingly at the opposite wall. For some strange reason Meg's death filled him with more emotion than he had known at the loss of either of his parents. He wondered if it was because of the resentment he had felt against his father for pushing him into a marriage he had not wanted, and with his mother because of the bitter quarrel they had had when she insisted on burying Weem Lowrie on land when James knew that his father's dearest wish was to be given back to the sea he loved.

Meg was different; Meg had always been different. A big woman with a big heart, she had only needed to walk into a house to set its very walls thrumming with her presence. And she had always met folk on their own level, James realised now, never judging, never criticising, always ready to accept them as they were.

For the past fourteen years she had been the head of the family, and with her dying she had handed that position over to James himself. Although he lived with death every time he took his boat out to sea he was suddenly reminded by Meg's passing of his own mortality. Who would follow him when his own days were over?

Adam had left his two letters, one envelope still sealed, on the table. James picked up the opened letter and glanced down at it, seeing only the beginning, 'Dear Adam,' and the girl's signature scrawled at the bottom of the page.

Dear Adam. He looked at the wall again, seeing with his mind's eye the young face beneath the shock of black curls that, like his own hair at that age, tended to tumble over the boy's forehead. And he railed against the knowledge that when he himself was gone there was no son to carry the bloodline forward.

No son, at least, that he could claim before the rest of the world.

Sarah had been right in saying that the sea journey home to the Moray Firth would be easier than the trip out to Lerwick. The sea was just as rough and the boat tossed as much as it had before but, buoyed up by the excitement of going home and memories of the good times she had had at the Lerwick fishing, Etta managed to get through the misery of seasickness without becoming too wretched.

They landed at Aberdeen, where Peter Bain, son of the farmer who had employed Zelda as kitchen maid before her marriage, was waiting to take the Buckie fisher-lassies home. Crowding onto the back of his lorry they roared out hymns and popular songs as they rattled and bounced along the coast to Buckie.

The local season lay ahead of them, and there was the English fishing to come after that, but at least, Etta knew, she would be able to sleep at home after a day spent slaving at the Buckie farlins. As for the move south, that journey would be made by lorry and train, with no more tossing about at the mercy of the sea.

Zelda was waiting down by the harbour with Annie, Sarah's twin, when the lorry arrived and began to spill its cargo.

'Where's Mary?' Zelda asked as the girls climbed to the ground.

'Milady decided to keep Peter company in the cab.' Ruth banged on the door, and Mary appeared, giggling as she was met by a chorus of cheers and jibes from the others.

'We've missed ye both!' Zelda ran to hug her daughter and then her niece. 'The house wasnae the same without ye!'

'Mither, how could you tell?' Mary wanted to know. 'There were still five bairns in the place – ye surely couldnae miss just two of us with all that noise goin' on.'

'I never feel right unless ye're all close by me,' Zelda said firmly. 'Peter, son, come and have a wee cup of tea before you go home.'

'I'd like that fine, but there's work tae be done, and my faither'll be waitin' for me. I said I'd get right back,' he said with genuine regret. Zelda had been his nursemaid when he was a child, and he still thought the world of her.

'Another time, then. Don't you forget, now.' She stood on tiptoe to give him a hug and a hefty kiss on the cheek, to another chorus of cheers from the fisher-lassies. 'Give my regards tae your mother and father, lad, and bless you for bringin' my lassies back tae me,' she said, and then as Peter climbed back into the cab and the lorry drove away, 'How did ye like the Lerwick fishin', Etta?'

'She liked it fine,' Sarah smirked. 'See that bonny wee shell necklace she's wearin'? Rory Pate gave it tae her.'

'Rory? Are the two of ye courtin', then?' Zelda asked eagerly. She loved a bit of romance.

'They've been walkin' out together,' Mary said.

'The necklace was for my birthday,' Etta protested, 'and Rory's just been showin' me round the place, and tellin' me the names of the birds.'

'Ruth's got an admirer too,' Sarah said, while Ruth giggled, well pleased with herself. 'He's a photographer mannie that photographed us at the farlins, and took her to the dancin'.'

'His name's Jack,' Ruth chimed in. 'Jack Morrison. He's takin' pictures for a book. I told him about Aunt Beth'ny's net factory and the smokehouse, and he's comin' tae Buckie tae take pictures of them.'

'You'll need tae bring him tae the house for his tea, Ruth. What about you, Mary? No boyfriend for you?' her mother asked wistfully. 'I'd fair like tae set up your weddin'.'

'I'm not in any hurry. It was terrible news about Auntie Meg,' Mary said, and tears sprang at once to Zelda's eyes.

'I miss her that much! But she went quick, and I suppose that's a blessin' for her, even though it's so hard on the rest of us,' she said, and then, scrubbing a hand across her eyes, 'Come on now, tell me all about Lerwick.'

She linked arms with her eldest daughter and they set off together along the street. As the other fisher-lassies followed in a ragtaggle group, Annie burst out, 'I'm that glad ye're back! I've made up my mind that I'm goin' back to the farlins, and if my mither wants any more help she can get it from you, Sarah, or from Ruth. We cleaned that cottage so much that it's a shame tae let folk live in it. It wasnae enough just tae wash the oilcloth on the floor – we'd tae take it up and put it outside so's we could get at the floorboards and give them a good scrub with bleach. Then the oilcloth had tae be cleaned afore it could be put back down, and I'd tae black-lead the fireplace an' scrub up the fender wi' steel cloth – I even had tae clean the ash pan afore it went back below the grate.'

'My mither did that every springtime,' Agnes said, 'And she had this big black kettle that had tae be blackleaded every week. It was never used for anythin', mind, it was just for show. You young quinies don't know the meanin' of spring-cleanin' nowadays.'

'I do now,' Annie said from the bottom of her heart, while Etta asked, 'D'you clean your own hoosie like that, Agnes?'

'Me?' The woman boomed out a hearty laugh. 'Away tae damty, lassie, d'ye think I've got the time for all that palaver? Not at all!'

'Then when the whole thing was finished,' Annie went on, 'I'd tae scrub the floorbrush and clean the shovel. I kept waitin' for her tae tell me tae wash the coal in the back bunker. And once it was all done tae her satisfaction she hung up one of they samplers she'd found in a shop, with "Home Sweet Home" stitched on it. Home, indeed – I'm certain that even if the King and Queen themselves were tae take that cottage for their holidays they'd find it cleaner than their own home. I tell you, the thought of standin' at the farlins all day guttin' fish sounds like Paradise tae me, after what I've been through!'

Rory Pate was no sooner home from Lerwick than his sister pounced, bursting into his room before he had time to respond to the swift, impatient tap at the door.

'She's impossible!' she stormed, standing over him as he sat on the bed, leafing through the nature notebook he had been keeping during his walks in Lerwick.

'Who?' he asked, though he knew the answer well enough.

'I'm not talking about Leezie, am I?' Her arms were folded tightly across her chest and her eyes were angry. Rory gave an inward sigh and laid the book of sketches and notes aside.

'Mother.'

'She's not our mother, she's our stepmother! Our real

173

mother wouldn't have treated me the way *she's* treated me. Rory, she's got me working in the net factory!'

'You're makin' nets?' He looked in disbelief at her hands with their neat polished nails.

'How would I know how to make nets? She's got me writing out the invoices and doing the wages and keeping an eye on the place – the things she used to do herself. She's making me *work*,' Ellen said, her voice filled with self-pity, 'and she's making me pay money into this place every week.'

'I pay for my keep, and I suppose Adam will, from the money he's earnin' at the fishin'.'

'But it's different for you; you've got the cooperage to run. I shouldn't need to work!'

'You have to do somethin', Ellen.'

'Why should I? We don't need the money. People only work when they need to.'

'Sit down, Ellen, my neck's gettin' stiff with lookin' up at you. The thing tae do,' Rory said when she had thrown herself into the only chair in the room, 'is tae find somethin' you like better. Work in an office, or a shop, mebbe.'

'But that's still work!' Ellen's fingers drummed on the arms of the chair. 'And I don't want to work – I don't need to! I've written to Uncle Nathan to ask for my inheritance early, but he'll not agree.'

'I don't see that he can, since our father's will says that you have to wait until you're twenty-one.'

'I must have that money, so that I can get away from this place.'

'Where would you go?'

'Aberdeen – Edinburgh—'

'And what would you do when you got there? There won't be enough money tae keep you in comfort for the rest of your life.'

'I'll find something more suitable once I get there. Rory,' Ellen coaxed, 'you could lend me money, just until I reach my twenty-first birthday and get my inheritance.'

He gaped at her. This was something he had not expected.

'You haven't spent it, have you?' she asked sharply. 'What could you have spent it on? You never go anywhere or do anything but work.'

'I put it in the bank.'

'Well then, you can take it out, or some of it at least, and give it to me. I'll pay it back.'

'How will you do that?'

'I'll find a way. Please, Rory?'

He hesitated, and then shook his head. 'I cannae do it.'

'Why not?'

'Because it seems tae me that Mother's tryin' tae teach you that we all need tae pay our way. And she's right, because—'

Ellen dismissed the words with a melodramatic wave of her arms. 'You're saying no? You're denying me, your own sister? Your own flesh and blood?'

'If ye really can't bear tae work in the factory, I can pay money intae the house for you until you find somethin' more suited—' he said, but his sister was on her feet and glaring down at him, her face screwed into an ugly grimace.

'Go to hell, Rory Pate,' she said, and then went out, banging the door so hard that he was surprised to see it remain on its hinges.

The cleaning frenzy that had plunged Annie into gloom had been balm to Stella Lowrie's soul. For the first time in a life spent in ministering to others – first of all her mother, who had more or less become an invalid after the loss of her three sons at sea, then her father, and then her husband and daughters – she was a woman of property, an independent woman who earned her own money by renting out the cottage that had been her childhood home.

And for the first time, as she banked the rent money, Stella began to wonder if her self-willed, difficult sister-in-law had, like her, railed against having to be dependent on a husband.

175

But it didn't soften the dislike she felt towards Bethany. Too much had happened for that to be possible.

'I don't know why we don't just bring our caff mattresses down here an' save the walk home and back again,' Andra's Jenny grumbled as she gutted. The boats had been low in the water on their return to Buckie on the previous day, and the women, after an early start, had been kept at the farlins until close to midnight. After a few snatched hours' sleep they were back to start the new day's work. 'Andra made a right fuss last night when I got home,' Jenny went on. '"Where have ye been?" he wanted tae know – as if I'd been out enjoyin' mysel'! I told him "once you take the fish from the sea they cannae be left lyin' overnight. That's what keeps the guttin' quines standin' at the farlins, and if ye want yer wife at home, then ye have tae stop catchin' so much fish. Ye cannae have things a' ways," I said.'

'Men aye think they can have things a' ways. He'll be pleased enough when the money comes in at the end of the season,' Agnes grunted, and Jenny brightened up.

'He will that, and so will I. We'll be able tae give the bairns a right good Ne'erday when it comes.'

To Etta's surprise, Rory continued to seek her company on his beloved walks along the shoreline and over the farming country behind Buckie. 'It's peaceful here, is it not?' he said one Sunday afternoon as they sat on a hillside, looking down on Buckie's roofs and chimneys, the boats crammed into the four basins of the harbour, and the great stretch of glittering water beyond.

'I'd have thought you would have plenty of peace in that fine big house you live in. It's not like our place, with bairns near sittin' on top of each other and folk comin' in and out all the time.'

Rory picked a stalk of grass, drew the inner stalk from its sheath, and began to chew on its soft flesh. 'I like Aunt Zelda's house. It might be busy, but it's friendly, not like our place. Adam's moanin' about havin' tae go back tae the university come September and Ellen's in a right takin' because our mither's makin' her oversee the net factory. She goes off tae work with such a sour face on her that I feel sorry for the folk that have tae work for her.'

Etta knew all about the tensions in the net factory, for her cousin Jessie, now fourteen and working there, came home every night bursting with tales of the day's happenings. Bethany had an aloof way with her, but her employees had accepted that because she was a mature woman, and although she was strict she was fair. Ellen was different; for one thing, many of the younger women found it hard to treat her as their superior since they were of the same age and she had played with them in the old days when, like them, she had lived in a cottage. Ellen put on airs, Jessie said, and looked down her nose at folk, and the workers resented this.

Etta wondered if she should tell Rory what her foster sister had said, then she decided that it was none of her business, and settled for, 'Everyone has tae earn their way.'

'Aye, and she's not the only one who cannae do what she wants.'

A sudden bitterness in his voice caused Etta to look up at him from where she lay comfortably on the grass, her head pillowed on her jacket. 'You're all right, surely, runnin' your own cooperage?'

Rory picked another stalk and examined it closely, using his thumbnail to split it lengthways. 'Aye,' he said at last. 'I'm fine. I aye knew that I was meant for the cooperage. It was what my faither decided for me when I was born.'

Then he tossed the grass stalk away, and as it was caught by the slight breeze and carried down the hill he leaned over Etta and kissed her, his mouth soft and warm on hers. She liked his kisses, but to her mind, they were more safe than romantic, and she tended to look on him more as an older brother than a sweetheart.

Sometimes Mary Lowrie and Peter Bain went walking with

177

Etta and Rory. During the summer fishing Peter had taken time from farming to become a horseman, the name given to the carters who carried salt and baskets of fish from the boats – or from the auctioneers if the fish were sold on the open market instead of being contracted to a merchant such as Jacob McFarlane – to the farlins, and took the filled and topped barrels away.

More than one fisher-lassie had paused from her work to smile up at the young horseman as he rode past, controlling the horse with a twitch of the reins and the occasional swift command, and standing up on the cart as straight and as proud as a Roman charioteer. His shirtsleeves were rolled up to show tanned, muscular arms and the breeze tumbled his fair hair about his square, pleasant face.

But Peter only had eyes for Mary Lowrie. The friendship that had begun when Mary travelled in the cab of Peter's lorry as he drove the fisher-lassies back from Aberdeen had grown swiftly, and by the end of August, when the fish were once again on their way south, the two of them were officially walking out together, to Zelda's delight.

17

Jack Morrison, the young photographer, arrived in Buckie just before the summer fishing came to its end. He took lodgings with a widow woman who lived in a cottage in the Yardie, not far from James Lowrie's home, and he and his camera became a familiar sight in the town as he photographed the fishermen mending their nets and the old men sitting down by the harbour, smoking their pipes and exchanging stories of their time at sea. He rose early in the morning to photograph the boats coming into harbour after a night's fishing, and was back in the afternoon to record them coaling in preparation for the next trip.

'Ye'd have thought he'd have had enough pictures of us at our work,' Agnes said when he arrived at the farlins.

'It's no' us that's the attraction,' Andra's Jenny told her, grinning, while Ruth, beaming into the camera lens, posed with an empty barrel hoisted above her head. 'It's that lassie there, the one that gets all dressed up these days just tae gut the herrin'. I never thought she cared that much about fish.'

Jacob McFarlane, who had a keen interest in everything and everyone, invited the young photographer to his house on several occasions, and as often as not Ruth went with him. The two of them were made welcome, as everyone was, in Zelda's kitchen, and Ruth even managed to persuade her mother to invite Jack to their home, though when her youngest daughter first broached the subject Stella said nervously, 'I don't know, Ruth, I'm not used tae entertainin' gentry.'

'He's not gentry, Mither, he's just a man that makes his money by workin', the same as the rest of us.'

'Aye, but he comes from a city, and they do things differently there. What would he want tae eat?'

'The same as everyone else,' Ruth said, exasperated. 'Just give him what we'd be havin' ourselves. Auntie Zelda treated him like one of her own, and so can you.'

'Aye, but Zelda has a different way with her,' Stella argued, 'and I don't know what your faither'll say. He's not over fond of visitors.'

'Then it's time he changed,' Ruth said firmly, and marched down to the harbour to face James in his own cabin, where he spent a great deal of his time when the drifter was not at sea. She swept across the gangplank and into the galley, then clambered down the ladder to find him enjoying a glass of whisky with Adam Pate and Innes Lowrie.

'Are you old enough tae drink that?' Ruth asked her cousin.

'I'll be eighteen next month, and anyway, it's none of your business,' he shot back at her, but she was already studying some of the pictures torn from magazines and stuck up on the cabin walls.

'Who put these photographs of women up there?' she wanted to know, and her father almost bit the stem of his pipe in two, while Innes laughed.

'No' me, I'll tell ye that.' James reached up and tore down the nearest photograph, crumpling it in his hand. 'It's the younger lads, and there's no harm tae them. Anyway, you shouldnae be burstin' in here without askin' my permission first.'

'And I suppose you're one of the folk that put those pictures up, are you?' Ruth asked Adam.

'I might have. There's no harm in lookin'.'

'Move along.' She pushed him along the bench and sat down. 'You neednae fret about pictures, Faither, or the whisky bottle, for I'll say nothin'. I'm here tae ask a favour. I want

180

tae ask Jack Morrison tae the house for his dinner, and my mither's in a fuss about it. Will ye tell her that it's all right?'

'Who the— Who's Jack Morrison?' James asked, confused. He never quite knew what to make of this quicksilver daughter of his, for she was quite unlike her mother and sisters.

Adam grinned. 'Ruth's sweetheart.'

'Sweetheart?' James took the pipe from his mouth. 'You're too young for that sort of nonsense!'

'Faither, I'll be nineteen years of age in another two weeks. I'm older than him,' Ruth exploded, giving Adam a hefty nudge in the ribs, 'and you're letting him sit there drinkin' whisky for all the world like a grown man.'

'Wait a minute – I've never heard of this Morrison loon. Is he from round here?'

'He's from Glasgow, and he takes pictures. Proper pictures, for a book,' Ruth added. 'Not the sort of thing you've got up on the walls there. You must have seen him about the harbour with his camera.'

'The camera with the long spindly legs? That man? You want tae ask him tae our house for his dinner?'

'Photographers need tae eat the same as the rest of us do. You and my mither should be pleased that someone's takin' an interest in me at last,' Ruth pointed out. 'You don't want me tae be an old maid, surely?'

'Damn the chance of that,' muttered Adam, rubbing his aching ribs.

'You're right,' his cousin agreed amiably. 'I'd ask the question myself before I'd die of waitin' for some man tae get round tae askin' it. So Faither, can I tell my mither that you said Jack can come for his dinner?'

'I suppose he can, if that's what ye want.'

'And you'll be there? Aye, you will,' Ruth said swiftly as her father began to argue. 'You'll want tae meet the young man I'm walkin' out with, surely?'

'Does he know that the two of you are walkin' out?' Adam enquired.

'If he doesnae know it now, he will when he gets invited tae meet my faither. How will ye find out, else, if he's suitable for me?' Ruth asked James. Then, before he could reply, 'And Adam, you could ask Aunt Beth'ny if she'll allow Jack tae take pictures in the smokehouse and the net factory for this book of his.'

'I don't think she'd object to that. I'll ask her tonight, and tell ye tomorrow,' said Adam, and she gave him a beaming smile and paused to ruffle his dark hair before hurrying back up the ladder to the galley.

'I'll never understand women,' James said when his daughter had gone, leaving little invisible whirls of energy in the air.

'Who'd want to?' said Adam.

'I've met this Jack Morrison that your Ruth's taken to,' Innes told his brother. 'He's been to our house, and he's a decent enough lad. You'll like him.'

James refilled his glass and held the bottle out to the other two, who both shook their heads. 'I never thought that fatherin' lassies was goin' tae be such a trouble.'

'Ach, it's no trouble, lassies are fine if ye just take them as ye find them,' Innes told him comfortably.

'It's a pity you never had sons, Uncle James, to follow you to the fishing,' Adam said, and then glanced uncertainly at the two older men, aware of a sudden tension in the cabin.

'You'd best be gettin' off home before yer mither starts lookin' for ye,' James told the lad abruptly, and Adam shrugged.

'Ach, she's got enough on her mind, with all the work she's taken on. It's Leezie who runs the house now, and she'll not be botherin' about me.'

'Ye'll soon be away tae Aberdeen and your studies, anyway,' Innes said, and the boy bit his lip.

'I wanted tae talk tae you about that, Uncle James.'

'Me? It's got damn all tae do with me!'

'Aye, but it has. I like goin' to the fishin', and I'm heartily sick of book learnin'. Will you talk to my mother?' Adam asked, leaning across the table. 'Will you explain to her that I come from fishing stock, just as she does? I've got the sea in my blood, and I don't want to go back to the university.'

'Indeed I will no'!'

'But you're the one that could get her tae understand that there's no sense in forcin' me in one direction when my mind and my heart's set on another way entirely,' the boy argued.

'What makes you think yer mither would listen tae me? Even if I tried, she'd be more set on the university than ever, just tae spite me for stickin' my neb intae her family business. No, no,' James said vehemently, 'I'll have nothin' tae do with it.'

'Uncle Innes—' Adam appealed, but Innes shook his head.

'Bethany's never listened tae me, laddie, and she'll not start now.'

'So you both want me to be miserable in Aberdeen, is that it?' Adam asked angrily, and when the two men glanced at each other uneasily, but kept silent, 'I'll do it anyway, in spite of the lot of you. If I have tae do the damned course I will, but as soon as I'm finished I'm comin' back to the *Fidelity* whether she likes it or not!'

'He will, you know,' Innes said when his nephew had stormed off the drifter.

'I hope he does, for by then he'll be too old tae be under Bethany's thumb.'

'He's damned near too old for that now, and his heart belongs to the sea just as much as yours does, James. Why won't you help the lad?'

James gave a short, angry laugh. 'Bethany's scarce looked my way for the past eighteen years. She'd throw me intae the harbour if I tried tae tell her how tae treat her precious son.'

'That's a pity, for the boy worships you. He does,' Innes persisted when his older brother looked up at him, startled. 'And he worships the sea, too.'

'He's a good enough seaman, I suppose.'

'From what I've heard from Siddy and the rest of them he's better than good. He's more flesh and blood to you and our faither than I ever was,' Innes said. Then, slowly and deliberately, 'There's little enough of Gil in his nature, would you not agree?'

James's fist, marked with old rope burns and the curved scars of dogfish bites, clenched the whisky tumbler so tightly that Innes expected to hear the sharp crack of broken glass. But the tumbler remained intact as he lifted and drained it. It even withstood being banged back down on the table.

'I've work tae do.' James lurched to his feet and made for the ladder. 'Go home, Innes,' he said over his shoulder as he began to climb. 'And mind your own business.'

Jack Morrison spent an entire day in Bethany Pate's smoke-house and arrived at Ruth's home that night with a parcel of kippers, which he presented to his startled hostess.

'I thought mince and tatties . . .' Stella said nervously.

'It sounds grand, Mrs Lowrie, but could I have a kipper as well?'

'Have you not tasted them afore this?' Annie asked in astonishment.

'I have, but this is the first time I've seen them being kippered. It would be grand to eat one right out of the smoke-house. Unless it's a bother to you?'

'No, no, it wouldnae be any bother.' Under his warm smile, Stella began to thaw. 'In fact, you're easy pleased. Would you like to come and stand by me and see how we cook them an' all?'

'You'll be goin' to the net factory next?' Ruth asked as the family sat down to their meal.

'I've to get back to Glasgow tomorrow, but I'll be in Buckie again to take pictures of the net making in a month or two.' Jack began to dissect his kipper carefully.

Ruth's face fell. 'You're goin' away tomorrow? I'll probably be in Yarm'th by the time you get back here.'

'If you are, I'll go on down to Yarmouth when I'm finished here,' he promised, then went on to talk enthusiastically throughout the meal about the day spent photographing the women splitting the herring, washing and pickling them, then stringing them on poles to be hung up in the kilns and smoked.

The family, so well used to the kippering process that they thought nothing of it, listened in silence, stunned and bewildered by this stranger's enthusiasm for such an everyday event.

It was August, time for the herring to spawn. The Moray Firth fishing season began to draw to a close and Adam Pate reluctantly put away his high, iron-studded boots and sou'wester and the fisherman's gansey that his cousin Mary had knitted for him, and departed for Aberdeen, neatly suited and with his curly dark hair slicked down.

Etta saw very little of Rory over the next two months, for he and the other men in the Pate cooperage were working from early morning until late at night to make barrels for the big English fishing to come. She had work of her own to see to; once the gutting crews broke up, the women had to find other jobs such as working in hotels and big houses or, like Etta, in the net factory.

She had enjoyed her two years in the factory between leaving school and becoming old enough to take up the gutter's knife, but she soon found that Jessie was right when she said that things were different with Ellen Pate in charge, for the young woman made no secret of her resentment at having to earn her living.

Bethany had toured the factory several times a day to make sure that all was well, but Ellen preferred to stay shut up in her tiny office all day, and if she had to leave it to attend to a problem in any part of the factory, she did so with an abrupt, impatient air that irritated the men and the women who worked in the place. Although she wore a plain blouse and skirt to work the garments were clearly well made, and far superior to anything that the female employees could afford. It was as though she was constantly reminding them, as well as herself, of the social gap that yawned between them.

Since she had learned well during her first stint in the factory, Etta was put to work in the mending room. The menders were a privileged group of women, chosen because of their skill with the bone mending needles. They checked the new nets coming straight from the looms, repairing any small flaws; the nets they worked were still white and clean, whereas the employees repairing used nets had a dirty job.

'It's not as if Ellen Pate knows one end o' a net from the other,' one of Etta's colleagues complained one day when Ellen had just passed through the room looking, as someone muttered once she had gone, as if there was a bad smell under her nose. 'At least her mither could handle a needle. Many a time when we were extra busy she'd stand in this very room hersel', mendin' the nets along with the rest of us. But I doubt if milady there could even mend her own stockin's.'

'Not her,' said another girl. 'She'd buy new every time!'

'She's all right,' Etta said uncomfortably, remembering the far-off days when they had all played wee houses with each other on the shore, using shells for cups and sea water for tea. Ellen had been good company in those days.

The other girl snorted. 'She's a right madam, that's what she is, and the sooner she realises that she's no better than anyone else in this factory the better!'

A great rush of activity around the harbour soon followed the brief lull enjoyed by the drifter crews at the end of the midsummer fishing in September. Paintwork had to be freshened up and boilers scaled, bilges cleaned and bunkers trimmed. Nets had to be barked and the leader ropes that controlled the nets as they were paid out and hauled in again had to be tarred.

The entire harbour area carried the strong but pleasant smell from the freshly treated nets hanging the length of McLaren's Brae and on every other stretch of fencing available in the harbour area, while canvas buoys used as floats for the herring nets were repainted to keep them water-tight and prevent marine growth, then hung on poles to dry, giving the place a festive air.

New chaff mattresses and pillows had to be made, for after three months of use, those made in May had been thumped into place so often and so vigorously that all the chaff had been pushed to the sides and the men were more or less sleeping on the boards of their narrow bunk beds.

Barrels were stacked high along the length of the harbour wall, ready to be loaded into the holds and piled on the decks of the drifters when they followed the herring down the southeast coast. Coal boats arrived daily, and when the great bunkers on the harbour were full, two old hulks anchored close by were pressed into use to hold the coal that the fishing boats would require.

Once the men had finished work on the boats the womenfolk arrived to give the living quarters a good clean.

'As if I've not had enough cleanin' tae last me a lifetime,' Annie moaned as she and her mother and sisters tackled the *Fidelity*.

'You're a woman now,' Stella snapped. 'Old enough tae know that cleanin' never stops. And none of us is leavin' this boat until it's spotless. I'll not have fleas or vermin runnin' about on any boat that belongs tae this family. And once we're done here there's the bakin' tae see tae, so's your faither can be sure of havin' some good, hearty food inside him when he's on his way tae Yarm'th.'

While his wife and daughters toiled to make his boat the cleanest in the entire Scottish fleet, James Lowrie sat in the cabin of his cousin Jem's drifter, reading and rereading a single-page letter that had come from Aberdeen. It was addressed to James himself, but had been sent care of Jem.

'It's no' bad news, is it?' Jem asked, his eyes bright with curiosity.

'No, no, it's just a wee thing I'd half expected.' James scanned the letter one last time before folding it slowly and carefully and replacing it in its envelope.

'I wondered, with it bein' sent tae me instead of straight tae you,' Jem probed, watching every deliberate movement. 'Mebbe the person that wrote it didnae know your own address.'

'Mebbe.' James put the envelope into his pocket, pushing it well down to make certain that there was no danger of it falling out and getting lost.

'Or mebbe it's from someone that didnae want his business – or her business,' Jem suggested, 'known tae your Stella.'

'It could be that, I suppose,' James acknowledged, his face expressionless.

'Damn it, man, I'm yer own cousin and the letter was entrusted tae me.' Jem's curiosity boiled over. 'Surely I should be told what it's about? I'd not want tae be connivin' behind Stella's back, would I?'

'Not if you knew what was good for ye,' James agreed, getting to his feet. 'So it's best that ye don't know anythin' at all. That way, ye'll no' be goin' behind her back, will ye?'

'Is there an answer, mebbe?' Jem had one last try when the two men were back on deck. 'Somethin' ye'd like me tae post for ye?'

James considered the offer, pursing his lips and gazing across the boats strung between him and the harbour wall. 'It's a kind offer, Jem,' he said at last, setting foot on the *Homefaring*'s gunwale. 'But I think that I'm best no' tae send an answer of any sort. I'll just bide my time, and see what happens.'

As he leapt easily from the *Homefaring* to the neighbouring drifter and began to make his way, boat by boat, to the harbour wall, he could scarcely keep the smirk from his normally dour face.

*

The special train carrying coopers and fisher-lassies down to England was so full that Etta had to sleep as best as she could sitting bolt upright and with her arms jammed by her sides. Sleep was not easy, for there was constant noise – people talking or singing, and children who were accompanying their mothers because there was nobody at home to care for them crying with overexcitement and exhaustion or running up and down along the narrow corridors.

Some of the lucky people, those who had made the journey before and knew what to do, had managed to board the train early and hoist themselves on to the luggage racks, where they could lie down, even though the constant noise below kept them from sleeping.

But at least the rocking motion of the train was much easier to bear than the corkscrewing and plunging of the steamer that had taken the gutting crews to Lerwick, and there was a festive air among the passengers that kept them all cheerful and made the lack of sleep bearable.

'Ye'd never think we were goin' tae work,' Agnes said from her seat opposite. Despite the cramped conditions she had managed to fetch her knitting wires out, and Etta watched, fascinated, as the stocking the woman was knitting for her husband grew before her very eyes. 'Goin' down tae England's more like holidays for the likes of us.' She winked across at Etta. 'The rich folk travel round Europe for their holidays while the likes of us just get a change of farlins. But it's nice, all the same. You'll see.'

Great Yarmouth, being a popular holiday resort during the summer months, held a large number of lodging houses. In the winter, when the summer trade had gone and the herring season arrived, the landladies offered accommodation to the fisher-lassies and fishermen and coopers and curers who poured into the town and took it over for as long as the herring shoals swam off the English shores.

Bethany Pate, mindful of her own days as a fisher-lassie and of the struggle to cope with work and domestic duties, housed her gutting crews in decent accommodation. Etta and her crew, Andra's Jenny and Sarah, shared lodgings with Agnes, Kirsten Taylor and Ruth. They had a decent-sized bedroom with two double beds, one for each crew, and they also had the use of the front room.

'It's a far cry from Lerwick, is it no'?' Jenny bounced on the bed and looked about the small, clean room with satisfaction. 'Better than a hut, and we've a landlady here tae cook our food. Bein' in Yarmouth's the nearest the likes of us can get tae bein' treated like gentry!'

'You'll no' be so chirpy when ye're standin' at the farlins at eight o' clock at night, up tae yer hurdies in mud and with the rain bouncin' off ye,' Agnes reminded her.

'Nothin' comes easy,' Jenny shrugged. 'An' until then, we can enjoy ourselves. I'm for a walk round the town before the fishin' starts in the mornin'. Come on, Etta, it's you and me for the shops. We can choose what we're goin' tae buy tae take home when the time comes.'

They set out on what was one of the women's favourite pastimes, window-shopping and making up lists of all the things they would buy if they had enough money left over by the time the fishing season finished.

'Ye don't have tae be too serious about it,' Jenny explained as she and Etta and Ruth wandered down Glass Row. 'There's a difference between buyin' and just lookin'. Now, I think I'll have that' – she pointed at a smart woollen costume draped across a stand – 'an' that nice wee scarf, and I'd need a pair of gloves tae set it off.'

'Kid gloves,' Ruth chimed in.

'Oh aye, they'd have tae be kid. I'd no' want knitted gloves with thae sort of clothes. And I'd need tae get my hair permed, and mebbe buy a nice smart bag tae hang over my arm.'

'And shoes,' Etta joined in the game.

'An' silk stockin's. We'll decide on the shoes first,' Jenny said and the three of them set off, arm in arm, to find a shoe shop.

Reality set in the next morning when the lorries arrived to take them to the Denes, where the farlins awaited them. Dressed warmly against the chill dawn, they knitted busily, their cloth-covered fingers flying along the needles, while they watched and waited for the boats to come up river.

It wasn't long before the first dark shape came nosing through the grey mist that hung over the river. The women pushed their knitting into the leather whiskers hung from their belts, and hurried to take their places.

It was a long day. At nine o'clock the lorries took them back to their lodgings, where Mrs Rogers, the landlady, had made porridge and a great pot of strong tea, and a platter of toast.

'Are you sure it's all right?' she asked, nose wrinkling as she watched her six lodgers spooning up their porridge. 'I couldn't take it myself.'

'It's grand,' Mary assured her through a mouthful. She had insisted on steeping the oatmeal herself the night before, with a liberal handful of salt tossed into the pot. 'Ye've tae watch the English where porridge is concerned,' she had advised Etta, 'for they'll put sugar in it if they're left tae make it themselves, and never as much as a shake of salt. They make it far too sweet.'

They had to eat and drink swiftly, for in no time at all the lorries returned to take them to the farlins. They ran out, stuffing what was left of the toast into their pockets, for if the catches were good they would probably not have time for another break before six o'clock.

18

'It's your own fault.' Bethany said without sympathy. 'Everyone knows that scalders turn into an itching powder when they die in the nets.'

'I didn't know it. How could I know it?' Ellen sniffled. Her hands, normally white and smooth, were red and puffy from frenzied scratching and tears poured from her swollen eyes.

'Don't!' Bethany and Leezie yelped in unison, as the girl lifted a hand to mop the tears away. 'That's the way you managed to hurt your eyes in the first place,' Bethany went on as Leezie snatched Ellen's hand out of harm's way and muffled it in a clean towel.

'But my eyes are itching as if someone's thrown a handful of pepper into them,' Ellen whined.

'For goodness' sake, lassie, what does it take to teach you a lesson?' Exasperation sharpened the edge of Bethany's voice. 'Your eyes are sore because you touched a net and then rubbed the stuff over your face. You're lucky you didn't get it in your mouth, or you'd have right sore lips into the bargain. As to you not knowing about the scalders, you should make it your business to know that sort of thing now that you're overseeing the net factory.'

'I can't be expected to learn everything. I'm just there to keep an eye on the workers.'

'Exactly, so why were you handling nets that had come in

for repair?' Bethany swept on as Leezie sponged the girl's face with clear cool water in an attempt to ease the stinging pain. 'That's not your job.'

'I was showing that photographer man around the place and he wanted a picture of the nets being repaired.'

'And you pretended to be working at one, just to get yourself in the photograph?'

'It wasn't like that at all! The net was there, and the needle was lying beside it, and I just—'

'And you just happened to be dressed like the rest of the beatsters.' Bethany indicated the girl's smart, green, knitted costume, its low-waisted jumper chosen to disguise Ellen's tendency to plumpness.

'Should you not fetch the doctor?' Ellen whimpered as Leezie bathed her face gently with a soft damp cloth.

'No, you'll be fine – eventually. Clean water's all you need.'

'I might go blind!'

'You'll not go blind. You just need to keep bathing your eyes and your hands until the dust's washed away. Have you never thought to ask why the women repairing the nets always keep buckets of water close by? It's because of the scalders.'

'Give it to me!' Ellen snatched the cloth from Leezie and pressed it to her face.

'That photographer must have been right impressed when you started to skip about the place screaming and clawing at your eyes. And the lassies in the mending room must be having a good laugh, too,' Bethany said. Then, as the girl threw the wet flannel at her and fled from the kitchen, 'Leezie, take the basin and go after her. And tell her to have a nice cool bath and a lie down.'

'You're over hard on her,' Leezie disapproved as she gathered up the basin of water and the towels.

'No wonder. She's not got the sense she was born with. This'll mebbe teach her a bit of sense.'

When Leezie had gone upstairs Bethany went into the

parlour and began to open the day's post, still lying unopened on her writing desk. Using an ivory paperknife that Jacob had given her she slit the envelopes open, drawing out their contents and giving each a swift glance before dropping it on to one of several different piles – one for bills, one for orders, one for payments and one for personal letters.

She paused, frowning, as she came to a letter with the University of Aberdeen's name at the top of the page. She read it once, and then again, in disbelief and growing anger. Her first instinct, after the second reading, was to seek Jacob's advice, but he had gone to Yarmouth on the *Fidelity* with James. There was only one person she could ask about this business, she decided, and stormed from the parlour into the hall, shouting for Leezie.

'What is it now?' the maid wanted to know, appearing at the bend of the stairs. 'I'm bathin' the lassie's eyes.'

'I'm going out!'

'How long will you—' Leezie began, then stopped as the front door slammed shut so hard that the stained-glass upper half shook in its frame.

'One of those days ye'll crack it entirely,' she murmured, before turning back to answer a wailed summons from Ellen's room.

It had been many years since Stella Lowrie had opened her door to find her sister-in-law standing outside. Surprise swept across her face and was immediately replaced by a cold, blank look.

'What do you want?'

'I want my son.' Bethany's voice was as frosty as Stella's gaze.

'He's not here, and if he was he'd no' be welcome.'

'Not by you, mebbe, but James is another matter.'

Stella's thin lips tightened as though she was trying to hold back a sudden spasm of pain, then parted just wide enough to say, 'James is in Yarm'th.'

'I know that, but who else is there with him?' Bethany's head turned to the left and then to the right, her gaze sweeping along the street in both directions before returning to her sister-in-law. 'Am I to be allowed in, or would you prefer the whole street to hear my business?'

For a moment Stella looked as though she was going to refuse, and then she stepped back, opening the door wider. 'I suppose ye'd best come in.'

'Thank you.' For the first time since her mother's death, Bethany Pate, nee Lowrie, stepped over the threshold of the house where she had been born and raised. The kitchen, at least, had not changed much, she saw as Stella closed the door. The big dresser that had belonged to her parents was still in place, and she recognised some of the pretty china plates upon its shelves. She still recalled her mother's delight when her father brought them home from his fishing trips to other ports.

'Sit down,' Stella said, and then, after a slight hesitation, 'You'll have some tea?'

'Thank you, but I'm not stopping long. Ellen was trying her hand at repairin' a net in the factory,' Bethany explained, sitting in a straight-backed chair at the table, 'and it had scalders in it. She didn't know to look out for them.'

The ghost of a smile touched Stella's face as she seated herself at the other side of the table. 'I thought everyone knew about them. We came across them often enough when we were mendin' the nets at her age.'

'Aye, we did, but Ellen never had to do that.'

'More money than sense,' Stella observed, and Bethany had to rein in a sudden spurt of anger.

'Mebbe so, but I'm here about my Adam. Where is he?'

'How should I know?'

'I thought he was at the university, at his studying. I've just had a letter from the place,' Bethany took it from her pocket, 'and it says he's gone away. They don't know where.'

'Aye. I've heard that he's a loon that likes to have his own way.'

195

'Mebbe he is, but while he's under my roof he'll go my way!'

The smile flickered across Stella's mouth again as she nodded at the letter. 'From what you say it seems that he's decided tae keep tae his own road.'

'I blame James for this! He's the one that encouraged the lad to go to the summer fishing and now he's enticed him down to Yarm'th! I'm sure of it. Did he say anything of this to you before he left?'

Stella shrugged. 'He never tells me what he's thinkin'. There's another one that goes his own way. They're well matched, are they no'?'

'Adam's father had his heart set on him going to the university, and so have I, and that's an end of it!'

Stella, throwing caution to the winds, leaned across the table, her brown eyes venomous. 'Adam's father? You know as well as I do, Bethany Pate, that if your son's father had his way of it the loon would be at the fishin', not at any university. And you're right – the fishin's probably just where he is at this very minute, along with James.' Then, as Bethany stared at her, white faced and open-mouthed, she got to her feet. 'I know it's been a good while since you and me last spoke tae each other, Bethany, but for myself, I'd prefer to keep it that way.' She swept across the spotless kitchen and threw the street door open. 'Good day tae ye!'

There was never a minute's peace in this house, Leezie thought. If it wasn't one thing it was another. This was supposed to be her day for doing the ironing, and the basket still waited in the kitchen, piled high with crumpled clothing. First Ellen, half blinded and squawking like a bairn, had been brought home by two sniggering lassies from the net factory, then the mistress had gone rampaging out of the house, only to return half an hour later with a black mood on her, and announce that she was off to Yarmouth.

She had gone round her bedroom like a whirlwind,

throwing clothes into a bag, and finally departed, leaving a great list of instructions. No sooner had she gone than Ellen had taken over as mistress, reclining on her bed, a damp cloth over her sore eyes, issuing orders and keeping Leezie scampering up and down the stairs. And now, just as she had finally got down to the ironing, someone was ringing the doorbell.

Muttering under her breath she went into the hall, tidying her hair as she went. A smartly dressed young man stood on the step, a bunch of flowers in one hand.

'Is Miss Pate in?'

'She is, but she's no' well.'

'Mrs Pate, then?'

'She's gone away on business,' Leezie said flatly. His face was familiar but she couldn't put a name to it.

'Oh. Perhaps you could tell Miss Pate that I called, and give her this.' The man drew an envelope from his pocket and handed it over. 'And these, of course.'

'I'll tell her.' Leezie took the flowers. 'Good day tae ye.'

'Who is it?' Ellen wanted to know from the top of the stairs as the housekeeper closed the door.

'I don't know. He sent these to you, and this.' Leezie held out the envelope and flowers, and then as the girl beckoned impatiently she trudged up the stairs for the umpteenth time that day. Ellen snatched at the envelope, tore it open, then said breathlessly, 'It's Mr Morrison. Fetch him back!'

'But you're no' well. You're in your goonie and he'll be away down the road—'

'Fetch him back at once! And show him into the parlour. Then put these in water. I'm going to get dressed,' said Ellen, and fled into her room, calling over her shoulder, 'And make tea— or wait, perhaps he'd prefer whisky, or port. Get two trays ready, just in case. And for goodness' sake, get after him before he disappears!'

As soon as the mistress came back, whenever that was, Leezie swore to herself as she ran out of the gate and down

197

the road after Mr Morrison, she was going to give in her notice and find another position somewhere else. Anywhere else.

When the gutting crews finished Monday's topping up, Mary and the others opted to go to the shops but Etta took the opportunity to stay behind in the lodgings to get some washing done. Since her boarders were free, for once, to see to their own evening meal, Mrs Rogers had gone out for the afternoon and evening and Etta was enjoying having the house to herself. Raised in her Aunt Zelda's busy household and, even at work, used to being surrounded by others, it was a joy to be all alone for once, with no sound but the ticking of clocks and the splash of water as she washed her clothes in the big kitchen sink.

She rinsed each item out, twisting it tightly between her strong young hands before running it through the big mangle, then hung it all up on the pulley to dry. When the pulley had been hauled up to the ceiling she tied the rope about the hook on the wall and stripped her clothes off before climbing nimbly from a chair to the counter and then stepping into the sink.

After a thorough wash she dried herself, dressed, and was mopping up the few splashes she had made when someone came hammering at the door.

Etta stood undecided, head tilted to one side. It couldn't be the postman, for the postman had already called and left letters for Mary and Ruth. They lay on the lobby table, Mary's envelope adorned with Peter Bain's square, firm handwriting and Ruth's from Jack Morrison, who wrote to her every two or three days.

While Etta was wondering if it was her place to open the door to folk when the mistress of the house was not at home the knocking came again, several pounding blows on the sturdy wooden panels. Such urgency couldn't be ignored, she decided, hurrying from the kitchen. If it was, the door might suffer permanent damage. It was just a blessing that whoever it was had at least waited until she was dressed.

The hammering began again, just as she went through the small lobby. 'I'm coming!' she shouted, drawing back the bolt and opening the door. As soon as it left the frame a firm hand from the other side swept it back, sending Etta staggering. As her shoulder bounced against the wall the door slammed shut again and the bolt was shot into place.

'About time – she near saw me!' Adam Pate said breathlessly, leaning back against the closed door.

'Adam? What are you doing here in Yarmouth?'

'Fishin', what else? Hello, Etta. Have ye got the kettle on?' he asked hopefully. 'I could fair do with a cup of tea.'

'You near broke the door down just to get a cup of tea?'

'No, no. Is Mary here? Or Sarah or Ruth?'

'They're all out but me.'

'What about your landlady?'

'She's out too.'

'Good.' Adam swept his cap off. 'You can make me that tea, then. Is the kitchen through here?'

'Why are you fishin' when you should be up in Aberdeen at the university?' she wanted to know as she followed his broad back through to the kitchen.

He picked up the kettle, shook it to make sure there was enough water in it, and then set it on the gas stove. 'Matches.'

'On that shelf. Adam!'

'I ran away.' He lit the gas ring before turning to face her, blowing out the match. 'I couldnae stand it there a minute longer, Etta. I was goin' mad stuck in those lecture rooms with no air tae breathe, thinkin' all the while of the rest of you gettin' ready to come to Yarm'th. So I sent a letter for Jem tae pass on tae my Uncle James, sayin' that I'd meet him here and work the season on the *Fidelity*.' He dropped the match onto the counter by the stove and hooked a chair out from under the table with one foot.

'Your mother's the one that'll go mad when she finds out

what you've done.' Etta picked up the spent match and put it into the rubbish pail Mrs Rogers kept by her back door.

'She did,' Adam said as he dropped into the chair. 'That's why I was in such a rush tae find somewhere tae hide. Uncle James told me tae stay out of sight when I wasnae on the drifter just in case she got old Jacob McFarlane tae bundle me back tae Aberdeen, but that meant bein' stuck in one room again, just like the university. So this afternoon I went out for a wee wander round the shops, and who should I see but my mither, chargin' along the street like a ship under sail.'

'Aunt Bethany's here in Yarm'th?'

'I got a shock, too,' Adam admitted, getting up as the kettle boiled. 'I'll make the tea.' He talked on as he scooped spoonful after spoonful of Mrs Rogers' tea leaves into the pot. 'She must have found out and come after me.'

'Did she see you?' Etta made a mental note to replenish the landlady's tea caddy.

'I didnae wait tae find out. I just about-turned and ran for my very life with the studs on my boots throwin' up sparks. I landed up in this street, and minded hearin' that Mary and the rest of them were lodgin' here.' He poured boiling water into the teapot and began to open drawers at random until he found a spoon. 'So I thought I could hide here for an hour or two, just until my mither gets tired of lookin' for me.'

'Adam,' Etta said nervously, half expecting to hear the door knocker being plied at any moment, 'she'll never get tired of lookin' for you.'

'Ye're right there.' For a moment his open, normally cheerful face clouded over, then it cleared and a grin broke through. 'But dammit,' he said, 'at least I'll give her a run for her money. Now then,' he whirled the chair about and straddled it, leaning his folded arms along the backrest, 'while the tea's makin', tell me what you think of Yarm'th.'

Bethany was certain that Adam had seen her, but he had melted into the crowds so swiftly that she had no hope of catching up with him. Instead, she made her way to Jacob's lodgings.

'You'll be lookin' for the lad,' he said as soon as his landlady had shown Bethany into the comfortable parlour, then added, his eyes suddenly narrowing, 'or is there some problem back in Buckie?'

'None, apart from that daft quine Ellen making a fool of herself in the factory and near burning her eyes out with scalders.' Bethany sank down into a comfortable armchair. 'Of course I'm here after Adam. Why didn't you send him back to Aberdeen when you found out what he was up to?'

'It's not my business. And the laddie's stubborn, Bethany. If his heart's set on the fishin' I doubt you'll get him back tae his books.'

'But what sort of life's that for a clever young man?'

'I did well out of it – very well. And so has James,' the old man reminded her.

'I know, I know, but I'd wanted something more for Adam, and so did Gil. If he was here now he'd give the loon a good thrashing and drag him back to the university by his shirt collar.'

Jacob's eyes glinted with amusement. 'Is that what you're plannin' tae do?'

'I'll have a damned good try at it if I catch him,' Bethany promised. 'I saw him out in the street half an hour since, but he was off before I could get to him.'

Jacob's landlady brought tea in, and when she had gone out again Bethany said, 'I want to see James as well. I've got things to say to that man. Where's he lodging?'

'Not far from here. What about yersel', have ye got somewhere tae stay?'

'Not yet. I've only just arrived. I left my things at the station.'

'Have your tea and then go to see James. There's a good hotel at the end of this street – I'll arrange accommodation for you there and have your luggage delivered,' said Jacob, a seasoned traveller as much at home in Yarmouth as he was in Buckie. He poured out the tea and brought a cup to her. 'Come round here for yer dinner tonight. I hope ye've brought a nice frock with ye?'

'I'd no' thought of dining out when I came here. I was just thinking of fetching Adam home.'

'I'm sure ye'll look bonny whatever ye wear, for ye always do,' Jacob said blandly. 'I've invited an Edinburgh merchant tae eat with me tonight, and now that you're here I want you tae join us. He's an important man and I'd like fine tae do business with him. You could help me.'

'You've changed your tune, have you not? It wasn't so long ago that you were telling me that business wasn't for women.'

'Aye, but ye're here now, aren't ye?'

'On my own business, not on yours.'

'Even so, ye might as well make use of your time and help me intae the bargain. I'm goin' tae leave it tae you tae tell the mannie why it would be worth his while buyin' his fish from Jacob McFarlane.'

'I don't need to wear a bonny frock to tell him that.' Bethany's voice was tart.

'Mebbe the frock's more for my benefit than his.' Jacob grinned at her. 'D'ye think ye can win the man over?'

'I've no doubt of it,' Bethany rapped back at him, doing her best to hide her rising elation. At last she was getting the chance to face a good challenge.

Jacob settled his heels into the rug before the fireplace, teacup in hand, and beamed down at her. 'Now you're here, my quine, I'm glad of it. Mebbe you were right in what you said back in Buckie; mebbe it's time for ye tae meet up with some of the folk I deal with.'

202

19

The lodgings that James Lowrie had found for himself and his crew were less comfortable than Jacob's, but suited them well enough. For once, James was taking his ease in shirt-sleeves and braces when his sister was ushered into the tiny parlour.

'I thought ye'd be down here after the laddie soon enough,' he said calmly, indicating a chair. 'Sit yoursel' down.'

Bethany stayed on her feet. 'Where is he?'

'I'm his skipper, Bethany, no' his prison warder.' James deliberately settled back into his comfortable chair. 'All I ask is that he's on the boat when I need him. The rest of his time is his own and that's the way we both like it.'

'I've come to take him back to Aberdeen.'

'No you've not, for I'll not allow it. He's contracted tae work out the season with me and I need him on the *Fidelity*.'

'You were a man short when you sailed from Buckie, because you knew he was going to meet you here,' she accused. 'You put him up to this!'

He rested his head against the back of the chair, looking up at her from beneath half-closed eyelids. 'Adam's a man now, Bethany, old enough tae go his own way. Nob'dy needs tae put him up tae anythin'.'

'He might be a man but he's still not got the sense to know what's best for him!'

'And you have?' James asked mildly.

'I'm his mother!'

'Aye, his mither, no' his keeper. How much heed did you pay to our mither when you were Adam's age? As I mind it ye never even paid heed tae her when you were a wee bairn. You always went yer own way and so does Adam.'

'I don't want him crewing on the *Fidelity*.'

'It's the family boat, and he's family. Dammit, you own part of it. It's where the laddie wants tae be; can ye not see that for yourself? He even spent the money he earned goin' out fishin' with me on lessons on navigation at the school in Buckie. And he never once missed a class, though he worked hard enough at hidin' from that damned tutor you insisted on hirin' tae get him ready for the university. Does that not show ye where his heart lies?'

'He's my son and I know what's best for him,' Bethany insisted, and then as her brother remained silent she rushed on, 'If that's the way you want it, I'll be waiting on the harbour for him when he tries to board the boat, and I'll take him back to Scotland with me. If you've any sense you'll tell him to pack his things and meet me at Jacob's lodgings before then.'

'You'll leave that lad be!' James came out of his chair, his face tight with anger. 'You've had yer time with him, Bethany,' he said. 'Eighteen years and more. Now it's a faither's guidance he needs, no' a mither's.'

'His father's dead.'

'That's what you've given him tae understand, but you know and I know that his father's very much alive!'

'How dare you! I know who fathered my own child!'

'Aye, ye should, and ye do, and it's time ye admitted the truth of it, tae me if tae no one else,' James said, and then as she flung herself round towards the door his hand caught her shoulder and turned her back to face him. 'There's just the two of us in this room, Bethany,' he said, 'so ye can stop yer pretence! Adam's not Gil's son and he never was.'

'Yes, he—'

'The sea's in that lad's blood, just as it's in mine and in yours. You can't deny that and it's time ye stopped tryin'. He's a fisherman tae the very marrow of his bones; he needs tae be with the sea, and I need him on my boat. It's my right and it's where he belongs.'

'I'll not have it!'

'Aye, ye will.' James's eyes blazed into hers. 'Stop tryin' tae make his decisions for him, Bethany. He's chosen his future and he's chosen my way, not yours. It had tae happen,' he went on, his fingers tightening as she tried to twist away. 'I've bided my time all these years, and I've held my tongue, because I was waitin' for the day when he'd make up his own mind as tae which road he wanted tae take. I knew that his choice would tell me who'd fathered him, and it has.'

'You're havering!' She wrenched herself free.

'And you're still lyin'. Face the truth, Bethany. Gil was never meant tae father a laddie on you, just as Stella was never meant tae bear one tae me. But you and me both wanted a son tae go tae the fishin' – and that's what's happened.'

Her face was as white as milk. 'You're talkin' of a mortal sin!'

'I know I am, but it happened all the same, and it happened because it was meant. We've both paid for it, me more than you,' James said. 'D'ye think it's been easy for me, watchin' the bairn grow up and hearin' Gil boastin' about him?'

'It's not been easy for me either. I wish to God,' Bethany said passionately, 'that you and me had never—' She stopped, unable to say it.

'If we'd both been more content with the folk we were wed tae it wouldn't have happened, but it did, and Adam's the result. Would you wish him out of the world?' James asked, then when she said nothing, 'Neither would I. He's here and now it's my turn with him. And I'll not let you deny me that!'

Fear leapt into her eyes and her voice. 'You'd not tell him? I'd sooner see us both dead than let Adam know.'

So would James, but, realising an empty threat was his only weapon, he hardened his heart and pressed on. 'I want him on the *Fidelity* with me, Bethany. I want a son tae take over from me when my time's done. If you agree tae let Adam go his own way he'll never know the truth from me, but if you keep crossin' him, and me,' he said, his voice as hard as iron, 'I'll tell the truth tae him and the whole of Buckie.'

'You'd turn him against the two of us!'

'Mebbe so, but I've got nothin' tae lose.' James released her and stepped back, his hands falling loose by his sides. 'Give Adam yer blessin', Bethany, or take the consequences. The choice is yours.'

'Oh, aye?' Andra's Jenny said when she and the others arrived back at the lodgings to find Adam sprawled at his ease in the parlour. 'I thought it was Rory that ye were sweet on, Etta, not his brother.'

'She's no' sweet on me, or me on her,' Adam grinned up at the girls standing round his chair. 'She took me in because I'm hidin' from my mither. Did ye see her when ye were out?'

'Aunt Bethany's here?' Mary asked in surprise. 'What's she doin' in Yarm'th?'.

'Lookin' for this one, I'd say. Are you not supposed tae be at the university, learnin' how tae be a fine clever gentleman?' Agnes wanted to know.

'I'd as soon be here, goin' out with the *Fidelity* and havin' a grand crack with the lassies when I'm ashore. And if my mither manages to get hold of me, that's just what I'm goin' tae tell her – when her anger's cooled a bittie. Now ye're back, we'll just have a wee cup of tea. Did ye bring any cakes?' Adam asked hopefully.

It was as well that Mrs Rogers was not due back until night time, for the cup of tea swiftly turned into an impromptu party. Adam was good company, and his stories of university and the folk he met there had them all laughing till they cried.

'Ye're a right tonic, laddie,' Agnes said when he finally announced that he had to get down to the harbour. 'And ye're bonny tae look at an' all. Mebbe we should just let ye go on hidin' here for the rest of the season.' She swung her hips and winked at him. 'Jenny and Kirsten and me share a bed, but I'm sure we can make room for you.'

Adam grinned. 'I'd like that fine, but my Uncle James wouldnae, for the boats'll be goin' out soon and I have tae get tae the *Fidelity*.'

'What if your mither's waitin' for ye? That's the very place she'd expect tae find ye,' Kirsten pointed out.

'We could always dress you up as a woman,' Ruth suggested. 'And then we could all go out together arm in arm, as if we're takin' a nice walk in the fresh air before we go to our beds.'

'Agnes's clothes would fit ye fine, Adam,' Jenny agreed.

'Aye, and what d'ye think Uncle James and the rest of them would say if I went on board dressed as a lassie? You come with me, Etta,' Adam said, 'and we'll walk casual like, as if we're just out for a stroll. If my mither's at the harbour you can keep her talkin' while I get tae the drifter. Once I'm on board Uncle James'll no' let her haul me off again.'

It was dark outside, but the streets were still quite busy. Adam pulled his cap well down to hide his face and drew Etta's hand through his arm. 'Just pretend we're sweethearts out for a nice wee stroll tae the harbour.'

'You're enjoying this,' she accused, and he chuckled.

'Of course I am, it's an adventure, like ye see in the picture house. Have ye been tae the pictures yet, Etta? I'll take ye next week if ye like. What sort of picture would you like tae see?'

'All I can think about is what I'm goin' tae say if we meet Aunt Bethany.'

'Ach, we'll worry about that when it happens,' Adam said cheerfully.

As they neared the harbour they became part of a steady

stream of men, all on their way to their boats. To Etta's relief, there was not a sign of Adam's formidable mother.

'You'll be safe now,' she said, halting.

'Are ye not goin' tae see me right tae the boat?' he teased. 'I might get lost between here and the *Fidelity*.'

'Aye – and end up at my door again. On you go and let me get to my bed.'

'Thanks, Etta, you saved my life.' To her astonishment, he stooped swiftly and kissed the corner of her mouth. 'Ye're a grand lass,' he said, and then he was gone, mingling with the dark shapes moving along the harbour wall.

After Bethany left James she went for a long walk round Yarmouth in an effort to work off her anger. It had been a long and arduous fight, but now he had won. She had no doubt that if she pushed him far enough he would keep his threat to tell Adam the truth, and so she had no choice but to let her son turn his back on academic life and go to sea.

After all, she told herself as she travelled along street after street, it was what she had wanted for him, originally.

As her anger abated and resignation began to take over, she remembered Jacob's dinner invitation, and the merchant whose business he sought. She had packed for the journey in a fury with no thought to socialising while she was in Yarmouth, and had brought very little with her; so she went into the first shop she could find and bought the first blouse she tried – a square-necked garment in a pale green material with dark green embroidery at the neck and on the cuffs of the three-quarter-length sleeves. The blouse was pouched at the waist; it would do well enough, she thought, with the plain black skirt she had packed.

Jacob had indeed booked a room for her in the hotel near his own lodgings, and her luggage was already awaiting her. She laid the skirt and blouse out on the bed, decided that they would serve their purpose well enough, and freed her hair from its usual knot at the nape of her neck. It crackled as she brushed it out, venting the last of her anger with long steady strokes. Then she pinned it up, stripped, and saw with dismay that the marks of James's fingers stood out clearly in blue and black on the white, smooth skin of her upper arm. She put a hand up to touch the bruising, matching the outline of each of his fingers with her own. Even after she had washed, scrubbing hard at her skin as though it was possible to wipe the bruising away, and then put on the new blouse, she fancied that she could still see the outline of his fingers even through the sleeve.

Waiting with Jacob in his lodgings was a tall, well-built man, grey-haired and clean-shaven. He had an interesting face, Bethany decided as Jacob introduced her to Lorne Kerr. Her first impression was of shrewd green eyes, as clear as glass, set beneath well-shaped black brows. He might have been extremely handsome had his nose not been a little too large and his mouth a little too wide. As it was, the mismatched features added up to a face that, while almost ugly, had an attraction all of its own.

'I am very pleased to make your acquaintance, Mrs Pate.' The merchant took her hand in a firm grip. His voice was deep and pleasantly mellow, and his smile warm. 'Jacob tells me that you're an able business partner as well as a good friend.'

Bethany inclined her head and said something appropriate, and all the time she could feel the bruises left by James's fingers tingling on her arm.

Two days later Adam stopped by the farlins on his way back from a night's fishing on the *Fidelity* and drew Etta aside, leading her behind a great pile of barrels waiting to be taken to the railway station. It was a day of overcast skies and chill winds, and it was good to be in the shelter of the barrels for a few minutes. Even so, she protested, 'I've got my work tae do, even if you're finished.'

'It'll not take a minute,' he said. 'I just wanted tae thank you for helpin' me the other day.'

She glanced nervously over her shoulder. 'Your mither's still about the place.' Bethany Pate had visited the farlins on the previous day, in the company of Jacob McFarlane and a man that Etta had never seen before. After one horrified glance at the trio, especially her aunt, she had kept her eyes on her work, convinced that at any minute she would be pulled aside to receive a tongue-lashing for hiding Adam, and possibly be dismissed on the spot. But nothing had happened, and she had been left waiting and wondering.

'I know, she's stayin' on tae see tae some business for Jacob McFarlane. But it's all right, I've met with her.'

'She's lettin' you stay with the drifter?'

He grinned. 'She couldnae do anythin' about it. I want tae stay with the *Fidelity* and Uncle James needs me, and that's that. She's agreed tae leave me in peace from now on. No more university for me, Etta – I'm a fisherman at last! Are ye still willin' tae go tae the cinema with me on Saturday night?'

'Cinema? Me?' Etta vaguely remembered him making the offer the other night as they hurried together towards the harbour, watching all the while for his mother. 'Why me?' Every lassie in Buckie, and probably most of the lassies in Yarmouth, would be happy to go out with Adam Pate, and he had never shown any interest in Etta before, other than to tease her.

'As a way of thankin' you for what you did.'

'You don't need tae—'

'Stop fussin', lassie – will ye come out with me or will ye no'?'

'Aye, I'll come,' she said.

'Good. I'll meet ye outside the Red Lion at the end of King Street at seven o'clock.' And then, as a shaft of sunlight found its way through the cloud above and touched her face he said, 'Ye've got salt on your mouth.'

'It gets everywhere.' She put a hand up to rub at her lips, only to have it captured in his large fist.

'Leave it be. It's sparklin' like the diamond brooch my faither once gave tae my mither, and there's fish scales glitterin' in your hair as well. You look like a fine lady decked out in all her jewels.'

'Mebbe so, but the salt can give me blisters and I don't want that.'

'Then I'll take it away,' Adam said, and kissed her. His mouth was cold against hers, and yet the kiss seemed to burn its way from her lips to the very tips of her toes. When he raised his head – too soon! – he said, smiling down at her, 'There, it's gone.'

She watched, mesmerised, as the tip of his tongue slid out to run along his upper lip, then the lower.

'Sparklin' kisses that taste of salt,' he said. 'Saturday night, then?'

Rory was at the farlins when she scampered back. 'Where were you?'

'A call of nature,' Mary said quickly. 'Even guttin' quines have tae answer them.'

'We didnae want tae tell him that ye'd gone behind the barrels with young Adam,' Jenny said when Rory had gone. 'He might get jealous, with him bein' your sweetheart.'

'He's not my sweetheart, we just walk out together.'

'One tae walk out with and one tae kiss behind the barrels?' Ruth said with a grin.

'It wasn't a—' Etta began, and then, as a jeering chorus of disbelief began to rise, 'He just wanted tae thank me for helpin' him tae hide from his mither the other day.'

'I helped tae hide him an' all,' Agnes said, 'and he can thank me behind the barrels any time he likes!'

Etta lay in bed that night listening to the snores and groans and mumbles of the other women and thinking of Adam; the touch of his hand on hers as he drew her into the shelter of the barrels, and his voice telling her that the salt on her mouth made it sparkle like diamonds. And then – her bare

211

toes curled against the lumpy mattress as she recalled his kiss.

She had only been kissed by one other man before – two, she suddenly remembered with a sense of disgust, but surely the desperate, greedy kisses of the Irish boy who had caught her alone on a dark night in Lerwick didn't count? The other man was Adam's own half-brother, Rory, but Rory had never ignited the sudden fire that blazed up when Adam kissed her. With Rory she felt no passion, no hunger, no yearning to be kissed again, and again, and for ever more.

Ruth suddenly sat bolt upright, said something so quickly that Etta, torn from her waking dream, could not make out the words, then flopped back down and turned over. Dreaming, no doubt, of her photographer sweetheart, Jack Morrison. Ruth was clearly in love with the man; since arriving in Yarmouth she had spurned the advances of more than one young fisherman, and she spent a large part of her free time writing long letters to Jack. She made no secret of her hope that once she got back to Buckie he would ask her to be his wife.

When she was certain that Ruth had settled down again Etta turned over carefully, so as not to fall off her side of the bed, and went back to thinking about the look in Adam's eyes as he spoke of the sparkle of salt on her mouth, and then . . . and then – his kiss.

20

The sooner the mistress was back home the better, in Leezie's opinion. With Mrs Pate and Rory both in Yarmouth Ellen had taken on the role of mistress of the house in Cliff Terrace, and Leezie was fair sick of being told to do this and do that and fetch the next thing as if she was new to her duties instead of a housekeeper with years of service.

True, Ellen was out at the net factory for most of the day, but with her stepmother away from home she tended to return earlier in the afternoons than usual. She had also taken to entertaining her friends to the evening meal, which now had to be served in the small dining room that had scarcely been used since Gil Pate's death. The big kitchen table had done well enough for Mrs Pate and her family, with the stove and sink conveniently close to hand, and a chair set in place for Leezie so that she could eat with the family.

Now she ate on her own in the kitchen while Ellen and her friends – a lot of silly, empty-headed idle folk, in Leezie's opinion, most of them the sons and daughters of well-to-do families in the area – chattered and giggled and played card games in the front parlour.

Scarcely an evening went by without Leezie being summoned time and again from her comfortable chair by the kitchen fire by the irritating tinkle of the little bell that Ellen had unearthed from the depths of some cupboard. The only time she got to herself in the evenings was when the young folk all went off in their motorcars, and even then Leezie could not settle to sleep until she heard Ellen returning, sometimes in the small hours of the morning. After those evenings, she knew that she would have a struggle to get Ellen out of her bed in the morning in time to go to work.

Jack Morrison, the young photographer, was a frequent visitor to the house. On several occasions he had been the only visitor. He was a pleasant enough young man, Leezie thought, with more manners than some, and it was becoming more and more clear to her that Ellen was smitten with him. When he was the sole guest Ellen always took special care with her appearance and insisted Leezie light candles all round the room. Leezie, who had to clean the solidified wax up in the morning, and who had been raised in a cottage where the only lighting came from candles, could not understand the attraction of candlelight. Proper electric lighting was clean and quick, and it let folk see what they were eating.

She considered herself to be caretaker of both house and inhabitants when Mrs Pate was away from home, and so she fretted about what was going on. She tried to speak to Ellen, but the young woman immediately flared up at her and told her to mind her own business.

'It is my business. Mrs Pate expects me to take responsibility for this house when she's not at home.'

'That might be the case when we're all out,' said Ellen, who was sitting at her dressing table rubbing foundation cream into her face. 'But when I'm at home I'm the mistress of this house.'

'Indeed? Then perhaps you'd like tae give me some more housekeepin' money, for I've had to spend all that was left for me on the fancy food that you keep orderin'. Your mither didnae know when she went away that you were goin' tae feed half the young folk in the district. She'll no' be pleased when she sees the bills waitin' to be settled when she gets back.'

'My *step*mother,' Ellen said icily, emphasising the word,

'can well afford to pay the bills when she comes back from Yarmouth. It's not my fault if she didn't leave enough house-keeping money.'

She leaned forward to study herself in the mirror and then, satisfied with what she saw, she picked up a black pencil and began to thicken the line of one eyebrow.

'You've not told me what you want tae eat tonight,' Leezie reminded her, 'or how many visitors ye've invited. I might have tae go out to the shops again, if there's not enough in. And I'll have tae ask for tick again.'

Ellen wet a finger and ran it along the line of the completed eyebrow. 'Wealthy folk always pay their bill at the end of the month,' she said grandly. 'The shopkeepers are used to that. And don't bother about dinner, for Mr Morrison's taking me out. You can go now, Leezie.'

Oh, I can, can I? Leezie thought, and it was all she could do not to smack the little madam across the back of the head for her impertinence. Aloud, she said, 'Did I not hear that Mr Morrison was walkin' out with wee Ruth Lowrie?'

'What?' Ellen swung round, her eyebrows, one exagger-ated by deft strokes of the pencil, the other as nature intended it, giving her face a lopsided look. 'That's nonsense!'

'I'm sure I've heard folk mention it. She's a nice wee lassie, Ruth. She'd be awful upset if she thought that someone else was makin' eyes at her laddie.'

'Jack Morrison's nobody's la— gentleman friend. He's free to choose his own company and so am I. And if you don't mind your tongue, Leezie, I'll have to turn you off!'

'Turn me off, is it? I came here when you were just a wee quinie, and a nice wee bairn you were in those days, so I don't know what's happened tae change ye. And as for turnin' me off, there's only one person can do that,' Leezie said, at the end of her tether, 'and that's Mrs Pate!'

'Then I shall write to her and complain about your behav-iour—' Ellen began, and then broke off with a squeal of dismay as the front doorbell rang. 'He's here – and me not

215

ready yet!' She turned back to the mirror and began to draw in the second eyebrow. 'Go downstairs at once, Leezie. Show him into the parlour and tell him I'll not be a minute. Go on!'

There was little Leezie could do but obey, but when she tried to usher Jack Morrison into the parlour he stayed where he was, in the hall, talking about the weather and about the photographs he had taken that day, and asking after Leezie's health. He was altogether too nice for Ellen, the way she had turned out, Leezie thought as she shifted from one foot to the other, trying to answer him and wishing that he would just go into the parlour and leave her to return to the familiar safety of her kitchen.

It was a relief when Ellen came hurrying down the stairs, wearing a smart frock that Leezie had never seen before, and with her bobbed hair sleek and her make-up immaculate.

'Jack, I'm so sorry, I was kept back. Such a nuisance,' she gushed.

'That's all right, Leezie kept me company,' he said pleasantly.

'That's good.' There was a brittle note to Ellen's voice, and the gaze she turned on Leezie was full of suspicion.

'We were discussing the weather. It always provides a grand topic of conversation in this country,' Jack Morrison said, taking Ellen's coat – also new, Leezie noted – and holding it out for her.

'Don't wait up, Leezie,' she said as she slid her arms into the sleeves. She made it sound more like an order than a request. 'I might be late.'

'But don't worry,' Jack added, 'I'll make sure that she gets back home safely.'

Ellen's scarlet Cupid's bow mouth curved into a warm smile. 'I know you will,' she said, and then they were gone, and Leezie was free at last to go into the kitchen and slump down in her usual fireside chair. At least she had the evening all to herself, for once.

As always happened when Ellen was out late, Leezie prepared everything for the night and then lay down fully clothed on her bed in the small back bedroom next to the kitchen, alert for the sound of the young woman's return. Ellen sometimes forgot to lock the front door, and so Leezie liked to make sure that the house was secured and, as often as not, pick up the shoes and coat and gloves and hat that Ellen shed carelessly on her way through the hall and up the stairs.

Tonight, possibly worn out by the confrontation she and Ellen had had earlier, she fell sound asleep, and woke with a start to find that the lamp still burned by her bedside and the house was quiet. A glance at the clock showed that it was after two in the morning. If Ellen had come home, then she had been quieter than usual, and if she had not—?

Leezie jumped up and hurried through to the hall, breathing a sigh of relief as she saw the smart new coat draped over the newel post at the foot of the stairs, and the hat Ellen had worn on the bottom step. Her shoes lay in the hall, where they had been kicked off, and the front door, though closed, was not locked. Leezie picked everything up, turned the key and went to bed.

Despite her broken sleep she was up bright and early the next morning. It was too early to rouse Ellen, so she set herself to putting the parlour to rights. She was on her knees, sweeping the hearth, when she heard a noise in the hall.

'Ellen?' There was no answer. It must have been the morning post falling onto the mat, Leezie thought, but when she went into the hall the mat was empty. It was also slightly askew, though she distinctly recalled setting it straight and locking the front door the night before.

The door, when she tried the handle, was unlocked. Surely, Leezie thought, puzzled, Ellen hadn't got up and gone out at this early hour? She opened it and went out onto the doorstep.

And was just in time to see Jack Morrison hurry off along Cliff Terrace, heading for the town.

*

It was Etta's very first visit to a cinema, and as she and Adam emerged her head was crowded with the images she had just seen of handsome men and beautiful women living in fine houses and leading lives that were so different from her own.

'They're only play actors,' Adam said, amused, when she wondered aloud at the splendour she had just witnessed. 'They were only pretendin'.'

'But surely their own lives must be grand.' She had skivvied for a brief time in one of the big houses in Buckie, and had marvelled then over the opulence and comfort of thick carpets and fine china and folk who could afford not only a bed just for themselves, but an entire bedroom each. But even these homes had not been as luxurious as those she had witnessed on the cinema screen. 'I don't suppose they live like ordinary folk – like us.'

'They live in America, so I suppose it's different there. Would you like tae live like the women in that film?'

'Aye,' she began, and then changed it to, 'mebbe. It would be nice, sometimes, tae have bonny things and nice clothes, and not have to work so hard.'

'I'd not want that at all,' Adam said firmly, and then, glancing up at the night sky. 'It's a grand evenin'; d'ye want tae go back tae your lodgings, or will we take a walk about the town?'

'A walk,' she said at once, and then, as they fell into step together, 'You could have all that – a nice house and a lot of money – if you went back tae the university like your mither wants you tae do.'

He gave a snort of disgust. 'Me? I've got the life I want right now, and I'd as soon sleep on a wooden bunk in the drifter than in a nice, soft bed. I want tae be like my Uncle James and my grandfather.'

As they walked, he talked about what it was like to be a fisherman, and Etta listened, enthralled, as he described the exhilaration of seeing the longed-for glint of silver beneath the tossing waves as they hauled the nets.

'There's no better thing tae hear than Uncle James shouting out that it's a good shimmer this time,' he said, 'and then when the nets are all inboard it's a race tae get tae the harbour and land the fish while they're still fresh.'

He proved to be a good listener, too, drawing out of her the story of the young father and mother she had never met and the harsh existence she had known in her grandfather's home – something that she would never entirely forget, not even if she lived to be very old – and being rescued and taken to live with Aunt Zelda and Uncle Innes.

'That was the best thing that happened tae me,' she finished.

'Aye, they're grand folk. It's a pity, though, that Uncle Innes could never thole the sea. He told me once,' Adam said, 'that my mither and Uncle James and my grandfather had little time for him because of that, and I can understand how they felt, for it's hard tae see how anyone can hate the sea. But even so, he's a fine man. He says that my mither never got over bein' born a quine instead of a loon, and that's why she took it hard when he turned against the fishin', when it was what she'd always wanted.' He paused, then went on thoughtfully, 'You'd wonder at her bein' so against me goin' out on the drifters, wouldn't you? You'd think she would have wanted me tae do what she'd have done herself if only she could.'

'But you're clever, and she's got the money tae send you tae the university,' Etta said. 'That means that you've got the choice. Not many folk have that.'

'I'm no cleverer than Rory, and university was never offered tae him.'

'That was because the cooperage was waiting for him, surely.'

'Aye, I suppose so. I'll tell ye this, Etta, if I have bairns, they'll damned well do as they please,' Adam said, and followed it up with, 'though I'd hope that the laddies would want tae go tae the fishin', like me.'

'And the quines?' Etta asked, and he laughed.

'I'd want them tae marry fishermen and breed more fishermen, of course. What more could a man ask of his daughters? Is that no' what you want for yoursel'?'

'I'd not mind it,' Etta said demurely. They had worked their way through all the main streets of the town, and now, as a church clock chimed ten times, she added, 'I'd best be gettin' back.'

'I'll walk ye to the door,' Adam offered. Then just as they turned into her street he suddenly caught her by the arm and whisked her into a darkened shop doorway and kissed her.

'Your mouth still tastes of salt,' he said when the kiss was over.

'So does yours, and no wonder, since we both work with the stuff.'

He laughed, and kissed her again, and this time she was ready for him and quick with her response. They clung tightly to each other, exchanging kiss for kiss, and Etta could feel his heart pounding against her breast. When Adam finally drew away from her he said, 'Ye're tremblin' like a wee bird I've caught in my hand. Are ye cold?'

'No,' she said, and drew him back into her embrace, unwilling to let him go.

The clock chimed the half hour and then the quarter before they finally stepped away from each other.

'D'ye kiss all the laddies like that?' Adam asked, his voice slightly unsteady.

'I've never kissed anyone like that. I didnae know I could.'

He laughed, then said, 'Are ye havin' a gatherin' in your lodgin's tomorrow?'

'Aye, after church, same as usual.'

'I'll see ye then,' he said.

As he went down the street, whistling, she ran the last few yards to the lodging house, where the other girls were either in bed or getting ready for bed.

'Has that Rory Pate been keeping you out late?' Annie asked with mock severity.

'No, and it wasnae Rory I was with anyway,' Etta said, and at once they all pounced, clamouring to know who her new sweetheart was.

'Is it one of our own laddies?' Mary pried when Etta refused to give them a name.

'I'm not sayin'.' She smirked at them, nursing her secret and enjoying the feeling of superiority it gave her.

'It's an English lad, or mebbe an Irishman,' Ruth guessed, while Jenny suggested, 'It could be a cooper, or mebbe even one of those folk that just come tae watch us workin' at the farlins.'

They were still guessing when they were all in bed, with the light out. But Etta kept her own counsel, knowing that part of the excitement that had turned her world into something as magical as the story she had seen unfolding on the cinema screen earlier was that only she knew the name of the man who had held her and kissed her so sweetly, and yet so passionately.

'I've not seen you for a while, Etta,' Rory said on the following afternoon. The weather was cold and wet, and the fisherlassies' parlour was filled with folk.

'You see me every day at the farlins.' Adam had arrived with his step-brother, but the place was so busy that they had not had a moment to speak to each other. She could see him at the other side of the room, talking to – flirting with, she thought to herself with a sudden pang – a pretty lassie from Fraserburgh.

'Aye, but we've scarce been on our own since we came tae Yarm'th. I've tae spend tomorrow evening with Jacob and my mother and some Edinburgh fish merchant that's interested in doin' business with us, but I'd like it fine if we could go for a wee walk on Tuesday night.'

'Aye,' she said, 'if we finish work in time.'

The afternoon dragged on and still she got no chance to speak to Adam, who finally left with only a casual nod in her direction. When the last of the callers went away the women had to set to and put the place to rights, and by the time they were done it was mid-evening.

'I'm away out for a breath of fresh air,' Kirsten announced, and Mary and Sarah decided to go with her. Jenny was out with her husband and Agnes was visiting local folk she had befriended on her first visit to Yarmouth years before. Ruth settled down with pen and paper to write to her sweetheart, Jack Morrison, and after mending a tear in her working skirt Etta decided that she could not stand being cooped up in the house for a moment longer.

She had walked a few yards down the street when a hand darted from a dark doorway and caught her elbow. She was whisked round and pulled into the shadows, while another hand was clapped across her mouth to stifle her squeak of surprise and outrage.

'Sshhh,' a voice whispered into her ear, 'd'you want the whole street tae start cryin' thief, or worse?'

Then there came a choked exclamation as she bit hard on one of the fingers that had been used to silence her, and the hand was withdrawn as swiftly as it had arrived.

'Damn it, Etta, d'ye have tae be such a vixen?'

'You think I'd be willin' tae be murdered without a fight? What d'you think you're doin', Adam Pate, hidin' in the dark and frightenin' folk that just want a breath of air?'

'I've been waitin' for you out here in the cold and the dark. Did you not see me noddin' at you when I was leavin'?'

'I thought you were just noddin' goodbye.'

'You've got a lot tae learn. I think ye drew blood,' Adam said, peering at his hand.

'Serves you right. You should be grateful I hadnae my guttin' knife with me. You couldn't even see me in the dark – you might have pulled anyone in here. Mary or Kirsten or Agnes. What would you have done then?'

222

'Thrown them back, the way we do when we catch the wrong fish in the nets.'

Etta giggled. 'I doubt if Agnes would have given you the chance tae throw her back. She's had her eye on you for a while.'

'There's only one lassie my eye's on and that's why I've been waitin' for her in the cold for the past hour and more.'

'I didnae know,' said Etta pertly, 'that that quine from Fraserburgh bided in this street.'

'What quine from Fraserburgh?'

'The one you were talkin' with half the afternoon.'

'Ach, I was only talkin' tae her because you were too busy seein' tae other folks' comfort tae spend time with me. Come for a walk with me next Saturday.'

'If you want.'

'I do want,' Adam said. And then, drawing her into his arms, 'And I want somethin' else as well.'

She returned to the lodgings an hour later, her mouth tingling from his kisses, and her feet scarcely touching the ground.

The fishing had been good but in the early hours of the morning the weather had turned cold and wet, and the incoming boats wallowing up the River Yare appeared suddenly through a grey curtain of rain. The gutting crews had started work at six o'clock in the morning and now, midway through the evening, they were still working by the light of paraffin lamps known to the women as 'bubblies'.

Rory and some of his coopers had managed to rig up a tarpaulin awning above the farlins but the women were only partly protected, for the slanting rain still drove its way in beneath the covering, and the ground was already water-logged. The women were ankle-deep in sticky mud; each time they moved they had to haul first one booted foot and then the other from its grip.

'I don't know why they can't give us sheds tae work in,'

Ruth complained as she struggled to fill a barrel by the light of a lamp, rain streaming down the oilskin hood she wore and finding its way inside her waterproof jacket to trickle down her neck. 'It's no' much tae ask, surely?'

'It's probably no' worth their while for the time we're here, though if *they* were the ones tae do the guttin' they'd soon get shelter put up,' Mary said.

'Some places manage tae have their farlins in a sort of shed,' Ruth argued. 'Even if they'll not do it for us they should do it for their precious herrin'. The way the rain's teemin' down I'm packin' these fish in more water than salt. I'd not be surprised if they came back tae life and started loupin' out the barrel.'

'That's no' likely, with their guts taken out.' Annie peered through the downfall at her younger sister, 'How's that hand of yours?'

'It's all right.' Ruth had cut a finger a week before and despite being packed with well-chewed bread the wound had still not healed.

'We'll have a look at it tonight, and if it's not any better you're goin' tae the mission nurse in the mornin',' Annie said firmly.

'Ach, it'll be fine.' Ruth had other things on her mind, for there had been no letter from Jack Morrison that week. 'I'll steep it in hot water when I get back tae the lodgin's.'

'We'll not be long now,' Agnes assured her. 'The boats are all in and the farlins are emptyin'.'

Just then a chorus of squeals and curses broke out at the end of the long farlin as one of the posts holding the awning snapped under the weight of the water collecting on the tarpaulin, sending an icy deluge over the women working directly beneath it.

21

By the time the farlins were finally emptied and the coopers had rolled the last of the barrels away the rain had turned to sleet. Water cascaded from the women's oilskins as they trudged wearily over to where the lorries waited to take them back to their lodgings. The younger, more agile women were first on board, turning to offer a helping hand to the others as they climbed up, hampered by mud-slicked boots that skidded and slipped as they tried to gain a foothold.

For once they were too tired and too miserable to sing as they went jolting back to their lodgings.

'Take your boots off before you go in,' Mary, ever the housewife, instructed the others. 'We don't want tae muddy Mrs Rogers's lobby.'

'But my feet'll get soaked!' Kirsten protested.

'Don't be daft, lassie, they're already soaked.' Andra's Jenny settled her backside against the house wall and stuck one leg out. 'Here, pull that boot off.' When Kirsten had done as she was told, Jenny took it from her and ordered, 'hold yer hands out and I'll wash the mud off them.' She turned the boot upside down and a stream of water poured from it and over Kirsten's hands. 'Now help me off with the other one,' said Jenny, 'then I'll help you off with yours.'

When they finally got inside, the house was filled with the tantalising smell of a rich meat and vegetable stew, and Mrs Rogers was waiting to fuss over them. 'I've been stoking the boiler all day and there's a hip bath in your parlour with pots of hot water,' she said, and then, proudly, 'It's lucky I've got a bathroom of my own.'

'Four of us in the big bath,' Agnes said, 'Two at a time, and the other two can take turns with the hip bath. And the oldest gets tae be the first!'

It was too dark to see anything from the window of the small, private dining room, but Bethany Pate stood watching the sleety rain run sluggishly down the darkened pane for a while before letting the heavy curtain fall into place.

'Winter's coming in,' she said. 'It was a good catch today. The women might still be working at the farlins, poor souls.'

'Poor souls indeed, but I suppose they're used to it.' Lorne Kerr sat back in his seat at the table and held his glass up to the light to admire the rich glow of the port. 'Are you sure you'll not take a glass with me? It's particularly fine.'

'Perhaps half a glass. And you never get used to working at the farlins in all weathers and all hours,' she went on as he lifted the decanter.

He paused in the act of pouring her wine. 'Jacob told me that you had been a fisher-lassie, but I found it hard to believe.'

'Really?' Bethany held out a hand to him. 'You can tell a fisherman by the scars he carries on his hands, Mr Kerr, and the same goes for a guttin' quine. Working in all weathers with sharp knives and fish bones and brine pickle can be hard on the skin,' she went on as he set the decanter down and took her fingers in his, examining the fine white lines left by old scars. 'So you and Jacob McFarlane have been discussing me?'

'I was curious, and Jacob has a great admiration for you. So have I,' he said, and she withdrew her hand from his, suddenly aware that he had been holding it for a little too long. 'You're a remarkable woman, Mrs Pate.'

'I'm a Buckie woman, Mr Kerr. We're all remarkable.'

226

Bethany seated herself opposite him and accepted the glass of port. 'You should come to the Firth and see for yourself.'

'I intend to, now that we're in business together.'

It had been a very enjoyable evening, one that had been planned to celebrate their new business partnership and to mark the end of Bethany's stay in Yarmouth, but Jacob had bowed out at the last minute, pleading the need to visit an old friend who lived locally and had fallen ill.

Bethany and Lorne Kerr had enjoyed a very good dinner, during which she discovered that he was a childless widower who, like Jacob, had devoted himself to building up a successful business. She wondered idly why a man with his money and personable character had not found himself a second wife. Perhaps he valued his freedom and independence, just as she did.

'Tell me something about your life in Buckie,' he said now, and she started to talk about the net factory and the smokehouse.

'Who's in charge while you're in Yarmouth?'

'I've a good foreman in the smokehouse, and my stepdaughter's overseeing the net factory, though goodness knows what she's been up to in my absence. She's not been in charge of the place for long.'

'If she has half your ability, I'm sure that she will be looking after it admirably.'

'Ellen,' Bethany said, 'is not a business woman.' She launched into the story of the net that had been covered with powder from the stinging jellyfish, and felt absurdly pleased with her own storytelling skills when Lorne roared with laughter.

'I'm sure she learned her lesson well,' he said when she had finished.

'Perhaps – but I have a feeling that Ellen needs more than one reminder. It's just as well that I'm going back tomorrow.'

'Your company will be greatly missed,' he said.

'I've enjoyed my time in Yarm'th. But now I must get back to my hotel. I leave first thing in the morning.'

A sudden gust of wind buffeted against the windows and Kerr got to his feet. 'I'll arrange for a car to take you back.'

'No need for that. I'm used to bad weather, and I enjoy walking.'

'Then I'll accompany you,' he insisted.

The sleety downpour was being driven before a strong wind and the umbrella Lorne had borrowed from the hotel porter threatened to be more of a hindrance than help. After only a few steps he folded it and tucked it under one arm.

'Are you certain about the car?' He had to raise his voice above the sound of the wind, and when Bethany kept to her decision to walk, he drew his coat collar up and took her arm, drawing her close to his side. 'Then walk we shall, Mrs Pate.'

Even above the wind they could make out the deep boom of waves racing up river, and in the lamplight, as they passed close by the shore, they caught the occasional brief sight of white-flecked spray being tossed into the air. Bethany shivered, and was glad of the warm, strong body close to her own.

'It's a bad night for the boats,' Kerr said when they had reached the doorway of her hotel.

'Aye, it is.' She thought of Adam and James, and had to fight back a tremor of fear. 'But the boats are sturdy, and they've weathered worse,' she said firmly. 'Good night to you, Mr Kerr.'

'Good night, and safe journey home. We'll meet again,' he said, and disappeared into the rain-soaked darkness.

The hotel sign just outside Bethany's window squeaked monotonously as it swung in the wind, but even if it had been oiled into obedient silence she would not have been able to sleep for worrying about the *Fidelity*, out at the fishing grounds on this wild night with her son and her brother on board.

*

228

The wind had come up with unexpected speed, and by the time the *Fidelity*'s nets were ready to be hauled inboard a howling gale shrieked vindictively over the drifter. As she reared and then plunged, lacy white spume ripped from the crests of the racing waves flew from the darkness to spatter over the crew, blinding them and chilling faces and hands.

'As fast as ye like,' James yelled, his voice all but snatched from his lips by the wind and borne away into the night. 'Get the nets aboard and we'll turn her head tae wind and try dodgin' out the storm!'

It was a nightmare task. All about them as they worked the waters boiled and seethed in a massive tantrum; it seemed to Adam that the sea had suddenly become tired of the puny men who had the audacity to wrest their living from it and had decided to swallow them and their boats whole and draw them deep down below.

One by one the nets came inboard, and for each net – each fish, even – the men strung in a line along the gunwales had to fight the might of the raging waters. The steam winch roared and struggled and as they leaned overboard to haul the nets in with their bare hands the racing, tumbling waves were only inches below. They were using the rolling of the drifter to help in their task – when she dipped precariously close to the surface the men hauled desperately and as she lifted again they leaned back on their heels, still gripping the net, in a bid to drag a few more inches inboard. The deck was awash and, with the occasional herring slipping from the meshes to the deck before it reached the hold, there was the increased danger of stepping on a fish and skidding.

James, unable to keep away from the action, had sent Siddy to the wheelhouse, and he himself was among the crew dragging the nets up from the deep, yelling orders all the time.

A wave broke over the boat and while it covered them, seeking to pick them off one by one and carry them overboard, the men could only hang on to the net they were hauling, dig their feet in to the angle of the deck and the gunwale, hold their breath and wait until the water subsided. As he worked, Adam spared a brief thought for the boy creeping around and around on his knees in the tiny rope locker, coiling in the thick rope. He knew from personal experience that the claustrophobic little cupboard would be awash and that the boy would be soaked to the skin.

The next wave came in hard and fast from another direction, lifting the boat up and then dropping it so quickly that it fell away from beneath their feet. Sensing nothing but water beneath his sea boots, Adam knew a moment's panic. For several vulnerable seconds he was entirely at the mercy of the sea; this was the moment where the net could pull him over the gunwale, wherever that was, as easily as if he were a fish caught on a line.

Rain and spray blinded him – then at last the deck came up beneath his feet, connecting with a solid thump that vibrated all the way through his body and clashed his teeth together hard. He was aware of a stab of pain as he bit his own tongue, and the tang of cold salt water was replaced for an instant by the hot, brassy taste of blood. But at that moment the pain and the blood were the most beautiful sensations he had ever known, and he heard himself tossing a whoop of jubilant laughter into the wind.

After a struggle they won back the net, but as the winch began to haul up the next net a figure struggled out of the hold and clumped James on the shoulder.

'The hold's fillin' with water,' the man yelled. 'If we don't cover it she's in danger of goin' down!'

'Fetch the axe,' James shouted back, and then, to the others labouring alongside him, 'Let the net go, lads, we're cuttin' it free!'

The moon suddenly appeared through clouds as torn and demented as the waves below, its pale, cold light striking silver from the sharp blade of the axe as James lifted it and then slammed it down on the thick messenger rope straining over the gunwale. Two hard blows almost had the rope parted;

he lifted the axe high again just as another big wave swept in. James, intent on releasing the nets, was not paying enough attention to his own safety and the wave caught him and hurled him back. Still clutching the axe, he slipped and went down hard; even above the noise of the storm Adam, beside him, heard the dull thud as his uncle's head hit the raised wooden ridge about the open hold.

As the wave receded James's oilskin-clad body rolled sluggishly down the deck and thumped against Adam's legs, almost felling him. Even as someone pulled the axe from James's limp hand and chopped at the rope another wave, crosswise to the last, came racing in out of the darkness and reared its foam-flecked head above the deck. As it crashed down, almost swamping the drifter, Adam threw himself across James, curling one arm tightly about the man and reaching desperately for some sort of purchase with the other. If there was nothing to grip, he well knew, the two of them would almost certainly be swept over the side and perhaps become entangled in the net that, once released, would disappear swiftly into the depths. And it would be the two of them, of that he was certain, for no matter what happened he was not going to let go of the semi-conscious man.

The wave broke over their heads just as a deckhand, who had anchored himself securely on one of the mast stays, caught Adam's wrist in an iron grip. It seemed to Adam, as the receding wave fought for the right to claim him, that his arm was being wrenched from its socket, but even so he managed to wrap his frozen fingers round his saviour's wrist and held on until the wave was gone. Then he was hauled to his feet, while someone else dragged James back from the side of the drifter.

'Are ye all right, lad?'

'I'm fine, what about my uncle?' Adam yelled.

James had already come round and began to stagger to his feet just as the messenger rope parted. As the remaining nets and the fish in them sank swiftly below the turbulent water, the *Fidelity,* freed from the weight anchoring her to the seabed, bounced and then steadied, and the seasick, miserable boy in the rope locker was sent sprawling in several inches of dirty water.

'Cover the holds! Turn her head to wind, Siddy!' James roared, taking command again.

The storm began to ease towards dawn, and as they headed for Yarmouth Adam, climbing wearily down the ladder to the cabin for a short and much needed rest, found his uncle sitting at the table, both hands cupped round a steaming mug of tea.

'How's yer head?'

'Loupin' like a salmon goin' upstream, but I've a thick skull. It'll mend fast. Siddy tells me that I'd be fish-bait now if you'd not hung on tae me.'

'It wasnae just me; if Walter hadnae got a grip of me we'd both have been over.' Adam poured tea out for himself. 'It's a funny thing, but while we were sprawled there I minded what you'd said about my grandfaither Weem believin' that a fisherman belonged tae the sea.' He sat down opposite James. 'I mind wonderin' if I should just let it happen, for at least we'd have gone down together.'

'Here.' James reached into a locker and brought out a bottle of whisky. Opening it, he poured a good dram into Adam's tea. 'That'll do ye good.'

'Thanks. But then I thought – I've got a lot of livin' tae do yet, and I want tae get the chance tae enjoy it afore I go. And as for you,' Adam took a deep swallow of the hot, laced tea and then grinned at James over the rim of the mug, 'I need tae have you around, for who else can teach me how tae take over the *Fidelity* when my time comes?'

And then he wondered why, just before his uncle cleared his throat and looked away, the man's eyes suddenly took on a strange shine. It was for all the world as though they were damp.

*

Bethany did not even realise that she had gone to sleep until a gentle tapping at the door awakened her.

'Yes?' She struggled up in bed, realising that she could no longer hear the hotel sign creaking as it swung. The wind must have dropped.

The door opened and the chambermaid's head appeared round it. 'If you please, ma'am,' she said in the rich rolling local dialect. 'There's a gentleman below wants a word with you. A Mr McFarlane.'

Terror clutched at Bethany's heart. 'I'll be down in just a minute,' she said, and as the door closed she sprang out of bed. Something serious must have happened to bring Jacob to the hotel at such an early hour. As she dressed hurriedly she prayed all the while that he had not brought bad news of her son.

'What's happened? Is it Adam?' she asked as soon as she went in to the small parlour set aside for hotel guests. Jacob, heedless of the dark prints his wet, booted feet were making on the rugs, was pacing to and fro, his face ashen.

'Adam's fine,' he said swiftly, 'and so's James, apart from a lump on the back of his skull where he got bowled over by a wave. The *Fidelity*'s already come up the river and I've spoken tae the two of them. It's the *Jess Lowrie*.' His voice shook and the tears began to run down his face unchecked. 'She's gone down, and her crew with her. We've lost them all, Bethany.'

It was a sombre group that gathered at Jacob's lodgings an hour later. James was there, and Jem, who told his story in a dazed, halting voice.

'We were fishin' near tae each other, the *Homefarin'* and the *Jess Lowrie,* an' we'd tae cut the last net loose because of the weather gettin' worse. We were the first tae head back tae harbour when the storm began tae ease and I gave the *Jess Lowrie* a shout on the loud-hailer when we were near enough. Willie Gunner said he was goin' tae manage tae take in all their nets and that they'd be in afore us.'

He stopped and looked down at his hands, fisted together between his knees and moving continually, the knuckles grinding against each other. 'That's what he said, that they'd show us a good run. I wish tae God we'd stayed by her, but there was no reason for it. She seemed tae be fine. We were just past her when the rain started again. It came down in sheets an' we lost sight of her almost at once.' Jem paused, his broad face haunted by the memory of that last sighting, and the last contact with the missing drifter.

'Go on, Jem,' James prompted quietly. Glancing at him, Bethany saw that there was a grey tinge to his usual tan and he looked exhausted.

'There's nothin' else tae tell,' Jem said helplessly. 'We got back without a sight of the *Jess Lowrie* or any other boat until we were comin' up tae the shoreline. She wasnae in when we arrived and I waited for her, thinkin' she'd be up the river any minute. We all waited, James and his crew too, when the *Fidelity* got in. But she never came back and no other boats have seen her.'

'Is there a chance that she might have gone into another port because of the storm?' Bethany asked.

'Aye, mebbe,' James said, but there was little hope in his voice.

'Seven of a crew,' Jacob said huskily. 'Six men and the boy.' He had suddenly aged overnight.

'The boy's the son of one of the deckhands. They come from Findochty.' Bethany could not bring herself to speak of the missing crew in the past tense. 'And the skipper's Willie Gunner from the Yardie. The others are Highlanders down for the fishing. Two of them are brothers, and their cousin's aboard as well. Could the sea have got into her hold and swamped her?'

James nodded, then winced slightly and put a hand to the back of his head. 'Aye, it could, and if it did she could have gone down fast – too fast tae fire off a rocket.'

'I'll stay on in case there's more news. If it's bad I'll have to contact the families when I get back to Scotland.'

'D'ye want me tae travel back with ye?' Jacob offered.

'No, you stay here and see the season out.' She could tell that the loss of the drifter he had named after her mother meant almost as much to him as the loss of her crew. 'I can manage on my own.'

'It's a terrible thing tae happen,' the old man said. 'When ye depend on the sea for your livin' ye know that the price can be high. But even so, ye never come tae terms with it.'

He went upstairs just after Jem left. Bethany looked at James, still slumped in his chair. 'Jacob said you hurt your head.'

'Aye, I was cuttin' the last of the nets free because the hold was fillin' with the water pourin' inboard, an' a wave came over and knocked me off my feet. It damn' near tossed me right intae the hold. The edge of it caught me on the head, and then the wave tried tae take me back out with it. If it hadnae been for Adam I'd be down there with the nets we lost.'

'Adam?'

'He held me back till the wave was by, Siddy says. I don't mind much of it mysel'.'

'Let me see.' Bethany moved behind his chair and he bent his head submissively. The tips of her fingers found the large lump easily, and she parted his thick, dark hair, damp from the rain and the spray and sticky with salt, so that she could have a closer look.

'It's fair-sized but you've not broken the skin. Mebbe you should go to the hospital and let the nurses have a look at it.'

'No need for that. It'll go down in its own time.'

'You should at least go back to your lodgings and have a sleep. I doubt the boats'll be going out again today.' She glanced out of the window; the rain was still falling from a heavy grey sky, though no longer driven by heavy winds.

'We'll be out all right, if we can manage it.'

Because of the darkness of the morning, lamps had been lit in the room, and the artificial light caught the silver threads liberally woven through James's black hair. Against her will, Bethany remembered a time when his hair had been free of silver, and soft and thick to the touch.

'Be careful, James,' she said.

'I'll no' let anythin' happen tae Adam,' he promised. 'The lad saved my life, and I'd give it away without a second thought in order tae save his.'

'I didn't just mean Adam, I meant—' Bethany stopped speaking, then said, 'I meant the crew, and the boat. We've already lost one drifter.' She stepped away from the chair and picked up her coat. 'Is Adam at the lodgings?'

'I suppose so.'

'I'll walk back with you and have a word with him,' Bethany said, hungry to see her son and to reassure herself that he was safe and sound.

22

Ruth, and therefore Agnes and Kirsten, who shared a bed with her, had had a restless night because of the pain in her hand. 'It was loupin' all night,' she complained as Mary unwrapped the bandaging in the morning.

'I'm not surprised.' Mary took her cousin's wrist gingerly between her thumb and forefinger and held the affected hand up to let the others see it. 'Look at that.'

'No packin' for you today, my quine,' Agnes said after one glance at the hand, which was puffy, with an ugly bruised look to the skin around the wound. 'We've some toppin' up tae do while we're waiting for the first of the boats tae come in, and it's that cold that we'll have tae break the ice on the barrels afore we can start. You'll just make that sore hand ten times worse if ye try tae work today. Anyway, I doubt there'll be much fish in, given the storms last night. The nurses'll have tae see tae ye as soon as the mission's open.'

Protests were waved aside and Ruth watched wistfully from the window as the lorries carried the others away to the harbour. It was a gloomy place that day, for the *Jess Lowrie* was one of three boats that had succumbed to the storm. One crew had been saved by a fellow drifter close enough to see its rocket signals. Thanks to excellent work from the skipper and his crew they had managed, despite the heavy seas, to go alongside and take every man aboard before the stricken vessel slipped beneath the waves. The other, like the Buckie boat, had simply failed to return.

Ruth arrived at the farlins in the early afternoon, dressed for work and with her hand bandaged.

Annie and Sarah pounced on their younger sister as soon as she appeared. 'Let me see your hand,' Sarah ordered, and when she saw the neat bandage, 'You're no' workin' with that. Ye'll loosen it.'

'Or it'll be covered with salt,' Annie chimed in.

'I can manage,' Ruth was protesting when Rory arrived with another barrel for the packer who was standing in for her.

'What are you doin' here, Ruth Lowrie?'

'She thinks she's come tae work,' Sarah sniffed. 'Tell her, Rory!'

'What did the nurse say?'

'It's just a wee bit poisoned. But she punctured it and took all the poison out and bandaged it, and it's not sore at all now.'

Rory's blue eyes, normally cheerful, stabbed into hers. 'I didnae ask what she did, I asked what she said.'

Ruth bit her lip and finally admitted that the nurse had told her to stay away from the farlins, and get the hand looked at again in two days' time.

'That settles it, then, ye'll no' be back before Monday,' Rory announced.

'I could wrap it in a bit of tarpaulin. It wouldnae come tae any harm.'

'How can you pack barrels one-handed?'

'I can pack them one-handed and with a blindfold tied round my eyes,' Ruth snapped at him. 'You know I'm good at my job.'

'I know that I'd not forgive myself if that hand got worse. And Aunt Stella wouldnae forgive me either, so you're goin' tae stay away until the nurse says ye can come back tae work.'

'I need the wages, Rory!'

'You'll get yer wages.'

'For not workin'?'

'Aye, because you're right – you're a bonny packer and you're worth every penny I pay ye. It's not your fault ye've been hurt. Now do as ye're told and get away home and look after that hand,' he ordered.

'Any more news of the *Jess Lowrie* and the other boat?' Ruth asked when he had gone. 'They were speakin' of them at the hospital.'

'No. I don't doubt they're both lost, and all the poor souls aboard them,' Kirsten said, and a sudden silence fell over the women as they worked on the fish that all too often came ashore at dear cost to the men who harvested them.

Despite her brave words Ruth was still in pain, and that night her hand was throbbing so badly that they had to tie her wrist to the bedpost in an attempt to ease it, and to keep it from getting knocked during the night. She was pale and drawn in the morning, and content to stay in the lodgings with no further argument. When the others returned from the farlins for their midday meal she looked a little better.

'He's a good, kind soul, Rory Pate,' she said, and Andra's Jenny agreed, 'He's a right gem.'

When they left for the afternoon's work, Ruth was settling down at the table with her writing pad.

'No' another letter tae that photographer? You wrote tae him just the other day,' Agnes pointed out.

'Aye, but he's not answered it yet. It's a good thing it's my left hand that's bandaged,' Ruth said; and then, frowning, 'I'm wonderin' if Jack's mebbe ill. I'd have thought he'd have written before now.'

'Mebbe he's found better things tae do with his time,' Kirsten suggested, and Ruth glared at her.

'He hasn't!' she snapped.

Two days later the others returned from the farlins to find her in tears.

'Ruth, what is it?' Mary flew to her cousin's side. 'Did the nurse say your hand's got worse?'

'N-no, she's lettin' me g-go back tae work on M-onday!'
Ruth looked up at them, her pretty face swollen with crying.

'Has there been a letter from home? Is someb'dy ill?'

Again, Ruth shook her head. 'It's Jack! I g-got a letter
from J-Jack—'

'That's a good thing, surely?' Mary said, puzzled. 'You
were worried because you hadnae heard from him, and now
you have.'

'I didnae mean this kind of letter!' Ruth shrieked. 'He's
gettin' wed! Gettin' wed – tae Ellen Pate!' She hurled a crumpled ball of paper across the room and then threw her arms
about Mary, almost knocking her backwards, and burst into
loud, noisy sobs.

'Ellen Pate and your Jack? Never! They scarce know each
other!' Kirsten stooped to pick up the paper, which had landed
almost at her feet.

'What does it say?' Etta and Agnes and Andra's Jenny
crowded round as she smoothed it out.

'It's right enough, he's got himself engaged to Ellen Pate
– of all people!'

'That cold lassie that runs the net factory? He's no' particular, is he?' Jenny said, and Ruth's wails redoubled.

'For pity's sake, someone, help me with the lassie,' Mary
begged, her voice muffled as she tried to cope with the weight
of the weeping girl.

It took all five of them, and a dram or two from a small
bottle of brandy that Agnes kept by her for emergencies,
before they could calm Ruth down.

'It's not the end of the world, hen,' Andra's Jenny said as
she poured out a second dram.

'It is for me.' Ruth's face was swollen, and her voice thick
with sobbing.

'Ruth, ye'd surely not want tae keep the mannie by your
side against his will—' Mary began, and her cousin turned
on her.

'You don't know what it's like tae lose someone ye care

240

for! Peter Bain would never do a thing like that tae you!'

'Lassie, we all know what it's like tae lose a lad,' Agnes told the distressed girl. 'If I'd a pound for every man that's slipped through my fingers I'd be a wealthy woman. But men's like herrin', there's always another shoal out there. Ye'll find that out for yersel' soon enough, for ye're a bonny lass. If ye've lost him it's because he wasnae meant for ye.'

'But he was!' Ruth hiccupped.

'What I want tae know is, what does he see in Ellen Pate?' Kirsten mused.

'She's made a play for him while I was down here in Yarm'th. She knew that him and me had an understandin', and she's deliberately taken him away from me, the nasty cat!'

'We'll have none of that talk, not about your own cousin.' Mary said sharply.

'She's not my cousin, she's my Aunt Bethany's step-daughter!'

'She's still family,' Mary insisted. 'I tell you what – we'll all go out tonight, and take a good look round the shops and decide what we're goin' tae buy tae take home.'

'I can't manage. I'm going somewhere else,' Etta said hurriedly.

'With Rory? Well, you can just tell him what I think about his sister when you're—'

'I'm not going out walking with Rory tonight.'

'There, ye see? Etta's discovered that there are plenty of men in the world,' Agnes cut in, and before Etta could protest, 'The rest of us'll go round the shops, then, and we'll mebbe go tae one of those music halls intae the bargain. What d'ye say, Ruth?'

'She says yes, and that's the matter decided,' Kirsten said, then sniffed the air. 'I can smell cookin'. I'm fair ready for my dinner!'

*

241

'Our Ellen, with that photographer fellow?' Adam asked in disbelief that night. 'Engaged to be married, did ye say?'

'So he told Ruth in his letter.'

'I can't imagine any man wantin' our Ellen.'

'She's a bonny enough lassie.'

'Mebbe so, but she's thrawn; the man'll find that out for himself, soon enough. And she likes tae have her own way.'

'Ruth's in a right state about it, the poor soul. She cared for him.' Recollecting the utter misery in the girl's face, Etta felt a shiver go through her. Adam's arm immediately tightened about her.

'Are ye feelin' the cold?'

'Just a wee bit.'

'Over here, then.' The storm had abated, but the sea was still rough and most of the skippers, the thought of the two lost drifters in their minds, had decided against putting out to sea. Adam and Etta were walking along the river's edge, the shingle crunching beneath their feet and the lights of Yarmouth falling away behind them. Now Adam veered away from the water, urging her towards the black hulk of an upturned dinghy. 'We'll sit here for a minute, out of the wind.'

'I'm wearin' my good skirt,' Etta objected, and he stripped his jacket off and spread it over the ground.

'There you are.'

'But you'll catch your death!'

'No I won't,' Adam said, urging her gently to the ground. 'I'll keep you warm – and you can keep me warm.'

He settled down beside her, leaning up on one elbow with his head propped on his hand. Thin clouds moved above them, parting now and again to show the pale moon and the frosty twinkle of far-away stars studding the black of the velvety sky. She could see the outline of his head against the stars and feel his eyes travelling over her face. The close examination, and his silence, began to unnerve her.

'What are you thinkin' about?' she asked, more to break the silence than anything.

242

'I was wonderin' why any man would want our Ellen when there's you instead,' he said.

'You're haverin'!'

'Shut up, woman.' Adam bent to stop her mouth with his own, then said, 'Your lips still taste of salt.' He kissed her again and then drew back, his fingers tracing a path from her forehead to her chin, down to her throat and then further down to the first button of the blouse she wore beneath her jacket. 'Salty lips,' he said, 'and sweet kisses.'

'Adam—' she said as the button was eased from its buttonhole.

'What?' The second button was released.

'You know what.'

'Ye like me, don't ye?'

'Of course I like you, but—'

'And I like you, Etta. I like you an awful lot.' He kissed her again, with passion this time, and the heat from his lips sped like a fire out of control down the length of her body. His fingers, though deliciously cool against the skin of her breast, did nothing to quench the blaze.

'I've never—' she muttered against his shoulder as he shifted position, slipping an arm beneath her so that she was raised up against his body.

His soft laugh tickled her earlobe.

'Neither have I,' he whispered. 'I've been waitin' for you, my bonny lass.'

As the blouse fell open beneath his determined fingers and the blaze that had taken Etta over flared out of control, her last coherent thought before she gave in to his need and to her own was a vague realisation that she should have done as Mary urged and put on a warm jersey before going out that night. If she had, he might just have been deterred from leading them both into such terrible, delicious wrongdoing.

Things had been happening in the house during her visit to Yarmouth, Bethany realised as soon as she stepped inside the front door. There was an uneasy atmosphere about the place and Leezie, lugging her mistress's bag up the stairs to the bedroom, almost radiated anger.

As well to get the air cleared from the start, Bethany thought. 'Right, then, what's been happening here?'

Leezie, who was as strong as a horse, heaved the bag on to the bed with a lot of huffing, as though it weighed more than a sack of coal. 'Nothin',' she said through a mouth as stiff as the slit on a post box. 'What could be happenin'? One day's much like another in this house.'

'Is it Ellen? Has she been difficult? Because if she has I'll have something to say to the lady.'

'She's been fine,' Leezie said, then added, 'I suppose.'

'What d'you mean, you suppose?'

'I mean,' Leezie snapped, 'I'm just the servant here, how should I know how she feels?'

'Don't be daft, woman, you know you're more than a servant. Has she been going to the net factory every day?'

'Aye. I'd expected you home long afore this.'

'I meant to be, but Mr McFarlane had business to do and he needed me with him. And we lost the *Jess Lowrie*.'

Leezie forgot her own grievances. 'Lost her? What about the crew? God rest their souls,' she whispered as Bethany said nothing. 'That's a terrible thing tae happen!'

'Aye. I've to go and see the families, and write to the folk up in the Highlands that had lads on the boat.'

'D'you want me tae hang your clothes up?'

'I've got two good hands, haven't I? I can see to my own unpacking. I could do with a cup of tea, though.'

When Leezie had gone downstairs Bethany went to the window, where she looked out towards the Moray Firth, a mass of surging white-topped water on this cold, grey day. Something had gone wrong during her absence; she knew it by Leezie's martyred air. Something that would have to be dealt with – once she had gone to the Yardie to see Mrs Gunner, widow of the skipper of the *Jess Lowrie,* and then visited the woman in Findochty who had lost a husband and a boy not long out of school.

A letter had to be written, too, to the relatives of the three young Highlanders who had come south for the fishing, and would not be returning home.

Leezie had taken the tea tray into the parlour and lit a fire in the grate. A pile of letters lay on the desk, and while she sipped at her tea Bethany began to open them. Soon she was involved in the business matters that had been gathering while she was away, while her second cup of tea cooled unnoticed close to her hand.

Ellen swept into the house as if she owned it, and was half way up the stairs before she heard Bethany call her name from the parlour. There was a brief silence and then the young woman came back down and into the front room, dropping her bag and gloves on to a chair and peeling her fur-collared coat off.

'You're back, then.'

'I'm back. That's a fancy coat to wear to the factory.'

'It's nice and warm on a day like this.' Ellen tossed the coat over a chair and then sat down, crossing slim, silk-clad legs and folding her hands around her upper knee. 'Did you find Adam?'

She was dressed soberly enough in a black skirt and long, warm cardigan over a white blouse but her hair, Bethany noticed, had been stylishly waved and she was wearing lipstick and eye shadow.

'I found him.'

'And is he back in Aberdeen, being a good laddie?' The sneer was subtle – too faint to cause open offence, but obvious enough to sting. The little madam knew the answer to that already, Bethany thought with a flash of annoyance, but she refused to be drawn.

'No, he's still at the fishing. It seems that Adam has no interest in getting a good education, so there's little I can do about it.'

'So my wee brother's won again.' Ellen moved her position slightly and a ring on one of her fingers flashed in the glow from the lamp by Bethany's chair.

'It wasn't a battle, Ellen, so nobody wins. Your brother's made a choice, and that's all there is to it.'

'Rory didn't get to make a choice.'

'Rory didn't have to; he always knew that the cooperage would be his as soon as he'd served his apprenticeship. That's what his father intended for him all along. Being the second son, Adam doesn't have a business to inherit and so it was only natural that I wanted him to do as well as he could.'

'And what about me? I didn't want to go into the net factory, but you made me.' Ellen's voice was sulky, and she shifted position again; it was irritating the way she could not keep still, Bethany thought. One minute her left hand was fidgeting with the buttons on her cardigan and the next it was smoothing her skirt over her knee. What was wrong with the lassie?

'You weren't doing anything at all with your life,' Bethany pointed out. 'It's not good for a healthy young woman to spend all her time trying to keep herself amused. I work, and so does Rory, and I am perfectly entitled to expect you to work as well. I thought I made that clear at the time. I hope you've been looking after the factory well while I've been away?'

'Of course.'

'Good,' Bethany said crisply. 'I'll take a look in there tomorrow.'

Ellen shifted in her chair yet again. Then as Bethany returned to the papers in her lap, she said, 'There is one thing I should tell you. You're going to have to find someone else to take my place as overseer in the factory.'

'Take your place? Have you found other employment?'

Ellen smirked. 'I suppose I have, and it's in Glasgow.'

'Glasgow? Ellen, what—' Bethany started to say, then stopped as the younger woman put her left hand up to her

246

throat and the light again caught the ring she wore. A ring that Bethany had not seen before. 'Is that— have you got engaged?'

'I thought you'd never notice. It's nice, isn't it?' Ellen stretched out her hand to display the ring, three diamonds in a row.

'But— who is it?' It was not often that Bethany spluttered, but she was completely taken aback, and she could tell by the younger woman's eyes that Ellen was enjoying her discomfiture.

'Jack Morrison. You know,' she said as her stepmother gaped at her, 'the photographer who came to take pictures of the women working in the factory.'

'But Ellen, you've only just met the man! You scarcely know him! I've not been away much over a week – how could you possibly get engaged in that time?'

'I've been seeing him every day while you were away. We bought the ring in Elgin yesterday and I'm going to Glasgow over the New Year to meet his family,' Ellen crowed.

'You can't promise yourself to someone as fast as that! Not with me and Rory away!'

'Jack doesn't want to marry you, or Rory,' Ellen got to her feet. 'It's me he wants, not my family. We're getting married in the spring and living in Glasgow. It'll make a nice change – lots of places to go and people to meet. Are you not going to congratulate me?'

'I'm happy for you, of course, if you're certain that this is what you want.'

'I've never been more certain. Jack's just right for me.'

A thought struck Bethany. 'Was Jack Morrison not walking out with Ruth Lowrie?' she asked, and Ellen shot her a hard look.

'They met when he was taking pictures at the farlins in Lerwick, and Ruth showed him around when he first came here. But she never meant anything to him.' She threw the last few words over her shoulder as she sauntered to the door. 'I'm off to wash my hands before we eat.'

'Ellen!' Bethany called, and when the girl reappeared, one elegant eyebrow arched in a silent question, she indicated the hat, bag, gloves and coat spread over the chair. 'You haven't picked up your things.'

'That's what we pay Leezie for. She's the maid.'

'She's the housekeeper. I'm the one who pays Leezie her wages, and it's not for picking up after you or me,' Bethany said evenly. 'We're old enough to do that for ourselves. Once you're a married woman,' she added swiftly, seeing the threat of open rebellion in her stepdaughter's eyes, 'you can make your maid pick up after you all day if you wish. That is, if your intended husband can afford a maid.'

Ellen glared and then began to snatch up her belongings.

'You've not asked what's happening in Yarmouth.'

'Was there anything worth asking about?'

'There was a storm,' Bethany said quietly. 'The *Jess Lowrie* was lost, with all her crew.'

'Oh.' Taken aback, Ellen stared at her for a moment before saying awkwardly, 'I'm sorry.'

23

When Ellen had gone upstairs Bethany went into the kitchen, where Leezie was banging pots and dishes about.

When Ellen had gone upstairs Bethany went into the kitchen, where Leezie was banging pots and dishes about.

'Why didn't you tell me that Ellen's to be married?'

'It's not my place tae talk about members of my employer's family. I'm just the maid.'

'You'd best watch your tongue, Leezie Watson, because I've nearly had enough for one day. It's been a quick court-ing, has it not?' Bethany probed.

'You know Ellen, once she makes up her mind to have somethin' she doesnae waste time. She's been like that from a bairn, as I mind.'

'So it's like that, is it? She saw the man and she wanted him, so she set out to get him?'

'I wouldnae know about that,' Leezie sniffed.

'D'you think she's making a mistake? I'd not want that to happen.'

'Since you ask, I think the lassie needs tae get out of here and intae a place of her own. And now she's got somewhere tae go. So if I was you,' said Leezie, 'I'd leave her tae it. And if you're lookin' for somethin' tae do, ye can drain these potatoes for me.'

'Etta,' Rory caught up with her as she left the farlins with the other women, and put a hand on her arm, drawing her aside. 'I've not seen ye for a while.'

'You see me every day.'

'Aye, along with all the rest of them. I was wonderin' if ye'd like tae take a wee walk round the town tonight.'

'I said I'd help Ruth with some mendin'. Her hand's still sore, and—'

'So it's true.' It was a flat statement rather than a question. 'You're walkin' out with our Adam, aren't you? I thought I saw the two of you comin' out of the picture house the other night.' Then as she said nothing, but just stared miserably at the top button of his jacket, 'Ye should have told me.'

'I know, and I tried, but I never found the right time.'

'One time's as good as another. Are you and him— d'ye care for him?'

'I like him – and I like you, Rory, it's just that—'

'The lorry's waitin',' Rory said, and turned away.

'It's awful bonny, is it no'?' Etta said wistfully.

'Are ye thinkin' of buyin' it?'

'I couldnae do that!'

'Ye've got the money for it,' Annie pointed out.

It was the middle of December and with the fishing season coming to an end the herring catches were small and dealt with in half a day. The fisher-lassies had been paid their wages, the reward for the long, hard hours they had put in at the farlins, working at times for up to fifteen hours in bitter weather, and now, in their free time, they were all buying gifts to take home.

'It wouldnae be right tae spend so much on myself,' Etta fretted.

'Ye've worked hard – ye deserve a wee treat.'

The afternoon was cold and dark, but the shop window the two of them peered into was brightly lit. Behind the glass, mannequins sitting and standing in elegant comfort, protected from the bitter wind, gazed aloofly out over the heads of the two girls on the pavement.

For the past month, ever since she first saw the dress, Etta

250

had gone back regularly to look at it, convinced each time that someone would have bought it. But it was still there, and the wages she had just received from Rory seemed to burn in her pocket as she looked at the dress. It was cotton, with a V neck and long sleeves; fawn and trimmed with blue round the neck and cuffs. It had been cut in a wraparound style fastened on one hip, with the skirt falling in soft folds from fastening to hem.

'It might not fit me.'

'Ye'll not know until ye try it on. There's no harm in that.'

'Oh, I don't know—'

'I'm not freezin' out here a minute longer,' Annie said decisively. 'Come on.' And before Etta knew it the two of them were inside the shop and Annie was saying to the saleslady, 'We'd like tae see that light browny frock in the window. The one on the lassie that's sitting down.'

Etta's fingers trembled as she took her jersey and skirt off in the tiny changing room. Part of her wanted the dress to fit while the other part hoped that it would be too small or too large, because that would put an end to the matter. But it fitted as though it had been made for her, falling into place with a soft sound that was almost a sigh of relief.

When she stepped outside the cubicle to where Annie waited, the older girl said, 'You look bonny! Ye'll have tae buy it, Etta.'

'It's two whole pounds!' Etta hissed at her.

'Ye've got the money, haven't ye?'

'Aye, but—'

'And ye've bought wee gifts for the folk in Buckie.'

'Aye, but I should be savin' my wages, no' spendin' them on myself.'

'Ye've worked for the money, so ye're entitled tae spend some of it on somethin' ye want. Here.' Annie took her hand and led her to a bank of mirrors near the front of the shop. 'Look at yerself.'

The mirrors gave Etta views from the sides as well as from

the front. The dress fitted perfectly, there was no doubt of that, and it felt better than anything she had ever worn before. She felt taller, slimmer, and as glamorous as any of the actresses she had seen on the cinema screen. But she had never spent money on herself before, and it went against the grain.

'I don't think—' she was beginning when the shop door opened and Adam said, 'Etta? I thought it was you.' He advanced across the carpeted floor with not a trace of embarrassment, his eyes fixed on her. 'You look . . . you look like a princess.'

'That's what I think,' Annie said. 'She's had her eye on this frock for weeks and now we've got our wages I think she should buy it.'

'So do I.'

'No, it costs too much.' Etta made up her mind. 'I'll go and take it off—'

'How much?' Adam asked the saleslady.

'Two pounds.'

He dug a hand into his pocket. 'Here ye are – she'll take it.'

'I can't let you buy me a frock, Adam!'

'Why not? Ye look – ye're beautiful.' His eyes drank in the sight of her reflected again and again in the long mirrors. 'It's my Ne'erday gift tae you, come early.' He thrust the money at the saleswoman, commanding, 'Away and take it off and let the lassie wrap it up and then I'll take the two of you tae a tearoom.'

Annie rushed after Etta as she returned, dazed, to the cubicle.

'So it's you and Adam, is it?' she breathed, her eyes dancing. 'Ye sly wee cat. Wait till I tell the rest of them!'

The drifters carried the bulk of the fisher-lassies' purchases back to Scotland together with their kists, but every passenger on board the special train taking them back to Aberdeen had packed a good dozen sticks of sticky, striped Yarmouth rock in his or her luggage.

Most of them sang and joked and chattered non-stop on

the long journey, too excited to feel tired. They could sleep once they were back in their own beds.

'The bairns'll have grown since I last saw them,' Andra's Jenny said wistfully. 'The wee one'll mebbe not remember me.'

'Ach, it'll not take her long for her tae get tae know you again,' Kirsten comforted. 'It's amazin' how fast a sweetie can sharpen their wee memories.'

'And it's amazin' how soon ye get used tae bein' back with them,' Agnes reminisced. 'When my bairns were wee I spent the first half hour back home huggin' them and the second half hour scoldin' them.'

'One of the best things about bein' a herrin' quine,' Sarah said, 'is gettin' tae travel and see different places.'

'Different farlins, you mean,' Kirsten sniffed. 'An' different herrin'. It's true that the fish we gut in Lerwick's the largest, and in Yarmouth they're the smallest. There's nothin' like havin' a change.'

'Yarm'th's different, though, with the shops and the picture palaces and the music halls,' Sarah argued. 'And even though its grand tae be goin' home again, come the summer we'll be itchin' tae get away on our travels.'

'I'll not,' Mary put in from where she was crowded into a corner.

'Of course ye will, along with the rest of us.'

'I'll not, Sarah.' Mary blushed scarlet and then said, 'That last letter I got from Peter— He says he wants tae marry me.'

Suddenly she had the attention of the entire carriage. 'And ye never told us? You're a close-mouthed one,' Annie shouted from the far corner. 'Have ye written back tae the laddie?'

'Aye.'

'And what did ye say?'

'What d'ye expect her tae say?' Agnes boomed. 'He's a fine laddie. She said yes, didn't ye, my quine?'

'Aye,' Mary confessed, red as a poppy, and they clapped and cheered and began to chant, 'She's goin' tae be a farmer's wifie!'

In the midst of all the excitement Etta realised that Ruth, sitting beside her, was silent, her hands clasped tightly in her lap and her head bowed. She reached out and touched the girl's wrist.

'Are you all right? Is yer hand sore again?'

Ruth lifted her head. 'I'm fine,' she said, her eyes bright and hard, her voice razor-edged. 'It's grand news about Mary, is it no'?'

'Ruth, it'll happen to you one day.'

'I thought it *had* happened tae me,' her cousin said. 'I never thought anyone would be able tae take him from me.'

'I'm sure Ellen didn't mean to do it.'

Ruth's mouth twisted into a thin, hard smile. 'Didn't mean tae? She's deceitful, that one. She meant tae take him, all right, as soon as my back was turned. How else could it have happened so fast? But I'm not bothered,' she went on with a pitiful attempt at a shrug. 'Who'd want a man that turned away from her as easy as Jack Morrison turned from me? You be careful, Etta – never trust a man, especially Adam Pate. He could have any lassie he wanted, and there's always bound tae be plenty after him. You should hold on to Rory, for he's the better of the two.'

She lapsed into a moody silence. The girl on Etta's other side started to talk to her, but as she answered, smiled, and even laughed, Ruth's words burned deeper into her brain.

As it happened, Peter Bain was driving the lorry that collected the Buckie women. At sight of him the women let out a concerted roar and the young man took an involuntary step back, gaping in confusion. Then as Mary was pushed towards him his face went crimson.

'Ye told them?'

'Aye,' she confessed, and buried her own flushed face in his shoulder as the others crowded round them, fighting to kiss the future bridegroom and demanding invitations to the wedding.

'There'll be no weddin' if we don't get ourselves home afore we all freeze tae death,' Agnes shouted above the uproar. 'Peter, where's yer lorry?'

Once outside the station, they boosted Mary up into the cab alongside her intended.

'And straight home, mind,' Kirsten yelled up to Peter. 'No stoppin' tae have a wee cuddle on the way, for it's cold for the rest of us ridin' up behind ye.'

'Aye, ye can do whatever ye want with him once he gets us home, Mary,' Andra's Jenny chimed in, 'but until then we've more need of him than you have.'

It was a cold ride home, but they were all warmly dressed, with scarves about their heads, and there were so many of them that they generated their own warmth. Singing lustily, they endured the journey which, as Sarah pointed out, was better than the farlins, for at least they were sitting on their luggage instead of standing, and they weren't having to work with salt and brine pickle.

A great cheer went up as they drove into Buckie, waving regally at the folk walking along the pavements. It was almost dark and the light pouring from shop windows and doorways created a sense of warmth and cheer.

'Look,' Andra's Jenny pointed, 'is that not Ellen Pate comin' out of that shop?'

'Aye, I think it is. Here, Ellen,' Agnes shouted, cupping her hands to her mouth. 'Give us a wave, pet, and show us yer bonny ring.'

Ellen's head jerked up. She cast a swift glance at the lorry load of shouting, singing women and then turned away.

'Snooty bitch,' someone said, and a few of the women began to sing, 'Here Comes the Bride'. People on the pavement looked around, wondering who the women were shouting at, while Ellen began to walk faster, outrage in the set of her shoulders.

'Stop the lorry!' Ruth's voice shrilled above the shouting and singing. She struggled to the front and banged her fist on the cab and then, as it slowed, turning in towards the kerb, she began to fight her way back towards the tailboard, pushing the others roughly aside as she went.

As soon as the lorry had lurched to a standstill she jumped off, almost losing her balance but only just managing to stay on her feet. Then she began to run along the street, shrilling, 'Ellen! Ellen Pate!'

The women on the back of the lorry stared after her in astonishment. 'She's lost her wits!' Annie said. Ellen finally turned round and Ruth, now only feet away from her, launched herself forward. Because she had been running, the final leap had much the same effect as a battering ram. Ellen reeled back, taken by surprise, and if she had not come up against a house wall she would have been sent sprawling to the ground. Ruth recovered first, grabbing her cousin's shoulders and shaking her hard while she yelled accusations and abuse at the top of her voice.

'Stop her, someone! She's making a right exhibition of herself!' Annie struggled to get through the mass of women now standing up on the lorry to see the fun.

'She's managin' fine, leave her alone,' Agnes said as Ellen, recovering from the shock, started to fight back. In no time at all her neat little cloche hat was rolling in the gutter and the two young women, hands locked in each other's hair, were staggering up and down the pavement. A crowd gathered as swiftly as seagulls round a fishing boat, and people came hurrying out of shop doors and running across the street from the opposite pavement.

Both of the cab doors flew open and Mary tumbled out of one side while Peter jumped from the other. The young farmer raced back along the road and began to fight his way through the crowd, Mary in close pursuit. A disappointed groan went up from the fisher-lassies as Peter caught hold of Ruth and hauled her back, still kicking and shouting and clawing at the air.

Someone took hold of Ellen, but unlike Ruth, she had no

wish to pursue the fight. Instead she slumped against her captor, her hair standing on end, while Mary and Peter hurried Ruth back to the lorry.

'Help her up, will ye?' the young farmer appealed, and as several hands reached down to haul Ruth onto the back of the lorry he grabbed his betrothed's arm. 'Intae the cab with you, Mary, and let's get out of here afore someone brings the police out!'

The doors banged shut and the lorry jolted forward, leaving the crowd behind. As it picked up speed the women gathered round Ruth.

'Ye fairly showed her, pet,' someone said admiringly, and Ruth, her hair all over the place and a bruise already coming up on one cheekbone, beamed, looking happy for the first time since she had received Jack Morrison's final letter.

'Aye,' she said. 'I did that!'

It was the second time that Ellen Pate had been brought home weeping and bedraggled.

'Are you going to make a habit of this?' Bethany wanted to know as she surveyed her stepdaughter.

'It was Ruth Lowrie – she attacked me in the street,' Ellen sniffled. 'Jumped off the lorry bringing the women back and just threw herself on me. For no reason!'

'No reason? Was she not walking out with Jack Morrison before she went down to Yarm'th?' Bethany asked, and the girl glared at her.

'I told you already, they weren't walking out together!'

'Mebbe Ruth thought that they were. Here,' Bethany said as Leezie brought a basin of warm water and a soft cloth into Ellen's bedroom, 'give it to me.' She took the cloth, dipped it into the water, and dabbed gently at a split on Ellen's lower lip. The younger woman winced.

'You're hurting me!'

'Not as much as Ruth did, I'm thinking. Leezie, give me the iodine.' Bethany dabbed it on liberally and Ellen shrieked, tears springing to her eyes. Then she put a tentative hand to her head.

'Has she pulled out my hair? Are there any bald spots?'

'Not that I can see. You're just lucky she didn't have her gutting knife to hand.'

Ellen got up from the bed, pushing her stepmother out of the way, and went to inspect her scalp in the mirror.

'I've a good mind to get the police to her,' she said vindictively. 'That would teach her a lesson.'

'Are you sure you should?' Bethany wanted to know. 'You'd not want Jack to know you were brawling in the streets.'

'I wasn't brawling, it was her!'

'And you just stood there and never even tried to defend yourself? I'd let it be, if I was you.'

'I'm going to write to Jack and ask if I can go to Glasgow early. I won't stay in this place a minute longer!'

'If I was you I'd wait until that lip gets better,' Leezie advised. 'Ye don't want tae meet yer future in-laws with yer poor mouth all swelled up. They might think ye've been fightin'.'

'Get out!' Ellen shrieked, and the housekeeper shrugged and did as she was told. As she left the room, Bethany was sure that her shoulders were shaking.

'Ye should never have set yer sights on someone like that photographer mannie,' Stella told her youngest daughter. 'My mother aye used tae say, "Take cats of your own kind and your kittens won't scratch." That means that ye only face trouble if ye marry away from yer own kind.'

'Poor Jack Morrison's marryin' a cat, right enough,' Ruth said pertly, examining her bruised face in the mirror with a certain amount of pride. 'And they're welcome tae each other.'

'Quite right. There'll be someone else meant for you,' Annie consoled her younger sister. 'Someone better than Jack Morrison.'

Ruth's shoulders suddenly slumped and tears welled up in her brown eyes as she turned to face her mother and her sisters.

'But I didnae want anyone better,' she wailed. 'I wanted him!'

True to her word, Ellen Pate went off to Glasgow to meet her fiancé's family, and with her going, the atmosphere in the house on Cliff Terrace lightened. Bethany promoted one of the older beatsters in the net factory to the post of supervisor, and to her relief the woman was quick to learn the bookwork.

'And she's got more interest in the place than Ellen ever had,' she reported to Jacob. 'The other workers like her and they trust her. I think I've done the right thing this time, which is just as well since we've got a lot of nets in for mending, and orders for new sets to be ready for the summer season. There's plenty of work to do.'

'That's fine, lass.' He stood by the window, looking out, hands in his pockets.

'You might want to take a walk down there tomorrow and have a word with the woman herself, just to set your mind at rest,' she suggested. 'After all, it's your factory.'

'No, no, whatever you decide suits me.'

She frowned at his back, disturbed by his lack of interest in his own business. The settling up had just been completed and the skippers engaged by Jacob had gone home, satisfied with the money they had received for the season. All in all the local boats had done well, though some were saying that the herring shoals were smaller than before. But it seemed to Bethany that since the loss of the *Jess Lowrie* Jacob had lost his usual enthusiasm and drive.

24

With a wedding to organise, Zelda Lowrie was in her element. She flitted about the village persuading neighbours to help with the baking for the occasion, and insisted on going round every home in the fishing community with her daughter to issue invitations to the wedding early in January.

Once they had been round all the cottages, mother and daughter, dressed in their best clothes, walked up the hill to call on Bethany, spurning her invitation to walk into the parlour and opting instead for the kitchen.

'For I've got a favour tae ask of your Leezie,' Zelda said, her still-pretty face glowing with excitement and cold air, 'and anyway, tea tastes better in a kitchen than in a front parlour. Leezie, will you help us with the bakin' and the cookin'? Mary and Peter'll be livin' in the farmhouse with his parents, and the Bains have said that the weddin' party's tae be held in their big barn – they're gettin' it all set up for the occasion – but I want tae do my full share of the arrangements and not leave it all on Mrs Bain's shoulders. Ye'd not mind, would ye, Bethany, if Leezie helped me? Ye've got a fine big range in here.'

'I don't mind, if Leezie's willing; I'd not have time to do much baking myself.'

'It'll be no bother tae me.' Leezie poured out cups of tea all round.

'And ye'll come tae the weddin', of course, Leezie, for

ye're as near tae bein' a member of the family as anyone,' Zelda said, and as the housekeeper glowed at the compliment she hurried on, 'I've been lookin' forward tae settin' up Mary's weddin' since the day she was born. Ye'll mind, Bethany, how my faither was set against me and your Innes gettin' wed because of me fallin' with Mary before we got a church blessin'. It meant a quiet weddin' for us,' she explained to Leezie, her face clouding at the memories, 'but now here's my own daughter gettin' wed tae the very lad I'd have chosen for her mysel'. So we're goin' tae make a right occasion of it!'

'She's so set on a real traditional weddin' that she's got me worried,' Mary confessed. 'She's even goin' tae have a bed-makin'.'

'Are ye?' Leezie was fascinated. 'I mind some grand bed-makin's in my young day.'

'Ye're more than welcome tae come tae this one if ye like,' Zelda said. 'It'll no' be quite the same, with Mary and Peter livin' in the farmhouse instead of havin' a wee place of their own, but we can still go up there the night before the weddin' an' set their bedroom tae rights for them.'

'I don't mind that part of it,' Mary said nervously, 'puttin' the furniture in place and that. It's the other bits of a bed-makin' that worry me, like fillin' the bed with feathers or thistles, or grabbin' me and Peter and blackin' our hands and our feet. I'd not want that sort of thing goin' on in front of Mrs Bain.'

'As if I would! I used tae work for the woman, so I'm not likely to misbehave myself under her own roof. All we're goin' to do,' Zelda assured her daughter earnestly, 'is put your room tae rights and make it all ready for the two of you. And Mrs Bain's asked us all tae supper afterwards. It'll be a very pleasant evenin'.'

Quite a crowd set out for the farm on the wedding eve. Mary's two younger sisters, Jessie and Meggie, and some of Zelda's own sisters were included, as were Leezie, Etta, Ruth, Annie and Sarah. They all carried an offering for the wedding – some had food while others were lending their good china. The night was clear and frosty, and although they shivered when they first stepped out of doors into the ice-cold air they were warm by the time they had climbed the hill to the farm, where Mrs Bain and her daughter Elizabeth were waiting to welcome them.

Peter had taken the lorry to Buckie earlier in the day to collect Mary's clothes and the few belongings she wanted to take with her to her new home, and in no time at all the womenfolk had put the place to rights. Mary hovered round her mother, eagle-eyed, but Zelda, as she had promised, was on her best behaviour.

Then they moved on to the barn that Mr Bain and Peter had cleared and cleaned out in readiness for the wedding party. The place had been decorated with great bunches of greenery and ribbons, trestle tables had been set up and a makeshift platform erected for the musicians. The women bustled around, decorating the kettles with bows of ribbon and setting out tablecloths and dishes and bowls and boxes of sugared almonds and the conversation lozenges that were a feature of every wedding. By the time they were done the barn was pleasantly festive, and the tables glittered with the beautiful china beloved of fisher-folk.

'It's all grand,' Zelda enthused when they finally sat down to supper in the large farm kitchen. 'It's goin' tae be a bonny, bonny weddin'.' She laid a hand on Mary's, her eyes suddenly bright with tears of emotion. 'This is what I've been lookin' forward tae since the day ye were born, my lass. I swore on that day that you'd have the sort of weddin' I'd have wanted for mysel' if only I'd not had such a dour father.'

'He was strict, I'll grant ye that,' Mrs Bain agreed. 'But he'd be right proud if he could see what a fine marriage you made, Zelda. And he was a grand shepherd, one of the best we ever had.'

'Mebbe he should have had sheep, then, instead of bairns,' Mary muttered.

'Who'd have thought, Zelda, when you worked in this very kitchen and looked after wee Peter for me, that one day he'd be marryin' with your daughter?' Mrs Bain said. 'It's a happy time for you and me both, so just you think on tomorrow an' forget about the past.'

'Aye, ye're right.' Zelda dashed a hand across her eyes, and beamed around the table. 'Now then, let's have a song.'

It was late, and they were beginning to think of going home, when the door opened and Peter came in. His mother promptly slammed the palms of both hands down on the table.

'At last,' she roared. 'Zelda, where's the boot polish?' And as Zelda triumphantly produced two large tins from her pocket, 'Come on, lassies, catch a hold of him – and Mary too!'

And the kitchen erupted into uproar as the bride and groom, protesting loudly, were pinned into chairs and their shoes, socks and stockings hauled off in readiness for the traditional foot blacking.

It was a fine wedding, fine enough to satisfy even Zelda. Mary, flushed and glowing with happiness, made a beautiful bride, and when the church service was over she and her new husband led their guests on the wedding procession to the Bains' farm.

Paraffin stoves lit first thing in the morning ensured that the barn was warm by the time the bridal party and their guests arrived. There was enough food to satisfy even the greediest guest, and at the tables set aside for the younger folk conversation lozenges were being passed around amid a lot of giggling and blushing.

Most chose their lozenge carefully, but when the dish was passed to Ruth she shut her eyes before dipping her hand into it, closing her fist about the sweet so that nobody else could see it. After reading it, she leaned across the table and presented it to Rory.

Startled, he glanced at the words, 'I Choose You,' and then stared at her. 'What's this for?'

'Because I want you to have it. And now,' she said cheekily as the musicians began to tune up, 'you can ask me up for the first dance, Rory Pate.'

Etta was wearing the dress Adam had bought for her in Yarmouth. 'You look bonny,' he murmured into her ear as he drew her onto the dance floor. 'I knew that that dress was just made for you. Here,' he slipped a conversation lozenge into her hand, 'I kept this one for you.'

'Be My Sweetheart,' the pink writing spelled out against the white background.

'D'you mean it?'

'Of course. Every man needs a sweetheart, and every lassie needs a beau. And I couldnae find one that said, "meet me outside in five minutes."'

'It's too cold to go outside.'

'There's a shed just a few steps from here, with some winter hay still in it. Would ye like tae see it?'

'Why would I want tae go and look at a shed?' Etta wanted to know, and he laughed down at her.

'Because it would keep us fine and warm if we were tae decide tae take a rest from the dancin'. I'm takin' a stroll outside after this dance, and if ye feel like takin' a bit of fresh air yoursel' in a minute or two, I'd be willin' tae show ye the shed.'

Once the dance ended he disappeared like a twist of smoke up a chimney, but it took some time for Etta to pluck up the courage to sidle towards the barn door. With every step she expected someone to call her back, or ask where she was going, but at last she reached it and slipped through it. A hand immediately came out of the darkness to grasp hers.

'Adam?'

'Who else were ye expectin'?' he said against her mouth. Then, when he had kissed her, 'No salt this time, just the sweetness. Come on—'

'I can't see,' she protested as he drew her away from the barn. 'I'm scared I'll trip over somethin' and fall.'

'You don't need tae see, and ye'll not trip. I'll look after ye,' Adam said, and stumbling over uneven ground, she followed where he led, trusting in him.

Bethany's faint hope that after Yarmouth, Adam might be content to return to his studies, was dashed when he announced his intention of going line fishing with Jem during the winter months.

She even approached Innes when the two of them met in the street a week after Mary's wedding, and suggested to him that Adam should be taken into Thomson's yard as an engineering apprentice.

His reply was a flat, uncompromising, 'No.'

'What d'you mean, no?' she asked, astonished. 'What's wrong with my Adam serving his engineering apprenticeship in the boatyard? Other laddies do it.'

'Other laddies *want* tae do it. Does Adam?'

'I'm sure he'd be pleased to get the chance.'

'The way you thought he'd be pleased tae get a university education?'

Bethany's temper began to rise. 'He's proved me wrong there, I'll admit that, and now I've accepted that his heart's set on going to sea. But an engineering apprenticeship would give him a better chance of being skipper of his own boat, or an engineer on a cargo boat or one of those big ocean liners. Is that not why your Will's serving his apprenticeship?'

'Aye, but Will cares more for the engines than the fishin'. He'd sooner be engineer on a drifter than a deckhand or even a skipper. He's like me.'

'How can he be like you when he's not afraid of the sea?' Bethany said waspishly, and regretted her quick tongue as soon as she saw the anger flash over her brother's normally placid features.

'I'm not afraid of the sea, Bethany.' There was a sharp edge to Innes's voice now. 'It makes me sick tae my stomach, just, and I see no sense in bein' sick day in and day out when I can be hale and hearty on land instead. And me and Zelda would never try tae force one of our bairns intae somethin' they didn't want for themsel's.'

He fell silent as someone brushed past them, then went on when they were alone again, with nobody in earshot, 'There's another thing – the townsfolk don't always take kindly tae loons from the fishin' community takin' more than their share of the engineerin' apprenticeships. Their own laddies are lookin' tae be engineers in land jobs, and sometimes they find it hard tae get in anywhere because of skippers takin' the apprenticeships for their own lads.'

'I just want what's best for my son!'

'What you're wantin', Bethany, is a way of takin' the laddie away from the *Fidelity* and away from James. I've always wondered,' Innes said, 'why you never sought an apprenticeship for Rory.'

'Rory had the cooperage, he didn't need anything else.'

'If he'd been allowed tae follow his heart, though, he might well have become an engineer, and a good one at that. He'd the right feel for it, just like Will. That lad used tae spend hours with me, gettin' me tae teach him about all the different kinds of engine. He could draw them well, too, and that's somethin' I never could do.'

Bethany suddenly found herself on the defensive. 'He never said that he wanted to be an apprentice.'

'I'd have thought you'd have noticed for yourself where his interests lay, but mebbe you were too taken up with what was tae become of Adam. Did you never think, Bethany,' Innes probed, 'that he could have taken on the cooperage instead of Rory? After all, he's Gil's son too – is he no'?' And then, as she stared at him, speechless, 'If Adam's still hungry for the sea our James is the best teacher he could have. And if you're so desperate tae come between them, why don't ye buy a drifter for the lad and be done with it? That way, once he's learned his trade he can go out on his own, instead of stayin' in the *Fidelity*. And now, if ye'll excuse me, I have tae get back tae work.'

He tipped his cap, and went loping off along the street, leaving Bethany in a state of confusion.

Innes's final words hung in her mind, gradually forming into the thread of an idea. After a week of deep thought, she called on Jacob.

'It's time we thought about another drifter.'

'Tae tell the truth, lass, I've no' got the heart tae think of replacin' the *Jess Lowrie*,' he said, the pain of his loss still raw in his voice.

'It's business, Jacob. We'll be a boat down come the summer fishing. We could have one built,' she suggested, eyeing him closely. 'The *Fidelity*'s a good age, and the *Homefarin*'s not far behind her.'

'They've still got years in them yet.'

'But mebbe this is the time for a new boat, built to our own specifications. If we commissioned it from Thomson's yard it would mean that Innes would be in charge of installing the engine, and there's few engineers better than he is. We could call her *Jess Lowrie II*,' Bethany coaxed.

'It would cost us.'

'I know, but I was thinking – if I could raise a third of the money, and you could raise another third, we could surely borrow a third from the bank.'

'How would you raise that sort of money?'

'I could take out a mortgage on the house. We'd be paying for the drifter as it was built, so we'd not have to find all the money at the one time.'

'Even so, if anythin' went wrong – if the next two seasons were tae be bad for us, say – you and your family could be homeless.'

Bethany shrugged. 'Ellen's already gone, and from the few

letters she's troubled to send she seems well settled in Glasgow and bent on staying there. No doubt Rory'll find himself a wife soon enough and want a place of his own, and I'd be just as happy in a cottage. After all, that's what I came from. As for Adam – he's old enough to see to himself. D'you think that you could persuade the bank to advance a third of the cost?'

'I think they can trust me.' A spark of interest began to glow in his eyes. 'After all, I've been dealin' with them for nigh on twenty years and I've never let them down yet.'

'You'll speak to them?'

'No harm in doin' that.'

'Then I'll find out how much I could raise on the house,' Bethany said. 'At least Gil had the good sense to leave it to me and not to his children.'

She raised the subject of the proposed new drifter one evening when Leezie was visiting cousins and she and Rory and Adam were alone at the kitchen table.

Adam reacted with enthusiasm, as she had hoped. 'It'd be grand, havin' a new drifter built to whatever specifications Mr McFarlane wants. Will Uncle James be skipper?'

'Mebbe. Jacob's not fully agreed to the idea yet, but I know now that I can raise my share of the cost, and I'm determined to coax him into it.'

'If he agrees, and if Uncle James takes her over, that means that I'd be crewin' on her.'

'Eventually,' Bethany said, 'you could take her over yourself – be her skipper.'

'Me?'

'The drifter's not even been commissioned yet. I was thinking – if you were to go to one of those nautical colleges for a year, you'd learn all you need to know faster than if you worked your way up from being a deckhand.'

His enthusiasm suddenly drained away. 'So that's what it's all about – more learnin'!'

'The sort of learning you want, though, that's the difference,' Bethany said swiftly. 'You'd learn about engines and navigation and the things that James has taken years to learn. And at the end of it you'd have all the knowledge you need to take over the new drifter.'

'Not the fishin' knowledge, though.'

'You're already getting that, aren't you? You've done a full season at the fishing now, and you'd still be able to go north in the summer, for the college year doesn't start till after that. You enjoyed those classes at night school, didn't you? This would just be more of the same. '

Adam chewed at his lower lip, then said, 'But this would be all the time, not just in the evenin's. It's still a lot of classroom learnin' and bookreadin'.'

'Will you just think about it?' Bethany urged, and he pushed his chair back with a swift gesture and got to his feet.

'Mebbe – but I'm not sayin' yes until I've had a chance tae think about it,' he said, and walked out of the kitchen. Almost at once, the front door opened and closed.

'Give him time tae himself,' Rory advised.

'Would you—?'

'If you're askin' me tae speak tae him about it, the answer's no. He'd give up the whole notion if we both started on at him.'

'But going on the way he is – it's such a waste of a good brain!'

'Waste? You call goin' tae the fishin' a waste? It was good enough for your faither and his faither afore him, and it's good enough for your brother. And it's the fishin' that keeps the net factory, and the cooperage and the boatyards goin'. It's the fishin' that made Jacob McFarlane the wealthy man he is!'

Bethany was startled by the sharp note in his voice. Rory never lost his temper, never even displayed irritation or impatience, but now he was looking at her with a mixture of both in his clear blue eyes.

269

'It's just that – Adam has choices,' she found herself trying to explain.

'Choices, no' obligations. There's a difference.'

'Are you thinking about the cooperage? That's what you wanted to do, isn't it?' Bethany asked, recalling what Innes had said about Rory showing an interest in engineering.

'It was what I was always meant tae do.'

'What choice would you have made if the cooperage hadn't been waiting for you?'

'I don't know why you're talkin' of me havin' choices when you won't accept Adam's right tae have one,' Rory said, and the accusation so stunned Bethany that she did not even notice that he had avoided answering her question. 'Anyway,' he went on, 'ordinary workin' folk like us are never asked what we want tae do with our own lives. We have tae make the most of what we're faced with and we have tae earn our food and the roof over our heads and the clothes on our backs, and that's all that's tae it. Look at you – I doubt if you married my faither of yer own free choice.'

Bethany gasped, floundered, and finally managed to choke out, 'Of course I did!'

'I never thought that, even as a wee laddie. It's my guess that you were expected tae marry with the first man who asked ye, and there was my faither, a well set up widower lookin' for a second wife tae care for his house and his bairns and see tae his own comforts. I mind once when I was on the farm with Peter,' Rory went on while she stared at him, completely taken aback, 'we found a wee bird that had got trapped under a bit of nettin' in his mother's kitchen garden. Peter took it out and gave it tae me tae hold in my hand. It didnae struggle, because it knew that there was no use in that, but I could feel its wee heart just burstin' tae be set free, and I could see the misery in its eyes. It minded me of the way you looked at times.' He spoke as if it made all the sense in the world. 'It wasnae fair on you, havin' tae take on two wee bairns you'd not birthed yoursel'. I'm no' complainin', mind,' a smile tugged at the corners of his wide, strong mouth, 'for you did a grand job and we'd some good times together, you and me and Ellen, when we were wee. But the best times were always when my faither was away from home.'

He was right, and there was no sense in denying it. Bethany could still remember the sense of freedom she experienced each time Gil was out of the house, and the feeling of being trapped the moment he stepped back over the threshold.

'I didn't realise that you saw so much and understood so much.'

He shrugged, and then said, 'You changed when Adam was born, though. You were more settled after that. Mebbe you just needed tae have a bairn of your own.'

'Do you ever feel trapped, Rory? Innes told me the other day that you could have served your apprenticeship as an engineer.'

He stared down at the table, then said, 'It's like I said – I was born tae be a cooper, like my father. And I like workin' with wood, for it's a livin' thing.'

The doorbell rang, and she put out a hand to stop him as he began to get up.

'I'll see to it.'

As she opened the front door Jacob stepped from the dark of the night into the light and warmth of the hall, ever confident of his welcome in this house.

'There you are, my quine. I'm glad you're at home, for I've brought you a visitor – a man willin' tae put up a third of the cost of havin' that new drifter built,' he said, and stepped aside to let Lorne Kerr enter.

25

Bethany burst into the kitchen, where Rory was cutting another slice of cake for himself. 'Jacob's here, and he's brought a fish merchant from Edinburgh,' she hissed.

'What's a mannie from Edinburgh doin' in Buckie at this time on a January night?'

'Jacob says he wants to put money into this new drifter – and look at me in my working clothes and my pinny!'

'Ye look fine.'

'I do not! Rory, I've put them into the front parlour; could you go in and see if they want whisky or port or mebbe tea, and talk to them for a minute or two – just until I get time to sort myself out?' Bethany begged, and fled up to her bedroom, where she tore off the apron and blouse and skirt and splashed water over her flushed face before pulling a suitable dress from the depths of the huge wooden wardrobe. Once dressed, she unpinned her hair and gave it a swift brushing before pinning it up again.

Her unexpected guests, glasses in hand, were seated on each side of the fire, which Rory had poked into a good blaze, and Lorne was questioning him about the cooperage.

'Ye're welcome tae come and see round it,' Rory was saying as Bethany came into the room. 'This is a busy time for us, ken, with all the new barrels tae be made for the summer fishin', but even so, you'd be welcome.'

'The busiest time is the best time to see how a place

operates,' Lorne said, and then as Bethany entered he scrambled to his feet and offered her his chair. 'I insist,' he said when she shook her head. 'I'll be very comfortable over there. Would tomorrow do for the cooperage?'

'Aye, of course. Ye're only here for a day or two?' Rory asked.

'I'm here for as long as I care to stay. I want to see everything that Jacob and your stepmother are involved with, and I'd like to go out on one of the drifters if I can.'

'Jem's line fishin' in the *Homefarin*',' Jacob said. 'I'm sure he'd no' mind takin' you out with him.'

'Why would you want to put money into a drifter?' Bethany asked when Rory had excused himself and gone up to his room.

Lorne fixed her with his clear green gaze. 'Speaking to you and to Jacob in Great Yarmouth made me realise that fish doesn't just appear in boxes at the markets,' he said. 'I've become interested in the people involved in the fishing process – those who make the nets, catch the fish, smoke and pickle them, the coopers who make the barrels – and when Jacob mentioned in a telephone conversation that you had persuaded him to commission a new drifter I realised that this was the perfect opportunity for me to become more closely involved.'

'So you've decided, Jacob?'

'Aye, I have. Ye've got a good head on yer shoulders, my quine, better than a lot of men, and if you think a new drifter's a good idea then so do I.'

'I would say that it's an excellent idea,' Lorne said, and then, raising his glass to Bethany, 'and I would also like to say that it will be a pleasure doing business with someone who has beauty as well as brains.'

Adam walked from Cliff Terrace along East Church Street to the town centre, where he took the road leading down towards the sea and then along the shore. He passed the rows of fishermen's cottages known as the Yardie and walked on to Buckpool where, in the Main Street, he knocked at a door.

It was opened by his Aunt Stella, her face darkening when she recognised the caller.

'Yes?' Her voice was flat and uncompromising.

'Is my Uncle James at home?'

'Aye, he is.'

'Could I speak tae him?' Adam gave her his warmest smile, and then thought to himself that he might as well have grinned at a rock for all the reaction he got.

'Wait here and I'll get him,' she said, and closed the door in his face.

There was no understanding his Aunt Stella, Adam thought as he paced up and down the street, hands thrust into his pockets. In any other instance he would have been invited inside, especially on a cold January night like this. When he visited his Uncle Innes's cottage he just lifted the latch, like everyone else, and walked in, sure of a warm welcome, but not here – never here. He got on fine with his uncle and his cousins, but for some reason Aunt Stella had never taken to him.

The latch lifted and James Lowrie came out onto the pavement, closing the door after him. 'Adam? Is there somethin' wrong?'

'No. Well, mebbe . . . I just need tae speak tae ye.'

James glanced over his shoulder at the closed door, and then jerked his head towards the narrow passage that led round the side of the house to the back yard. 'We can stand in here, out of the cold,' he said, and led the way. Once in the passage he said awkwardly, 'Your aunt's givin' the kitchen a bit of a clean and she doesnae like folk tae see the place in a mess. What's troublin' ye?'

'It's this drifter that Jacob McFarlane's havin' built tae replace the *Jess Lowrie*. You'll have heard all about it?'

'He told me. Tae my mind he could have bought a boat just as easy, and had it in time for the new herrin' season,'

James grunted, 'but if he feels he can afford tae build a new drifter, then that's his business.'

'It's not just him that's payin' for it; my mither's puttin' up some of the money, so they'll own it between them.'

'Bethany? Where did she find the money for that?'

'I don't know, but she has. She told me and Rory all about it just this evenin'. She's not certain that Mr McFarlane's goin' along with the idea, but—'

'Wait a minute,' James interrupted, 'are you sayin' that this is all Bethany's idea?'

'It seems so. The thing is,' Adam hurried on, 'now she wants me tae go tae one of the nautical colleges in the autumn. She says that if I do that I'll learn enough tae be able tae take over the new boat when I'm done.'

'Does she now?'

'I don't care for the idea of more studyin', but my mither might be right. What d'you think I should do?'

'Don't bring me intae it. It's between you and your mother.'

'But she doesnae understand how I feel, and you do,' Adam argued.

'I think,' his uncle said after a long silence, 'that you should take yer time over yer answer. And if ye want, we'll talk about it again, later. For now, it's too cold tae stand here.'

Even so, he stayed where he was for a while after Adam left, turning the boy's news over in his mind. Since Bethany was behind the plan to build a new drifter, then it seemed clear to James that she hoped to use it as a way of getting Adam away from the *Fidelity* – and from him. He could easily talk the younger man into turning down the offer of a college place, but if he played Bethany at her own game then Adam, the person who mattered most to both of them, would become little more than a pawn, and James didn't want that.

'What was he after?' Stella asked as soon as he stepped inside the door.

'Nothin' important,' he said, and she bit off the end of her sewing thread with a vicious snap of the teeth.

Lorne Kerr became a familiar sight about Buckie in the next two weeks. He toured the net factory and the smokehouse and the cooperage, and he went line fishing on the *Homefaring* with Jem and Adam.

'I'll say this for him – even when the boat took a bit of a tossin' the man did his fair share of the work, though he looked a bit green about the mouth,' Adam reported in the Pate kitchen as he downed a large plate of meat and pota-toes.

The day after his fishing trip Lorne asked Bethany to drive around the area with him. 'I've hired a car for the day, but it's not the same without a companion. It would be helpful to be with someone who knows the place. You can tell me something of the villages along the coast.'

'Jacob can do that, and he's got more time than me,' she pointed out, and he grinned down at her. When she first met him in Yarmouth, and when he first arrived in Buckie, he had been immaculately dressed, but during his stay on the Moray Firth he had reverted to more casual wear, and now he was clad in a thick gansey of the type the fishermen wore. He had allowed the wind to ruffle his normally immaculate hair; the result gave him a slightly piratical air.

'Are you scared to be alone with me, Bethany Pate? I could always hire a chauffeur if you want a chaperone.'

'Of course I'm not scared!' She felt herself reddening, and hated herself for it.

'Good. I'll collect you from the house at two o'clock this afternoon,' he said.

Lorne Kerr was a pleasant companion, though it took Bethany, unused to dealing with a man on a social footing and unused to being driven in a car, some time to relax as he drove along the coast, weaving in and out of the fishing villages –

Findochty, Portknockie, Cullen and Portsoy – strung along the coastline.

'You must be ready for a cup of tea,' he said some time after they had started out.

'I'm fine, and anyway, there's nowhere around here that serves tea. We're not in Edinburgh,' she pointed out. 'We don't have hotels waiting to cater for folk.'

'We brought it with us. Jacob's housekeeper very kindly made up a basket for me.' Lorne drew the car into the side of the road at a spot high above the Firth. 'It's in the back.'

As well as tea in a thermos flask the basket held neatly cut sandwiches, biscuits, scones and a sponge cake, together with milk, sugar, napkins, cups and all the necessary cutlery.

'I think Mrs Duthie enjoyed making it up,' Lorne said as he unpacked it. 'She used to be a housekeeper to some titled people, and I think she misses the little niceties that the lady of the house demanded.'

'I didn't know that. How did you find out?'

'I'm interested in people; I always have been. I take after my mother in that way, though my sister says I'm just inquisitive. Sugar?'

As they had their tea he told her about his sister and her family, and about his late wife, who had been fond of music and had encouraged him to learn to dance.

'It's a pleasant pastime and I miss it now that I no longer have a partner. Do you dance, Bethany?'

'We never had much time for such things,' Bethany said dryly. 'There was always more important work to be done.' And then, with a sidelong glance, 'Speaking of work, I would have thought you'd be needed back in Edinburgh by now.'

'I have well-trained employees. There's no sense in building up a business only to become its slave. I always made sure along the way that I taught others to work well for me. And why should I hurry back to the bustle of the city when I can enjoy a good long holiday in a bonny place like this?' He paused to indicate the Firth stretching to the horizon, glittering in the sharp January sunlight. 'Very bonny,' he added, turning to survey Bethany. 'Though now that I've done all I came to Buckie to do, I suppose I must think of returning.'

'Your sister and her family will be glad to see you back home.'

'I'm sure that it will do them good to be rid of me for once,' Lorne said easily. 'Sometimes folk feel obliged to keep offering hospitality to a man on his own. The one thing I regret in my life is that Margaret and I never had children. I would have liked to have had a daughter to spoil, or a son to follow me in the business. I enjoyed my fishing trip with Jem and I enjoyed working alongside your Adam. He's a competent fisherman.'

'Fishing's not what his father wanted for him, but he's set on going to sea.'

'We work hardest at the employment we want most.'

'He says you did well on the drifter,' Bethany said, and Lorne laughed.

'I don't know about that. Look.' He held his hands out, palms up, and she saw the fresh calluses where he had been handling the ropes. 'I'm too used to soft living. And I had to swallow hard a few times, I can tell you, when the waves grew and the boat began to toss. I'd a sudden notion to say that I'd just get off now, but there was nowhere to go. So I had to persevere, and it worked out well in the end. Though I was glad to see the shoreline appearing as we made our way back. I'm trusting you not to repeat anything of this to Adam, mind.'

Two days before Lorne Kerr returned to Edinburgh the entire Lowrie family was invited to dinner at Jacob's house to celebrate the commission of the new drifter.

An extra table had to be squeezed into the dining room in order to accommodate the twenty-one people, including Lorne Kerr, Mary's husband Peter Bain and Jacob himself, and extra staff was hired to help Mrs Duthie in the kitchen. The older members of the family, including the newly-weds, sat at one table with Jacob and Lorne, while the younger members were at the other table.

'Have you any news of Ellen?' Zelda asked Bethany, who cast a swift look over her shoulder at the other table before answering. Seeing that Ruth was too busy tormenting Adam to listen to their talk, she said, 'She seems to be well-settled in Glasgow, and the Morrison family have taken to her.'

'She'll be comin' back tae Buckie for the weddin', though?'

'From what she says, I think she'd prefer to marry in Glasgow.'

'She'd be well advised tae do that,' Stella said stiffly.

At the other table, Etta had been seated opposite Adam. Every now and again he smiled across at her, and once she thought that his foot had pressed hers beneath the table, though she could not be certain. For the most part she sat silent while the others chattered and laughed all about her, toying with her food.

'Etta, are ye all right?' asked Jessie, sitting beside her. 'You're not sickenin' for somethin', are ye?'

'No, I'm fine. Just not hungry,' Etta assured her, and looked across at Adam again. He looked, she thought enviously, as though he hadn't a care in the world.

'That man's taken a right shine tae Bethany,' Stella said as she and her husband walked home at the end of the evening.

'Lorne Kerr? Away, woman!'

'I'm surprised you didnae see it for yoursel'. He'd be a grand catch for a widow woman; I've heard that he's got as much money as Jacob McFarlane, and a fine big hoosie in Edinburgh. Your sister could do very well for hersel'.'

'Bethany has more sense than tae get tied down tae another marriage,' James said roughly. 'Would ye listen tae the noise these lassies are makin'?' He nodded at their daughters, walking ahead of them. 'They've no consideration for the folk that's tryin' tae sleep!'

279

He pulled up his coat collar and quickened his pace, and Stella hurried after him, well pleased with the thought she had planted in his mind.

'I've been watchin' our Mary,' Zelda said. 'It's been more than a month since she and Peter wed, but I've not seen any signs of a bairn on the way.'

'It's surely too early for that.'

'Oh, it just takes the once. And I can tell the signs early – sometimes before the lassie herself knows it. For instance,' Zelda said with a sidelong look at Etta, 'I might not see them in our Mary yet, but I can see them in you clear enough.'

'What?' They were working in the little wash house built on to the rear of the cottage. Etta had been hauling the dripping clothes out of the boiler and lowering them into a tub of cold water so that her aunt could plunge them and then wring them out by hand before putting them through the mangle. Now she dropped the tongs, which hit the edge of the boiler before bouncing off and disappearing into the steaming hot water.

Sweat had been running down her face; now it turned to ice, and a chill went down her spine as she stared at her aunt. 'What are you talkin' about?'

'About you carryin' a bairn. I'm not blind, lassie,' Zelda said as Etta began to shake her head vehemently. 'And I'm not angry either. I've been waitin' for ye tae tell me. You surely knew it yourself?'

'I wondered,' Etta whispered through numbed lips. 'But I thought mebbe I was wrong.'

'Ye're not wrong, and hopin' won't do a bit of good. Come on,' Zelda said gently, 'the washin' can wait while we have a nice cup of tea and a bit of a talk.'

She took Etta's hand and led her to the kitchen, which was empty, for once, and poured two cups of tea from the pot on the hob, adding a dollop of condensed milk to both. She also put several spoonfuls of sugar into Etta's cup. 'Tae help tae settle yer nerves,' she said comfortably, sitting down at the table. Then, carefully, 'Are ye willin' tae tell me who the faither is? I'll not force ye if ye'd rather keep silent.'

Now that Etta's secret fears were confirmed there was no sense in keeping anything back. She needed help, and Aunt Zelda was the only person she could turn to. 'It's Adam,' she said huskily.

'Oh, pet!' Zelda covered one of Etta's hands with her own. 'I thought it might be, but I was hopin' I'd the wrong way of it.'

'Why?' Etta looked up sharply. 'What's wrong with him?'

'Nothin' at all – I'm as fond of the lad as I am of you and all my bairns. It's Bethany; Adam's the apple of that woman's eye, and I'm sure she'd her heart set on him marryin' with some rich man's daughter.'

'He loves me!'

'Has he said?'

'No, but I'd not have—' Etta hesitated, then rushed on, 'not if I thought he didnae love me.'

'Does he know about the bairn?' Zelda asked, and then, when Etta shook her head, 'He has tae know, pet. Why haven't ye told him?'

'I – I wasnae certain myself, and I wanted tae wait until . . .' Etta's voice trailed away, then the tears began to flow. 'Aunt Zelda, what'll I do if he refuses tae marry me?'

'You'll stay here with me and your Uncle Innes, and you'll have the bairn and we'll help ye tae raise it, that's what you'll do.'

'Does Uncle Innes know?'

'Of course not. I'd never say a word tae him without speakin' tae you first. But he'll not be angry, and he'll agree with everythin' I've said. We both know what it's like tae be in your situation, my quine. But the first thing tae do,' Zelda finished, leaning forward and stroking Etta's hair back from her forehead, 'is tae tell the laddie about the wee one.'

'Aunt Bethany—'

'We'll worry about her when the time comes. No need tae go seekin' trouble before then.'

At almost the same moment, Bethany was staring in disbelief at Lorne Kerr, who stood in the middle of her front parlour, hat in hand.

'Come with me,' he had said as soon as the door closed behind Leezie. 'Come to Edinburgh.'

'Why should I do that?'

'Because I want you to meet my family and my friends.'

'I can't.'

'Can't, or won't?'

'I can't,' Bethany said again. 'I've too much to do. The house, for one—'

'You have a very capable housekeeper.'

'There's the net factory, I need to keep an eye on that.'

'You have an overseer, and Jacob will be here to watch over it. After all, it is his factory.'

'And there are the financial ledgers as well.'

'Again, I'm sure that they could be left to Jacob. In fact, I know that he would be quite willing to take over all your duties for a week or two.'

'You've spoken to him about this idea of yours, even before you spoke to me?'

'Last night, when all his guests had gone home. I knew exactly what you would say when I asked you,' Lorne said, putting his hat down on a table, 'and I wanted to make sure that every argument could be defeated. So yes, I did speak to Jacob.'

'I'm not a possession!' Bethany sought refuge in anger. 'I can make my own decisions.'

'Then decide to come to Edinburgh with me. I want you to see my home, which I hope will be to your liking, and to meet my sister and my friends. I want you to realise that you could be just as content – perhaps even more so – in Edinburgh as in Buckie.'

282

'You make it sound like a proposal of marriage.' Bethany suddenly realised that her fist was still gripping the pen she had been working with when Lorne arrived, and that it was beginning to hurt her fingers. She put it down, glad of the excuse to turn away from him.

'We haven't reached that stage yet,' he was saying now, 'though I'd not mind if we did, for we're very well suited, you and me. For the moment, though, I'm just asking you to visit Edinburgh. I know that my sister would be happy to have you as her house guest; the two of you would take tea with her friends and visit the theatre together and spend hours in the shops. You would love the shops in Princes Street, Bethany. Edinburgh would suit you, I'm sure of it.'

'I'm very content with what I have now.'

'Are you? Your children are grown. You had to work to support them and yourself when you were widowed,' Lorne said, 'but they no longer have need of you. I know what a good business partner you've been to Jacob McFarlane; you could help me to build my business, and' – his eyes travelled over her in a swift, all-encompassing glance – 'you would be an asset in my home. My first marriage gave me a taste for the companionship and the pleasures of sharing my life with a woman. We've both been alone for too long, Bethany. A woman of your beauty and your temperament should not be on her own.'

'As it happens, my temperament is well suited to the single life.' Bethany rose from her chair. 'My marriage was more of a business arrangement than a love match, as Jacob has no doubt told you, and I've no wish to repeat the experience.' She held out her hand. 'I wish you a good journey, Lorne.'

'I've offended you. That was never my intention.'

'I'm not offended.' She drew her fingers from his as soon as was decent, clasping them tightly in her other hand.

'If you change your mind you only need to let me know.' He picked up his hat. 'Now I must go and spend a little time with Jacob. He has been a very good host.'

'Why don't you invite *him* to Edinburgh, then?'

'Perhaps, one day,' Lorne said, with just a glimmer of a smile. '*Au revoir*, Bethany Pate. No need to trouble the housekeeper, I can let myself out.'

As the front door closed behind him Bethany relaxed her hands and held them out before her. As she had suspected, they were shaking; whether from shock or from anger she could not tell.

26

A cold wind swept in from the sea, and Etta, huddled behind
a pile of coiled ropes and lobster pots, had long since begun
to shiver. She had watched from the shadows as the crew of
the *Homefaring* came ashore, but there had been no sign of
Adam, and if he didn't come soon, she thought, she would
have to go back home.

She was on the verge of leaving when at last two men
came along the harbour wall. One was unmistakeably Adam,
his voice and laughter giving him away, and when the other
spoke she realised that it was Jem.

She shrank back, dismayed and unwilling to let anyone
witness her meeting with Adam. Then, as they began to draw
level with the lobster pots, her fidgeting uncertainty caused
one of the pots to rock and topple. The two men stopped,
peering through the darkness.

'Who's that skulkin' about?' Jem barked. 'Come on out of
it and show yersel'!'

'It's only me.'

'Etta? What're you doin' out here?' Adam wanted to know.

'I was waitin' tae have a wee word with ye.'

'It must be an important word tae keep ye waitin' about
here in the cold and the dark. I'll see ye in the mornin', lad,'
Jem said. 'Good night tae ye, lass,' and he walked on as
Adam took Etta's hands in his.

'You're frozen. How long have ye been waitin' here?'

'Long enough. I'm fine,' she added hastily as he began to take his thick jacket off.

'Your hands are like ice. And your face too,' he said, the back of his hand warm as it brushed across the tip of her nose. 'Here.' He put the jacket about her shoulders and she clutched at it gratefully, burying her face in it to inhale the smell of him.

'Is somethin' the matter?' he asked as his arm crept round her, 'or is it just that we've not seen much of each other lately? You know what it's like in this place; when I'm not on the boat, my mother keeps—'

'I'm expectin', Adam.'

'Expectin' what?'

She had been fretting over her condition for weeks, and she had been trying all day to summon up the courage to tell him about it. Now that the news was out, his total lack of awareness infuriated her. 'A bairn, ye daft loon,' she said sharply. 'What else would I be expectin'?'

'A bairn?' His arms fell away from her and he took a step back. 'A bairn?' he said again, and then, 'Are ye sure?'

'Of course I'm sure. And if I'd any doubts, they're gone for good now, since my Aunt Zelda's noticed it for herself.'

'Are you sayin' that it's mine?' Adam asked, and then yelped as the toe of her boot cracked against his shin.

'Ye devil!' she screeched, too angry to keep her voice low. 'Sayin' such a thing tae me! No, get away from me!' She pushed him away as he tried to take her into his arms again. He staggered back and almost tripped over the lobster pot she had earlier dislodged, and as he danced about in an effort to keep his balance Etta started walking quickly away, so blinded by tears that she could easily have gone over the edge and into the water below.

'Wait – Etta, wait!' Adam caught up with her and grabbed her arm, turning her towards him. She fought him off, knotting her fists and lashing out at him, her blows catching his face, shoulders and chest.

'Etta!' he protested as he tried to ward off the assault, but she was too far gone to listen, or to care. By the time he finally managed to capture both her hands in his the two of them were breathless, and the tears were dripping from Etta's chin.

'I'm sorry – I'm sorry, I shouldnae have said that. It was just the shock of hearing you say— Etta!' he said as she kicked out at him. 'Cripplin' me isnae goin' tae make things different.'

He was right; Etta stopped fighting him and stood submissively in his grip, sobbing out loud now, like a child in abject misery.

'Oh, lass!' Adam said, and began to kiss her forehead, her wet cheeks, her nose, and her mouth. 'Ye taste of salt again,' he said, wiping the tears away with the heel of one hand.

'But this time there's no sparkle tae it,' she meant it to be a witty remark, but the half sob, half hiccup that followed spoiled the effect.

'Aye but there is, for yer eyes are glitterin' up at me. Here.' The jacket had slipped from her shoulders; now Adam lifted it from the ground and settled it snugly round her shoulders again. 'Come to the *Homefarin'*,' he said. 'There's nob'dy aboard her, an' at least we'd be out of this wind.'

There was another boat between the harbour and the *Homefaring*. Adam went down the iron ladder first, and Etta followed slowly, her feet settling cautiously on each rung while he guided her with a hand on one ankle. As she put her foot on the gunwale he lifted her as though she was no heavier than a baby and carried her across the deck.

'Adam, let me down! You'll have both of us in the water if you try tae carry me across between the two boats!'

'I'm not goin' intae any water on a cold night like this, with nob'dy about tae fish me out, and I'll not let you fall in either. Hold on!' he ordered, and she wrapped her arms about his neck and buried her face in his thick knitted gansey, pressing her cheek so tightly against his chest that the special pattern, which told the initiated of his family history, dug into her skin. She could feel the steady thump of his heart, hear the rumble of his breathing, and sense the sudden lift as he stepped onto the gunwale. He leapt the gap, and she was jolted in his arms as one foot thudded onto the *Homefaring*'s gunwale and then the other landed firmly on the deck.

She held on, wanting to stay safe in his arms for as long as she could, until he said into her hair, 'We're here now, and I'll have tae put ye down if I'm tae open the galley door.'

The galley stove was out, but the iron casing still held some heat and Etta was grateful for the warmth as she followed Adam into the blackness.

'Over here,' he said, and his hand sought and found hers. 'We'll go down tae the cabin.' And then, when she hung back, 'I cannae light the lamp up here, someone might see it. We'd be able tae have a light down below.'

'We don't need a light, we're fine here.'

'If ye're sure,' he said, and guided her over to where a wooden bench was fastened to the wall. They sat close together, his hands holding hers. 'Now then,' he said, 'about this bairn—'

'It's yours, Adam Pate.' The anger returned, sharpening her voice. 'Mebbe you don't know about how bairns start, but there was that time in Yarm'th in October, when we went walkin' on the beach, only we didn't walk all that far. And then there were another two times on that same bit of beach. And there was the hay shed at the Bains' farm the night of Mary's weddin', though by that time I was beginnin' to know what had happened.'

'Why didn't ye tell me then?'

'I wasnae certain, not until Aunt Zelda faced me with it. She knows about these things, but don't ask me how.' Etta said, and then, her voice trembling, 'And anyway, I didnae know how you'd be about it.'

'I don't rightly know mysel',' Adam admitted. 'I never thought of it.'

'Mebbe you got away with it when you were with other lassies,' Etta said, and was startled by the jealousy that stabbed through her when he didn't deny what she was saying. He had told her, that first time at Yarmouth, when he had loved her in the shelter of an upturned dinghy, that it had been the first time for him, too, but she had not believed him. She knew that Adam went with plenty girls before her, and he had known just what he was about. 'I suppose I never thought of the consequences myself,' she said dismally. 'I wish now that I had.'

'D'ye – d'ye want me tae marry ye?'

Her heart and her body all shrieked at her to say yes, yes, and yes again, but her mind was in control, for all that day she had been imagining the different ways in which he might react to the news she had to tell him, and she had carefully worked out an answer to every eventuality. So while her heart raced she forced herself to say calmly, 'I'd not want you tae marry me just out of pity. Aunt Zelda says that the bairn and me can live with them if I want it that way. So ye don't need tae provide a home for us, or tie yerself down. We're both young yet, Adam, and mebbe there's more ahead of us than marriage tae each other.'

'You're awful cold about it!' He sounded quite shocked.

'I've had more time than you tae think about it. I have tae be practical,' Etta said, while her heart quailed within her at the thought of being left to bear and raise a child without his love to sustain her.

'D'ye want the bairn?'

'I've no' got much choice, have I?'

'I've heard that there's ways—'

'Not for me, and now that she knows, Aunt Zelda would never hear of such a thing. I'm – I'm willin' tae birth it and rear it, for what's happened isnae the poor wee mite's fault.'

'No, I suppose not.' He released his hold on her hands and drew away slightly. They sat for so long in silence that Etta's heartbeat began to slow and her blood to cool. She became aware that the galley was not as warm as she had first thought, though the chill that gradually crept over her as Adam remained silent was not entirely due to the cooling of the big iron stove.

'You neednae worry,' she said at last, resigned to her fate. 'Nob'dy will know who the faither is. I'd not want tae do that tae you.'

Adam stirred. 'What?' he said, sounding as though his mind was returning from somewhere far away.

'I said I'd never tell folk the faither's name, so you've no need tae worry about—'

'Are ye willin' tae marry me, Etta?' he asked. 'D'ye want tae marry me?'

Etta had been so sure that he was going to leave her to face the town alone, with only her aunt and uncle for support, that her carefully nurtured serenity and self-reliance deserted her there and then. 'Yes,' she said, 'oh yes, Adam, it's what I want most in the whole world!'

'That's it settled, then,' he said, and reached for her.

'What about your mother?' she asked when he finally gave her the chance to speak. 'She'll not be pleased.'

'What makes you think that?'

'Aunt Zelda said – she said that Aunt Bethany would want you tae marry with some rich lassie.'

He laughed, his breath warm on her cheek. 'That would never have happened! I'll tell her tomorrow, but it doesnae matter what she thinks. You're all that matters now, Etta. You, and the bairn.' One hand reached beneath the jacket still about her shoulders, to stroke her belly. 'It's more comfortable down in the cabin,' he suggested.

'We'd better not—'

'What can happen that hasnae happened already? Besides, we're goin' tae wed, aren't we? As soon as we find a wee cottage and the banns are called in the kirk. Come on, Etta.'

Adam drew her to her feet and over to where the vertical ladder led down to the drifter's cabin, and she followed her man.

'It's true what they say,' Bethany said tartly. 'Men *do* turn into gossiping women when they get older.'

'What makes ye think that, my quine?'

'You've been talking to Lorne Kerr about me and my business.'

'He was talkin' tae me about you,' Jacob corrected her mildly. 'Wantin' tae ken all about ye, he was.'

'He invited me to visit his sister in Edinburgh.'

'And why not? You work too hard, Bethany, you deserve a wee holiday.'

'I had one when I was in Yarm'th. Anyway, it wasn't just a visit he was thinking of.'

'Did he say that?' Jacob asked, delighted.

'In a roundabout way. He thinks that we're suited.'

'And you sent him away with a flea in his ear?'

'I told him that I preferred to be single, if that's what you mean.'

'That would explain why he downed such a lot of my whisky on his last night. He went away with a right sore head – and a sore heart too, mebbe.'

'His heart had nothing to do with it,' Bethany sniffed. 'He made it sound more like a business proposition than a marriage. All the man wants is someone who can look after his fine house and warm his bed.'

'There's a lot to be said for . . .' Jacob took one look at her face and finished the sentence with 'companionship.'

'I've no wish to marry again, Jacob! In any case, I'm too old and set in my ways.'

'Nob'dy's ever too old tae want a bit of happiness. Tell me this, Bethany – have you ever known real passion for a man?' Jacob asked, and she stared at him, taken aback.

'What a question to ask a body!'

'You're a passionate woman; I can see that, and mebbe Lorne Kerr saw it as well.'

'I doubt that, for he didn't seem to be interested in passion – and neither am I,' Bethany said hotly. 'That's one thing we're agreed on.'

'If ye don't need that sort of warmth in yer life, lass, then

291

all the more reason tae consider Kerr, for he could make ye very comfortable for the rest of yer days.'

'I've no wish to leave Buckie. It's my birthplace and my home. And there's Adam. I'm not easy in my mind about him,' she confessed.'I still feel that he could do better in his life than being a deckhand.'

'Ye'll need tae think up a very good ploy tae get that laddie tae dance tae your tune instead of his own, for he's as stubborn as you are yourself.'

'I know that.' Now that Lorne Kerr had disappeared from the conversation and they were on safer ground, Bethany felt more comfortable. 'I've suggested to him that he should go to one of the naval colleges. By the time he comes out the new drifter'll be on the water.'

'You're never suggestin' that the lad should come straight from college tae skipper the new boat?'

'No, but he'd have all the knowledge, and according to James and Jem he's a good fisherman. He could go on the new drifter as mate until he's proved himself, and then take her over.'

Jacob rubbed his jawline, considering the suggestion. 'Aye, I suppose it might work out,' he said at last, and Bethany, having sowed the seed in his mind, was content.

'So what are ye goin' tae do about it?' James asked.

'I've said I'll marry her, as soon as it can be arranged.'

'Is that what ye want?'

'Tae tell the truth, when she told me last night it came as such a shock that for a while I just wanted tae run away from Buckie and away from her, as far as I could go,' Adam admitted, staring at his hands, fisted loosely together on the *Fidelity*'s scarred cabin table.

'That's the way most of us feel at the beginnin'. Men never seem tae be ready for fatherhood and domestic responsibilities.'

'Then when I thought about it, I realised that it could work out tae my advantage,' Adam went on enthusiastically. 'If

I've tae marry Etta Mulholland soon tae give the bairn a name, then I cannae go away tae college, can I? I'll have tae find somewhere for us tae live and stay on at the fishin' tae support the lass. And that'll put an end once and for all tae my mother's nonsense about me gettin' some learnin' instead of stayin' here in Buckie.'

'You'll be a deckhand, on a deckhand's wages. Her plan would see ye bringin' in more money eventually,' James pointed out. Opposed as he was to Bethany's college scheme he wanted to make sure that the lad made his own decisions.

'We'll manage. Besides, I've already said that I'll marry Etta. I cannae go back on my word now – Aunt Zelda would have the scalp off me, and once she was done, Uncle Innes would no doubt start on me.'

'That's mebbe nothin' tae what yer mother'll do when ye tell her ye're marryin' a fisher-lassie that works in the net factory, instead of some fine Aberdeen lassie with a father that has his own shop.'

'She cannae stay angry with me for ever,' Adam said confidently. 'And even if she does I'll be out of the house and well settled with Etta, so it'll not matter.'

James stayed silent for a moment, then lifted his head and looked the younger man in the eye. 'I tell ye what I'll do,' he said. 'Siddy's gettin' too old for the fishin', he's said that himself. When the summer fishin' starts you'll come back tae the *Fidelity* as deckhand, and I'll train ye up so's ye can take over from Siddy as soon as we can manage it.'

Adam's face glowed. 'D'ye mean it? I'd as soon be mate on board this old drifter than any fine new boat.' Then, hopefully, 'I don't suppose—?'

'Oh no,' James said emphatically. 'You've admitted that you're faither tae this lassie's bairn, and that makes you a man now. Bein' a man carries responsibilities, and the first of them is facin' up tae yer mother and tellin' her about yer change of plan.'

*

293

Zelda could scarcely wait for Innes to get home from work. As soon as he and Will set foot in the door she ordered Teena, only weeks away from her twelfth birthday, to keep stirring the broth and make sure the potatoes didn't burn, and then dragged her husband into their bedroom, the only room in the tiny house where they could find some measure of privacy.

'What's amiss?' he asked in alarm as she closed the door behind him.

'Nothin's amiss – it's the other way.' Her eyes were dancing and her still-pretty face wreathed in smiles. 'Innes, there's tae be another weddin' from this house!'

'But Jessie's no' fifteen yet – or is it Will? The laddie never said a word tae me down at the boatyard.'

'No, ye daft loon – it's our Etta!'

'Etta's gettin' wed?' Innes said in wonder, taking his cap off and scratching his head. 'I never even knew she was courtin'.'

'Neither did I, but she's been courtin' for the past three months. Since she was in Yarm'th, I'd say. Imagine, Innes, two weddin's from this house in the space of a few months,' Zelda said excitedly. 'The first thing tae do's tae find some-where for them tae live—'

'Is she stayin' on in Buckie, then?'

'Where else would they live?'

'When you said she met him in Yarm'th I thought mebbe it was a laddie from those parts.'

'No, no, it's Adam!'

Innes gaped at his wife, lost for words. 'Adam Pate?' he said at last. 'Bethany's lad?'

'Of course, and I didnae say they met in Yarm'th. I said they probably started courtin' there, for there was no sign of it before then. Unless it began during the Lerwick fishin',' Zelda began, and was interrupted.

'Does Bethany know?'

'If she doesn't then she soon will, for the weddin's tae be held as soon as they can find a place tae live and get the banns called.'

'She'll never agree tae it.'

'I don't see why not, for the lad could do a lot worse than our Etta. She'll be a grand wee wife and he's lucky tae have found her.'

'She'll not have it, I'm tellin' ye. Bethany's got her sights set higher than our Etta for her son.'

Smirking, Zelda played her trump card. 'The choice isnae Bethany's, though, for there's a bairn on the way.'

'A bairn? Etta's carryin' Adam Pate's bairn? Are ye sure of this?'

'I knew about it even before she did. I could see the signs. I couldnae tell ye till I got the chance tae speak tae the lassie. And Adam's agreed that he's the father.'

'A bairn!'

'Ye neednae sound so shocked about it, Innes Lowrie. They're two young folk with all the hot blood that runs in young veins. Ye've surely not forgotten that you gave me a bairn before ye gave me yer name and yer gold ring. You and me arenae in a position tae judge others.'

'No, of course not, and I never would. But Bethany won't like it,' Innes repeated.

His wife put her two hands on his shoulders and went up on tiptoe to dab a kiss on his lips.

'Bethany,' she said smugly, 'will just have tae like it, because for once she's not goin' tae get things all her own way.'

27

Despite his brave words to Etta, Adam was finding it hard to tell his mother about his new plans. Once or twice on the following morning he went into the front room where she worked at her desk but she looked so busy and so businesslike that his courage failed him and he retreated without saying anything.

Finally, not knowing what else to do, he went down to the cooperage. It was mid-morning, and within the rough shed the air was hot and stuffy, for the braziers were still burning, providing hot water to soften the barrel staves. Coopers and their apprentices were busy all about the three-sided shed, each group or duo working on a different barrel at a different stage. No sooner had Adam gone in than his ears began to ring with the non-stop noise.

Rory was working on his own, circling a barrel rapidly and continuously, forcing the final hoop into place with hard, evenly spaced hammer blows. The barrel, open at both ends, stood over a small brazier filled with burning chips of wood; the heat was needed to keep the well-soaked staves of wood pliant enough to be drawn together to make the traditional shape. Rory's free hand, supporting the barrel, was precariously near to the flames, and sweat ran freely down his face and dripped from his hair as he worked.

When Adam approached his brother a brusque nod signalled him to stand out of the way. Watching from near the open end of the shed he marvelled at the way the coopers could work in such heat and noise. Give him the fishing life any day, with the fresh wind in his hair and on his face, and the open waters all about him. He was glad that he had been born the younger son, and not his father's direct heir.

He had not long to wait before the barrel was finished, its hoops in place and the staves bent to the cooper's will. Rory deftly twisted it away from the flames without damaging it or toppling the fierce fire, then came to Adam, buffing sweat from his hair and face with a rag. His eyes, irritated by the smoke from the burning wood chips, were red-rimmed and streaming with tears.

'What is it that can't wait till later?'

'I've got a favour tae ask ye.'

'And I've got more barrels tae finish before the day's end, so out with it.'

'I want ye tae stand by me at my weddin',' Adam said, and Rory stared at him in disbelief through eyes that were still watering.

'You? Marryin'?'

'Aye, as soon as it can be arranged, and I'd like ye tae be my best man.'

'Who's the lass?'

'It's Etta, Etta Mulholland. We've been walkin' out together for a month or two now.'

'Ever since Yarm'th.' Rory's voice was suddenly flat.

'Aye,' Adam said, 'that's right. Ye knew about it?'

'I knew somethin' of it, but I didnae know it was serious. She's not the first lassie ye've courted, not by a long way.'

Adam grinned. 'She's the first tae catch me, though.'

'I thought you were goin' tae naval college. How can ye do that and get wed as well?'

'That's the good thing about it,' Adam started to explain. 'I wasnae sure at all about this new idea of Mother's because tae tell the truth, I'd rather just stay in Buckie and keep on with the fishin'. But now that Etta's expectin' a bairn—'

'Etta's carryin' your bairn?'

'Aye, that's what I'm tryin' tae tell ye,' Adam said, impatient with the interruption. 'Don't ye see? My mother surely can't blame me for doin' the right thing by the lass, and if I'm havin' tae get married, then I can't go tae the college, can I? Mother'll just have tae go along with it whether she likes it or not. Etta's solved my problem for me. It couldnae have happened at a better time for—'

The world suddenly exploded in a great burst of stars against a crimson background, and pain shot through his jaw as he went staggering backwards, arms flapping in a bid to keep himself upright.

'The fire – for God's sake mind the fire!' he heard a voice yell from far away. Adam felt his heel catch on something and as he fell heavily his left hand hit against something hard. Then the back of his head bounced on the ground, sending another great rush of stars flashing before his eyes. They passed in an instant, and then everything went black.

He came round within seconds to find himself being rolled roughly about the ground and slapped at by what seemed to be a host of hands. For a moment he lashed out feebly against his tormentors, under the impression that he had become embroiled in some sort of a fight, then he gasped as a panful of cold water was dashed into his face.

'What the—?' He came to, choking and spitting, to find himself lying on the ground in the cooperage. Several men were gathered around, looking down at him.

'Ye were burnin', man,' one of them said. 'Ye went right back and fell against one of the wee fires an' knocked it all tae damty.' He indicated a spot not far away, and Adam, cranking his head around carefully, saw that the ground was littered with smoking wood chips. 'Some of them caught yer jacket and if we'd not slapped the flames out ye'd have been a torch. Christ,' the cooper went on as Adam began to struggle to his feet, 'Rory fairly hit ye a right crack, man. I've seen him lose his temper once or twice, but I've never

298

known him lift a hand tae a livin' soul afore this. Here.' He reached down and caught Adam's arm, jerking him to his feet with one swift, hefty pull. When Adam was upright, he added softly, so that nobody else heard, 'I don't know why he hit ye, but if I was you I'd not let him get away with it.'

'Get back tae yer work,' Rory roared, storming through the group and sending them scattering. 'I don't pay ye tae stand about gossipin'!'

He glowered at them as they slunk back to work, then turned on his brother: 'As for you, get out of here before I throw ye out!'

Adam put a hand to his jaw, which throbbed and felt as though it had swollen to twice its normal size.

'I'll go when ye've told me what the hell ye mean by this.' It hurt to speak.

'Ye'll go now,' Rory said, his hands loose by his sides and his face, despite the sweat that still dripped down it, as hard as if it was hewn from stone.

Adam's head was not yet completely clear, and his jaw hurt abominably, but aware that the men were watching from the corners of their eyes while appearing to get on with their work as their employer had ordered, he took a swift step towards Rory, knotting his right fist. Rory fended the blow off easily, then caught Adam's gansey in his two hands, bunching it tightly and dragging Adam towards him so that they were almost nose to nose.

'Don't be a fool,' he said, his voice thick with loathing. 'I'm just as strong as you are, mebbe stronger, and if you try tae start a fight with me I'll kill ye, I swear tae God I will.'

'What's wrong with ye?' Adam asked, bewildered. 'All I asked was—'

'That's what's wrong with me!' Rory released him, taking his arm instead and hustling him to the wide doorway. 'I'm heart sorry for Etta and I'm damned if I'll stand by yer side and watch you makin' use of her for yer own ends. Find

299

someone else – and for the meantime,' he added roughly, pushing Adam outside, 'get out of my sight!'

Adam, reluctant to face his mother's fussing, spent the rest of the day on a secluded part of the shore, bathing his face and head in sea water in a vain attempt to rid himself of the bruising and swelling on his jaw as well as the throbbing knot on the back of his skull, where his head had hit against the ground. His left hand had been burned when it hit against the small iron pot holding the wood chips, and although the salt water stung at first it eventually helped to ease the pain and prevent a blister from forming.

Between times he sat on the shingle, huddled against a rock large enough to provide some shelter and privacy, his knees drawn to his chin and his arms wrapped tightly about them as he puzzled over his half-brother's uncharacteristic behaviour.

As a boy he had always run to his Aunt Zelda when he was involved in a fight or had hurt himself through some daredevil prank. Aunt Zelda was good at soothing scratches and bruises and helping to disguise them, too. And in her house there was always room at the table for hungry visitors. But Etta lived with Aunt Zelda, and no doubt she would start to fuss over him and to ask questions, the way women did when they owned a man – or thought they owned him – through motherhood or betrothal.

His intention was to sneak back home when everyone had gone to bed, but darkness, cold and hunger forced him back to Cliff Terrace long before that, stiff-limbed and chilled to the bone.

As ill luck had it, his mother was coming downstairs just as he let himself into the house.

'Where have you been?' she asked at once, and then as he looked up at her and the light shone on his bruised and swollen face her voice rose. 'And what in the name of God's happened to you?'

'Nothin'.' Dinner was almost ready, and the smell from

the kitchen made Adam's mouth water. He tried to escape to his bedroom, where he could at least wash his face and brush his hair and change out of his scorched gansey, but Bethany blocked his way, shooing him before her to the kitchen.

'Sit down there. Leezie, fetch the vinegar and a cloth, and make up a hot compress.'

'I would, if I'd more than just the one pair of hands,' the housekeeper said from the stove. 'But as I've no', ye'll just have tae follow yer own orders.'

'I'm fine,' Adam said irritably, going to the sink to wash his hands.

'Fine? Look at you! Have you been fighting?' She caught his sleeve and pulled his arm away from the sink so that she could examine the angry red patch on the back of his hand. 'Is that a burn? How did you get that?'

'It was just a wee mishap,' he said, and then yelped as Bethany caught his bruised chin and pulled his face round towards the light. 'That hurts!'

'I'm not surprised, for someone's hit you a right hard blow. Who was it?'

'Nob'dy. It's my own business.'

'It must have been somebody, and I want to know who?'

'It was me,' Rory said from where he leaned against the frame of the kitchen door.

'You?' Bethany and Leezie said in unison. 'You hit your own brother?' Bethany asked.

'My half-brother.'

'What in the world did you do that for?'

'That's for him tae tell ye – if he's got the courage,' Rory said with cool contempt. 'I'm goin' out. Keep my dinner hot, Leezie, I'll have it when I get back.'

'Rory!' Bethany shouted after him, but the front door was already closing behind him. 'What's going on between you two?' she asked in despair. 'Why did he hit you? Rory's never hit anyone in his life before. What did you do to him or say to him to make this happen?'

For hours Adam had been trying to think of the right way to break the news to his mother; now, thanks to Rory, it had all gone wrong and there was no longer any need for a careful approach.

'I just asked him to be my best man. That's all I did, as God's my witness.'

'Best man?' Bethany's voice was faint with shock. 'You're getting wed?'

'I was goin' tae tell you tonight.'

'Who is she?'

'Etta Mulholland.'

For a moment the only sound in the kitchen was the clash of pots from the stove, where Leezie worked with her back turned but her ears flapping. Then Bethany said, 'Leezie, keep the dinner warm for a wee while. Adam, come into the front room.'

'She'll hear all about it anyway,' Adam protested as he followed his mother's straight back and squared shoulders. 'We could have talked about it while we were eating. I'm starving.'

'Even if Leezie does hear it all later it starts in here, between you and me. Close the door,' Bethany ordered. 'As for food, you can just starve a bit longer.' Then, as he came further into the room, 'Etta Mulholland? Zelda's niece? A guttin' quine? You're marryin' with a guttin' quine?'

'You know fine who Etta is, and a guttin' quine was good enough for my father,' Adam pointed out coldly. 'I don't see why you should take against the lassie like this.'

'I've nothing against her, but she's not for you, Adam.'

'I think she is.'

'But you could do better for yourself! Why else d'you think I wanted you to go to the university, or the naval college? You'll still be going to the college, won't you?' Bethany said swiftly. 'The two of you can get married after that, if you still want to. It'll give you a wee while to think things over and make sure of your feelings.'

302

'We'll be gettin' wed as soon as we can, Mither. We have tae, for Etta's havin' a bairn.'

One of Bethany's hands groped about as though the room was in darkness, then found the back of a chair. Her ability to seat herself slowly and gracefully, her body folding itself while her back remained ramrod straight, had always fascinated Adam, but tonight she dropped into the chair as though her knees had given way and could no longer keep her upright.

'Your bairn?'

'Aye.'

'Are you certain, Adam? It could be anyone's.'

'Etta says its mine and I think she's tellin' the truth,' he said sharply. 'I've said I'll marry her and I will.'

'But if you marry now, how are you going to get to college?'

'I'm not, I'm stayin' here in Buckie. Uncle James is goin' tae arrange for me tae crew on the *Fidelity* and he's said that when Siddy leaves the boat I'll be mate.'

'You told James about this before you told me?'

'He was easier tae tell,' Adam said bluntly, 'and I wanted tae get the future right in my mind before I spoke tae you.'

'You can't do this.' Bethany's voice was suddenly strong again, as cold and as hard as iron. 'I'll not let this happen to you. I can help the girl – I'll give her enough money to take care of herself and her child, rent a wee place for them to live in if that's what she wants. You can still go to college and then you can take over the new drifter—'

'It's all decided, Mother. I'm marryin' Etta and I'm crewin' on the *Fidelity*. I'm old enough tae make my own decisions.'

'Old enough?' Her eyes blazed up at him. 'You're a fool, that's what you are! Where are you going to live, you and this future wife of yours?'

'We'll find somewhere to rent.'

'You needn't come asking me for the money to pay for it!' Bethany raged.

'You've just offered tae find a place for Etta and the bairn.'

303

'That was for her, while you were at the college. But if you're so set on marrying her now then you can support her. I'll not pay good money to see you ruin your life before it's properly begun!'

'Then I'll borrow the money, or I'll find work on one of the farms until the new fishin' season starts. And there's the line fishin' with Jem. I'll pay my way somehow. I'm nineteen, Mother, and in less than two years I'll get my inheritance from my faither. We'll manage until then, me and Etta and the bairn.'

'D'you love her?' It was a challenge rather than a question.

'Aye, I do,' Adam lied, looking his mother straight in the eye. He had always been able to lie convincingly; not even Bethany could tell his lies from his truths.

'Very well,' she said now, rising to her full height, a good six inches short of his. 'Ruin your life if you must. But I tell you here and now that you'll live to regret it – bitterly. Tell Leezie I don't want any dinner. I'm going to my bed.'

When he was alone Adam let his breath out in a long sigh of relief. It was done – not in the way he had intended, but at least she knew now.

Despite the throbbing in his jaw and at the back of his head he was cheerful as he went into the kitchen.

'My mither's gone tae her bed, Leezie, and she doesnae want any food. So that means more for you and me. I'm right famished. Serve it out now and I'll tell ye what's been happenin'.'

'Rory?' Etta asked in disbelief. 'Rory hit you?'

'Aye, he did that. Near knocked me into one of the fires in the cooperage, too.' Adam displayed the red weal across the back of his hand. 'My gansey got the worst of it, though, for the wood chips landed all over it.'

'I'll knit ye a new one,' she promised at once. 'I'll start on it tonight. But what was Rory thinkin' of?'

'You, seemingly. He doesnae think I'm good enough for ye, Etta. Now I'll have tae find another best man. Mebbe Will would stand with me,' Adam said, brightening. 'I'll ask him.'

'Aunt Zelda'll be pleased about that. She's fair delighted to have another weddin' tae arrange.'

'Tell her no' tae make it a grand event like Mary's, because we can't afford it.'

'Have you told Aunt Bethany yet?' He had waited outside the net factory for her at the end of the working day, and now they were walking slowly back to Innes's cottage, hand in hand.

'I was goin' tae tell her carefully, but when I went home lookin' like this' – he gestured to his face, still swollen and now, as the bruise matured and spread, looking very colourful – 'she started tae fuss the way women do. I was tryin' tae make little of it when that fool Rory came in and said that it was him that hit me, and I'd tell her why. Tell her? I still don't know the reason for it mysel',' Adam said. 'So that was that.'

'How did she take it?'

'She was a bit upset,' he admitted, and she bit her lip.

'I told you she doesn't think I'm good enough!'

'No, no, it's not that.' Adam slid into another lie. 'She was a guttin' quine hersel', so how could she think ye werenae good enough? It's me stayin' in Buckie instead of goin' tae the university or the naval college that's botherin' her.'

'I've spoiled everythin' for you, Adam.' Etta felt tears prickling the backs of her eyes. 'I've wasted your chances!'

'Ye've not! I'd far rather stay here with you than go away from here.'

'You're not just sayin' that tae make me feel better?'

'No!' It was only a half-lie this time, for unwittingly, she had saved him from another year or so of classroom learning. He drew her into the shelter of a house end, taking her into his arms. 'I'd a million times rather stay here with you.'

305

'Oh, Adam!' She planted a passionate kiss on his lips, and then recoiled as he let out a yelp of pain. 'I'm sorry, I forgot you were hurtin'!' She reached up and touched the bruise gently, the tips of her fingers feeling the nasty swelling along the jawline.

'It's all right, ye just took me by surprise.' He kissed the corner of her mouth, a delicate butterfly kiss that, sedate as it was, sent an unexpected tremor through her. 'Now then – we'll have tae find somewhere to live, for there's certainly no room at Aunt Zelda's. Have ye any savin's, Etta?'

'No, have you?'

'No,' he admitted.

'Aunt Bethany?'

'She says not – because of me not goin' to the college,' Adam added hastily.

'We'll find somewhere. One room would do at first, just as long as we're together.'

'Mebbe my mother'll calm down soon. My room at home's big enough for two, and a bairn.'

'No!' Etta said sharply. The thought of living in that grand house in Cliff Terrace, under Aunt Bethany's roof and, worse still, under her disapproving eye, filled her with terror. Nor could she bear to be in the same house as Rory. She knew, even if Adam didn't, why the young cooper had reacted so badly to the news of their hurried marriage. 'No,' she said, 'I'd as soon live in the old shed in our back yard than in your house. At least I'd be welcome in the shed.'

'I'm not livin' in any shed!'

'Other folk have, when they've had no other way of putting a roof over their heads. Come on, Aunt Zelda'll be wonderin' where I am. You can stay for your dinner if you like.'

'I will – but don't tell them how I got this.' Adam indicated his bruises. 'I'll tell them I fell in the dark and hit my face against a wall.'

The family were already eating when they arrived, and there was an immediate banging of spoons on the wooden

306

table and a disjointed rendering of 'Here Comes the Bride', while Zelda jumped up at once and came to Adam, her arms outstretched.

'I'm the happiest woman alive! Tae think that you and my wee— for goodness' sake, laddie, what's happened tae ye?'

'Have ye started bossin' the man around already, Etta?' Will shouted.

'She has not, and she never will. I'd a bit of an accident in the dark last night.'

'Celebratin' yer engagement? Why didn't ye invite me along?'

'It wasnae that – I just turned clumsy-like and fell over against the corner of some house.'

'Aye,' Innes said, 'I heard about that already today, from one of the coopers.' Then, as the young couple looked at him in horror, he added to his noisy brood, 'and a hurt face is nothin' tae laugh about, so we'll have no more of it. Though there's just one thing – I hope tae God nob'dy thinks that I did that to ye because ye've got this lassie—' he glanced at the younger members of his family, then said, 'because of you and Etta gettin' wed.'

Zelda was already busy at the stove. 'Sit in, the two of ye,' she instructed. 'Matt, Meggie – move along and make room.'

'I was wonderin',' Adam said as he and Etta settled themselves at the table, 'if you'd be my best man, Will.'

'Our Will? But what about Rory?' Zelda leaned over their shoulders so that she could set plates of food in front of them. 'Surely your own brother's the one tae stand by you on your weddin' day?'

'He's— he'd be happier for me tae find someone else,' Adam mumbled. 'You know Rory, he's a bit shy about things like that.'

'Then you'll do it, won't you, Will?'

'Would I have tae wear a suit?'

'Aye ye would, and have your hair brushed, and cut your

307

fingernails, since it's the only way tae get rid of the oil that's always caught beneath them.'

'I'm no' sure it would be worth the bother,' Will began, and his mother cuffed the side of his head.

'He'll do it, Adam, and he'll do it right – I'll see tae that.'

'Where are ye goin' tae live?' Teena wanted to know, while Jess asked, 'And what about your bridesmaid, Etta? Can I do it?'

Meggie and Teena immediately began to claim the honour, and the noise only abated when Innes thumped on the table and announced that if a man could not enjoy a peaceful meal in his own house at the end of a day's work, things had come to a pretty pass.

'Yer father's right.' Zelda settled back into her own seat. 'No more weddin' talk – me and Etta'll sort it all out in our own time. Samuel, pass the bread.'

'Now then, where are the two of ye goin' tae live?' Zelda asked later that night. Innes had stepped out to the back yard, as he always did, to enjoy a final pipe of tobacco in peace, and the others had gone to their beds.

'I don't know.' Etta felt her lower lip begin to tremble. 'Adam says that Aunt Bethany won't help him, seein' as he's disappointed her over not goin' tae the college,' she said, her voice little more than a whisper, 'but I think it's because she's angry that it's me he's marryin' and not someone she can be proud of.'

'Don't be daft, lassie.' Zelda put her arms about her niece and hugged her close. 'Any woman that has you for a daughter-in-law's blessed. We'll find somewhere for you and Adam tae live. Now, about your bridesmaid – I was thinkin' that if you choose one of my lassies it's only goin' tae cause trouble with the other two, and in any case, they'll all end up standin' as bridesmaid tae each other in time – if I'm fortunate enough tae get the lot of them married off. What about Ruth? You like her, don't you?'

'I do, but d'you think she'd agree tae it, with the disappointment she's had?'

'I think it would be the very thing tae help her tae get over her own hurt. You ask her,' Zelda advised. 'And let me sort out the weddin' arrangements.' She dropped a kiss on the top of Etta's head before releasing her. 'I'm good at that!'

28

Ruth almost burst with excitement and pride at the prospect of being Etta's bridesmaid. 'It'll be the best day of my life,' she declared, her eyes alight for the first time since she heard that Jack Morrison was to marry Ellen Pate. 'We'll have such a good time, you and me and Adam and Rory!'

'Will's to be the best man. Rory's too shy for it, Adam says.'

'What? Not standing by his own brother at his marriage? We'll see about that,' Ruth said, and the very next day she marched into the cooperage and tapped Rory on the shoulder.

'I want a word with you. Outside, so's we can hear each other.'

He followed her out. 'What's amiss?'

'What's amiss is you not standin' by Adam on his weddin' day. Etta says you're too shy tae take on the job, and it's tae be Will instead. And I only agreed tae be her bridesmaid because I thought you'd be best man.'

'I didnae care for the job,' he said shortly. 'Will's welcome tae it.'

'Please yerself, but I'll still want a dance from you at the celebrations after.'

Rory bit his lip, shuffled his feet and looked over her head at the grey sea beyond the harbour. 'I'm no' sure I'll be there,' he muttered at last.

'Not be at your own brother's weddin'?'

310

'He's my half-brother, no' my brother.'

'Don't be so daft, Rory Pate – Etta's cousin tae Will and Mary and the rest of them, and that's further apart than you and Adam, but they all call her their sister. And why wouldn't you go to his—' She stopped, understanding dawning in the hazel eyes that were a mixture of her father's grey eyes and her mother's brown eyes, then said, 'It's because you still care for Etta, isn't it?'

'That's none of your business, Ruth Lowrie!'

'It is my business, for we're all related, even if it's only by marriage. I knew the two of ye were walkin' together, but Etta said it was just in friendship – though from the look on your face,' Ruth said shrewdly, 'it was more than that tae you.'

'I have tae get back tae work.' Rory made to walk away, but she danced quickly to one side, putting herself between him and the cooperage.

'No ye don't, not until we get this business sorted. Rory, it's Adam she's marryin' because it's Adam she cares for, and the sooner you accept that the better.'

'You don't know what ye're talkin' about!'

'You say that tae me that had tae stand by and see your own sister steal away the man I cared for? There's nothin' you can teach me about the pain of losin' someone ye wanted tae spend the rest of yer life with.' Ruth's voice was suddenly fierce, her eyes bright with loss as well as anger. 'But as I see it, what's done's done, and mebbe Jack was never meant for me after all. Mebbe I'm supposed tae get someone a hundred times better than Jack Morrison. That's what I tell myself, and that's what you have tae think too. And never mind how you feel about Adam – I'll not let you spoil our Etta's weddin', Rory Pate, and it *will* be spoiled for her if you're not there, for she counts you as one of her dearest friends. And I'm still goin' tae have that dance with ye, even if I have tae come out of the hall and along tae your house and drag ye intae the street and make ye dance with me there, in front of all your fine Cliff Terrace neighbours. And wouldn't that just upset yer mither!'

311

There was a short, angry pause, during which Rory glared down at the small, bristling figure before him, and Ruth glared back.

'So ye'll be at the weddin', then?' she asked at last.

'Aye.'

'Good. And mind that dance you owe me. Forget it and I'll make ye sorry for the rest of yer life.' She stepped aside and said graciously, 'Ye can go back in now.'

'And you'd best get back home. Your nose is red with the cold.'

'It's not the only bit of me red with the cold, but we'll not discuss that any further,' Ruth said pertly. As he went into the cooperage she called after him, 'Mind that conversation lozenge I gave ye at Mary's weddin'?'

'Aye.'

'Have ye still got it?'

'Aye,' Rory said without thinking. Then he blushed.

'Good,' Ruth said. 'It'll be your turn tae choose one for me when Etta gets wed. Make sure it says the right thing, for I'm awful particular.'

Bethany's anger with James was so great that she had to wait for two whole days before she could allow herself to confront him. She sent a note, asking him to call at the factory to have a look at the set of new nets he had ordered for the *Fidelity*, and when he arrived she took him to where the first of the nets had been hung for his inspection.

'They're fine. A grand job. Ye'll have them ready in good time for the new season?'

'Of course.' Bethany led the way back to the tiny office, a route that took them through the mending room where Etta Mulholland worked among the other menders. James nodded affably to her, while Bethany offered the girl no more than a dip of the head.

'Ye're no' very friendly tae the lassie that's tae be yer new daughter,' James said as she closed the door, shutting

312

the two of them away from the eyes and ears of her employees. She had already arranged for the woman who had taken over from Ellen as overseer to be busy elsewhere for the morning.

'The lassie that's to be Adam's wife,' she corrected. 'She's one of my employees. It wouldn't be seemly if I was seen to be favouring her.'

'I doubt there's any danger of that; just as I doubt that you only wanted me here tae look at a few nets.'

'You're right. Adam tells me that you've promised him the mate's job on the *Fidelity* when Siddy leaves.'

'I think he'll be ready for it.'

'You'd do anything to get him to turn against my wishes and go along with yours, wouldn't you?'

'I just want the laddie tae follow his own inclinations, Bethany. Not mine, and not yours.'

'You probably approve of him marrying Etta Mulholland.'

'He's acceptin' his responsibilities,' James said levelly, 'the same as the two of us had tae do all those years back.'

'Can you not see that he's making a mistake? He's going to regret this, but by then it'll be too late!'

'We all have tae put up with the consequences of our own mistakes.'

Bethany looked at her brother for a long moment and he met her gaze without flinching. She was the first to look away, turning to the desk to fidget with the papers lying there.

'I just want him to be happy.'

'Etta's a decent enough quine, and if she cannae hold on to the lad, that'll be her worry, not ours,' James said, and when she did not reply, he got up and went to the door, turning for one last comment.

'My greatest regret is that you refused all those years ago to come away with me to some place nobody knew us, and start again. But you'd not have it – and now you have tae deal with the result, Bethany.'

*

313

'There's a wee cottage for rent in the Catbow,' Bethany said that night to Adam. 'Two rooms and a sail loft, just, but I think it might do you and your— and Etta, if the two of you would care to have a look at it.'

'What rent are they lookin' for?'

'That needn't concern you. If you want it I'll pay the rent for two years. That'll see you through till you inherit the money your father left in trust.'

He gaped at her, and then asked cautiously, 'What're the conditions?'

'There are no conditions. It's my wedding present to you. You'd best go and tell the lassie. Now's as good as any other time,' Bethany added sharply as he started to speak. 'Best to see it before someone else takes it.'

Now that Bethany had found them somewhere to live and Ruth, by some piece of cunning she would not divulge, had managed to get Rory to come to the wedding, Etta felt that life could not be more perfect.

She and Zelda and her foster-sisters threw themselves into wedding plans; the banns were called, the church hall booked for the reception, the local fishing community invited, and every night the kitchen table was taken over with patterns, stretches of cloth, ribbons and buttons and lace. Mary spent more time at her parents' cottage than she did at the farm, while Meggie and Teena and Samuel, still at school, were banished from the big kitchen table and had to do their homework as best they could in the two small bedrooms upstairs.

'It's not fair,' Samuel raged. 'We always have the kitchen table for our books – why can't Etta use a bedroom? Why does it have to be us?'

'Because we need the big table tae cut out the cloth,' his mother pointed out.

'We need it too. There's more beds than floor in the bedrooms,' Samuel argued. 'Why did ye have tae have so many bairns?'

'Because your father and me like bairns – though there's times when I wonder if we did the right thing,' Zelda said, and then, suddenly repentant, she drew her youngest, and most dearly loved for it, against her and kissed his mop of unruly curls. 'It'll not be for long, just till the weddin's over.'

'And then it'll be Jessie's weddin', then Meggie's, then Teena's!'

'I hope so, but by the time Teena gets wed you'll be a workin' man, mebbe with a wife and a house and bairns of your own, so you'll not be bothered about my kitchen table.'

'Not me,' Samuel said, disgusted by the very thought. 'I'm never goin' tae get married. Can I have a scone with raspberry jam on it tae help me tae do my homework?'

Thanks to the generosity of the local folk, the little cottage that Bethany had rented for her son and Etta acquired enough furniture to suit their basic needs. Jacob McFarlane gave them a brand new bed, and the girls in the net factory contributed bedding. Zelda and Innes gave them dishes and cutlery and someone donated an unwanted table, complete with four chairs. Two comfortable, if well-worn, armchairs came from someone clearing out her dead parents' home, together with some rugs for the floor.

Ruth, Annie and Sarah helped Zelda and Etta to scrub out the house and get it ready for the furniture, which would be moved in on the day before the wedding, and put in place that night as tradition demanded. There would be no feet-blackening however, for Adam, warned by Mary and Peter, had decided to stay well away from the cottage that night.

'I'm goin' over tae Elgin with Will and Peter and Uncle James and Uncle Innes – and Rory, if he'll come,' Adam said when he and Etta were working in the cottage. 'We'll have a wee drink tae set us up for the weddin'.'

'Not too much,' Etta said, worried. 'I don't want you too drunk tae say ye'll marry me when the minister asks ye.'

315

'I doubt my uncles'll allow that.'

'Uncle Innes surely wouldn't, but I'd not be so sure of Uncle James. It's bonny, isn't it?' Etta looked round the empty kitchen, eyes shining. 'Our very own home!'

'It's no' much, is it?'

'It'll do to start with,' she said, stung by the criticism in his voice. 'We can't manage anythin' near as grand as what you're used to at Cliff Terrace. But once the new fishin' season starts and you're bringin' in more money we can get things we need – a cradle for one.' She looked away, suddenly too shy to meet his gaze, then went on with mounting enthusiasm. 'And I'll get wee bits of material tae make baby clothes. Aunt Zelda says she can let me have a bonny shawl, and a few other wee things.' She put a hand on his arm. 'We'll be all right, won't we, Adam?'

'Aye, of course we will. It's a fine, sturdy place, with thick walls and a good roof. We'll be snug in here whatever the weather.'

'I meant you and me – and the bairn when it comes. We'll be happy, won't we?'

'I don't see why not,' Adam said. 'Other folk seem tae make marriage work, so I expect we will, too.'

On the day before her wedding Etta came face to face with Stella Lowrie in the street. For a moment the older woman hesitated, as though she wished she had had time to cross the street or disappear into a shop, and then she stopped, hefting her shopping basket from one arm to the other.

'Etta.'

'Is Ruth all ready for the weddin'?'

'As ready as she'll ever be.'

Etta smiled tentatively into the grim face. 'We're goin' tae get the house ready tonight. Would ye like tae come with us?' she asked.

'I've got enough tae do without that.'

According to Zelda's reminiscences, the younger Stella

Lowrie had been a gentle girl, happy with her lot as a wife and mother. Etta could see no sign of that girl in the woman confronting her. Sometimes she wondered what had happened to change Aunt Stella so much. Since Stella showed no signs of walking on, she persevered.

'Are you lookin' forward tae the weddin', Aunt Stella?'

'A weddin's a weddin' and if ye ask me, the only folk that look forward to it's the couple gettin' wed,' the woman said bleakly. 'I hear ye're expectin'.'

Etta's hand flew to her stomach, which had only just begun to fill out.

'Aye,' she said, and the older woman sniffed.

'It's one way tae catch a man, I suppose,' she said, and then, with a thin smile, 'and the other's tae have a father with property that the groom's family needs.'

'Adam's marryin' me because he cares for me,' Etta said, stung.

'Ye think so? Ye're goin' tae rue the day, lassie. Like father like son – and that lad you're promisin' yersel' tae is a right copy of his father. The only two things he loves are the sea and himsel', an' ye'd be a fool tae trust a word he says. Go ahead with this weddin' and the day'll come when ye find yersel' lyin' in a lonely bed and wishin' ye'd never walked up the aisle tae meet him.'

'But Adam's not— Uncle Gil surely didn't—' Etta said, bewildered, then she was brushed aside as Stella continued on her way.

The cottage that would be Etta's home from tomorrow night had been set to rights. Innes was still out with the groom's party, and the others had gone to bed. Zelda watched as Etta tried on her wedding outfit – a crêpe de Chine petticoat beneath a pale blue blouse and an oatmeal coloured woollen skirt with box pleats down the front.

'It is all right?'

'Aye, it looks grand,' Zelda said, head to one side. Then,

as Etta stood mutely before her, 'Lassie, what's wrong with ye? Ye've not been yersel' all evenin'. Are ye ill?'

'I'm fine.' Etta had made up her mind to say nothing about the ugly confrontation with Stella Lowrie. It had been a long and difficult evening, trying to smile while everyone else enjoyed the fun of putting her new home to rights, and the supper that followed – herring and potatoes served from the cooking pots onto newspaper spread on the kitchen table, and eaten with the fingers since the dishes would not be unpacked until the bride and groom were living in the house.

'You're not fine at all. I don't know what's wrong with you, but if ye're beginnin' tae have doubts about this weddin', ye don't have tae go through with it.'

'But everythin's been arranged!'

'It's still not too late. You know we'd be happy for ye tae stay here, and the bairn too. It'd be grand tae have a baby in the house again, and if that's what you want, ye just have tae say the word.'

The love in her aunt's voice took Etta to the verge of tears; she swallowed hard, then said, 'I love Adam and I want tae be his wife more than anythin' in the world.'

'That's all right then. The drape of the blouse and the skirt pleats are perfect,' Zelda went on briskly. 'Nob'dy would know you were expectin'. Now try on the jacket and the hat.'

'Everyone knows I'm expectin' anyway,' Etta said as her aunt helped her on with her straight, hip-length jacket. 'Aunt Stella mentioned it when I met her in the street on the way home.'

'Stella!' Zelda, who had picked up the blue felt cloche hat trimmed with a small bunch of artificial cream and blue flowers, put it down again. 'I might have known. What's she said tae upset ye?'

'She didn't say—' Etta began, and then the treacherous tears filled her eyes and overflowed before she could stop them. 'Oh, Auntie Zelda!'

'It's all right.' Zelda opened her arms, then just as Etta

was moving into them she said, 'Wait a minute!' and seized a clean towel that lay, folded, on top of the pile of newly ironed clothes. Shaking it out, she tucked it carefully about her foster-daughter's shoulders. 'Tae stop the bonny jacket gettin' marked,' she said apologetically, and then, sweeping Etta into her embrace, 'Now tell me!'

The story came pouring out along with the tears. 'I don't know what she meant,' Etta wept.

'Who knows what's in Stella's mind?' Zelda said helplessly, stroking the girl's back. 'She's changed. There's been a bitterness eatin' away at her for years now, and I can't for the life of me think what's brought it on her.'

The door opened and Will burst in, his cap and the shoulders of his jacket damp. 'It's rainin',' he said, taking the cap off and shaking it over the hearth. The hot iron range sizzled as the cold drops hit it. Then, turning and seeing the two women, he asked, 'What's amiss?'

'Nothin'.' His mother moved forward, putting herself between him and Etta.

'But our Etta's been cryin'.'

'That's what women do when they're happy.'

'Are ye certain that that's—'

'Will, get tae yer bed,' his father said from the doorway. 'Go on now,' Innes added sharply as the boy opened his mouth to argue. Will closed his mouth again, shrugged, and went up to his bedroom in what had once been the sail loft.

'It's somethin' Stella said tae the lassie today,' Zelda said, low-voiced, when her son was out of earshot. 'It's upset the lass.'

'On the eve of her weddin'? That's no' right.' Innes stripped off his damp cap and jacket and handed them to his wife. 'Come here, my quine.' He settled himself in his fireside chair and drew his foster-daughter down onto his knee, just as he had done in the past when any of the children in his care were upset. Zelda moved to stand behind him, with one hand on the back of his chair. 'Now then, tell me what Stella said tae ye.'

His face stilled, and then darkened as Etta, still clutching the towel about her shoulders, stammered out the story.

'We cannae make head nor tail of it,' Zelda said when it was told. 'Like faither, like son? Gil Pate was a decent, civil soul. A bit sharp with his coopers, mebbe, and with the guttin' quines working at the farlins from what I've heard, but there was never any badness in the man.'

'It's somethin' of nothin',' Innes said firmly. 'Take my advice, lass, and don't give it another thought.'

'I know James married her because him and his faither wanted her family's fishing boat,' Zelda said, 'and I can understand her feelin' bitter, since we all know that James isnae exactly a perfect husband, but—'

'Somethin' of nothin',' Innes said again, patting Etta's shoulder. 'We'll say no more about it, none of us. Not tae Adam or anybody else. Now stand up, lassie, and let me have a look at ye. By God but ye're goin' tae be a bonny wee bride,' he went on as she stood obediently before him. 'I'm not so sure of the wee cape, though.'

'It's a towel, ye daft loon.' Zelda snatched it from Etta's shoulders. 'It was tae keep her from cryin' on her fine jacket.'

'There's no need of it now, for the tears are all gone, aren't they, Etta?'

She smiled at him, comforted by his presence and his gentleness. 'Aye, they are. Is Adam—?'

'I took him right tae his door and saw him inside. And he had just enough drink in him tae be merry, and tae make him sleep like a bairn so's he'll be fresh for tomorrow,' he said, and then, with a wink, 'Mind you, it was a lot of work, for Will and James were determined tae get him as drunk as a lord.'

'Was Rory there?' Etta wanted to know.

'No. There's another one that's actin' strange. Ach well, it's not our concern,' Innes said, and began to pull his boots off. 'Time we were in our beds. It's goin' tae be a busy day tomorrow.'

*

320

'Ye don't think,' Zelda said in the darkness of the bedroom half an hour later, 'that Stella was hintin' that Adam's not Gil's son?'

'Eh? Stop haverin', woman, how could that be?'

'I don't know, but if I'm right, then Stella is in on it. Do you know anythin', Innes?'

'Aye, I do. I know that if you don't stop your tongue and let me get some sleep I'm goin' tae carry ye intae the kitchen and make ye spend the night on top of the table. Get tae sleep!'

Long after his wife had done as she was told Innes Lowrie lay against her warm, soft back, his eyes wide open and his mind full of secrets that he wished he had never discovered.

29

Bethany was disconcerted when Lorne Kerr returned to Buckie in the middle of June.

'I wanted to see how the new drifter's coming along,' he told her over dinner at Jacob's, where he was staying. 'And I'd a notion to see the start of the herring fishing. Jacob and I took a stroll down to the harbour just after I arrived – the place is buzzing like a beehive.'

'Aye, there's a lot of work tae gettin' the boats ready. I mind in my own young days,' Jacob reminisced, 'what an excitement it was after bein' on shore for a few months – unless ye were at the white fishin', but that's no' got the same feel about it if ye're a drifter man tae trade. Man, it was grand – like bein' let out o' the school after a long hard day spent wi' yer books!'

'I was speaking to your brother down at the harbour,' Lorne said. 'Your brother James. He says your Adam's sailing on the *Fidelity* with him.'

'Yes.' Bethany crumbled a bread roll with restless fingers, wishing that she had never accepted Jacob's invitation. Lorne seemed to be completely at ease, but every time she looked at him or heard his voice she recalled their last meeting and his almost businesslike suggestion that she should visit Edinburgh to find out if the two of them were suited.

'Adam's wed now, tae a right nice wee quine,' Jacob

boomed. 'Ye've met Etta, Lorne – she's foster-daughter tae Innes and Zelda. She'll be havin' a bairn just about the end of the summer fishin'.'

'You'll be looking forward to that event, Bethany.'

'Yes, indeed,' she said flatly, and was saved from having to say more by Jacob, who chattered on, 'And Ellen – Bethany's stepdaughter – has got married in Glasgow since ye were last here.'

Bethany felt her mouth tighten at the girl's name. Ellen had married Jack Morrison in a quiet, very private ceremony, and now sent her stepmother brief but triumphant letters every other week, bragging about her new flat and her maid. Her overworked maid, Bethany thought, feeling pity for the servant that had to put up with Ellen as a mistress.

She dragged her mind back to her surroundings and her companions, and asked Lorne, 'Have you seen the new drifter? She's nearly ready.'

'Not yet. We're going to have a look at her tomorrow.'

'I just wish James would agree tae be her skipper,' Jacob said, 'but he's determined tae stay with the *Fidelity*. I suppose, since she's his own boat, I cannae argue about it.'

'What about Jem?' Bethany suggested.

'He's no' as sharp a skipper as James. I cannae think of any man as good at handlin' a boat an' findin' a good shimmer o' herrin' as James. But if he'll no' do it, then it should by rights be Jem, for he's competent enough and I'd sooner find someone else tae take the *Homefarin'* than put a man I don't know on the new boat.'

'Ye'll never make me believe that that mannie's only back in tae see how the *Jess Lowrie II*'s comin' along,' Zelda said sagely.

'What other reason could there be?'

'Tuts, Etta, the man's fair daft about Bethany.'

'Aunt Bethany?' Etta still could not bring herself to refer to her mother-in-law by any other title, and Bethany herself

323

seemed to be quite content to leave things as they had always been. 'You can't be right!'

'If ye're thinkin' of their age, then let me tell you that gettin' older doesnae mean losin' interest in livin' altogether,' Zelda said with a twinkle in her eye. The two of them were sitting in the back yard of the little cottage Bethany had rented for her son and his new wife. Etta was knitting a new gansey for Adam and Zelda had the basket of mending that never seemed to be empty.

'If ye'd looked close enough when the mannie was last here and we were all invited tae Jacob McFarlane's for our dinner,' Zelda went on, 'ye'd have seen that he couldnae keep his eyes from Bethany. Not that you'd have noticed,' she added, the twinkle broadening into a grin, 'since you were only interested in Adam.'

Etta laughed. 'I was.' The sun was warm and the little flagged yard, newly swept that morning, was neat and clean. Snowy washing hung on the line strung across the tiny drying green and a pot of flowers she had lovingly grown from seed stood by the house wall, glowing all the colours of the rainbow. The baby kicked in her belly, and at that moment she would not have changed places with anyone in the world.

'You're shinin' like a star in the sky,' Zelda said just then. 'Marriage suits you.'

'I just wish Adam wasnae goin' away. I'll not see him for six weeks.'

'That's what bein' wed tae a fisherman means, my quine. Will ye miss goin' tae the farlins this year?'

'Aye, but gettin' things ready for the bairn'll keep me busy enough. Aunt Zelda, what if it comes while Adam's gone?'

'There's little fear of that,' Zelda said comfortably, 'since ye've still got six weeks tae go and a first bairn's usually late. Mary was two weeks past her time and I was near demented by the time she arrived. You wait and see – the last month's the longest. Anyway, we'll look after you, ye know that, and you can come and stay with us any time ye're worried about bein' on yer lone.' She reached out and patted Etta's hand. 'Imagine, I'm goin' tae have two wee ones tae nurse now that Mary's expectin' as well. I'm well blessed, Etta!'

'And I'm thirsty.' Etta rolled her knitting up and got to her feet slowly and clumsily.

'I'll make the tea.'

'No you won't, you just sit there. I want tae see that the stew for tonight's dinner's doin' well while I'm in the house,' Etta said, and then gave a startled cry as her toe caught on a raised flagstone. Burdened by her swollen belly, she stumbled in an attempt to stay upright, but lost her balance completely and fell forward, desperately reaching out with her two hands to break her fall and ending up on hands and knees.

'Etta?' Zelda threw down the sock she had been mending and rushed to her aid. 'Etta?'

'I'm fine, I'm fine,' Etta wheezed. 'Just – leave me for a minute till I – catch my breath.'

It was a minute or two before she felt strong enough to start lumbering to her feet. Once she had managed it Zelda helped her up and into the kitchen, where she sank down on to the comfortable armchair that had become Adam's.

'Are ye sure ye're all right?'

'Aye. I just got a bit of a fright.' Etta looked up into her aunt's worried face and managed a shaky laugh. 'I must have looked a right sight, down on the ground like that. It's lucky you were here tae help me up again or I might have had tae wait there till Adam came home for his dinner.' She made to stand, but Zelda pushed her back into the chair.

'You just sit there and rest, my lassie, and I'll see tae the tea.'

'Have a look at the stew first.'

Zelda opened the oven door and a fragrant smell drifted out. 'It's fine,' she reported, shutting the door and reaching for the tea caddy.

'I've made a right mess of my stockin's,' Etta mourned, examining the damage the fall had done. 'They're well torn, and my knees'll be black and blue in the mornin'. And my hands—' she held them out to show the grazes to her aunt.

'Just let me get the tea goin' and then I'll take a wet cloth tae them, and mebbe some iodine if ye have it.'

'In that wee cupboard. I'll get it,' Etta said, and began to get up. Then she stopped, gasping, as a sharp pain lanced through her back, gripping her in crab-like pincers for a long moment before vanishing.

She fell back into the chair, clutching at her belly, her face suddenly drained of colour. 'Aunt Zelda,' she said feebly, 'I think . . . mebbe ye'd better send someone tae find Adam.'

Adam paced the back yard until dark, when Zelda sent him off to his mother's for the night.

'It's goin' tae take a while, and with me and the midwife stayin' with Etta there's no room in the place for you.'

'Ye'll let me know as soon as anythin' happens?'

'Aye, but I doubt if it'll be before mornin'. Go on now, I've work tae do,' his aunt said, shooing him out. 'Yours is already done.'

The baby arrived the following afternoon, a tiny dark-haired scrap of humanity, loudly expressing his fury at being launched into the world before he was ready for the big journey. Exhausted though she was, Etta only needed one look at him to know that her life had changed for ever, and for the better.

'At least he's greetin',' the midwife said as she put him into his mother's arms. 'That's a good sign for an early bairn.'

'He's – he's awful wee, is he no'?' Adam asked when he arrived an hour later. He peered at his son and heir, well wrapped up and lying in the crook of Etta's arm. 'And awful red intae the bargain.'

'Just think where he's been these last months.' Zelda stroked the baby's face gently with the back of one finger.

'Red or not, he's bonny, and he'll grow intae a right lusty loon, just you wait and see, Adam. We'll need tae look after him well for a while, though, with him bein' so early. And it'll be a week or two before Etta's strong enough tae look after him and the house,' she added later when she got Adam on his own. 'She's had a difficult time of it and she's worn out.'

They named the baby Daniel, after the father Etta had never met. Weak and emotional after childbirth, easily moved to tears, she wept when Adam suggested the name.

'I thought you'd want him tae be called Gilbert after your own faither.'

'I wondered, but when I said tae my mother she didnae seem taken with the idea. Anyway, it's mebbe better tae let Rory have that name for his own firstborn son, seein' that he's the oldest. And when Aunt Zelda said that your own father that was killed in the war was named Daniel, I thought it went well enough with Pate,' Adam explained, adding, 'But I'd like him tae have Lowrie as his middle name.'

'Daniel Lowrie Pate.' Etta spoke the name aloud. 'It sounds grand.'

'Mebbe a bit much for such a wee thing,' Adam said doubtfully.

'He'll grow.' Etta wiped the tears away and gave him a shaky smile. 'One day he'll be as big and strong as you are, and then the name'll suit him handsomely.'

'I suppose ye're right.' As yet Adam had refused to hold his new son, terrified that he might drop him or damage him in some way. 'When he's older,' he kept saying, but in truth, he didn't feel in the least like a father. Etta seemed to have taken to parenthood but he himself had not changed at all. He had asked his Uncle James, the only person he could safely confide in, about it, and James had sucked thoughtfully at the stem of his pipe and then said, 'There's some born tae be fathers, like Innes, and some who never seem tae take tae it, like me. Though I have a right likin' for our Ruth.

She's a bright wee quine, and if only she'd been born a laddie I think her and me would have got on fine together.'

'I think I must be like you,' Adam said, and stopped worrying about his lack of feeling for the mewling little scrap, no larger than a kitten, that had taken over his home and all his young wife's attention. Being like his Uncle James had always been the main ambition of his life, and now, with the two of them sitting in companionable silence in the *Fidelity*'s cabin, he was glad that within the next week they would be off to the Shetlands for the fishing, leaving their domestic concerns behind them.

Daniel Lowrie Pate was christened a few days before the fishing fleet left Buckie, and on the day they sailed Etta was strong enough to manage the walk down to the harbour to see them off. Zelda was with her, pushing the baby in the brand new pram Bethany had given them.

Etta clung to Adam on the morning of his departure to the fishing ground, and wept. She was always weeping, he thought in despair. Aloud he said, 'Etta, quine, you know I have tae go. Uncle James has kept the *Fidelity* back for as long as he could tae give you time tae get yer strength back, but he can't wait any longer and he's dependin' on me. And we need the money, with the wee one tae see tae now.'

'I know, but I'll miss you,' Etta wept, her arms as tight around him as possible.

'You'll have Aunt Zelda for company, and my mother.' Not that his mother had been of much help. She had called in at the cottage to inspect the baby, and said how bonny he was. She had sent Leezie with nourishing food to tempt Etta's appetite back, and had given them baby clothes and the pram. But there had been no warmth – not that he had expected that from his mother. She was quite unlike Aunt Zelda.

'I know they'll still be here, but it's you that we want – me and wee Daniel,' Etta wailed.

Adam sought further words of comfort, and found them.

'Siddy's talkin' of stayin' ashore when the boat goes tae the English fishin' in November. I could be mate of the *Fidelity* within the year. And when that happens I'll get more money.'

'You'll be careful, won't you?' Etta pleaded. 'All the time?' Since Daniel's early birth she had suddenly become aware of the fragility of life. Less than a year ago she had had nobody to think of but herself, but now . . . if anything happened to her man or to her bairn, she thought, she would not be able to bear it.

'I'm always careful.' Adam disentangled himself and picked up his seaman's kist and his bag. 'I have tae go, Etta.'

'Aunt Zelda's comin' for me. We'll walk down to the harbour together, with the wee one. Mind and wave tae me – and mind and write,' she added.

'Of course I will.' He cast a glance into the crib and then put a finger into the palm of the tiny hand lying on the pillow. To his astonishment the baby's fragile fingers closed on it, and held on. 'Look at that!' Adam said, delighted. 'He's got a hold of me!'

'He's gettin' stronger already.' Pride dried Etta's tears, which could vanish as swiftly as they arrived. 'And he wants his daddy tae stay with him, don't you, my wee mannie?' she added to the baby.

'He's got a strong grip for such a wee thing, right enough.' Adam began to feel affection stirring deep within him for the little creature that had disrupted his life. 'But can ye get him tae let go now, Etta? I'm feared tae try in case I hurt him.'

As the *Fidelity* surged through the harbour entrance, one of a long line of boats moving gracefully towards the open sea, he remembered to look up at Etta. She was crying, as he knew she would be, holding a handkerchief to her face with one hand and waving the other so hard that it was a blur. Adam waved back. Over the past few months he had at times had his doubts about the wisdom of marrying so young. Who would have thought that a kiss and a cuddle with a pretty quine could lead to a man being tied down to such responsibility? But now, looking up at Etta and remembering his son's tiny, fragile fingers gripping his, he felt that marriage could suit him after all.

His Aunt Stella and her three daughters stood further along the harbour, well away from Etta and Zelda. Ruth and her sisters waved to their father and to Adam, while their mother simply stood motionless. As the *Fidelity* passed by them Adam saw his uncle, leaning out through the wheelhouse window, doffing his cap and nodding slightly to his wife, who nodded in return.

As James Lowrie took the drifter that was his very life through the harbour entrance Adam was surprised to see his mother, who rarely came to see the boats go out, standing there with Lorne Kerr. She was smiling down at him, and when he gave a tentative wave she waved back. It looked as though she had begun to forgive him for refusing to dance to her tune. Glancing at the wheelhouse he saw James salute them both, then the drifter was through the entrance and prancing slightly as she met the larger waves. To Adam it was almost as though she was giving a shiver of excitement and anticipation at leaving the confines of the stone harbour walls. He knew just how she felt, he thought as she settled down, her forefoot biting into the sea as she turned towards the horizon and the herring shoals.

It was ironic, Bethany thought as Adam beamed up at her from the deck of the *Fidelity*, that at one time all she had wanted was to see her son, her flesh and blood, going to the fishing just as she would have done had she had the chance. There was no denying that he belonged to the sea. But she had lost him to it, and to James, and there was nothing she could do about it.

'I must go back to Edinburgh,' Lorne said as the two of them turned to walk from the harbour. Boats were still sailing out; it would take some time for the harbour basins to empty, but already the first of the fishing fleet, the *Fidelity* included, was scattering across the face of the Moray Firth, and becoming smaller to the eye every minute.

'When?'

'Tomorrow morning.'

'Do you always arrive unexpectedly and leave unexpectedly?'

'I like to cultivate a certain air of mystery; it keeps me in folk's minds. Dine with me tonight. I've not seen much of you during my stay.' Lorne had spent most of his time with Jacob, visiting the yards where the nets were barked before being dried and then carried down to the harbour and put aboard the boats, and talking to the fishermen and the coopers and the carters and the old men, former fishermen, who congregated down at the harbour. He had watched the boats being painted and cleaned and coaled in readiness for the journey to northern waters.

'Come to the house for your dinner,' Bethany said on an impulse. Rory had already gone south, and the house Gil had bought for her and his children suddenly seemed too large, and too empty.

Leezie, pleased to have someone new to cook for, excelled herself, and after an excellent meal Bethany and her guest settled in the front parlour. A tea tray stood by Bethany's chair while Lorne enjoyed a glass of port.

'Bethany, I owe you an apology,' he suddenly said. 'The things I said to you just before I left for Edinburgh that last time – the words I used – it was clumsy of me, and wrong of me.' He held up a hand to stop her when she tried to speak. 'Give me time to say what I have to say, please. I realised after I got home that I had gone about things entirely the wrong way. You're a businesswoman and so I thought, foolishly, that it would make more sense if I spoke in a business-like way. But I ruined everything, and I offended you. I can't apologise deeply enough.'

'You invited me to see Edinburgh for myself, and I declined. That was all.'

'It was not all, and you know it. I was so intent on sounding practical that I ignored the fact that you're a woman – a very beautiful and passionate woman. I should have spoken to that woman. I should have said, Bethany Pate, I believe – no, I know that I love you, and I hope that you love me, or that you can bring yourself in time to love me. Because I think that we could be very happy together, and I want nothing more in life than to make you happy.'

Then, as she stared at him, he stood up, set his glass down on the mantelshelf, knelt before her and took her hands in his.

'Bethany,' he said, his voice gentle now, his eyes pleading, 'will you marry me? Will you please marry me and be with me for as long as we both shall live, and with me wherever we may go after that, for all eternity?'

'I – but—'

'I hope you're not going to say that this is so sudden,' Lorne said with a faint smile. 'Because I'm sure you knew what I meant that last time, even though I put it so badly. You don't have to give me your answer now. You should visit Edinburgh and meet my sister and my friends. I want you to see my home and I hope that you will feel that you could live there, with me. If you don't care for it then we can find somewhere more suited.'

She moistened her lips, drawing her hands free of his. 'Lorne, this is most flattering, but I've been married once and I've no great notion to take on another husband.'

'Then you must have married the wrong man,' Lorne said, rising from his knees and moving to stand by the mantelshelf. 'In my case marriage gave me a taste for the companionship and the pleasures of sharing my life with a woman, especially if she is the right woman. Let me introduce you to those pleasures, and that companionship. You've been on your own for too long, Bethany. You need – you deserve – so much more than you have now. I know that you would hate to do nothing else but look after a house, and so I'm offering you a partnership in every way. I want you to share my business interests as well as my bed.'

She fumbled through her mind for a defence but could only come up with, 'I'm needed here.'

'No, you're not. Your children have lives of their own, and Jacob can find someone else to work for him. You're using these folk to hide behind, Bethany, and the person you want to hide from is you. How long have you been widowed now? A dozen years or more, isn't it? Far too long for a woman of your temperament.'

His eyes caressed her face and then moved down over her body, and she felt the heat of his gaze on her skin.

'What you're suggesting,' she said, her voice uneven, 'might prove to be a mistake for one or other of us.'

'My dear, is that not what life's all about – taking risks and finding out if they have succeeded? And if such a move does turn out to be wrong for either or both of us, I promise that you will be free to seek happiness back here or somewhere else. I would never hold you against your will.' He drained his glass and set it back on the mantelshelf. 'Take time to think over what I've said. In the meantime I hope that you'll come to Edinburgh on a visit, at least. Now, I must go.'

Bethany got up to lead the way to the door, and was taken entirely by surprise when he caught hold of her arm and deftly spun her round and into his embrace.

His kiss was demanding, probing, and not to be denied. Almost against her will Bethany found her lips parting beneath his, while her arms lifted of their own volition to hold him. When he finally released her she was breathless and dizzy with shock at the strength of her emotions.

'As I thought,' he said huskily. 'How can such a passionate woman deny herself for so long?'

If he had bent his head towards hers again she would not

333

have been able to stop herself from responding, but instead, he released her and stepped back.

'I'll let myself out,' he said, and then he was gone.

For several long minutes Bethany stood where he had left her. When she finally moved, it was to put a hand to her lips; they felt soft and swollen, and when she looked in the mirror above the fireplace she saw that they had a new fullness, ripeness, to them. Her entire body felt different. She moved about the room, unable now to stand still, or to sit down.

With one kiss, Lorne Kerr had awakened something that had been dormant for years, something that she had thought was dead. He was right, she did have passion; only one man had awakened it before, and that man was not her husband. She had managed after a terrible struggle to subdue it, but now . . .

'Is Mr Kerr gone, then?' Leezie asked from the doorway, and Bethany jumped guiltily.

'D'you never think to knock?' she snapped.

'I've never had tae do it before. Why, have ye got somethin' tae hide all at once?'

'Don't be daft, and don't be impertinent!'

'I'm too old tae be impertinent. He's gone, then?' Leezie asked again, and when her employer nodded, she came into the room. 'I can take the tea things away, can I? Or would that be imposin' on ye?'

'Take them, and then you can get to your bed.'

When the housekeeper had gone Bethany noticed that the glass Lorne had used still stood on the mantelshelf, overlooked. She picked it up to take it to the kitchen and then, on an irrational impulse, she ran the tip of a finger round the rim then put it in her mouth. It tasted of brandy, and it tasted of Lorne Kerr.

'Daft quine!' she muttered, and put the glass down so sharply that it almost broke. Then she put the lights out and went upstairs to bed.

30

Bethany spent a lot of time on her own over the next few weeks, walking all around Buckie, visiting the net factory and the smokehouse and the cooperage, which was quiet now that Rory and most of his men were in Lerwick.

She went down to the harbour every day and stood gazing down into the dark waters where once, a lifetime ago, she had swum with the laddies. Then she looked up and over the Firth to the horizon where the *Fidelity* and the other boats had vanished on their way to the northern fishing. She climbed the hill to Rathven and visited the cemetery where her parents and Gil Pate had been laid to rest.

Once or twice she visited the little cottage in the Catbow, to Etta's surprise and alarm, and sat nursing little Daniel, who was beginning to thrive.

'I'm not a motherly woman,' she found herself confessing one day. 'Though I always loved Adam dearly.'

Etta, who now understood what it was to be a mother, nodded and said, 'I know. It's different when ye've birthed the bairn yerself.' And then the two women smiled at each other over the baby's dark head, and formed an understanding that, although not close, was as close as they could ever reach.

Finally, Bethany spent two weeks visiting Lorne Kerr's sister in Edinburgh. True to his word, Lorne left her in peace to get to know his family and his city and his handsome home and never once asked her, even when he was saying goodbye to her at the station, if she had come to any decision.

'I'll write to you,' she said from the train window. 'Whatever happens, I'll write.'

'I look forward to your letter. And, if you decide to stay as you are, I hope that I can look forward to your friendship, at least,' he replied, and when she leaned from the window to look back as the train left on its journey, he was still standing there, his eyes holding hers even as he dwindled and disappeared.

'Lorne has asked me to marry him and live with him in Edinburgh,' she said to Jacob two days later.

'I thought he might, eventually. The man never stopped talkin' about ye the times he was here.' He put down his pen, folded his hands on his desk, and said, 'I hope ye said yes.'

'I've not said anything yet. It's a big step, Jacob. I've never lived anywhere else but Buckie.'

'I thought I'd spend all my days on this Firth,' he mused. 'But marriage took me away, too – only for me, it was yer mither's marriage tae Weem Lowrie that did it. I never thought I'd survive bein' away from here, but I did.'

'And now you're back, and a wealthier man for being away.'

'Money can bring its own comforts,' he said placidly.

'The thing is, how would you manage if I went away?'

'Tuts, lassie, ye mustn't put my well-being before yer own happiness. Ye've put good overseers intae the smokehouse and the net factory, and I'll surely find someone tae see tae the books for me. James has a good head on his shoulders; I've been wonderin' about askin' him if he'd take on more of the business, so's he can take over from me when the time comes. He deserves it.'

'I think the two of you would work well together. As to the gutting crews – if I'm not here to hire them next year, Sarah Lowrie could do the job just as well. Mebbe even better.'

336

'What would ye do about the house?'

'Rory's the only one living there now, apart from Leezie and myself. His father bought it, and it should pass on to him.'

Jacob reached for his pipe and his tobacco pouch. 'Mrs Duthie wants tae settle down in a wee place of her own. She says she's got enough money tae live in comfort, so as ye can see, I've been payin' the woman far too much. If your Leezie should be lookin' for another position I'd like fine tae have her as my new housekeeper – if Rory doesnae have need of her, and if she's willin'.'

'I've not gone yet, or said I would go, Jacob McFarlane! Would ye take my grave that fast?' Bethany wanted to know, and then when he grinned at her, 'If it comes to it, I could speak to her for you. But only if it comes to it.'

'Aye, aye. Let me know when you've made yer decision.' Jacob finished filling the pipe and put the stem into his mouth, striking a match. His hands, lumpy now with rheumatism and scarred from his days as a fisherman, fumbled slightly and the first match dropped to the desk.

'Here.' Bethany found the match and struck it, then put it into his hand.

'Speakin' for mysel',' Jacob said when the pipe was lit to his satisfaction, 'I think ye should tell the man yes. Ye deserve a bit of happiness, my quine.'

Bethany kept her own council until the fishing fleet returned to Buckie in August, and then Rory was the first to hear that she was going to marry Lorne Kerr and move to Edinburgh.

His reaction was swift. 'Good. I thought that the man liked you and I'm glad he's had the sense tae do somethin' about it.'

'You needn't worry about having nowhere to stay, for I'm giving the house to you. Ellen won't come back here, and Adam and Etta seem happy enough in their wee cottage.'

'I don't want the house. You're not the only one gettin' wed,' Rory said proudly, though his face went brick red.

337

'Ruth?'

'How did ye know?'

'Leezie's always saying how well suited you two are. If you're certain that you don't want the house—'

'Can you see Ruth Lowrie livin' in a place like this? We'd be happier in somethin' smaller.'

'Then I'll sell it and give the three of you equal shares of the price I get.'

'Even Ellen?'

'She deserves to be treated the same as you and Adam. And I'm sure,' Bethany said, a gleam in her eye, 'that she'll find something to do with the money. I'll write to Lorne tomorrow, and tell him that I'll join him in Edinburgh next week.'

During the next few days she quietly told her news to Adam, Zelda, Innes, and everyone who needed to know. She missed out just one person, for she could not bring herself to tell him of her forthcoming marriage face to face.

She knew that word would travel swiftly round the community and that he would soon come to hear of her departure from Buckie, but she hoped that he would do nothing about it. It was a foolish hope.

On the day before she left, she was working at her desk when Leezie came into the front parlour.

'It's yer brither James. He wants tae see ye.'

'Tell him that I'm not at home.'

'Tell me that yourself,' James said from the doorway, and she spun round, and then got to her feet. He brushed past Leezie and then bundled the astonished woman out to the hall and shut the door.

'And tell me tae my face,' he said. 'Don't let me hear it from other folk, the way I heard that you're goin' tae Edinburgh tae marry Lorne Kerr.'

'I thought I'd leave it to Stella to tell you. I knew she'd enjoy doin' that.'

'Is it true?'

'Yes, it is.'

'Why?'

'Because I've come to the end of my time here. Because Lorne's a good man and I'm tired of being on my own.'

'Does he love ye?' he asked, his face expressionless, his hands hanging by his sides, the fingers slightly curved. 'D'you love him?'

'Folk our age don't talk about love. Lorne . . . cares for me,' Bethany said, choosing the words carefully. 'He'll look after me, and mebbe that's what I want now.'

'I cannae bear the thought of not seein' ye.'

'We scarcely see each other anyway,' she said. 'Most of the year you're at the fishing grounds, or in Lerwick or Yarm'th and even when you're here, we don't spend time together.'

'But at least I know ye're here. Even when I'm far away I know ye're here.'

'James, I have to make my own life. I have to go away,' Bethany said wildly, unable to bear any more. 'And I have a lot to do before I go.'

If he stayed for much longer she knew that she would change her mind about Lorne, and Edinburgh. She would stay, as he wanted, as she herself wanted, but nothing would change. The torment would just go on, as it had done for the past nineteen years and more.

She walked quickly past him to the door, opening it, waiting, with her back to him, for him to walk past her and leave.

'Don't go,' James said from behind her, his whole heart in his voice.

And it was then Bethany knew that she must.

Etta Pate stood on the shingle, looking out on the Moray Firth. It had been a bright November day, a good day for the fleet to start their long journey south to the English fishing, but now that the sun was setting it had lost what little heat it had, and there was a sharp chill in the air.

The *Fidelity* had left the harbour in the company of the new drifter, the *Jess Lowrie II*, and Adam had been so excited at making his first journey as mate to his Uncle James Lowrie that he had almost forgotten to wave to her as she stood on the harbour wall, drinking in the last sight she would have of him for weeks, trying to burn the image of him into her memory. He had finally seen her, and waved, and then he was gone.

Daniel, possibly sensing his mother's misery, had been difficult all that day, grizzling when she tried to put him down in his crib to sleep, and so she had dressed him in the coat and pantaloons and hat and mitts she had knitted, and wrapped a shawl about him for greater protection against the cold before carrying him, so well wrapped that he felt like a bolster in her arms, out along the shore road to a spot where there were no houses and they could be alone.

He had fallen asleep as soon as she started walking, but now she heard a soft murmur of sound, and saw that the change in motion as she left the road and began to walk carefully over the shingle had woken him. Just then the fiery early-winter sun broke through thin cloud and suddenly a broad crimson carpet, glittering as though embroidered with rubies, spilled across the sea, reaching from the horizon almost to where Etta stood. The horizon itself was suffused with rich pink, shading to a pale rose colour and then rising into soft grey.

'Look, Daniel.' She angled her arm to lift him up slightly, turning so that he too was looking out to sea. His eyes, as dark as her own when he was first born, but now showing signs of turning grey like his father's, widened beneath the knitted cap pulled down over his forehead.

'Yes, it's pretty – and it's all for you.' She made for a conveniently placed rock and sat down, glad of the chance to rest. Daniel had made good progress since his premature